CODE RED

A ROGUE WARRIOR THRILLER

IAN LOOME

Published by Inkubator Books
www.inkubatorbooks.com

ISBN (eBook): 978-1-83756-121-6
ISBN (Paperback): 978-1-83756-122-3
ISBN (Hardback): 978-1-83756-123-0

CODE RED

n.

1. A condition of heightened alert against imminent danger
2. Unauthorized extra-judicial punishment meted out within the military

1

CHICAGO

The alley was quiet as evening approached, its dirty asphalt speckled with oily puddles.

Behind a forest-green dumpster near its North Peoria Street end, a refrigerator box was wedged into a gap between it and the brick wall. Droplets from gutters high above dripped steadily onto two rough sheets of opaque plastic draped over the box.

The box quavered as its occupant roused from his slumber. He listened immediately for any noise that might have prompted him awake. The streets could be dangerous; noise meant he had to pay attention.

He was an old hand at avoiding trouble.

The man pulled himself up to a half-sitting, half-lying position. His body was big and lean. It had been muscular once, too, but that was years earlier, and the hard asphalt pressed against his tailbone.

He dragged himself backwards, through the top of the box. He sat up on his haunches. Despite years on the street, he ate regularly at a mission, walked constantly, did his exercises every morning. He was happy to be in okay shape. It was enough.

He slumped down along the wall, using the old brick as a backrest. His breath felt short, anxiety and stress suddenly present.

They'd said he had PTSD, long ago, when that shit seemed important. Given what he'd seen and done, a little anxiety just made sense.

He leaned over and thrust an arm into the box, fumbling until he found the bottle. But it was empty. Depression began to settle in.

Need a drink, bad, he told himself. *Have to get up at some time anyway. Got to get to the soup kitchen and eat twice today. Missed supper yesterday; promised myself...*

He pushed his way through the narrow gap and into the alley. There was a corner store a few blocks away that over the years had supplied vanilla extract. It clocked in at about thirty-five percent alcohol.

But the owner, Mr. Lam, was cruel and had stolen his change, aware he couldn't complain. That had to be worth a single bottle.

It's not stealing. He owes you a buck forty-seven.

BOB REACHED THE STORE. The bell chimed as he pushed the front door open. It was warmer inside, the air sterile, silent aside from the hum of the tube lights.

The large rectangular space was divided by horizontal racks. There was a young man minding the front counter, behind a plexiglass protective shield. It wasn't the same young man, but his name tag also read 'Daniel.' *A younger brother?* A large round clock on the wall read seven forty.

The kid looked up from his phone.

"Hey! You have money?"

Bob nodded twice as enthusiastically as he could.

"Fine. Just... don't touch anything you aren't buying. I already have to clean nonstop; I don't need you getting your stink on things."

Insults were customary and easily ignored. Bob nodded again, then shambled towards the back of the store.

He reached its back wall of refrigerators, the shelves opposite his target. He knew where the vanilla was from his last visit. It had been big bottles, enough to get hammered if he could get it down in one sitting.

He spotted the brown containers, down low, next to racks of kitchen and bathroom items: rolls of plastic wrap and foil, bottles of detergent and drain cleaner.

Bob gazed over the racks to the front of the store. The clerk was still on his phone.

He looked down at the vanilla extract. The sticker read "3.99." He picked one up, turning it in his hand. Then he put it down again.

That's it, isn't it? That's why you're here, being a useless piece-of-shit alcoholic bum. Because you always do the wrong thing...

But it was hard. The walk had triggered thinking about the bad old days. He couldn't have that shit hanging around.

He reached down and grabbed the bottle, then stashed it in the overcoat's side pocket.

There. It's done. See? No bolt from above, no sudden retribution...

The entrance chimed. Bob looked its way, in time with the clerk.

The door swung open. Three teenagers walked in, stocky kids, the boy in front with a bandana on his head, gold front teeth.

Bob ducked below the last row of shelves.

They were loud, laughing and joking, harassing the clerk. The boy with the bandana flicked his hand across a display of potato chips, knocking bags onto the floor, which he then stepped on.

"You know what we want, you little shit, so hand it over."

At the counter, the kid moved away from the countertop and the small half-oval hole designed for passing money through the shield. He backed up against the wall, out of reach.

"You don't think we can bust in there, little man?" Gold-teeth snarled.

The boy reached down quickly and withdrew a sawed-off shotgun from under the counter. He raised it unconfidently. "Please..." he pleaded. "I don't want to hurt anyone..."

"You've got to come out here to use that. Then I'll take it away from you and blow your brains out."

"I already rang the silent alarm, so the police are coming."

Bob peered through the tiny gap between the shelves. The clerk couldn't have been much more than fifteen or sixteen and was terrified.

"Yeah? So...? Po-po slow. We've got about an hour to trash this place before they get here, do a lot more damage than whatever's in your till..."

The kid shook his head defiantly.

Give them the money, kid, Bob thought. *Don't make this worse for everyone.*

One of the other two teens had moved to the side wicket and was shaking its locked latch and the plexiglass furiously.

The kid with the gold teeth looked his way and smiled, then scowled at their other friend. "We're going to fuck this place up," he said. He drew a switchblade from his pocket and popped it open, a seven-inch knife edge swinging free. His friend followed suit, drawing a hunting knife.

They began to puncture chip bags, slashing magazines, knocking over containers, contents spilled.

"No! Please!" the clerk called out. "My father will kill me..."

At the wicket, the second youth was ripping at the door, giggling. "The latch is giving..." he suggested.

Bob could see where the confrontation was heading. He scanned the contents of the shelves ahead of him. He reached up and grabbed a jar of thumbtacks, measuring its weight.

Time to even up the odds a little.

2

Gold-teeth giggled. "I'm going to carve my name in his forehead."

The latch gave way, and the gate burst open.

The terrified clerk wheeled towards the onrushing teen with the shotgun but froze, unable to shoot someone in cold blood.

The older youth grabbed the shotgun by the barrel and yanked it away. "Give me that, you piece of…" He paused for a split second before slamming the gun's butt end into the clerk's stomach. The boy collapsed to the ground.

Gold-teeth nodded their way. "Go ahead. Do it!"

"Eric…"

"I want that cash, homes. Don't be a pussy! Shoot the little shit, or I'll do him and your chicken ass, too!"

The clerk was begging for his life, sobbing. "No, please! Please don't! Take what you want. The police are coming. The police…"

His attacker shook his head. He raised the shotgun to eye height, sighting down the barrel. "Man, I got to do what I got to do…"

His finger flexed slightly on the trigger. The clerk shut his eyes tight and threw up both arms in front of his face, as if it might stop a shell from close range.

Bob had seen enough.

"HEY!"

The three robbers turned in unison towards the call from the back of the room.

But there was no one there.

Gold-teeth looked nervous. He glanced back at the clerk, then towards the back of the room. He shook his switchblade in the sound's direction, then eyed the clerk again. "Who you got here with you?"

The boy shook his head, terrified. "N-n-n-nobody..." he stammered. "There was a bum, a-a tall guy..."

The ringleader's eyes narrowed as he considered the possibility. "Whoever you is, you best come out before we smoke your little homie..."

Gold-teeth craned his head from side to side, looking for movement.

"Go ahead, Eugene, kill him," the ringleader suggested. "You hear that, dude? This your kid? We're going to light his ass up... okay? Unless you come out right now...."

Before he could end the sentence, an object slid along the vinyl floor, between the rows, from the back of the room to the front.

All three men jumped back a step.

But when they looked down, it was just an oversized white plastic bottle, lying on its side, "Professional Strength Liquid Drain Cleaner" written across one side in block capitals.

The third boy walked over to it. "Man, it's nothing..." He reached down, the bottle suddenly beginning to swell in size.

Inside the half-emptied bottle, the drain cleaner had breached the small sponge Bob had shoved in ahead of the thumbtacks and balls of uncoated aluminum foil. The sodium hydrochloride oxidized the aluminum within seconds, creating hydrogen gas.

The gas expanded, the bottle swelled, then exploded, the hundreds of steel tacks expelled at thousands of feet per second, the boy screaming as the steel tacks cut his hand to ribbons. Acid sprayed across Gold-teeth's jacket as he threw up his hands to shield himself.

The ringleader took off his coat frantically. "FUUUCK!" he screamed. Their friend was lying facedown, barely moving, blood pouring from his badly wounded hand.

His shotgun-wielding partner was shielded by the plexiglass. He snapped out of the moment of surprise and looked around.

A bearded, disheveled man strode towards them, down the center aisle.

"Don't make me shoot you, man..." the kid with the shotgun threatened. "Back off!"

Bob continued apace. The kid stepped through the open counter gate and raised the shotgun to eye level.

Bob's hands came up from his midsection, his right using the Bic lighter to ignite the bottle of vanilla. He continued apace, arm arcing upwards as he flung the flaming liquid in the boy's direction.

The shocked youth squeezed the trigger even as he yanked the barrel up and away to avoid the arcing flame. The wayward blast from the shotgun sprayed the ceiling and back wall with pellets, a windowpane cracking, the alarm now piercing.

The kid used his free hand to try to beat the flaming liquid off his cheap polyester Chicago Bulls jersey.

Bob spun on his heel to his right. Gold-teeth was striding towards him, switchblade at the ready. The window damage had been minimal. *Rock salt?* Bob thought in mid spin, a raised elbow slamming into Gold-teeth's jaw, dazing the kid and knocking him to the ground, a glittering cap flying out in a crescendo of blood.

Bit his tongue. Bob turned back to the counter. The kid with the shotgun had beaten out the burning jersey. He raised the gun just in time. His eyes were wide with fear, the gun shaking in his hands.

Bob lowered his profile, turning side on and taking a half step the boy's way, his left hand grabbing the barrel, wrestling it upwards. The gun went off again, his hearing reduced to a high-pitched whine as the ceiling tile above them burst into a shower of plaster chunks.

He drove his right elbow into the kid's solar plexus, wind instantly gone, a panicked look as he gasped for air. Bob stripped the shotgun from his grip, tossing it to the ground.

The boy swung a feeble hook, and he ducked it. With a punch thrown from just a few inches, he struck the kid on the side of the chin with a flattened right palm.

The boy's eyes swam; his legs turned to spaghetti as he collapsed, bewildered that the last thing he'd seen was a bum.

Bob's ears were beginning to recover, the high-pitched whine replaced with a familiar rushing sound of air. He moved behind the counter and reached down to help the clerk.

"You okay?" he asked, too loudly.

The kid nodded, but his eyes were still wide, terrified. He scuttled backwards on all fours like a crab, pushing himself up against the under-counter safe door.

"I'm not going to hurt you," Bob said.

He saw motion out of the corner of his eye and acted on reflex, ducking below the countertop and retreating to the gate's door. He looked around the corner.

Gold-teeth groggily grabbed the shotgun and raised it.

"Give me the gun, kid, or this is going to get worse," Bob suggested as he stood up. "You may not believe it, but this is the luckiest day you ever had in your life."

The young man peered through squinted eyes. "Man... what the fuck are you talking about? I got the gun..."

"You're lucky to be living in the here and now. Ten years ago, you'd already be dead. Before you rose from the floor, I'd have snapped your neck. Your nervous friend? He'd have that cardboard poster tube on the bottom shelf jammed through his eye socket, into his brain."

He took a half step forward, through the gate and away from the protection of the plexiglass.

"Don't come any closer!" the kid barked.

"Like I said, it's your lucky day. Because that was ten years ago. I'm not that guy anymore. So you get a choice." He took a few steps closer.

"Yeah?" The kid pumped the shotgun's breach and chambered another shell. "What's that?"

"Drop the gun and walk away... or you'll force me to relive old times. You get to—"

The shotgun barrel kicked explosively once more. It sprayed its contents, the full load of rock salt catching Bob square in the chest.

He slammed to the ground, chest wounds already seeping through his shirt and coat.

3

Gold-teeth looked at the prone man in front of him as his dazed friend behind the counter staggered to his feet. His expression suggested he'd never shot a man before, and the notion filled him with terror.

His mouth dropped open, and his eyes widened in panic. The young punk dropped the shotgun at his feet. "Oh fuck," he mumbled. "Fuck, fuck, fuck, fuck..."

He ran for the front doors and out, leaving his two friends. A few moments later, they followed him, the boy from behind the counter helping up his dazed associate, hand mangled from the blast. He hustled them through the door to the trill sound of the alarm, a trail of blood behind them.

The terrified young store clerk rose to his feet, the air filled with the smell of gunpowder and hydrogen gas. The store was a wreck, ruptured inventory littering the floor, the acrid smell stinging his nostrils.

The clerk gazed over at the open gate. Just past it, Bob lay on his back. Police sirens were getting closer, multiple cars from the sound.

He ran over to the bum. "Buddy! Oh shit! Oh shit! I think he's dead! I think..."

Bob raised his head slightly, one eye closed as if struck by a migraine. "Hmm... what...?"

"Stay still, mister! You've been shot."

Bob pushed himself up onto his elbows, feeling the sting of the rock salt pellets.

He looked down at his chest slick with blood. "Rock salt. Won't... kill me. I... need to go," he said. He began to rise.

"Mister, please... you're hurt real bad, and the police are coming."

Bob could hear the sirens. That was attention he didn't need.

He used one arm to push himself haltingly to his feet. "I have to go..." he repeated.

He stumbled towards the entrance, a hand clutched to his chest wounds as if it might help.

The kid grabbed his free left arm. "You need to sit down, wait for help."

Bob shrugged off his grasp and staggered towards the door. He paused at the counter. "You... you got a Charleston Chew?"

The kid nodded numbly before trotting back to his post by the register.

He fumbled under the counter and produced a bar, sliding it under the partition gap.

Bob grabbed it and tipped it in the boy's direction. "Appreciated." He took two more hesitant steps towards the door and noticed the still-standing, rotating rack at the end of the counter. He smiled for a moment, as if caught in a fond memory. Then he plucked a pale blue plastic hair scrunchy off it. He slipped it over his hand and onto his wrist, like a bracelet.

The kid looked puzzled.

"Just... ancient history," Bob mumbled. "Okay?"

The kid nodded, his expression blank from shock. "Dude... you totally saved me... take whatever the fuck you want. Who the fuck ARE you, anyway?!"

Bob pushed the door open. He played with the scrunchy for a second, tugging on it, letting the elastic snap it back into place on his wrist. "I'm... I'm not important. I just wanted a drink, is all," he said.

He staggered outside, the boy calling after him.

IN ANOTHER LIFE, Bob had owned a townhouse in trendy Kennedy Park. But for a decade, on and off, the streets and alleys of Chicago's West Loop had been his home.

The storefronts were struggling. The restaurants and patios were doing better. The neighborhood provided things Bob could use: food, bottles, mildly drunk patrons' donations.

Bob shambled south, darkness settling in. Sidewalk traffic was sparse in the early evening. He knew it was late August or early September, as he'd seen a newspaper a few weeks earlier.

He passed the corner draft bar. They had live blues bands in sometimes, and he'd taken Maggie, back when he was semi-respectable. Sweaty crowds dancing and drinking until the wee hours, Maggie sashaying onto the dance floor, beckoning him with a crooked finger so sultry it was practically smoking.

Maggie.

Her tiny one-bedroom apartment had been three blocks east. He hadn't thought about her in days, he realized.

He stopped momentarily. He used his teeth to rip open the chocolate wrapper, then took a big bite and began to slowly chew the sticky nougat.

He resumed his walk.

Sugar will help for now.

He checked each store window as he passed, left hand clutched to his chest wound as he used the oblique reflections to look for police squad car lights behind him.

From the sirens, they were approaching quickly, almost certainly headed to the corner store. He needed to get out of sight.

He turned at the first side street, went a half block south, ignoring pedestrians' stares, then continued west again. If he'd gotten it right, the free clinic's back entrance would be...

There.

The alley was dimly lit. Outside the free clinic's back door, a pair of white-coated lab techs from the neighboring business were smoking cigarettes. He pushed past them and up the steps.

"Hey!" one yelled. "You can't go in that way. You have to—"

His friend used an arm to restrain him. "Let him be! I think he's bleeding."

Bob pocketed the chocolate bar. He pulled the gray metal door open and stumbled inside.

He'd been that way once before, when Nurse Dawn had insisted that he meet her secretly so she could give him new socks and a new coat for winter. That had been... what, four winters previous?

He leaned on the wall for strength as he wobbled down the long corridor. The clinic's interior was impersonal white plaster and tube lights, cheap carpet.

He was about to pass the last exam room when a familiar face inside, crouched beside a patient, spotted him.

4

Nurse Dawn's big brown eyes widened at the sight of his blood-slicked shirt. "Oh, my Lord... Bob!" She turned back to her patient. "Excuse me, sir, for just a minute, okay?"

The nurse was stocky but quick. She moved to the door and put Bob's right arm over her shoulder to help steady him, though he had to stoop slightly due to their height difference, wincing in the process.

"Have you been shot!?"

"Rock salt, from a shotgun."

"Here: come into the exam room, and let's take a look," she said. She guided him to the room across the hall.

Bob collapsed into an office chair, next to an exam table. "Sorry... about this," he said through gritted teeth. "God-damn, that smarts."

"Don't blaspheme," she counselled. "You know I don't like the bad language. And don't apologize! That's what we're here for."

"Sorry." He'd forgotten her religious streak. "How bad...?"

He flinched slightly as she pulled the top two buttons open.

"Your coat took some of the steam off it, so it's mostly surface, but some of the chunks are pretty embedded. I'm going to have to take them out with forceps, and you're going to need some stitches. Look... perhaps I should call Dr. Girard—"

"NO!" he snapped. He caught himself and lowered the tone. Nurse Dawn was good to street folk, didn't ask questions. That made her invaluable. "No. Sorry. It's just... you know what I think of doctors. And... he has to report it..."

"And you don't want to deal with the police."

"We have some history."

She moved over to the basin and opened the cupboard above it, taking out a chrome bedpan and forceps. Then she took a cloth and soaked it in hot water. "I'm going to wipe the blood away, then take out the salt pellets with the forceps, okay?"

He nodded. "You're okay with handling this?"

She put the items down next to him on the examination table, then went back to the sink and washed her hands. She turned and picked up the damp cloth, then wiped his chest diligently for about ten seconds before raising the forceps. "Seen worse. This is going to hurt quite a bit," she warned. "I can get a local..."

"No needles," he said.

She sniffed, then wrinkled her nose theatrically. "Your breath smells like candy. You drinking vanilla again? That stuff will kill you, you know."

"Really? Now? Besides... it was a chocolate bar." It wasn't technically a lie.

"Uh-huh. Always looking out for you, Bob." She began to pick out the peppercorn-sized chunks of salt, little rivulets of crimson blood following each one. She expected him to cry out or shrink away, but he remained stoic throughout, as if trying to hear a conversation a world away. She dropped each chunk into the bedpan with a metallic "clink."

It took ten minutes, dozens of little pieces removed. He was silent throughout, just staring ahead.

Dawn mopped at the cuts with alcohol swabs to sterilize them. She tried not to think too much about the last time she'd tried to staunch a serious gunshot wound. That just brought back painful memories.

"I'm going to apply some antiseptic cream with a numbing agent to stave off infection, and then a big bandage. Is that okay?"

He nodded. He was oddly brave in his attempts to remain stoic and unmoved. He really was a strange man, Dawn had treated any number of street people, but Bob was the only one who'd offered to teach her "Canadian Air Force exercise techniques."

The cream stung almost as badly as the alcohol, the disheveled man grimacing just slightly throughout, one fist clenched hard as if offering some diversion.

"Okay, that's it," she said. "Hold on here while I get you some painkillers and talk to my other patient."

He nodded as she rose and moved to the door. Bob felt his head swimming, a combination of fatigue and pain conspiring to overwhelm him.

By the time she looked back, he'd passed out, his head leaning slightly against the basin pedestal next to his chair, mouth lolling slightly open, breathing regular.

5

WASHINGTON, DC

The man on the other side of the one-way glass was trained to handle pain.

The room wasn't much bigger than a walk-in closet. Strapped to a chair, his wrists manacled to an iron loop in the middle of the interrogation table, he'd withstood two days of conventional torture.

That surprised his observers. Michael Smalls had once been a field agent, a member of the CIA covert operations group Team Seven. But he'd been a technical whiz, a reconnaissance specialist. His resilience had been questionable, they'd assumed.

He was smaller, at five five and a hundred and forty pounds. His cherubic face, thinning blond hair and spectacles made him look like a high school chemistry teacher.

They'd taken his glasses away, and he was squinting slightly, though that was at least partly due to the bright light they'd shined in his eyes for forty-eight straight hours.

They'd tried shock therapy, along with painful attacks on his genitals and anus, as well as nerve pressure to excruciating clusters along his hands, feet, and neck.

He'd given them nothing.

It was time to step things up, his captors had decided. An oversized bucket of water sat on the table ahead of him. In a few moments, they would soak the flannel cloth next to it and place it over his nose and mouth.

Then they would pour water over it in a slow, steady stream, his manacled arms unable to prevent the sensation of drowning as water filled his sinuses and the top portion of his throat, held back ever-so-precariously by a strip of absorbent cloth.

"You don't have to do this," Smalls was suggesting, though it sounded more like a plea. His breathing was rapid and shallow. He sounded exhausted, the fight beginning to fade. And he knew what waterboarding was.

He knew enough to be afraid.

Life had been difficult lately. His wife didn't entirely trust him anymore, and his work had suffered as his debts mounted.

But he still wanted to live.

"Look, it's like I said right after you brought me in… I was talking out of my ass. It's all bullshit. I swear to God…"

On the other side of the glass, Gerald Dahlen's expression was stoic, hands in the pockets of his gray suit trousers. His puffy, middle-aged face and beady blue-gray eyes revealed nothing.

Smalls had stolen something from him. He wasn't sure what yet, or how. But the little man thought it was leverage, information serious enough to warrant demanding a million dollars in cash.

Dahlen swept back the thin mop of gray-silver hair that still covered his scalp, then leaned forward and pressed an intercom button.

"Michael, it does you no good to insult my intelligence. It's my business, after all. Give us a location. Let's start with that. I don't need to know yet what you found; what you took from me. I'm sure we'll recognize it when we find it."

Beside the interrogation table, a stocky man with a dark buzz cut and a scar running from his nostril to his chin reached down to pick up the washcloth. He held it in the bucket for a moment, soaking it down.

"I'm telling you!" Smalls implored. "I got in deep with a 'made' guy in Vegas, a big debt..."

The man approached him.

Dahlen hit the button once more. "Hold off for a minute, Mr. Krug. Michael, we know you owe the Gabelli crime family a half-million dollars. We know everything about you."

Dahlen's family was a generation separated from Denmark, and he had a formal mid-Atlantic tone to his voice, a slightly British inflection. He liked to think people found it disarming.

"What I don't know, but must be sure of, is what you've got hidden away somewhere."

Smalls looked genuinely panicked as Krug soaked the rag once more.

"Look, Gerry... Mr. Dahlen, please... I swear to GOD I was bluffing. I know you've got more money than you can count now; I figured it was nothing for you to just make something go away. So I just took my shot..."

"I don't believe you. I've known you a long time, Michael. You've always had a duplicitous streak."

Dahlen released the button and glanced sideways towards his broad-shouldered bodyguard and personal valet, Gustav, who stood by the main door, hands clasped ahead of him like a soldier at ease. "What do you think? Lying?"

"Of course."

Dahlen pressed the intercom button. "Go ahead, Mr. Krug."

A pair of hands reached forward from behind Smalls as Krug's assistant pulled back on a leather strap, holding the terrified man's neck tight to the chair back. Krug reached down and picked up the rubber mouth bit. He crammed it between the smaller man's lips, over protestations, forcing them open.

He slapped the cloth over Smalls's mouth. Then he picked up the bucket and leaned over their captive.

He began to slowly pour the water, Smalls trying to thrash about in the chair but failing. His fight was useless against his restraints.

Krug smiled slightly, dark eyes wide, a dreamy look coming over his face as his gurgling subject tried to scream.

6

It was early evening. Dahlen had left Smalls in Krug's capable hands to take care of some business. Gustav had called the house to make sure that Cook had lamb and roast potatoes ready for him when he returned to his palatial home in the Kalorama neighborhood of northwest DC.

It had taken a half hour to deal with work. He'd returned to the interrogation room, straightened his wool knit tie, then leaned on the intercom button once more. "Mr. Krug?"

Smalls was sobbing, crying gently like a distraught child.

"No luck yet, sir. Again?"

It usually only took one, Dahlen knew. Being waterboarded was the most terrifying sensation most people could experience, an intense panic as they slowly felt themselves drowning.

But... Smalls had surprised them, holding up under repeated assaults. "Really? Nothing at all?"

"No, sir. He insists he made it up, that he has no information about Tehran at all other than the rumors at the time."

Dahlen knew those stories already, the stories about his days as Team Seven operations director.

Fifteen years had passed since the team's greatest failure, which could only have been due to a leak.

Dahlen knew that, despite his resignation a month prior to the mission, he had been suspected.

If Smalls had evidence confirming him as the Iranians' source, it could ruin him.

Critical Safety Management, his intelligence and mercenary outfit, relied on government contracts. He'd used his CIA and family connections to build it into a business worth more than $200 million per year.

He stared through the one-way glass at the demoralized former agent.

He was probably telling the truth. But perhaps what he really needed was an appeal to his mortality rather than pain.

He pressed the button. "Mr. Krug, I think Mr. Smalls has outlived his usefulness. Shoot him in the head, then get rid of him."

Smalls pushed hard against the leather restraints and began kicking and straining to break free once more. His thinning blond hair flopped about as he tried desperately to pull away from confinement. He was trying to say something, spittle flying from the gap in the middle of the rubber bit.

"Take out his mouthpiece for a moment," Dahlen ordered.

Krug complied, setting it on the table.

"KILL ME AND YOU WON'T KNOW FOR SURE!" Smalls insisted frantically. "Kill me, and... you won't ever be sure. I'm not the only person who has information. There... There are others; there are people who know that if I don't go home..."

Dahlen leaned on the button. "There are no others, Michael. I don't know how you were missed when the Team cleaned house, but we're going to rectify that now. You're a foolish little man, and you're going to die."

"There are others who know what you really are... a traitor to your country. How do you think that's going to look on the front page of the *Post*, Gerry? Huh?"

"The only people you knew from Team Seven are all dead, Michael."

Smalls was breathing hard, practically panting as he tried to convince the businessman of his story. "They missed me though, didn't they? There are others."

That prompted a moment of pause.

Dahlen considered it. He'd been assured years earlier by one of his lackeys that the survivors of the Tehran mission had met the same fate. They'd been fired by the agency, then systematically erased, as if they'd never existed.

If he was lying about having any evidence to begin with, he was almost certainly lying about that, too. "I don't believe you."

"Then explain why I'm still around, huh?" Smalls insisted, his desperation obvious. "I know who was tasked with cleaning us up... and that didn't go so well."

If he was telling the truth...

But that was impossible, Dahlen decided. Someone else would have broken cover by now. It had been a decade, slightly more. There had been five surviving members of the Tehran mission, Smalls and Krug included.

And there had been three who didn't come back.

"If they're still alive, where are they?" Dahlen demanded.

Smalls breathed in sharply, a sense of triumph creeping across his face. Dahlen sounded irritated, genuinely concerned. And the ex-spy knew it.

"For that... for that we need to talk about my million..."

Dahlen allowed himself a tiny smile, knowing his old

colleague couldn't see him. He certainly had guts... or was recklessly foolish.

"Mr. Krug, give Michael ten seconds to give you the location of the first team member. If he doesn't, shoot him in the groin. Let's see how many bullets it takes to loosen his tongue, or whether he dies first..."

Krug drew a nine-millimeter pistol from the speed holster clipped to his belt.

He chambered a round, then pointed the gun at Smalls's crotch. "Ten... nine... eight... seven..." He began to count down.

"If you shoot me, you get NOTHING!" Smalls spat. "You need me, and you know it."

"Six... five... four..."

"IT'S NOTHING TO YOU, for Christ's sake!" Smalls raged, straining against his bonds again, his face reddened. His tone reverted to a sad plea. "Gerry... I'm begging you..."

"Three... two... one..." Krug's finger found the trigger.

"WAIT!" Smalls barked. "Just... just wait."

"Well?" Dahlen said. "Last chance."

"I... I don't..."

"Ah!" Dahlen cautioned from the observation room, raising a knowing index finger even though Smalls could not see it. "Ah now! Be careful what you say next, Michael. I've always thought your name suited you. You're a small man, a little fellow, inside and out."

"Gerry, please..."

"You never really had the balls for the job, but you had one skill at which you were exceptional: you knew how to stay alive. And it's going to disappoint me; it's going to disappoint me, Michael, if you don't even have that to offer the world anymore."

Smalls scowled, his forehead wrinkled and forlorn. "I... I

don't know where they are. But they're alive, and they know what I know, and if you kill me, they'll..."

"Mr. Krug, shoot him in the head, please."

"Wait, NO!" Smalls yelped. "If... if..."

"If you don't know where they are, they don't know where you are, Michael. That's how it works. So... they either don't exist, or you haven't contacted them. Either way, you still have nothing. Go ahead, Mr. Krug."

"I..." Smalls attempted to get another word in.

Krug pulled the trigger once, the gunshot loud even through the glass, the bullet passing through the middle of Smalls's forehead and brain, his face frozen in a look of utter shock.

To be certain, Krug walked over and put the gun to Smalls's temple and pulled the trigger.

Blood and brain matter sprayed across the one-way glass.

Krug looked towards it. "What about what he said? What about the others?"

Dahlen wasn't sure.

"I don't know how he wriggled his way to safety, but I imagine they've been dead for years. Still... put the word out to everyone we know. If Smalls was truthful, it's possible there's another threat out there."

"And?"

"If there is..." He held the button down for a final moment. It was time to go home for some lamb. "Eliminate it."

7

CHICAGO

Bob stirred, awakened by the bruising sting of his chest wound.

He drank in the sterile air before opening his eyes slowly, tilting his head either way to take in his surroundings. The room was stark white, glaring, a fluorescent tube light blaring down at him from the tile-panel ceiling.

I'm at the free clinic.

A kid shot me with rock salt.

He could hear voices from the hallway, two women talking through the ajar door, voices muffled.

Dawn glanced back into the room to ensure her patient was okay. She noticed Bob had awoken. "I've got to handle this..."

"Later, girl," the other voice said. "Are you doing aquafit Saturday?"

"I plan to, I do. I'll call you this evening."

"Uh-huh."

She turned his way. "Great, you're awake." Nurse Dawn entered and sat down across the small room at a computer terminal. "We close in ten minutes, and insurance says you need to be gone then anyway..."

"I passed out?"

"You did. On the plus side, your wound looks mostly superficial, although I imagine it won't feel as such when the topical wears off."

She turned her office chair fully his way. "Look... Bob... I know your instinct is going to be to get out of here and find somewhere to be alone..."

"I have a flop. Good spot, too..."

"From the way your hands are shaking, I'm guessing you haven't had a drink in some time."

He glanced down. She was right. His hands were trembling. He pulled them tight to his body self-consciously, using his fingers to pull on his jacket cuffs, steadying them.

"Ran out of money and booze. Went to the corner store to... to pick up some vanilla extract instead, because of the price..."

"And you walked into a robbery. I had to convince Dr. Girard not to call the police. It was on the news; the store was completely trashed. They've arrested one of the little jerks who hit the place, in case you were curious. He lost most of his left hand to some kind of explosion and is up at Methodist in the ICU..."

"He made a bad choice." Bob pulled himself up and slung his legs over the edge of the exam table. "Now he gets to live with the consequences, like the rest of us."

She nodded and studied him as he talked. "Uh-huh. I get the sentiment, Bob; I just don't agree with it. People make mistakes all the time; shouldn't cost them a hand. My brother Carl was in jail for eight years, but it beat him being dead, I guess. My son, Maurice, wasn't so lucky."

"You had a son?"

"Uh-huh. Had him at eighteen, a surprise. His father was not much of a person, but at that time, maybe neither was I."

"He was in a gang?"

"My boy? No. He was a good kid. But he had friends who weren't. I tried to keep him away; did everything short of sending him out of state. Took a bullet when he was fourteen, just playing basketball with the wrong people. People make mistakes. Doesn't mean they deserve to die or be permanently maimed."

"I guess, yeah. Wait... fourteen? So that wasn't long ago?"

"Five years last month." She realized how raw it still was and changed the subject. "The clerk at that store... he said gang members tried to kill him, but he was saved by a street person. Officially, for when the police ask, you wouldn't know anything about that, I assume?"

Bob shrugged. He liked her, but her world didn't need to come into his orbit of misery. "It's news to me," he said.

She smiled and shook her head gently. "I don't believe you, not with that chest wound. But you've always been a good person, at least while visiting us. So I didn't say anything."

"Thank you."

"They'll pull his security camera data, you realize..."

"It looked pretty low rent. I doubt it'll help much. I don't have a record, just a few nights in the drunk tank," Bob said. "Can't imagine they'll look too hard for me."

"Uh-huh." She chewed on her lower lip for just a split second, nervous about broaching personal space. "I took a peek at your file while you were unconscious. Four years, I've been treating you. Four years of cuts and scrapes and sores and minor illnesses from exposure to the elements."

"I'm grateful," he said. "It's more than I deserve."

She frowned at that. Then she gently gripped his forearm.

"You don't have to live this way, Bob. I can help you find a recovery center where the money isn't the biggest obstacle..."

"Don't need it. Tried it once. Didn't take. Got my squat..."

"Squat?"

"My flop. It's not far. Got two squares a day with protein and veg from the free kitchen, when I remember."

"That's not living, not really."

She didn't, and couldn't, understand his choices. He pushed himself to his feet. He straightened his clothing and buttoned up his shirt. "I have to go. Like you said, you're closing."

She rose quickly, surprising him with her speed. She put a hand on his arm. No one had made physical contact with him in years other than to treat a wound, and Bob shrank back slightly.

"It's okay," she said. "I think you know I only want to help, Bob. Anyone who would take a risk like you did today... that's a good person. You're only forty-three years old! You have years ahead of you, and there's so much more to life that is worth—"

"Not my life," he interrupted. "Some of us, we deserve exactly what we get..."

"I don't believe that..."

"Yes... but you don't know me," Bob insisted tersely. "You don't know the things I've done. Now... can I go? Please?"

She crossed her arms. "I'm very worried about you."

He smiled thinly at that, a forlorn expression. "That's because you *are* one of those people, the good ones who deserve to be happy. But my train went off the rails a long time ago. You can't unmake my bad decisions by caring about me, okay? It's better not to try. I'll just let you down, and you'll get hurt."

"Booze... you know it's not an answer to anything..."

"I know that I drink it, and then I don't think straight, and

I can sleep. And then I wake up, and everything hurts, especially my head. I like that it takes me out of everything and then makes me feel like shit for it. I escape, and then I pay, and I figure maybe each day out there saves me a day later in Hell."

Her mouth hung open, and her expression was crestfallen. "Oh... Oh, Bob, that's no way to live..." She put a comforting hand on his forearm as he rose.

He shook it off. "No pity, thank you. I have to go." He ambled towards the door, right hand subconsciously massaging his bruised and lacerated chest. "I can't be here anymore."

She turned quickly towards the table bearing the computer, her purse adjacent. She grabbed it. "At least let me give you enough money to make sure you eat properly..."

She turned back his way in time to see the door swing closed behind him.

8

HICKORY HILLS, TWENTY MILES WEST OF CHICAGO

It had been a long, rare walk home for Marcus Pell.

He wasn't unfit or tired. It was only three miles from Amos Alonzo Stagg High School to his family's house. But it wasn't a walk the seventeen-year-old ever needed to make.

His mother had been picking him up after the 3:05 bell for years.

She rarely deviated.

He'd tried her phone, with no text back. Then he'd tried calling, because although he hated using a phone as a phone, it beat not knowing.

He'd gotten a busy signal repeatedly, then the dreaded voicemail. After fifteen minutes, he knew whatever was keeping her had to be important.

His friend Parker waited with him, because Parker didn't mind walking. Parker's parents were relatively poor by the affluent suburb's standards. Marcus's Levi's were clean and new; Parker's had a knee patch his mother had sewed in to save them for one more semester. Marcus was fit and usually healthy; Parker was developing a weight problem and knocked back sugar like it was water in a desert.

The morning had been cool and crisp, but by afternoon, the temperature had picked up, humidity noticeable. A flawless light-gray sidewalk carried them past homes that cost more than most Americans would make in twenty years, five- and six-bedroom colonials, pools in the backyard, manicured gardens tended by immigrant gardeners.

The driveways were filled by Porsches, Teslas, BMWs, Jaguars.

Parker was accustomed to making his own way. Sometimes, Marcus was jealous of the fact that his friend's parents were utterly uninvolved in his life.

But not often.

"Your mom's some kind of saint, giving you a ride every day," Parker said as they strolled. "Even with all the money around here, most kids are taking the bus. My old man says most of the people in Hickory Hills are assholes."

Marcus's parents didn't like the man and wanted him to stay away from his friend's home after dark.

But friends were friends. "He's not wrong," Marcus said, wishing he'd worn something lighter on the warm afternoon than the wool-collared denim jacket. "I mean... shit, man, I don't know. I like most people here well enough. But they're pretty serious, pretty snobby."

He didn't raise his nagging sense of alienation, that he belonged somewhere less privileged. Parker didn't need to hear that.

And he didn't need to know that Marcus always felt out of place, even in his own home.

"You don't see them when they're at their shittiest," Parker suggested. "He does. They know nothing about him, nothing about the piece of shit *his* old man was... but they're just fucking mean, bro, casually. Every day. Some of the judgmental shit they say to him… I'm telling you: rich people are the worst."

At the end of the block, a side street separated the homes from a corner-lot apartment building. It was an unassuming, boxy four-story brownstone walk-up, built in the 1950s.

Parker nodded towards it. "Home sweet home." He frowned on seeing his father's dented Toyota quarter-ton truck outside. The box was filled with mattresses, old furniture and other detritus from his sideline hauling oversized items to the dump.

"He's home already." Parker sighed. "It's going to be a long night."

"Sorry, man, I wish I could help."

"Nah… it's okay. You going to the career fair on Sunday?"

"It's basically mandatory," Marcus said. "Principal Steiner said it was voluntary, but that he'd be keeping an eye out for me."

"What booths are you going to hit?"

Marcus shook his head gently. "Man… I have no fucking idea. Do they have a booth for people who don't know what they want?"

It was good just getting a few minutes to talk, with no social pressures involved, no group chats, no DMs. Perhaps that was the upside to his mother not showing up.

He wanted to invite his friend over for a few hours' respite. But he knew Richard and Janet wouldn't approve.

His parents thought it a privilege to live in relative affluence, with other relatively affluent people. They thought it a privilege that he was allowed to use their first names, and had encouraged it since he was young.

But he hated it, hated the fact that he felt like a stranger in his own home. It was never "Mom and Dad," always "Richard and Janet."

He paused on the sidewalk, watching Parker make his

way up the apartment walk to the front door. He waited until his friend's door buzz was acknowledged by the click of its electronic lock. Once Parker was inside, he continued on his way.

The house was three more blocks away. He guessed his father would be home already. He'd been back by four every day of the summer, heading directly into his study to pretend he wasn't drinking.

They were like that, his parents. Richard was the more secretive, but they both had private selves, characters they reserved for isolated moments. It contributed to Marcus's unease, on the outside looking in.

While his father sipped scotch in his study, his mother would flit about the house, ensuring the maid, Lucretia, had dusted, cleaned the bathrooms, restocked everything.

Then she would restraighten all the books on the shelves, making sure they were in alphabetical order and rotated the same way, a habit of her obsessive-compulsive disorder.

It took five more minutes to get there. At the corner, with their house three properties away, he could already see his parents' cars. His father's Mercedes C-300 was parked at the curb, a jet-black success brag, with a slope-back roofline and an oversized corporate emblem on the onyx front grille.

That was weird. He always pulled into the attached two-car garage.

His mother's burgundy Subaru station wagon was in the driveway, which wouldn't have been strange... except that she seemed to have forgotten him.

He made his way to the front door and tried it. It was unlocked.

He pushed the door open, the hinges smooth and silent. "Hello?" Marcus called out. "Anybody maybe forget something today? Or somebody?"

It was strangely quiet, and he took a step forward onto the dark hardwood floor. He left the front door ajar.

The wide, open atrium led to a double staircase directly ahead. He heard heavy footsteps on the second floor. Marcus walked to the bottom step and put one foot on it. "Richard? Janet?" he called out. "I'm home."

His mother came barreling out of their bedroom suite.

She looked over the rail to the atrium below and saw Marcus. She headed directly for the stairs and hurried down them. She snatched his arm and dragged him up the first step. "Go to your room now, take your gym bag out of the closet, and pack two changes of clothing. Do it now. I don't have time to argue."

Janet was small, dainty. But her grip on his forearm was like a vise. "What's going on?" he demanded. "What's wrong? What happened?"

"Just do as I say!" she barked. "We don't have much time." She guided him past her and up the stairs.

His father came out of the bedroom carrying a soft-sided suitcase. He tossed it to her without pause before noticing his son. "Jesus Christ!" he agonized. "You forgot the kid?!"

"WE forgot the kid," she said, hauling the case down a few more steps, then sliding it to the front door.

Marcus paused in front of his bedroom. "What's going on? Somebody tell me, please!"

"Listen to your mother," his father said, hurrying back to the master bedroom. "We only have a few minutes. Get ready and we go, as quick as you can, now!"

Marcus obeyed. His father was no stern disciplinarian, but he wasn't soft, either. He hurried into his room and found the blue gym bag with the Nike swoosh on the side, buried under two inches of laundry in his closet.

He sniffed it reflexively. He'd used it for the three-on-three basketball summer league, and it reeked of sweaty armpits. He went back to the door and called out, "Janet! My gym bag is gross..."

His mother had just come back into the house, the soft suitcase gone. She left the door open as she hurried back up the stairs. "For God's sake, Marcus, just use it! We have to go right away!"

He took a step back into the room. She'd never yelled at him like that, like he was some sort of idiot.

His parents were brainiacs, and Marcus had always considered himself a little dumb. Great at tearing apart an engine block, not so hot at math, despite an accountant father. He grabbed a handful of clothing and shoved it into the bag, then added a few pairs of underwear.

Marcus hurried back to the landing at the same time as his father, watching Richard toss another suitcase down to the ground floor. His mother dropped it, then picked it up and made for the entrance. "Last one coming," he said.

She pulled the door open, then slammed it just as quickly. "We're too late. They're here," she said, frantically engaging the deadbolt and main lock.

Richard Pell turned to his son. "Marcus, go down to the basement. Hide behind the woodpile, cover it and yourself with the orange tarp on my workbench. Got that?"

"Richard... Dad... I..."

His father grabbed his upper arm forcefully. "Do as I say! There are men here who want to hurt us – to hurt you. Go! Now!"

Marcus nodded frantically and made his way down the stairs. He headed for the basement door. He felt numb, unable to process the sudden threat. He heard a telltale clicking, the sound of a pistol's slide going back, like something out of a Bourne movie. "Is that...?" he began to ask.

His mother shooed him towards the door. "Go! Now!"

He opened the door, the hinge creaking. Then he paused, intent on finding out what the hell was going on.

"How many?" his father asked.

"Black SUV, four occupants," his mom said. "We can assume four more through the back..."

Marcus's eyes widened as she drew a pistol from her purse. "Janet... I don't..."

"GO!" they both yelled in unison.

Years of following their instructions kicked in. He hurried down the stairs.

The basement was open plan, with a low ceiling, the room broken up only by the furnace in the back corner. His father's workbench was along one side wall, the woodpile next to it, slightly away from the wall to ward off dampness.

He picked up the orange tarp and made his way over to the stack. Marcus turned sideways and carefully hid, crouched, behind it. He spread the tarp over it and himself, anxious about knocking over the pyramid of lumber.

His heart was racing, his breath short and shallow. Their lives were boring, even by Hickory Hills standards. None of it made any sense.

A heavy thump broke his panicked spell. He looked up, though the tarp cut off any view. It sounded as if it came from the front of the house.

Another heavy thump followed, this one shaking the basement ceiling. A third bass thud echoed, followed quickly by a crashing noise, the worst of it drowned out by the distance and floor between them.

Is someone... breaking down the front door!?

He had his answer immediately, the gunshots less muffled, a pair of loud cracks followed by silence for a split second.

Then all hell broke loose.

Marcus covered his head with his arms in fearful shock as

machine-gun fire echoed through the house, followed immediately by two more single shots, a heavier thump, this time like someone falling over. Footfalls crossed the ceiling above in strange, precise unison.

It was quiet for a few moments, and he realized he was panting, the only sound coming from his heavy breathing, the anxiety and fear overwhelming, his heart pounding faster and faster. The single light bulb near the front of the room hummed gently.

He heard another crash, this time due west, in the direction of his mother's study and the kitchen. There were two more shots. More heavy footsteps followed, fading quickly though still there if he concentrated enough to pick them out.

Multiple people going... upstairs?

More gunfire, staccato automatic rounds, glass breaking, single shots following. It was muffled, like the background noise in a war correspondent's TV news piece, the cracks barely audible from two floors away.

Then louder gunfire, right above. Another heavy fall. More crashes, items knocked over, more glass breaking. Marcus didn't know how to react, his mouth hanging open. He was beginning to hyperventilate, and he tried to slow his breathing.

The basement door hinge creaked.

9

It had gone suddenly quiet upstairs, the gunfire subsiding.

But the door had creaked once; he was sure of it.

Perhaps he'd left the door open, and it had simply shifted an inch. He tried to slow his breathing, mouth closed, nostrils flaring to double-time gasps.

What...!?

It was the barest of echoes, a wooden step protesting with a slight, squeaky whine as someone put their weight on it.

Marcus held his breath and listened closely, fear beginning to course through him.

Had he imagined it? He began to breathe again, gently, in through his nose and out through his mouth, as his father had taught him.

Calm down. You're imagining things.

Another stair squeaked.

The squeak was louder this time, perhaps a footfall.

He tried to slow his breathing again, but it became uneven, as if he couldn't concentrate on listening for more sounds while also controlling his breaths, as if thinking about it made his breath shorter, more ragged.

Panic began to set in, pulse racing, an electric shudder running through his body.

If someone was coming down, did that mean his parents were...?

He pushed the thought away. His father was an accountant... but he'd always sensed a toughness in him, an instinct for self-preservation. He had begun teaching Marcus martial arts years earlier, as well as forcing him to go hunting, to learn to shoot.

He hadn't taken to any of it naturally; violence wasn't in his character. But Richard had insisted, making vague joking references to a zombie apocalypse or the collapse of democracy.

None of it mattered in the moment, frozen in place, hidden from sight but equally unable to see. His heart pounded in his chest like a kick drum.

He wanted to lift the tarp, take a peek over the woodpile. But Richard had taught him while hunting about how easy it was to spot movement against a still background, how they could use it from a deer blind to spot game.

It had been a side of his father he'd never expected, an uncomfortable willingness to kill a defenseless animal, not for food or even sport, but to prove a point.

Specks of light bounced off the tarp, a flashlight beam impeded by the logs, thin rays shining through gaps in the pyramid.

Someone was searching the basement. The beams danced around from side to side.

But there wasn't much to search, Marcus knew. If he moved at all, whoever it was would spot him. If he stayed there, they'd eventually make it to the back of the darkened room and check under the tarp.

He looked to either side. His father sometimes left the hatchet for log splitting buried in the old wooden block to one side of the pile. He tried to reach over that far, but realized to do so, he'd have to let the tarp move slightly.

Grab it. Defend yourself. If they're close enough, you might have time to...

To what? Hatchet someone? The idea was crazy.

Marcus knew his lack of aggression was another thing he didn't share with Richard. He'd had his shot, in the woods of Northern Michigan's Upper Peninsula, on that first hunting trip. He'd had a six-point buck in his sights, but had been unable to pull the trigger.

His father had been more kind than normal about it, telling him it was a good thing he had a hard time killing, but that for some people, it was necessary to survive.

He'd thought Richard meant harvesting game.

In the moment, he was no longer sure.

"You down here, kid?" The man's voice was unfamiliar. "The sheet said three of you. Your parents can't help you, so you might as well come on out from wherever you're hiding. Can't be too many places..."

He felt his body quiver from fear, the shaking difficult to stop. If he had to defend himself...

I need to know what I'm facing.

He reached ahead a few feet and gently, ever-so-slowly, lifted the edge of the tarp.

The gap was tiny, less than an inch. But it was enough to reveal the figure approaching, dressed in black clothing, barely visible but for the flashlight – which was attached to the sight rail of a submachine gun.

The man seemed to look straight at him.

Marcus dropped the edge of the tarp and held his breath.

His adversary chuckled. "Pretty dumb, kid. Old man

should have taught you how to keep still. Never know; I might've been lazy, might not have checked back there."

He was less than twenty feet away. Marcus wondered if he could reach the hatchet, throw it at the man, perhaps shelter behind the logs again from the inevitable gunfire.

"If you're thinking of going for that hatchet over there, I'd think again," the man offered. "Just come on out. I won't hurt you."

A distraction? A distraction of some kind. That was his only shot, something to draw the man's attention away from the woodpile. He dug into his side pocket and found his phone, frantically scrolling to the timer app and setting the clock at five seconds, the sound to "explosion."

He reached around the right side of the pile and slid it across the concrete floor with as much force as he could muster, plastic scraping concrete.

Marcus stood in one motion, throwing off the tarp and reaching down the other side of the pile for the hatchet's blue rubber handle, his grip finding it as his assailant watched the cell phone slide by.

Its timer went off, and it released a feeble, underpowered explosion tone.

The man laughed as he began to turn back the boy's way. "Is that all you've—"

Marcus hurled the tiny axe sidearm with all his strength. It flew end over end towards the other man's chest before the man could raise his gun.

Instead, the gunman raised his free hand in a flash, judgment true, fingers finding the handle. He caught the hatchet, then dropped it disdainfully, the metal head clattering on the floor.

"Stupid," he said. "Sorry, kid. If it were up to me..."

He raised the submachine gun to eye level, and Marcus closed his eyes and threw up both arms, as if it might help.

The crack of the gunshot was the loudest yet, and he took another sharp, desperate lungful of air in, anticipating pain.

The gunman collapsed to his knees, his free hand coming up to his chest, the hole through it just below his collarbone and above the edge of a flak jacket, blood pouring from the wound. He stared at the blood on his gloved hand for a moment in disbelief. "Well... well, what do you know..." he muttered.

A second shot sounded, Marcus seeing the muzzle flare near the bottom of the stairs, the darkness pushed back for just enough time to see a smaller figure.

Janet.

The gunman pitched over face-first, dead before he hit the ground.

"We need to go, NOW!" she barked.

He stood unsteadily, pushing his way out from behind the pile, not worrying about spilling a few logs.

"Quickly!" she hissed through gritted teeth.

He stumbled towards her, looking down with horror at the dead man.

She grabbed him by the wrist and led him to the bottom of the steps. "We don't have time for feelings right now if we're going to survive. Understood?"

He nodded, dazed.

"We're going to go upstairs. The rest of these guys are searching the bedrooms."

"Where's Richard?" he mumbled. "Dad..."

"Your father's dead," she said coldly. "No time, Marcus! We grieve later. When we get to the top of the stairs, we're going to make a run for the door. Got it? Here..." She slid a set of keys into his hand. "Whichever one of us reaches my car first takes the driver's seat and starts it. If I don't make it..."

"If you... Dad!?" he interrupted. "Janet... Mom..." He'd

begun to cry without realizing it, hot tears tumbling down both cheeks.

"Shhh! There's no time for that now. If I don't make it, you drive. You drive as far and as fast as you can, get away from here. Are you wearing your locket?"

He reached down to his chest absently, feeling the heart-shaped jewelry under his shirt. He nodded.

"Behind our picture, there's a piece of paper with a name and an address. You go there and find him. He can help. Got it?"

He nodded again. "But..."

She slapped his left cheek gently. "Snap out of it. NOW! This is life or death, Marcus, you hear me? Up the stairs! I'll be right behind you. On the count of three, you shove the door open, and we run. Clear?"

He nodded again. She pushed him towards the staircase. He began to climb the steps. His heart was still pounding, breath short, brow riveted with sweat. His skin felt numb, as if he'd stepped away from his own body.

They reached the top step. He felt faint, a dizzying sensation from hyperventilating. "Ready?" she whispered. "GO!"

He shoved the door open and ran, not looking back, reaching the front door split seconds later and throwing it open, stepping around it and outside. He glanced over his shoulder as he made for the Subaru, seeing her reaching back with the pistol, rounds fired in quick succession.

Marcus reached the driver's door and yanked it open, fumbling with the keys to fit them into the ignition, pulling the door shut simultaneously. Through the windshield, he saw his mother backing up a few steps more towards the car, firing off two more shots in the process. She turned to approach the passenger's side.

The machine-gun bullets cut her down where she stood,

the gunman leaning around the edge of the doorjamb. She fell sideways, collapsing gracelessly to the asphalt.

"MOM!" Marcus screamed in abject horror.

The figure in the doorway raised something. He could barely see through his tears.

The crack of the gun's muzzle came a split second after the bullet pierced the windshield. The bullet went straight through the front passenger seat, spraying the back of the car with a mist of foam, stuffing, and faux leather.

Instinct took over, panic urging him on. Marcus threw the automatic gears into reverse and stood on the accelerator, the car rocketing backwards, bouncing heavily as it found the asphalt of the street.

He shifted to drive and stood on the gas, anticipating another bullet that did not come. His fingers gripped the wheel like a man hanging from a cliff, knuckles white as he blew through the first stop sign, a horn sounding from the car coming the other way, suddenly cut off.

Marcus drove without looking back, pointing the car east towards Chicago, unable to think straight as he headed for the anonymity of the busy interstate highway.

10

WASHINGTON, DC

If it had been anyone else insisting on setting the time and place, Andrew Kennedy would have been angry.

As the deputy director of the Central Intelligence Agency's Special Operations Group, he had a fearsome reputation for tightly controlling his time.

But former colleague Gerald Dahlen was the agency's top private security contractor, and the private sector didn't respect agency protocol with the same rigorous standards.

Dahlen wanted to meet at Trattoria Giovanni, Kennedy's favorite eatery. No one else at the agency, to Kennedy's knowledge, frequented the restaurant, which meant they were unlikely to be seen together.

Dahlen wasn't the kind of man with whom he wished to be seen.

Kennedy studied the menu, occasionally pushing up his square, steel-framed eyeglasses. The chef at the restaurant was adventurous, and the menu was different each time he visited, it seemed.

He lowered the menu slightly and considered the room. It was mostly composed of smaller two-person tables, most customers young people, the under-fifty set in their finery, schmoozing each other for business.

He could see the barest reflection of his own face in the menu's plastic cover, the crown of white hair, the worsening jowls. The other patrons made him feel even older than his seventy-two years.

But the food was fantastic, the jazz music relaxing and cool, the décor a stylish throwback to the supper clubs of his childhood. It was all so elegant, so utterly unsuited to a man like Gerald Dahlen, a man who was rich but bought suits off the rack. The kind of man who preferred news radio to jazz.

He hadn't seen Dahlen in four years.

He watched the other man cross the busy restaurant towards his table.

Kennedy couldn't stand him. He'd helped oust the former Team Seven operations director nearly fifteen years earlier, just prior to the Tehran debacle.

That didn't change the fact that Critical Security had men on the ground in Afghanistan, in Iraq, in Colombia.

If he'd had a choice between trusting the Danish-American tycoon or an angry rattlesnake, Kennedy supposed he'd have gone for the snake.

Still... assuming he's always lying at least makes him predictable, he told himself as Dahlen and his brick wall of a bodyguard reached the table.

Kennedy rose and proffered a hand. Dahlen took it in two of his own and shook effusively.

"Old friend," Dahlen said, his smile revealing two rows of perfect, tiny teeth. "It's been too long."

"Please..." Kennedy said, gesturing to the other chair.

Dahlen waited while his man pulled out the chair for him, then took a seat. "You can wait for me in the car, Gustav," he suggested. The bodyguard nodded once and headed back towards the front of the restaurant.

"Now..." Dahlen began as he unfurled a neatly folded white linen napkin and placed it over his lap, "... what could possibly have arisen that requires this sort of private tete-a-tete? Hmmm? It's been... what... three years since we last had a face-to-face?"

"Four." *And it remains too soon.* "The trouble in Tikrit."

Dahlen nodded, a distant, smug expression on his face, as if staring through his dinner companion to a window into the past. "Again, not our finest moment. Also, not our fault."

"Twenty-nine dead civilians, including women and children, counts as somewhat worse than just 'not a fine moment.'"

"But we paid off the families, and the job got done with minimal additional loss of life," Dahlen said. "And we paid back a portion of the contract, as agreed."

"You did."

"So everyone's happy."

Kennedy had never been sure if Dahlen was an opportunist or just an out-and-out sociopath. Certainly, he'd never had much time for politics or ideology. But unlike most men of action whom the CIA veteran knew, his preoccupation with self-enrichment was damn near legendary.

It might well have amounted to the same thing, as a consequence. "You have a team in Chicago right now." He didn't phrase it as a question. Kennedy had long ago learned to control conversations with decisive certainty.

"We do?"

"You do. Operating on American soil. That's strictly against the rules, Gerry..."

Dahlen smirked slightly, his gaze drifting away again, as if puzzled. He crossed his arms and shook his head. "I'm not sure I'm aware of anything like that. That doesn't sound like our kind of thing at all."

"Our intel on this is really solid. We know you've had an

eight-man team there since this morning. They left the city heading towards the western suburbs this afternoon at two o'clock in a pair of black Cadillac Escalades, claimed from your holding facility there. We've lost them since, but we'll pick up their trail again in short order, I imagine."

Before Dahlen could deny it, he added, "Why? I'm not here to turn this into a pissing match. I just want to know what could be so important that you'd risk your contracts with the department."

Dahlen rubbed his chin thoughtfully. "Let's suppose there was something we had to take care of..."

"Again, domestic ops are—"

"Not an operation. Cleaning up an old mess."

"Potentially even worse," Kennedy said.

A waitress stepped up to the table, tray balanced on one arm. She was young and chipper, with ruddy cheeks. "May I bring you gentlemen a cocktail to start with, or something from our—"

"Go away; come back in five minutes," Dahlen ordered, not bothering to turn his head.

The waitress looked nervous and quickly skittered away.

"Unnecessary. She's just a kid working for a living," Kennedy said.

"Point taken. But best to get business out of the way before we eat. I hear the oysters here are—"

"Fresh daily, yes. The cleanup?"

Dahlen bobbed his head slightly from side to side. "It's a little of this, a little of that. Nothing you'd benefit from knowing about."

"End it. Quickly."

Dahlen squinted at his lunch partner. "Was that an order, Andrew? You're aware I don't work for the agency anymore? I believe you had a little something to do with that..."

Kennedy ignored the jab. It had been a long time,

although Dahlen had evidently never let it go. He removed his glasses and breathed on the lenses to fog them, then cleaned them methodically with his napkin.

"Team Seven is... essential to our ability to counter terrorism where it lives, to protect Americans from attack. Any effort that serves to undermine that mission, including having one of the group's principal contractors in the news domestically..." He put his glasses back on. "Well, that won't sit well with my superior. This doesn't have anything to do with the Team... does it, Gerry?"

"Perish the thought." Dahlen's gaze drifted to neighboring tables, as if lured by the clinking cutlery and wineglasses.

"Because any effort that might undermine the team will also be met with... substantial resistance."

Dahlen returned his attention to the CIA man. He took a sip from his water glass, then set it back down on the table. He straightened his knife and fork setting. "Now who's talking about breaking mandates? The team isn't allowed to operate on US soil, either, is it? Unless things have changed dramatically, the team doesn't officially exist. So it's not sanctioned anywhere..."

Kennedy did not respond immediately. He let the comment hang between them, the restaurant cacophony of muttered conversations and steel forks against plates filling the void.

He leaned back slightly in his chair and propped his arms on his stomach, arching his fingers. "Think about that, Gerry. Consider what that could mean for you. We didn't hesitate to do what was needed when you were my ops director. That hasn't changed. If anything, we're more determined than ever."

The implicit message, Dahlen knew, was that the Team was not to be trifled with. It left him in a difficult position because former team members had information that could hurt him. "Give me a week."

"That's a negative," Kennedy said. "Eddie says—"

"Eddie doesn't need to be involved in this, in any way." Kennedy's current ops director was his former Clandestine Operations head, Edward Stone. Like Kennedy, he was in his seventies, a Vietnam veteran who'd run CIA missions around the globe for thirty years.

The two men had supported each other's careers for decades. "Besides… isn't he mandated to retire by now? Aren't you both, technically, bound by the rules for law enforcement and foreign service?"

"Well… you know how some rules are more flexible than others. We make it work."

They both knew Dahlen's spotted, suspicious history and about Tehran. He'd been under unofficial investigation for weeks before his resignation. That had been more than fifteen years ago. Now, he was a powerful man.

"Five days," Dahlen countered. "And I'm not asking for favors. Just… don't put anyone on it until then."

The waitress returned, wearing a nervous expression. Before Dahlen could dismiss her again, Kennedy cut him off. "Ah! I think I'm ready. I'll have the salmon with dill sauce, and scalloped potatoes. My friend is too busy to stay."

Dahlen rose, the nervous waitress taking a step back. He put his napkin down on the table. "Remember, Andrew: respect is a two-way street. Give me my five days, and we can both go back to only seeing each other every few years."

"And if not?"

Dahlen didn't elaborate. But the expression suggested the result would be more or less inevitable. He buttoned his suit coat. "Have a good evening, Andrew." He turned and walked out of the dining room.

Kennedy watched him go with a dispassionate, stoic

expression. Internally, he seethed a little. He knew that no matter how soft the jazz and how strong the scotch, future visits might prompt him to think of Gerry Dahlen.

I need to find a new Italian restaurant.

Across the room, an elderly man – his fit build evident through his mock turtleneck and square-shouldered corduroy jacket – sat and observed the conversation breaking up.

A moment later, Edward Stone rose from his chair and pushed it in, then walked over and sat down next to Andrew.

"Eddie."

"Andrew. Did he explain?"

"Not really. Whatever it is, it has him spooked, big time. He wouldn't risk blowing the new contract with Homeland Security unless he thought everything could go ass over teakettle. Keep an eye on him. I don't doubt that if Gerry Dahlen feels cornered, he'll scramble until he overturns the boat."

"He still blames you for his departure."

Kennedy shrugged. "He's not wrong. As soon as I was made SOG director, you were getting his gig. Be wary of this one, old friend. He's a special kind of poison."

11

CHICAGO

The address in the locket offered nothing other than a name and location.

Marcus sat in the Subaru station wagon, parallel parked between a black Audi and a red Jeep. He'd been lucky to find the spot in front of the brownstone townhouse.

When he'd first arrived, he'd sat with the car in park for ten minutes without even looking around or turning off the engine. He'd been lost in grief, memories of his parents back to his earliest days flooding back.

The radio was on so that he could listen to the news, and the sudden switch away from music to a newsreader's voice snapped him out of his trance.

The brownstone stood tall among similar townhouses and fourplexes, on a tidy residential block of West Drummond Place, in Kennedy Park. Across the street, most of the block was taken up by a prep school soccer pitch behind a black chain-link fence.

He stared at the tiny slip of paper, scribbled years earlier in his mother's handwriting. Above the address was the only other piece of information he had to go on:

B. Singleton.

The locket made him think of his parents. He'd spent years feeling irrelevant to them, even though they'd always shown him that he wasn't.

But they were dead, and he felt ashamed, guilty at ever doubting them.

He felt lost without them, and for all his frustrations at their choices when alive, now that they were gone, he could only remember the special times: the skinned knees his mother had nursed when he was a boy; being carried as a six-year-old, half asleep, into the house on Christmas night by his father; going fishing with Richard at dawn, just the two of them.

Marcus began to cry again, the third time since fleeing Hickory Hills.

He'd arrived in Kennedy Park twenty minutes earlier, the setting sun casting long shadows across the tree-lined streets, the pale green, aged copper dome of St. Clements's Church a few blocks away towering over it all.

It had taken him a few minutes to work up the nerve to ring the doorbell. But there had been no one home, and he'd quickly scampered back to the car, self-conscious in the city, worried passersby were studying him.

But he had nowhere else to go, and no one else who he knew could help.

He had no other family that he knew of; he'd thought about calling his friends Parker or Ellie – then realized he'd left his phone on the basement floor of the house.

By the time he'd bought a new smartphone with

preloaded credit, he'd realized he couldn't involve either… or call the police.

For all he knew, the men at the house *were* police. They'd looked official, dressed in the kind of black body armor he'd seen worn by movie SWAT teams and paramilitary outfits.

Richard and Janet had known they were coming. That was the other problem. If the police were safe to involve, they'd have called them before the men even arrived.

Parker's old man had been arrested for drunk and disorderly at least twice to his memory and gotten a beating both times despite, in his words, the fact that he "didn't do shit to them."

It left Marcus without options other than to follow his mother's advice and find "B. Singleton."

He wiped tears away with his sleeve, his cheeks hot and flushed.

Why hadn't they warned him or told him what was wrong? Why hadn't they told him where he was going, who this person was, who the people were who wanted them dead?

Dead.

The five-thirty news report had called it a "murder-suicide," the whereabouts of a third family member unknown after a pitched gunfight between an angry married couple.

Marcus could only imagine the work they'd done to cover up the scene, make the story work. The place must have been a wreck.

The memory of the house brought back the memory of his mother, eyes empty and vacant, lying dead in the driveway.

The notion of them never coming back struck him again, and he felt an awfulness, a hollow, empty sensation he'd never encountered before, as if a cold spirit had stolen a piece of his soul.

He hadn't known his grandparents; they'd died before he was born, according to his parents; and there was little loveable about them. But it also meant he'd never experienced losing family.

He wiped tears away once more, embarrassed for not having more control.

A car pulled up in front of the townhouse, two spots ahead, a dark blue Volvo. The day running lights faded out as the driver switched off the engine.

A moment later, a man with close-cropped, dark salt-and-pepper hair got out. He had heavy features, a thick nose and round cheeks, and even twenty feet away, Marcus could see the lines and creases of age, a weathered complexion.

He was older than Richard, Marcus figured, maybe over fifty.

The driver looked both ways for traffic before rounding the car. He pulled off a pair of black leather gloves and stashed them in the pocket of his round-collared coat.

That was weird, Marcus thought. As with body armor, leather gloves were the domain of movie cat burglars, not something people actually wore outside of winter.

The man mounted the curb and followed the sidewalk to the four-step flight in front of the townhouse.

Now. Go talk to him now before he goes inside and you have to ring the bell.

Marcus opened the car door and climbed out, closing it firmly behind him. The man looked back towards the sound for a split second. Then he raised his key ring and tried the lock.

"Sir!" Marcus called out, and he jogged across the street. "Mister!"

The man looked back at him but ignored the request. He opened the dark-green front door and stepped inside.

The opportunity was evaporating. "Mr. Singleton!" he called out, not knowing what else to try.

The door stopped halfway.

It swung back open, and the man leaned out, just past the doorframe, no more than his head and neck exposed.

"Who's asking?"

"My parents..." Marcus fumbled with what to say as he approached the bottom of the steps. His stomach was growling, and he felt tongue-tied. "I mean, my parents, they know you, I think. I mean... they did."

"I doubt it," the man said. "Where'd you hear that name?"

"I mean... I didn't hear... What I mean is... my mother wrote it on a slip of paper. She said if anything happened to her, I should come see you."

The man looked down and away for a split second, as if irritated by his own curiosity. "Your mother?"

"Janet Pell. My parents... Richard and Janet Pell. Sir... I mean... I'm in a lot of trouble."

At the names, his expression shifted to surprise. It was only there for a moment, but it was obvious.

"You know them, don't you?" Marcus pushed the point. "I mean... knew them..."

"They're dead?" He said it bluntly.

Marcus nodded. "Earlier today."

Once again, the man checked the street in both directions. He nodded towards the Subaru. "That their car?"

The boy nodded fervently.

"Take it a few blocks from here and park it, then come back, and we'll talk. Okay?" The man retreated inside and closed the door.

Marcus looked back at the car, then at the door. *What...!?*

Life was falling apart, and this guy was worried about a parking space.

He had no other option. He made his way back out to the street, opened the driver-side door, and climbed behind the wheel.

12

It had taken ten minutes to find another parking spot, five more to walk back to the townhouse.

Marcus was afraid from the man's surprised initial expression that when he returned, the door would remain firmly shut.

Instead, the man opened it before he'd reached the top step. He peeked out again, but this time for even less time, a bare glance down the street each way.

"Let's go; get inside," he advised, motioning for Marcus to join him.

Marcus jogged up the steps.

The townhouse was unremarkable, whitewashed plaster and hardwood floors. The hallway walls were decorated with art prints, a mirror hanging over a telephone side table.

"What's your story, kid?" the man asked after closing the door.

"I'm Marcus. Marcus Pell. I mean... you knew that part..." Adults generally made Marcus nervous, as if he had to wait for another shoe to drop.

"I'm Mr. Temple," the man said, walking past him and to a wide opening along the left wall. He nodded towards it. "Grab a seat on the couch there. You want a pop or something?"

"Yeah... I mean... please, yeah... sure."

Marcus entered the living room and sat down on the three-seat cream sofa. The room was sparsely furnished, a pair of matching armchairs across from him, as well as a low, circular coffee table.

Across the room, another door led into what he guessed was the kitchen, and Temple exited through it.

On the wall next to the kitchen door was a black-and-white framed pencil sketch of Superman. Below it was another nine-by-six-inch picture, someone in a Marine's dress uniform, getting a medal from...

Marcus furrowed his brow and squinted.

Is that George W. Bush?

Under the picture, in a similar-sized black frame, was a brassy-looking medal in the shape of a cross. It had a deep-blue ribbon with a white stripe.

From the other room, he heard a refrigerator door open and close. Temple raised his voice to be heard. "I haven't seen or talked to your parents in a long time," he said. "What happened, exactly?"

Marcus wasn't sure how to begin. Everything up to that point had been a total shock, to the point that he felt numb. Temple emerged from the kitchen with a mug of tea in his right hand, a can of Coca-Cola in the left. "You need a glass...?"

Marcus shook his head. Temple handed him the drink. "Start at the beginning. Tell me everything you can." The aging former Marine sat down in the other armchair.

"I don't even know how to explain," Marcus said. He took

a drink and swallowed; he hadn't realized how dry his throat had become after hours of crying. "I got home from school, and they were all, like, desperate and stuff, talking about we had to get out of there right away, to grab my things..."

Temple sipped from his mug. He nodded slightly, thinking things through. "Then men arrived, I'm guessing. In suits or body armor..."

Marcus's eyes widened. "That's it! That's what happened... How did you...?" He looked around quickly, suddenly insecure. He had the horrifying thought that maybe this man was involved somehow with what he'd just said. "My mother said I should meet B. Singleton here..."

"He doesn't live here anymore." The man sipped his tea once again. "But she was right to send you here. Don't worry about me, kid. I'm not going to hurt you."

"Then who..."

"Singleton? Bob. An old friend of your parents. We all used to work together more than a decade ago."

"Doing *what*? My father... Richard... he's an accountant."

"You called them by their first names." Temple seemed to find that curious.

Marcus shrugged. What was so important...? "These guys showed up and killed them. They just... murdered them both, in our home..."

"You live in Hickory Hills?"

Marcus nodded.

"Then they hadn't moved recently or done anything to attract attention? Run for public office, anything like that?"

Marcus shook his head again. The man was so calm it added to his frustration. "What does this have to do with someone...? Someone murdered my parents, Mr. Temple. And I don't know what's going on. And... and I'm kind of scared." He wiped away more tears.

"It's natural to be upset, kid..."

"My mother didn't mention you. She didn't write down your name, I mean..."

Temple ignored the boy's show of suspicion. "Bob used to own this place. I moved in to... keep an eye on him when he was sick, help him out for a while. But he didn't want to stay, so he signed it over to me."

"He... signed it over...? You mean he sold it?"

"Leased for a dollar a year, technically. We're close, sort of like family. We were in the Marines together. Listen, that's neither here nor there. He's not coming back anytime soon."

Marcus felt his stomach sink. "My mom... before she died..."

"She sent you to Bob. Yeah... I can understand that. He was sort of her husband's boss for a while, and she trusted him. But Bob's not an option. He's not available. And we still need to figure out how to deal with this. You have any other family, anyone else who knows you came here?"

There was an edge to the question, a determination that unsettled Marcus.

He felt like he should lie, tell the man he'd made arrangements in case anything happened to him or something. But the right lie wasn't springing to mind, his nerves shot.

"No."

Temple nodded to the soda. "You've barely touched your Coke." He rose. "You want a sandwich or something? You should eat while we weigh options."

"I'm fine," Marcus said. He couldn't help himself, glancing towards the main hallway.

Temple's head sank for a split second. When he looked up again, he said, "Marcus, the reason I asked you to move the car is so that no one knows you're here. If you couldn't trust me, I wouldn't have done that. The guys who came after your parents, if they're who I think, would only need that license plate number and a few hours of digging around to pinpoint your exact location. You understand?"

He did. The man could have turned him in immediately if he'd wanted. Instead, he was offering a sandwich.

"I could eat..." Marcus offered nervously.

It took Temple five minutes to make his meal. "Here," he said, re-entering the room plate in hand. "It's cheese and tomato. I didn't have cold cuts or anything. Sorry about that."

Marcus gratefully took the sandwich and extracted a massive bite from one half. "Fn-ank ou..." he mumbled through a mouthful of food.

He looked up at the medal again as he chewed. "You won that?"

Temple looked over his shoulder to clock what was attracting the kid's attention. "Yeah... yeah, part of my time in the Marines. Not such a pleasant discussion."

Marcus frowned, puzzled; on the wall adjacent to the medal and the Superman art was a hand-drawn picture of Thor, another comic book character. He swallowed bread and tomato. "You... have a drawing of Thor on your wall," he managed.

"Drew that back in... oh man, must've been seventy-three, seventy-four. I was a kid, not even in my teens yet."

"You draw comics?"

"Not for a living. I teach. No... that was a tough period for me. Like Bob – like a lot of folks in the Marines, if I'm honest – my folks died when I was pretty young. I wound up living with my uncle, and he was pretty busy. Ran a car wash in Cicero. Anyhow... pretty much worked himself to death, so I had to find something to do."

"It's really good. Like, you could draw actual comics and stuff. Is your uncle still..."

"Nah. No, he was in his forties even back then, so he'd have been about a hundred now. Didn't make it past fifty. Bad ticker, lots of debt, dragged down by all the bums and losers he insisted on helping, working two jobs. It's an old story, kid, and not a fun one."

"I'm sorry, I didn't mean..."

"Water under the bridge." Temple nodded towards the hall. "Hang tight and finish that while I make a couple of calls, check a few things out. Okay?"

Marcus nodded again as the older man left the room.

The sandwich was simple but delicious. It was past six, and he hadn't had anything since breakfast. He took another big bite and chewed it up rapidly.

Something occurred to him. He frowned as he set the sandwich and its plate down on the coffee table. There was a telephone just inside the front door. Instead, Mr. Temple had gone to another room, farther up the hall, to make calls in private.

If it's about me, why doesn't he want me to...

He shook off the thought and chastised himself. The man had been nothing but kind, despite some crazy kid related to an old friend showing up on his doorstep. After everything that had happened, Marcus supposed, a little paranoia was normal.

Still...

His curiosity ate at him.

I need to stay on top of anything that could hurt me. That's reasonable, right? That's what Richard would want.

He rose from the sofa and went over to the hallway, following it past the stairs to another door, to the right. It was slightly ajar, an inch of space between it and the frame. He thought about just pushing it wide open and walking in, as if he'd made a mistake and picked the wrong room.

Dude... this guy is helping you. Give him a little credit...

He put his ear to the door crack.

"Yeah... Yeah, I know what I said. I was there, remember? I'm the guy who said it." He sounded irritated. "How...? I don't know. I told you at the time, it was done and dusted. Did I... what, personally? It was complicated. You know how those things go. What? Maybe twenty minutes. Look, this isn't a problem..."

The man on the other end was angry. Marcus couldn't hear the words clearly, but the voice coming through Temple's phone was yelling, vicious. He pulled it away from his ear for a moment to adjust. "Just cut the shit, okay? My guess would be the Family Health Center near Warren... I mean, that would be the last place with a record of seeing him. What? No! He doesn't care, that's what I'm trying to tell you. He's still using 'Singleton' instead of an alias..."

They were talking about Bob, the man he'd been sent to see, Marcus supposed. Temple had made seeing him seem out of the question.

"Look," Temple continued, "you can get all pissy with me all you want, but you never said how or... I know that! Don't you think I know that? I've got a kid sitting twenty feet from here in my living room. I'm acutely aware of... What!? No! Forget it, pal; that's not how this works..."

Marcus felt his stomach turn again. Mr. Temple was telling someone about him. At least, that was what it sounded like from half the conversation. He glanced over his shoulder at the front door.

"I can go down there," Temple continued. "But the kid stays here... That's not a world for an innocent kid... Hey! HEY! Screw you, pal!"

Marcus had heard enough. Temple was plotting something, with someone, and he was in the dark.

What had he called the place... the Family Health Center?

He looked back at the room one more time, his host still talking, animated.

Marcus headed for the front door.

If he was lucky, he figured, the place wasn't far off.

Either way, Temple's need to make plans would buy him some time.

13

Dawn Ellis's day had been even more difficult than usual.

She finished rolling up an elastic bandage and stored it in the white particle-board cabinet under the exam room sink. Then she began disinfecting the tiny area, using a spray bottle of bleach, rubber gloves up to her elbows, an absorbent cloth wiping diligently.

Along with the usual roster of angry drunks, drug addicts, beaten prostitutes and desperate single parents, she'd spent a half hour talking to a police officer.

Word had gotten around that she'd treated a street person who'd been shot in the chest, which was about as precise a description as police needed before getting involved.

She'd lied to the man, thrown him off the path, because she'd promised Bob that she wouldn't turn him in.

That didn't sit well.

She had issues with how the police treated folks in her neighborhood; however, they'd been wonderful when her son was shot, moving mountains to catch and prosecute the young man who'd ordered the drive-by.

But... she had a special feeling about Bob, that maybe he was worth the effort as a person. For a man who barely said a word on his two or three annual visits, he'd managed to make her worry more about him than her job.

That was a mistake, she suspected.

She wrinkled her nose at the bleach fumes wafting off the cleaning fluid.

The early morning visit by the officer had been followed by an array of patients with vicious injuries and unpleasant turns; a bottle picker caught on razor wire; a senior with toe fungus; the greasy fruit merchant from a few blocks down the street who did nothing but stare at her chest and make tasteless innuendoes.

On a slow day, she'd be required to just assist Drs. Girard or Fawcett. But that never happened anymore, and her array of responsibilities to their overloaded waiting room guests seemed to grow weekly.

There was a knock on the exam room door. A moment later, a hand pulled it slightly wider ajar, and a head poked around.

It was a boy, probably late teens. He had a mop of brown hair and an anxious look. "Nurse Ellis?"

She held her cloth aloft in a rubber-gloved hand. "You're not supposed to be back here..."

"I had to lie to the desk and tell them I needed to find my father's nurse." He looked sheepish, hands shoved into the side pockets of an old denim jacket, the kind kids loved in old '80s movies, the fleecy, white wool collar turned drab and gray.

"Sorry," he muttered. "Like... I mean... it's real important."

"Who..."

"The guy... I mean, the man I need to find... he's not my dad. My mom told me I needed to find him in an emergency and... well... I mean... I've got a real big one."

She put down the bleach bottle. “And someone told you...”

“They said up front you know Bob Singleton.”

Dawn couldn’t help but show her surprise.

She composed herself. “I can’t discuss patient information with someone who’s just walked in off the street.”

“I think he might be in danger. I think... I mean, I know I am.”

She put her cloth down next to the sink. Dawn walked over to the door and put a hand on the boy’s back, gently ushering him towards the hall. “Then you need to call the police is what you need to do.”

“I... I can’t. They might be involved.”

The kid was troubled, at best. “Do you have a number for your parents? Someone I can call...?”

“They’re dead. They... Before she died, my mom told me to find Bob Singleton. They...” His distress was growing, and he was talking around something, avoiding information. She didn’t want to push him into running away. But...

“Look, even if I wanted to help you... Bob is of ‘no fixed address,’ as they say. He doesn’t have a home, child. So...”

The boy looked puzzled. “He lives on the street?”

She smiled gently and nodded despite his terseness. “Uh-huh. It happens to people, believe it or not. Quite a few like Bob who choose to stay there, too. There’s kind of a Good Book on the subject; it counsels us to ‘judge not, that ye be not judged.’”

That added to his befuddlement. “The Bible?” He clearly wasn’t sure.

“Uh-huh. Now, like I said, I can’t help you any more than that...”

“Please!” He grasped her arm, then saw her concern and let go. “I’m sorry! I didn’t mean anything by that; it’s just... I need to find him. I’m scared, okay?”

She sighed. She cared about Bob, like all her patients. But he'd caused her two days of trouble. Maybe the kid *was* his. Either way, he was his problem.

"I can't tell you much; but six months ago, at the end of last winter, when the big storm came in, I followed him to his crash pad – his flop, he calls it – to make sure he was living okay. An alley off North Peoria and Hubbard, just off the Expressway. That's the best I can do. Now... why don't you let me call someone for you..."

The kid backed away quickly down the hall. "Thank you! You... Just, thank you." He turned and sprinted out of sight, into the waiting area and towards the front doors.

Dawn stared blankly down the hall and pondered whether she'd done the right thing.

She could hear voices blending, the sounds of movement suggesting the waiting room was busy as day dragged into evening.

After a few moments, she let it go and went back into the exam room.

Not going to disinfect itself... She grabbed the spray bottle and got back to work.

Can't get involved. Can't be worrying about every kid who comes through the community...

But it was hard not to. The West Loop and Greektown had been her work and home communities for a decade. She cared about the folks there.

He'd seemed desperate.

She finished wiping down the taps, then set the bottle aside once more. She walked over to the door and looked down the hallway towards the entrance.

You're tired and need days off. That's why you didn't ask him more questions.

She felt guilty about leaving him to his business.

Her introspection was interrupted by another person entering the hall, a man, older...

"Sir... you can't be back here."

"Nurse Ellis?"

"Uhhh-huh." *What now?*

"I'm Allan Temple; I'm an adjunct professor at Loyola. Have you talked to a teenage boy recently? A little bit shorter than me? He's a friend of a friend, and I'm worried about him. I think he might be in a lot of trouble."

14

The evening had set in, but streetlamps and rear-exit bulbs made Marcus's search a little bit easier.

Most of the businesses in the area were restaurants or small boutiques, the odd clinic or dental suite. There were four blocks east and three north between his position and where the nurse said Bob Singleton liked to sleep.

He covered the area methodically, circling each block, alternating between sidewalks and back alleys, keeping an eye out behind dumpsters and bushes.

The dark of night had crept in, pedestrian traffic thinning. He pushed down feelings of isolation and loneliness. Richard wouldn't have wanted that. He'd want him to persevere. To fight.

He was determined to get an answer from Bob Singleton, whether he was someone who could help or not.

Twice, he felt a sense of immediate fear; two men were standing around a burning oil drum behind a row of restaurants, though the evening wasn't that cool. They looked hard, skin tanned and weather-beaten, clothes disheveled and dirty. The younger man, in a knit cap and with dark, uneven facial hair, looked at Marcus as if the teen were a meal. His older friend had pale gray eyes and a white beard, and his gaze was empty and lifeless.

Marcus had scurried by, glancing back to keep a wary eye on them, more worried about what they might do than what they might think. At the end of the alley, he turned north, repeating the search a block farther.

A few minutes later and a few more blocks east, a car screeched to a halt at the end of the alley and stayed there, as if someone he couldn't make out in the half-light was studying him. He froze in place.

It remained still, though he could hear its big engine rumble. After a few tense moments, his heart beating faster, it moved on.

When he finally reached North Peoria, the alley was narrow and wedged tightly between three- and four-story buildings.

He walked the length of the alley twice, but there was no sign of any camp or... what had she called it? His "flop"?

The area wasn't exactly a hellscape, Marcus thought. It was cleaner than most of the other alleys he'd checked, albeit with giant dumpsters near each end. Bicycles were chained to a rack behind one of the blocks, suggesting apartments. It was dark, just the streetlights at either end keeping the gloom from gathering, their washed-out orange glow reflected in the tiny puddles left over from the morning.

Still... I mean... What a place to live. I guess this is what happens when no one cares about you.

He walked ahead a few feet, then chose a back door around which to begin searching. He lifted a pair of trash cans and moved them to one side, then followed suit with some crates and boxes.

Nothing.

He repeated the search at the back door across the alley. He carefully restacked the three crates he'd temporarily rearranged.

He was beginning to worry the nurse's information was too old to be useful, that the man had moved on again.

He walked past the second dumpster, to his left. There was just twenty yards of alley left before North Sangamon Street. It ended there, the block across the road an unoccupied building lot.

Marcus turned around slowly and looked back down the alley. He continued to turn in a full circle, hoping for movement or something that stood out.

But there was nothing.

He crouched on his haunches for a moment, his legs starting to tire. He'd been standing and moving for most of the prior five hours. The stress was overwhelming, a combination of grief, confusion, and anxiety. He buried his head in his hands for a moment, closing his eyes tight. *What am I doing here? What am I doing in a dark alley in downtown Chicago at night?*

Why? Why would anyone kill my parents? Why didn't I stay, find out what Mr. Temple was doing? He knew them. He knows Bob Singleton. He has answers.

He walked back to the east end of the alley, eyes peeled for anything he'd missed. He tried to let the emotion go.

The city was never quiet, even with no one immediately around. The air was filled by a low-level hum of cars, horns, the occasional emergency vehicle siren. Every few seconds, a whip of air would follow a car passing the alley's exit.

He'd always felt something off about his relationship with Richard and Janet. They loved him, but they didn't connect to him. They didn't ask about his thoughts or feelings or his private life at all. They didn't seem to worry, ever. Not until the insanity of that afternoon.

But now they were gone, and their absence felt blacker than the night sky above.

He felt near his wit's end, running out of options. He turned on his heel and looked back down the alley. There was nothing out of place, nothing...

He spotted a glare of light. It was just a small flash as he'd turned to his right. Plastic or something, by the back corner of the second giant dumpster. He considered the container's shape, its sloped walls...

There's space behind there.

Marcus checked his perimeter one more time. His stomach fluttered, nervous about sticking his head into a dark, unfamiliar place.

He walked over to the spot and crouched on his haunches again, pulling aside the piece of clear plastic.

Under it was a container of some sort, a large cardboard box, maybe from furniture.

He hunted in his pocket for the phone and used its flashlight app to cast some light into the interior, bracing himself against disturbing someone's slumber.

It was empty save for a blanket and an empty rum bottle. The box said "LG'" in big letters on one side. It had been wrapped several times in packing tape to hold it together, the plastic acting as a drop sheet, allowing water to run off it without damaging the cardboard underneath.

This is it.

It has to be.

But he's not here.

He turned off the flashlight app and checked the time.

8:39 p.m.

He probably always comes back here.

If he knows it's safe and hard to see...

His best bet was probably to wait. But the sensation of not knowing anything made him want to keep moving, to find help right away from someone... anyone.

From farther up the alley, he heard the sound of a can being kicked.

15

CHICAGO

The can rattled as it settled and came to rest on the alley concrete. Someone was coming.

Marcus felt a swell of hope that it was the elusive Bob Singleton. He was about to stand and look over the dumpster when a voice spoke up in obvious irritation.

"Dummy! We're supposed to be operational, here."

His voice had a drawl like a character in a gangster show. Was that New York? New Jersey, maybe? The footfalls suggested two people, perhaps three. Marcus crept to the front corner of the dumpster and peeked quickly around it.

The two men were both wearing dark suits, dress shirts and ties. They could've been going to a business meeting if not for the strange locale.

"Would you relax, for Christ's sake... Look around us, Phil: you really think this guy is any real issue? You read the intel: the guy is a bum now, a wino. Easiest job we ever had."

The can kicker was short and stocky with a pie-shaped face. The man next to him was tall and blond, his hair crewcut like a recent military recruit. "Besides, I'd be happy to let him know we're coming if it speeds this shit up..."

"You've got somewhere to be, I take it?"

They slowly approached the dumpster. "My brother's union has its annual beer bash and barbecue tomorrow in Brooklyn. If I'm not home tonight, chances are..."

"Yeah? Well, keep your mind on the job, okay?" the taller man said. "You want to tell Krug we missed this guy, then you be my guest. But I have a close affinity to breathing and to getting paid, so that's on you."

The shorter one stopped walking and looked around. "Looks bare. I don't like this, running a grid search with weapons secured..."

"Eight guys walking around alleys don't really attract attention in a city the size of Chicago. Eight guys carrying sidearms leads to immediate phone calls, police presence, problems. Just... shut the fuck up and do your job, okay? It takes a split second to draw your weapon."

Eight!? Marcus felt his stomach flip slightly. That meant they'd be all over the surrounding blocks. They obviously knew roughly where Bob was supposed to be... assuming they were there for Temple's friend and not him.

The latter prospect left his fingers and toes feeling suddenly numb: that they were merely cleaning up what they'd begun with his parents.

"I still don't see why this guy makes Krug so nervous. He's one old bum; even if he was something once upon a time, it's been more than a decade, according to his file..."

"He was dangerous once; he could be dangerous again." The taller man drew a penlight from his suit coat pocket and turned it on, then shone the thin beam around the trash cans and boxes across the alley, near the apartments' back door. "Bicycles. I swear to God, you fucking shoot me if you ever see me riding a ten-speed in the city. I mean, what kind of loser hippie..." He lowered the penlight. "You ever see anyone make Krug nervous before?"

The shorter man shook his head.

"Then that should tell you something, because Bob Singleton spooked him."

The taller man turned quickly, the penlight beam sweeping across the alley and directly towards Marcus. It cut across the back end of the dumpster, the tiny gap between it and the wall.

Marcus ducked out of the way just in time.

"You see anything?" the taller man said.

"Nah."

Marcus heard footsteps, one of the men approaching his hiding place. "What about the dumpsters? This one's on an angle, sort of." He lowered his voice. "Be quiet! Might be a spot behind there..."

Marcus's heart began to race. They were walking right over to him, and he had nowhere to go but into the packing box.

If they looked inside, there was no way he could get through it and the tiny gap between the dumpster's far corner and the wall before they caught him. If he darted out and tried to run, they were so close they'd either catch him quickly or gun him down.

Think, think, think, Marcus. You need some space, cover, a way to...

He remembered the basement, distracting that gunman.

The bottle.

He reached inside the box, and his fingers sought out the glass neck of the empty rum bottle. He patted the cardboard, unable to find it.

The footsteps got closer, beginning to slow.

Marcus's fingertips hunted frantically.

"Maybe we get lucky, maybe he's back there, we put two in the back of his head, ba-da-bing ba-da-boom, we're done for the night."

Oh damn, please...

His index finger brushed something glass. Marcus stretched slightly and grabbed the bottle neck. He turned on his heels and hurled it, overhand, in a high arc, away from the dumpster and towards the far end of the alley. The bottle shattered moments later.

Heels scraped concrete in unison as the two men turned to check the source.

"What the fuck was that?" the stocky one blurted.

"That was close, maybe twenty yards. Someone's behind us."

Marcus heard rustling sounds, followed by the click of pistol slides being drawn back. The taller man lowered his voice. "Take the other side. I'll take this one. We backtrack."

He counted to five, until their footsteps were no longer immediate.

He rose into a sprint, heading for the near end of the alley.

"HEY!" a voice yelled from behind him. "STOP!" There was more, but Marcus couldn't hear it, his sneakers pounding the asphalt as he blew across the street to the far sidewalk and turned south.

After a half block, he turned left into another alley, towards Green Street. If he zigzagged enough, he reasoned, they'd have a hard time spotting him in the dark.

The alley was long, running for several blocks. It was poorly lit, the darkness shrouding its contents in shadows, reducing them to vague shapes. It stank of decay. He stumbled as he tried to find his way past debris: broken wood pallets, boxes, a half-full garbage bag that caught his feet, almost tripping him.

Three-quarters of the way along, a truck backed into the alley's other end, blocking it, its reverse alarm shrieking over the chug of its diesel engine.

Marcus cursed inwardly and turned. In the half-light, he could see two shadows growing, creeping over the pale brick wall across the alley, making furtive progress in his direction.

"You there, kid? We won't hurt you," a man's voice called out. It sounded like the tall guy. "We just want to talk, is all..."

Marcus crouched behind a business's trash cans. He looked back frantically the other way, but the truck was still there.

"That was pretty slick with the bottle. You seem like a smart kid. Come out, and let's figure this out," the tall man said.

They were nearing his position. The tall man switched on his penlight once again, the beam dancing around the alley, tracing both sides, looking for anything out of place.

Marcus tried not to breathe too hard; but as in the basement, the more he attempted to slow his gasps for air, the more ragged they became.

The pair walked towards the trash cans. Marcus felt panic kicking in. His brain told him he had to run, but his legs felt numb. He checked the end of the alley, but the truck was still blocking it. There was nothing to distract them this time.

The shorter man drew a pistol from his waistband once more. Before his partner could protest, he muttered, "We know he's here somewhere."

Marcus tried to turn in his crouched position, looking for a back door along the series of businesses, an entry that might have been left ajar, anything that could be an escape route. But the doorways were unlit, two of three boarded over.

The clink of glass on asphalt surprised him, the heel of his sneaker catching an empty, discarded jar. It rolled to and fro for a moment.

His gaze shot down to the object in dismay, then back to the two men.

They'd heard it, too.

They strode quickly towards him, covering the last ten yards in a trot, pistols raised. The tall man with the blond crewcut swung wide, giving him a view behind the garbage cans.

Marcus locked eyes with him. There was no satisfaction in the man's face, just grim professionalism. He took aim at the prone youth. "Sorry, kid, but... better you than me, I guess."

BOB HAD STAYED ten yards behind the two men he'd followed from his squat, intent on finding out what they'd been up to. He'd seen their partners two blocks south.

But they'd called out now for someone twice; he huddled in the shadows, looking for movement in the darkened depths of the alley, between the debris and the dumpsters.

The two men heard something, a bottle chinking not far off. They rounded a series of trash cans; one raised his pistol.

Out of time. Have to act.

He grabbed the trash can lid at arm's length and took a three-step run-up before winging it, reverse Frisbee style, his index finger using the raised edge to guide it.

He didn't pause, following its flight as it slammed into the man's arm, throwing his aim off and forcing him to step to one side. Bob stepped in from behind the man, hammering his gun hand with an open-palm strike, the pistol clattering to the dirty asphalt, disappearing into the shadows.

His partner was already turning Bob's way, and he shot out a short side kick, the man's knee flexing inwards awkwardly. Bob threw his full weight at the man, driving his head down and off the cement.

He rolled sideways immediately, anticipating his colleague's attempted stomp. He stayed low, swinging his leg wide, tripping the man. The gunman hit the asphalt hard, but immediately scrambled for his pistol. Bob skittered forward and kicked out, kicking the pistol farther away.

The other man kicked backwards. Bob caught his foot and twisted hard. He jumped to his haunches and sprang sideways, dropping his elbow hard down on the back of the man's neck as he attempted to rise, following it with another elbow strike, driving his chin into the asphalt.

Down the alley, beams of light flickered.

He rose quickly and ran over to the figure hidden by the trash cans, looking around for the second gun but not spotting it. He offered the kid a hand.

"No time to argue, kid; there are more coming," he said.

The kid took his hand. Bob took off, practically dragging the kid towards the next building over. "Follow me, keep up and run, no questions," he said as he put his shoulder to a back door that appeared nailed shut. The boards over it cracked on the second attempt, splintering inwards in a V, the door behind them flung open.

In his periphery, Bob saw the first gunman rolling over, trying to regain his feet. He yanked on the kid's collar again, pulling them both inside.

It was dark, the room divided by tall shelves, barely visible with just the bare glow from the emergency exit signs. "Go, run!" Bob said, pushing him ahead.

Marcus didn't need a second invitation, trying to put distance between them and the door, heading due north. Shelves stacked with wooden crates cut them off, and he turned left, then right, then left again, cutting between storage aisles.

They reached the other side of a vast warehouse room.

"The door to your left along the wall," the man ordered. "Take it."

Marcus ran over to it. He yanked open the door, footfalls echoing from the hallway behind them.

The door led them into an office area, gray metal desks shrouded in shadows. His rescuer slammed the door and threw its deadbolt.

"The door on the north wall. Go, go!"

"I don't... I mean, who..."

His rescuer cut him off. "These warehouses are rarely visited. By the time he figures out the door we took and gets past that lock, we might be able to find a safe way out of here..."

"Who are you?" Marcus demanded.

The man ignored his question, moving to the front window of the room and pulling a wooden slat aside to check out Wayman Street. "I saw you at my flop, pinned down. Using the bottle was clever. But they won't be alone."

"You're Bob? Bob Singleton?!"

The man glared, as angry as surprised. He was broad shouldered, well over six feet tall. He had a full beard of dark tangled hair, like a gothic St. Nick. His hair was down to his shoulders, lanky and greasy.

"Who the hell are you?" he demanded. He strode towards Marcus like a man possessed, grabbing the young man by the collar on both sides, turning him in mid-stride, shoving him back another ten feet and pinning him to the wall. "Talk, now! Or this gets uglier really quickly."

His stare was penetrating, dark eyes cutting through Marcus with merciless intent.

"I'm Marcus... Marcus Pell. You knew my parents!"

Bob's face shifted quickly from anger to shock. "Richie and Janet?"

Marcus nodded. Bob was still holding his collar. The realization broke him out of the surprise of the moment. He let go.

"They're dead," Marcus said. "My mom, before she died... she told me to come find you."

Behind them, the door rattled a few times as someone tried the handle. "No time to talk," Bob said. The door shook with a thunderous bang as their pursuer laid a shoulder to it. Bob scampered back to the front door and checked the window again. "Shit. They're planning."

"Huh?"

"By radio. There are three in front of the doors; they have earpieces so that they can co-ordinate. Who are these guys?"

"I have no idea. I came home from school, and they attacked our house. They... they shot my mom and dad."

Bob ran over to the far wall and tried the handle on the door. It creaked open. "I've only been in here once before, during the bad snap last winter. I don't know where this goes."

Marcus looked over his shoulder. "We have a choice?"

"Nope. Stand clear." He pulled the door wide before leaning to check around one side of the door frame. "More storage, I think. Come on." He pulled Marcus inside, then slammed the door behind them.

He made sure it was locked. Bob looked around, surveying the room. It was too dark to see across and divided by tall shelves, reaching two-thirds of the way to the ceiling twenty feet above. It appeared to be crammed full of household items and furniture.

"Anything you can lift or roll or shove, in front of the door, now."

Marcus pushed a chaise lounge over, the feet squeaking on the concrete from resistance. Bob dropped a filing cabinet on top of it. Then he moved five feet to a larger object. "Here, help me with this," Bob asked.

They slid the roll-top desk into position, then tipped it end-over-end onto the top of the pile.

"This and the lock will only buy us a few minutes once they realize force will work," he said. "We need to find another route out."

They circled the furniture in opposite directions, cutting between the shelves as they looked for an advantage.

A crash sounded from next door. It sounded like they were through the first deadbolt.

"Anything you see that could help," Bob advised. "A weapon, a door or other passage, a window we can break through..."

Marcus stopped searching. "What about this?"

Bob rounded a tall row of shelving, his eyes alighting on Marcus's prize. He allowed himself a small smile.

"That could do it."

16

A half block away, Edson Krug sat in the front passenger side of a black van, watching as his team attempted to breach the front door of the old warehouse without attracting attention from passing drivers.

They'd taken a set of bolt cutters to a padlock and chain. "We're almost through, sir," his earpiece squawked.

Krug tapped it. "Team three, come in. What's your position?"

"I think they're in an adjoining room, sir. Wait..." He heard a crash as the door gave, and the three men out front hurried inside. "Team one is with me now, sir."

"What are you seeing? Talk to me."

"It's a vast, open storage area, maybe sixty feet across, forty or fifty deep. There's a set of stairs up to another level, but it's hard to see. Two doors that we know of, maybe another on the far wall..."

"Send two men to the upper floor. The rest of you breach that door. He'll stay on the same level moving laterally if it's his fastest route away from the teams. We play the odds. And keep an eye out; if he spots an available trap, you can be sure he'll leave it for you."

"Yes, sir."

"Advise me when you're through that door."

"Understood."

Krug had considered going in with them but had no intention of sticking his neck out if it was really Singleton.

"Should we go in, sir?" his number two, Jensen, asked from the driver's seat.

"That's a negative."

"Sir...?"

"This is a very special target. Forget what the intel said about his present circumstances. We need at least two people outside."

"In case he runs?"

In case nobody else comes out alive. Someone has to explain what happened. But Jensen was new, young. "Precisely... not that that should happen." He tapped his earpiece. "Team two, where are you?"

"We're on the second floor, sir. No sign yet."

"Keep me advised. Team one, are you through that door?"

"Any minute, sir. Fletcher has the battering ram..."

"When you breach, be prepared to gun down anything that moves. Hold down a crossfire suppression pattern and smoke the room, you got me? Nothing lives."

"Acknowledged."

Krug allowed himself a moment of grim hope. He'd thought Singleton long dead, and it had been years since he'd harbored notions of revenge.

His earpiece squawked. "The door's about to give, sir... it's cracking..."

Jensen had heard the call. He looked over at his boss and smiled confidently.

He's lucky he's not in there, Krug thought.

"I like our chances," Jensen said, smiling grimly.

"That's because we're in the van," Krug muttered.

Jensen frowned. "He can't be that good..."

"He is," Krug said.

"Who *is* this guy?" the young driver wondered aloud.

Krug sighed and took out a cigarette. He lit it using a disposable lighter, closing his eyes briefly to avoid the glare. "He's the thing that goes bump in the night."

ALEXANDRIA, VIRGINIA
OCTOBER 17, 2004

THE TRAINING FACILITY sat under an unassuming office block on the corner of King and Cameron Streets, less than an hour from DC.

Officially, it was a call center, a plausible explanation for two dozen employees who came and went at all hours. Past the front doors and one level down to the basement, visitors were greeted by a single receptionist and security doors.

Had an interloper decided to come in shooting, they would've found the doors were made of armor-thick safety glass, and that the receptionist, a fifty-something veteran US Marine, was a sharpshooter with blistering reflexes.

Past the doors, a long corridor led to a series of rooms, including a shooting gallery. Beyond it, the corridor reached a vast, one-hundred-by-one-hundred-and-fifty-foot open gymnasium. Free weights and universal gyms filled one corner. Judo mats and a boxing ring occupied another, along with heavy bags strung from chains. The rear south corner was home to a glass-cubicle room filled with desks and whiteboards.

Edson Krug sat on the edge of the boxing ring and removed the open-fingered grappling gloves. Sweat rolled off his brow, down his shoulders and back, a half-moon of perspiration staining the dark-blue tank top.

He wiped the sweat and grime from his hands using his black shorts. Ten feet to his right, an older man in a white golf shirt helped his sparring partner limp away.

The old man stopped, his young charge's arm over one shoulder, using his body for support. He looked back at Krug. "You could've taken it a little easy..."

Krug sniffed contemptuously. "He could've worked on his defense. Life doesn't always work out the way we wanted."

The trainer shook his head with resigned disgust as he led the young recruit off. Krug watched them go.

The kid needed a beating, he figured. He'd only been with Team Seven for three months, a former soldier whose pro boxing career had been waylaid by a detached retina a year earlier. He was cocky, arrogant.

Well... he was cocky and arrogant.

Was.

Getting his ass beat by a thirty-two-year-old man probably nipped that in the bud, Krug thought.

He looked up at the clock above the main doors. They'd finished just in time. The newest recruit was due to arrive in five minutes.

The doors swung open. The man who walked in was older, hair graying at the temples. He had a ramrod-straight posture, a product of years in the military, but wore a well-cut navy-blue three-piece suit. He carried a plain brown manila folder.

He walked over to Krug, nodding a greeting. "Alpha."

"What's shaking, boss? New guy here yet?"

"He's filling in paperwork." Team Seven didn't officially exist, but staff still needed to be paid and insured. Officially, they were an advisory branch of the Central Intelligence

Agency, bureaucrats too insignificant to warrant offices at Langley.

Krug sniffed, then raised a finger to his nostril, pressure blocking it so that he could blow a small chunk of loose, bloody mucus from the other.

"Charming," the ex-soldier said.

Krug shrugged. "I just went four rounds with a former Golden Gloves. He's doing a lot worse." He nodded at the folder. "That the new guy's file?"

The older man handed it over. "You have a copy in your email already. I suspected you wouldn't bother reading it in advance, so..."

"Huh." Krug weighed the folder's heft. It was a half-inch thick. "Electronic mail. It'll never replace paper, you realize. Besides, you suits have been all giddy about this dude for a month. I don't get it."

"Let me fill you in on some of the pertinent details, then." The soldier took the file back and opened it. "Robert Singleton, twenty-four years old. Six feet two inches tall, two hundred and twelve pounds. Recruited from the US Marines following his tour in Afghanistan, where he was field-promoted to sergeant..."

"Uh-huh. Another grunt who couldn't make the SEALs..."

"Awarded the Navy Distinguished Service Cross for courage under fire during a firefight in Kandahar, in which he single-handedly held off nearly a dozen Taliban insurgents, allowing time for his injured comrades to be evac'd..."

Krug rolled his eyes. "Okay... we're going to do the heroic résumé, I guess."

"Awarded the Silver Star for gallantry after the bombing of an Afghan forces base. The commissioning note says he rescued four friendlies trapped in a half-collapsed, burning barracks."

"So he's a little nuts and chooses his friends poorly..."

"Awarded a Purple Heart for the burns he sustained going back in to check on anyone he might have missed, at which point he located and rescued a pair of civilians."

"Is this all supposed to be impressing me?"

The soldier sighed slightly. Krug's reputation for callousness was less irritating when it wasn't in a man's face. "I wasn't finished. Completed his first tour last December, then spent thirteen weeks at sniper training at Camp Pendleton. Requested a return to duty in Afghanistan, citing his concern for former comrades and his ability to use his new skill set to protect them. When rejected, requested a return to duty in Iraq instead."

This time, Krug said nothing, and the ex-soldier allowed himself a small smile.

"He was three months into his second tour when he intervened in a dispute between a local chieftain in a small village and the family of the girl the chieftain was attempting to force into marriage via rape. Having failed to prevent a similar incident a month earlier, near the village of Al Mazrae, he took the matter personally. After leaving the man with permanently debilitating injuries, he was rostered out and offered to the agency's Clandestine Operations branch."

Krug shrugged. "A bleeding heart. Great."

The older man ignored him. "His parents died when he was sixteen, in a car accident. By then, he already had a black belt in karate and had been trained by his father in Jeet Kune Do, the precursor to mixed martial arts. In eight short years, he has since added a dominant level of expertise in judo, jujitsu, traditional wrestling, white crane kung fu... and boxing."

Krug smiled. "Now that's a little more interesting. He must like to spar..."

"He's a specimen, as dependable a living weapon as the team is ever going to find. He's also the new Gamma."

Krug winced. "What!? You're just giving him the number two slot? I had to get my ass shot off in Nicaragua just to get a sniff at that!"

"He's smart; he's driven by passion for his country and an unshakeable desire to punish wrongdoers. He follows orders, and he gets the job done."

Krug nodded. He sat back down on the edge of the ring, crossed his arms and leaned back against the ropes. "As long as he knows that if he comes for the top job, all the medals in the world won't help him."

Across the gym, the main doors swung open again. The man who entered was in civvies, a plain pair of gray dress trousers and a white shirt, the sleeves rolled up.

"Here he is now."

He had a stiff gait, as if accustomed to marching. He gestured towards the ex-soldier. "Mr. Stone."

"Bob," Eddie Stone said with a nod. "I understand Ops Director Gerry Dahlen sent you along to see us today. This is your group leader, Alpha."

The new arrival held out a meaty hand to shake. "Bob Singleton."

Krug ignored the hand. "Uh-huh." He sized the man up. Then he nodded to the ring behind him. "You up for a little sparring?"

Singleton held the man's gaze, his dark eyes unblinking. The challenge was obvious, an immediate attempt to stamp authority.

He let slip a tiny, mischievous smile.

17

CHICAGO

Bob stared down at Marcus's discovery with a wry sense of satisfaction.

In truth, he'd never been farther inside the building than the first room and had no idea how they'd deal with the tactical imbalance.

But now, perhaps, they didn't have to.

It was burnt orange and black, an early seventies Dodge Challenger, with a raised hood intake for an oversized engine block and a black vinyl roof.

The car's frame was bulky and aggressive, with a wide wheelbase and angular side panels that sloped inwards slightly, like a gunboat. Its paint job had been protected with a coating of car wax, buffed to a reflective shine even in the dull light of the warehouse.

Its mag wheels were wider than the norm, a sturdy base to support all that muscle. A power cord extended from just under the hood to an extension cord plugged in to a wall outlet nearby.

"Get in," Bob said.

Marcus headed towards the driver's door, but Bob caught him by the arm and redirected him. "Other side, genius."

They tried the door handles.

Locked.

Across the room, a jarring crash shook the dust off their pile of furniture. A desk chair slid off the top and to the ground.

Another crash. The door shook on its hinges.

"Battering ram," Bob said. "We need to be quick." He quarter-turned, then drove his elbow sideways, smashing the driver's window. He reached in and undid the manual lock, then climbed in and opened Marcus's door. The teenager joined him.

The interior smelled like the plush black leather had just rolled off a 1971 assembly line.

A high-pitched series of cracks echoed from the door side of the giant storage space. *Gunshots.* "They're shooting the deadbolt, trying to speed up the process," Bob explained.

He searched above the sun visor for the key. "Check the glovebox and under your seat. We need a spare key. The cord from the engine block says this is long-term storage, so maybe it's here."

"Just hotwire it," Marcus said.

"No time."

"Here..." the boy offered. He leaned over the gear shift and pulled out a pocketknife. He jammed the blade into the plastic housing of the steering column, and half of it popped away from hidden clips. "I have kind of a gift for this stuff."

Another thunderous jolt and crash. The filing cabinet crashed to the ground.

"WE DON'T HAVE TIME FOR THIS," Bob hissed.

Marcus felt under the column. "Can't... really see... Just need to find the right leads..."

"Jesus Christ..." Bob muttered.

The door crashed partly in; the deadbolt hasp ripped out, the wooden frame splintering. Only the desk and chaise lounge prevented them from pushing inside.

"Kid, for the love of God, we're out of—"

The engine fired to life, a guttural roar that chugged in idle.

Marcus let out a stressed lungful of air. "Battery wasn't dead."

"Trickle charger," Bob said. He put the car into gear.

The door crashed open, two figures bursting inside, pistols raised.

He hit the gas.

The car shot forward as he threw it almost immediately into second gear, barreling furniture and crates aside.

Their pursuers opened fire, slugs tearing through the back window at an angle, the safety glass shattering.

"Hang on!" Bob yelled.

Marcus's eyes widened. "That's a wall. Ahead. A WALL. Hey! THAT'S A—"

The Challenger smashed through the boarded-up former picture window and the wood shutters beyond, debris spraying the sidewalk and road outside.

Four wheels slammed two feet to the ground, rubber screaming on asphalt as Bob tried to yank the wheel to the left, the car sliding, drifting into a wide turn on the neon-draped street.

"GET DOWN!" he bellowed, leaning over to shove the boy's head down, ducking himself as a volley of bullets chewed noisily through the trunk of the car. A slug crashed through the windshield between them.

Bob stood on the accelerator, engine racing.

A cross street approached, the signal red. He ignored it, flooring the pedal, cutting just between two cars as they entered the intersection, both spinning out to avoid him, almost crashing end to end as the Challenger squeaked through the gap.

He threw the wheel to the left again, the car sliding wide, onto North Halsted Street, tail end momentarily fishtailing, a cacophony of sirens and alarms fading behind them, drowned out by the rising pitch of the big-block engine.

18

Bob put two miles between them and the warehouse before he felt safe pulling the car over.

He inched its wheels to the curb, between two sedans, across the street from Humboldt Park.

The park was dark, near empty, the sidewalks barren, the giant field house from a century earlier a tall shadow against the cloudy, dim horizon.

They sat in silence for a moment.

Marcus wondered what his Samaritan was mulling over. But he wasn't sure what to say. "Where are we?" he eventually managed.

"Humboldt Park. It's the park and the neighborhood around it." Bob's tone was tense and terse. "When I was a kid, it had a reputation for Puerto Rican gangs that made people worried to go out at night. But it's like most places these days; gentrification and housing demand took over."

"Like Hickory Hills."

"Sort of. Hickory Hills started out that way. Humboldt's still en route... Look, kid... We need to talk..."

"Okay."

His discomfort was obvious. He leaned on one hand, elbow on the door frame. The luminescence from a nearby lamppost lent a soft glow to the side window glass, framing his bushy, pirate king beard. To Marcus, he seemed powerful and lonely.

"Do you have other family?" Bob asked.

"No. My grandparents are dead. I don't have aunts or uncles or anything."

"Nobody?"

The boy shook his head.

"Damn. What about friends, close friends of your parents? Maybe someone you go to school with?"

Is... he trying to get rid of me? Marcus wasn't sure what he could offer that the man would want to hear. But he had to know, had to realize how desperate he was. "My mom insisted I come to you. Who are you, Mr. Singleton? I mean... how did you know them?"

"That's ancient history. Look... kid, I know you have a lot of questions, but if you trust me at all, after I saved your neck back there, trust me now when I tell you... you won't like the answers. Your folks and me... we have baggage going way back, bad choices. But things you don't need to know."

"But I—"

"No buts! Look what it got them. Look what you just walked into! Those goons back in the alley weren't there for you, Marcus. They were there for me."

"But I deserve answers! I need... I need to know what's going on. At the very least, I should be able to know if they'll come after me, too."

"They won't. You're nobody to them..."

"I saw them kill my parents! I may just be a kid to you, Mr. Singleton, but I'm not an idiot. I watch mysteries on Netflix. They always come after the witness."

"They... wait a second... How did you find me?"

"My mom gave me your old apartment address. I waited outside until somebody came home..."

"You talked to Al Temple?"

"Yeah. Is he the reason those guys came..."

Bob chuckled and shook his head. "Nah, Al's one of the good ones. He was my mentor for years. More likely, they followed you somehow. You have a phone?"

"A burner."

Bob grimaced sardonically. "So... you've seen *The Wire*."

"I mean... not really. It's a prepaid. But I figured I needed browser access, so I got a smartphone."

"Great. What about a ride?"

"My mom's Subaru. It's parked back near the Family Health Center..."

"That would be it, then. The men after me have connections, programs that let them track plate and VIN numbers, that kind of..." He noticed the kid's befuddled look. "What?"

"Programs?"

"Apps," Bob said. He pinched the bridge of his dirt-stained nose. "I'm so old. Look... I know what your mom told you, kid, but I can't help you. My time with them... that life... it's all ancient history. All of this... this bullshit is just old grudges, bad business, some of it from before you were born." He glanced over at Marcus, his look tinged with doubt. "How old are you?"

"Seventeen."

"Eighteen when?"

"Like... nine months..."

"At eighteen, you're legally an adult. You can make your own way. At seventeen, you're a problem."

"Make my own way?!" Marcus repeated. "You'd just let me handle this... because I'm a problem?"

"Why not? I was on my own at eighteen. So was your father. Don't kid yourself and think he had an easy road. Lots of people out there, too many, who have it rough. They make it on their own, and so can you. Your father was a practical man..."

"You see! This is why you have to help me. We should help each other because you really knew them."

Bob gave him a cold stare. "That's not how life works. Someone has to help you because, legally, you're still a kid. But it doesn't have to be me. I've done my time, played my part."

Marcus felt despair creep in. "So that's it? Just like that? You tell me you know why my parents are dead, but I don't get to know. I don't get any help from you?"

"Hey, I saved your life, kid..."

"WHAT LIFE!?" Marcus's eyes welled with tears, his anger building. "The only people who ever loved me are dead! I might not be safe again, and the radio says my parents killed each other! But I was there! I saw what those men did."

Bob looked uncomfortable. "I..."

"You won't help. Yeah... I get it. You'd rather go back to being a bum." Marcus reached down and unbuckled his seat-belt. "Look, I'll just get out here and do this on my own..." He leaned towards the door.

Bob's exasperation was obvious. "Just... put your belt back on, okay? I'm not going to let you wander off alone."

"You don't want to help me. You're just working some angle out..."

"I'm not, I swear. Look... maybe I don't want you involved, but I'm not just abandoning you, kid..."

"Then you'll help?"

"I'll figure out who to drop you with is what I'll do. This stuff is too dangerous for a kid to be around..."

"I'm not a kid. I'm seventeen. Like you said, in nine months..."

"Huh. Nine months too long." He started the engine

again. “I need to think about this, find an authority of some sort who can take you.”

Marcus’s eyes widened. “The Subaru…”

“Yeah… probably how they found us. Good job, kid.”

“No… I left it near the clinic. But if I could find you there by talking to Nurse Dawn…”

Bob closed his eyes and mouthed a silent curse. “Then they can find her, too.”

He started the car.

“We’re going back?” Marcus said.

“Buckle up,” Bob suggested.

19

The evening had turned gray and drizzly, occasional droplets of rain coming down on Dawn Ellis as she walked home along West Randolph.

Although it was past eight o'clock, the wide, triple-laned road was still busy, restaurants and bars every few blocks keeping the flow going after most businesses had closed. She kept a solid pace.

It made her feel better to have people around, the hum of traffic, the smell of exhaust. She'd contemplated taking the bus. But the half-hour walks always calmed her nerves and relieved the day's stress.

It also helped her get Maurice off her mind. She thought about her son every day, but managed usually to dwell on the good things, what a nice boy he'd been, and how she was sure he was in Heaven now.

But Bob Singleton's being shot had brought it all back: the pain, the heartache that lasted for two straight years. The guilt that she hadn't been able to prevent it despite trying her hardest. The constant, gnawing emptiness that visited her when she was tired or at loose ends.

It had been that kind of day. First, she'd dealt with the fallout from helping Bob. Then there was the weirdness with the kid and the man looking for him, Allan Temple. She'd given him the same directions and advice as the boy, and he'd disappeared before she could get a phone number to even check back.

You can't go getting involved with every crazy kid who runs away or something. Day like today, with nothing but headaches and hardcases, you deserve a reward. Ice cream... pedicure or something. A "me" day, Dawn Marie...

She gazed at a clothing store window as she passed, realizing she was near Halsted Street. There was a little Indian restaurant there that made the best smoked pork belly, cooked in a tandoor oven. Her friend Justine had refused to try it because it was pork and against her beliefs. But it was melt-in-your-mouth tasty. It was across the street somewhere...

She took a longing look towards the eatery. In the intersection, a black van pulled an illegal U-turn. It passed her and drove another fifty yards before slowing, as if looking for a parking space at the curb.

Dawn ignored it. She'd never liked driving, although she had her license. Drivers were rude, and she was usually only going a few blocks anyway. The price of a car would buy a lot of bus passes, she figured.

Hmm. The van was next to an open spot, but was pulled over just slightly as if dropping someone off, still blocking the lane – not a big deal in light traffic, but it struck her as rude.

The side door slid open. She was still twenty feet away, and it seemed odd that no one got out. She slowed her pace.

It almost felt like they were waiting for her.

Probably some ol' dirtbag, make a nasty-ass comment... That was the way of the world, it seemed. People didn't respect privacy anymore. People didn't respect *respect*. She looked behind her, but there were no other pedestrians nearby.

Her walk slowed to an amble, then a complete stop.

Maybe if I cut a wide berth around them... The sidewalk was broad there, plenty of space to get nearer to the buildings. She changed her direction to a slight northeast slant to put a few more feet between her and the road.

A man climbed out of the van.

He had a dark suit on and was younger looking, a tall white guy with straw-brown hair. He straightened his tie, and she noticed he had leather driving gloves on.

Well now, that's fancy...

"Excuse me, ma'am? Do you have a minute to help me find something?" he said, raising his voice slightly to account for the fifteen yards between them.

Dawn felt her tummy rumble. Something felt badly off. She looked past him, into the van. Another man was crouched in the darkness, betrayed by the glint of streetlights off his watch and glasses.

Panic took over. Dawn broke into a run, clutching her purse tightly like a running back with a football.

She could hear the man behind her, his shoe heels clipping along, getting closer. After a moment, a second pair of steps joined his.

Dawn had never considered herself athletic; she was wide-hipped, beefy and short legged, although being on her feet all day kept her in shape. But the man was young and looked fit. She felt older than her thirty-nine years, regretful of the extra pounds.

Panic surged through her, dragging her forward, legs wanting to move faster than they normally could, faster than she could process.

A man walked out of the building she was about to pass.

He turned slightly and saw her desperate expression, along with her pursuers.

"Help me!" Dawn pleaded.

He looked shocked for just a moment, then ran in the other direction.

Gah... coward! They would be on her in mere seconds, she knew. She looked around, praying someone else would help. But there was no one, just cars passing as if nothing was going on.

The door. She ran for the door the man had just used. She flung it open and ran inside.

It was a nightclub, large and open plan, music thumping electronic drumbeats at eardrum-bruising levels through bass subwoofers. A central bar was crowded by patrons. The lights were low, and blue neon encircled a large dance floor to one side, the other sections crowded with round, busy tables.

She looked for a doorman or waiter, anyone she could ask for help, but they were all dealing with customers, their voices competing with the deafening sound system.

She moved between the tables, glancing over her shoulder in time to see the two men enter.

My phone. I can call the police...

It was never her first choice. Her family had grown up in a neighborhood that generally feared police interaction, and despite the police officers' attitude about Maurice, the gentleness they'd shown, she'd seen plenty of other civilians treated terribly.

But there wasn't much option. She rummaged in her purse for her phone as she wandered towards the back of the room, trying to pay attention to her pursuers.

Phone, phone, phone... Oh, Lord, please help me find...

Then she remembered: She'd taken it out just before closing, to check the temperature outdoors before her walk.

It was sitting beside the exam room basin at the clinic.

A young man shoved her accidentally but just pushed by without acknowledging her. She tried to look through the sea of bodies, but she was shorter than most and couldn't make anyone out. A hand grasped her elbow and gently turned her.

It was the younger of the two pursuers, the good-looking boy with the crewcut who'd called out to her. She looked down to where his hand clasped her arm and saw the pistol pointed at her belly.

She reacted in a second, out of instinct, five years of working with handsy intensive care unit patients at her first job kicking in, her heel coming down hard midfoot. It caught him by surprise; he yelped with pain, hopped onto one foot, then tumbled over, between the patrons.

Dawn ignored their calls of concern for the man and pushed her way towards the back of the room.

It was muggy, the air scented with sweat and perfume. There had to be a rear exit. Failing that, a weapon of some sort to protect herself. At the very least, if they wanted a fight, she'd give it to them.

She reached the back wall, following it to a narrow corridor in the middle of the room. The odor of urine suggested it led to the washrooms, but there had to be a door there somewhere, she knew. She turned the corner and saw the illuminated red Exit sign.

She felt something hard press against the back of her head.

"If you fucking move, I'll shoot you dead where you stand," the young man muttered.

Dawn's tummy flipped from anxiety. Her legs felt weak, her hands quivering. She'd held her breath at the barrel's pressure, but now was having trouble resuming breathing, her fear overwhelming, her limbs beginning to tremble.

His friend joined them. "We need to take this somewhere quiet," he advised.

"She broke my fucking foot."

His friend chuckled. "You puss—"

"It's not funny, goddamn it. It's loud in here; no one's paying attention..."

"They're not going to miss gunshots, idiot. Take it outside."

They led her down the hallway to the back door and pushed it open. The cool air hit her immediately, and she realized how sweltering the club had been.

They were going to kill her, Dawn knew.

She didn't know why or really care in the moment. She felt a sudden, strange sense of calm. *Maybe it's God,* she told herself, *keeping things real, letting me know it's going to be okay.*

"You don't have to do this," she said. "I'm just a nurse. I don't have any money..."

One of them snickered. "Are you shitting me? She thinks we're muggers."

She turned around, not waiting for permission. They were both younger, in their twenties, wearing identical black suits. If it had been a Saturday afternoon at her apartment building, she'd have assumed they were nice white boys on a mission to spread the good word, Mormons or Jehovah's Witnesses or something.

"You broke my fucking foot," the younger one snarled. He had a sneer to him, a meanness to his tone.

"You stuck a gun into my stomach. Did you expect me to kiss you?" She felt a surge of energy, fear subsiding as anger took over, as if making it clear how little she thought of them gave her powers they couldn't understand.

He pulled back the pistol's slide and cocked it, chambering a round. "Yeah... well, if you can cross five feet of space before a bullet, you can try again."

The feeling of empowerment dissipated rapidly. "Do I get to know why, at least?"

He shrugged. "Your guess is as good as mine, lady. We're just doing a job... that's all." He raised the pistol to her forehead. "Bye-bye, sweetheart."

20

CHICAGO

Dawn shut her eyes tightly, expecting the moment of pain that ended her life.

A car engine roared behind her.

She turned to look out of reflex, the gunmen's attention also drawn to the end of the alley, forty feet away. The pale, red glow of rear brake lights cut through the darkness.

"Did you call in?" the first gunman asked.

His partner shook his head. "He can't even see us from there," he suggested. "Go ahead; let's finish this."

It started slowly backing up, towards them.

"Is... it moving?"

The first gunman nodded. "Yeah, backing up in idle, like he's looking for something..."

"Do it now, then. Get us out of here before we have a potential witness."

He raised the pistol to her head. "Bye-bye, nursey."

They heard the car's engine pick up slightly. "Is he...?" his friend began to ask.

The car shot backwards; paper and debris swept into the air in its wake, the driver flooring it in reverse.

"Does he even see... holy shit!" the younger man yelled.

All three hurled themselves clear as the car barreled through the spot on which they'd just stood, its brakes screeching it to a halt between Dawn and the men.

The passenger door opened. "Get in!" a man's voice barked.

She couldn't see him in the darkness of the alley, but she was out of options. Dawn practically dove inside, the driver gunning it. The open door slammed off a full trash can and swung closed as the car skidded out of the alley.

She heard the crack of pistol shots as she righted herself and looked up at her rescuer.

"Bob!"

He looked over briefly and had a sort of twinkle in his eye, the kind people get when their joke really surprises someone. "Okay, so I never told you I can drive," he said. "What else would you like to know?"

"Uh... Hi."

The voice from the back seat startled her. She threw herself sideways slightly as she looked over her shoulder.

The boy from the clinic.

Dawn's mouth hung open for a second as she composed herself. "Well... damn," she said. "Oops." She clasped a hand over her mouth. "My apologies for the language."

"I think we'll be okay," Bob said. "I mean... you seem so polite normally, but..."

She punched him in the upper arm.

"Ow! I'm driving here, okay?"

"What the heck is going on!?" Dawn demanded. "Who were those men?" She looked over her shoulder. "Is this why you were trying to find him at the clinic?"

Marcus nodded but looked sheepish, almost embarrassed. "These guys were looking for Mr. Singleton, and I think maybe me..."

"Definitely you too," Bob interjected.

"... because I'm sort of a witness and everything. I mean... so are you, I guess."

She gave Bob a hard stare. "What in the name of all that's holy is he yapping about, Bob? And where are you taking us?" Her anger had begun to bubble to the surface. "What the h-e-double-hockey-sticks have you gotten me involved in?"

He wore a pained expression. "I'm genuinely sorry about this, not that it helps. I didn't ask for any of this..."

"Who were those men? Why were they chasing me? WHY WERE THEY TRYING TO KILL ME!?"

He steered the Challenger into an open lane, slowing the car to a stop at a red light. "You talked to Marcus. They planned to kill both of us, making you potentially the last person he talked to. He might have told you something incriminating about the murder of his parents by the same people – we think – yesterday in Hickory Hills."

"Hickory... that's miles from here!"

"Yeah, well... not really a matter of geography. More like ancient history," Bob said.

"Well... we have to go to the authorities, the police."

"Not an option," Bob said. "These guys may work for the government. At the very least, they'll have strong police contacts, if the people behind this move in the circles I suspect. And they can track police bandwidths and communications. We wouldn't last a day."

She saw him glance over and realized her mouth was hanging open. She clamped it shut.

Hold yourself together, girl. Find out what these fools have done before you make a move.

She'd had two elder half brothers growing up, both of whom had gotten in trouble in school, mixed up in crime. They'd straightened out as they got older, as most folk did.

But she'd experienced with Maurice the damage hoodlums and gangsters could do.

"Then what is this? What is this all about?"

"I need to get us off the road, somewhere discreet..." Bob murmured, watching the busy lanes of traffic ahead, the lights from the surrounding high-rises glinting off the windshield.

"My apartment is two blocks behind us..." she said, immediately regretting the suggestion.

Why? Why do you always have to help?

Her daddy had been a hard man, an emergency trauma surgeon who brought any failures home and visited terror upon his family. But she'd also seen his softer side, when he drank and cried about the lives he couldn't save.

She'd always understood that, the need to make it better for others... and the inability to save some. The passage of recent years and tears had driven it home.

"Out of the question," Bob said. "They'll know your name by now, your address. They'll have a couple of guys like the two you just met guarding it."

"Turn right at the next corner," she commanded. "Take Wabash south for a while. I may know somewhere."

Bob did as commanded.

"There's a motel my cousin used to work at, south of East Twenty-Sixth. It ain't much to look at, but it's cheap, and they don't ask questions about the patrons."

She watched Marcus scoping out the neighborhood as they approached the motel. It had signs of renewal: an old yellow-brick apartment block gentrified into condos, a newer factory built in red brick to match its older neighbors.

But he was frowning. The signs of indifference were everywhere, from the grass growing routinely through cracked sidewalks, to the overgrown "commercial lot" with four-foot-high foliage and a dilapidated, collapsing chain-link fence, long rusted through.

She saw him staring at the empty lot. "That's some prime prairie right there..."

"Something here seems... off about this street, or whatever," Marcus said. "Not quite right. It's like it's..."

"Neglected?" Dawn offered. "You'll find that whenever you get near poorer neighborhoods in Chicago, the parts that the city and the rich business owners are supposed to take care of. For some reason – mostly money, I guess – they get put up on a shelf. Cross the river a few blocks south of here, and things take a real bad turn. Lots of folks trying, though, good people trying to turn it from a bleak industrial dump into something to be proud of. Lots of politicians who don't care enough, landlords and businessmen who see no profit in that."

She didn't tell him what that really meant. He didn't need to hear what it had been like in a cold-water flat near Soldier Field, trying to study for school with no power because her father, still in school, couldn't pay the bills. There were times when it had been so dark, so desperate and violent, it was as if light couldn't penetrate the yellow-brick walls and boarded-up windows.

That had been a long time ago.

"The residents are trying; their efforts are there. It's working, just slowly," Bob added. "You'll see homeowners' pride; you'll see small businesses tucked away here and there."

Dawn eyed him slyly sideways. "Yeah... it's almost like they refuse to give up. There's probably some sort of message in that."

"Yeah, well... maybe," he agreed, a sheepish expression setting in. He reached over with his right hand and tugged on the pale blue hair scrunchy around his left wrist.

Dawn frowned. "I noticed you had that on when you

came to the clinic. What's that about, anyhow? I mean... it's pretty and all if you're a twelve-year-old girl..."

"It's just a reminder," Bob said. "It's... never mind. Better days."

He'd always been strange, as little as she knew him as a street person. She knew she had to watch herself, be careful about getting close to the pair. They'd saved her in the alley, but presumably from problems they'd helped create.

She needed answers. And then, likely, she needed to get away from the two lunatics who'd dragged her into their mess.

21

She hadn't lied about the motel, Bob decided.

Getting a room in the decrepit, dirty building had been just sixty dollars for the night... although he had the impression most people rented for a few hours at most and brought customers.

He closed the room door behind them. The place smelled as if someone had peed in a giant ashtray. The room housed a single queen-sized bed, a pair of side tables, a bureau and a luggage rack. The TV looked twenty years old.

He wrinkled his nose. "Well... you weren't kidding about the privacy," he said. "I'm guessing there are police never too far away."

"I grew up not far from here, the projects down by Soldier Field," Dawn said. "We moved when my daddy got his medical degree, but this was my part of the city until I was nearly ten years old."

Marcus walked across the room to the rear window and looked out at the view behind them. "You can see the river from here. There's, like... junk everywhere."

"Like I said, a lot of folks care," Dawn said. "Some do not. I try to concentrate on the former."

Bob curbed his tongue. He didn't know the nurse well, but he respected her. And he'd dragged her into his troubles.

Marcus sat down on the end of the bed. "So... who gets the bed and who—"

"I get the dang bed!" Dawn declared. "Y'all can sleep in the tub, for all I care! Now, explain to me, Mr. Bob Singleton, why a group of heavily armed men are chasing a bum. Yeah... I said it! We can go down the road a ways into discussing that, too, if y'all want. I'm mad as heck right now, pardon my language."

Her expression suggested she'd doubt anything he had to say. Whatever it was, it was trouble, and not her trouble.

"It's complicated."

"Everything in life is complicated if you dig deep enough," she said, sitting down next to Marcus on the end of the bed.

"This... this runs pretty deep." Bob slumped into the ratty wooden desk chair by the chest of drawers, next to the old tube TV. "It's hard to know where to start."

"The beginning is always good."

He nodded. He had to explain. They deserved at least that much. "When I was younger, I was a very, very different person than I am now. I was in the Marines for several years, overseas."

"Afghanistan?" Marcus asked.

"Iraq. When I got back, the government decided that I had skills they could use in a less... overt manner."

"You were a spy?" Marcus asked.

"Yeah... I mean, sort of."

"You were a spy who killed people?" the boy suggested.

Dawn looked at him with some alarm. "You got THAT from 'I had skills...'?"

He shrugged. "Like Martin Blank." Marcus must've noticed her baffled expression, quickly adding, "In *Gross Pointe Blank*? It's a comedy about a hitman..."

"I really don't think we want to be talking about comedies right now." Dawn's head snapped back to Bob. "You were a government HITMAN?!"

"Not... exactly."

She stood up, exasperation building, hands perched on her hips in indignation. "OH! Okay then! And just what in the name of good mercy does 'not exactly' mean?"

"Just... please. Please sit. I promise it wasn't like that. Or... it wasn't supposed to be, most of the time. I killed people for the government, yeah. But I was part of a team, a military and espionage unit designed to infiltrate foreign governments, agencies, companies, paramilitaries. We were there to tear down groups that promoted terrorism, sometimes to rescue other people fighting it."

She sat down again, crossing one leg over the other and her arms, as if trying to protect herself. "You were a soldier, then."

"Basically, yeah. Just... specialized."

"That sounds real noble and all, but in the end, it was still your job to kill people."

"Yes. If it makes you feel any better, I pay for it every day, or I try to."

"By being on the street?"

"By walking away so that I can't hurt anyone else."

Marcus interjected, "And my parents?" He was crying again, a single tear tracking down the right side of his face.

Dawn put an arm around him and gave him a prolonged hug, squeezing tight. "It's okay, child... you'll be okay."

After a few seconds, he broke away and wiped the tears away with his sleeve, looking self-conscious. "Janet... my mom... she always tried to give me good advice, you know?

Like, she never wanted me to feel lectured. She had a cross-country skiing injury that made her limp, but she wouldn't let it, because she didn't want me to see her fail. At least, that was what Richard said."

"They sound like wonderful people."

"Richard is... was... always kind of quiet, I guess. Just, always thinking. He taught me to hunt and to defend myself, and that I wouldn't get what I wanted out of life without hard work. But..."

"But?" Bob asked.

"This is all insane. My father's an accountant. My mother's a part-time librarian. I mean... they were."

"They... weren't always."

The boy looked up, wiping away the tears with his sleeve.

"The team had eight members, including your father, who went by Richie Johnson back then. Your mother was an intelligence analyst – a desk job – at Langley, Virginia, at CIA headquarters. It wasn't the most senior role, but she was good at it. If analysts are off their game, people invariably die. But she saved most of the people she tried to help."

Marcus's mouth hung open. "Unbelievable."

"It's the truth," Bob said.

"So... what happened?" Dawn asked. "I mean, I'm guessing it came apart at some point..."

"Fifteen years ago, we were given an assignment. An Iranian nuclear physicist wanted to defect to America. The physicist had been working under house arrest for five years, but we were informed he was being relocated, from the nuclear power plant at Bushehr to a government office in Tehran. They sent us in undercover to get him out, and..."

"What?" Marcus said. "What happened?"

Bob hung his head. "Well... that's how things were back then. Things... they never really went according to plan."

22

TEHRAN, ISLAMIC REPUBLIC OF IRAN - JUNE 5, 2006

Bob stood atop the aging whitewashed apartment block, eight stories up and hidden from side views by twin chimneys.

Tehran was sweltering hot and the sky perfectly clear, as always seemed the case. He watched the thousands of celebration-goers begin to pack Imam Hossein Square below, a throng of young and old, all men, some in traditional kaftans, most wearing suits or short-sleeved dress shirts.

A stage had been set up on the opposite side of the square, a hundred and fifty yards from his location. A crew was arranging temporary seats and a lectern with a microphone.

His earpiece squawked.

"What are you seeing, Alpha?" Al Temple was in the Swiss Embassy's adjunct office for American diplomats, breaking a sacred covenant with its government to not use their guest space for espionage.

The handler was only supposed to plan and advise, which was fine with Bob. Al hadn't been in the field in years.

"Crowd's starting to build. Plenty of hubbub. They're

already diverting traffic off Damavand and Enghelab Streets. Dignitaries inbound in t-minus thirty-two minutes. The package should be moving ten minutes later."

The two streets were major arteries, and the traffic diversions, three blocks before the convoy reached the square, would cause major backups.

He lowered his binoculars. His skin was tanned dark and his beard full. He wore a pin-striped navy suit, indistinguishable from hundreds similar in the throng below.

"Things are looking solid," Al said. "We'll keep it open for now; go silent five minutes prior. Okay?"

"Roger that." The earpieces ran off satellite uplink and were encrypted. Even if the conversation were picked up, its meaning and location would be garbled.

A voice to his left interjected, "Is he happy?"

Bob turned towards the speaker.

Ten feet away, Edson Krug crouched near the edge of the roof. He wiped his forehead with the back of his hand, beads of sweat from the hundred-degree weather running down his temples, past his gold-rimmed aviator shades.

He wore a white short-sleeved shirt and dark tie, like a strangely beefy schoolteacher. He was carving his initials into a brick with a long-bladed sheath knife.

"Cut that shit out," Bob ordered. "We're not here to vandalize local property."

Krug scoffed slightly at the reprimand, but put the knife away. "Oh, yes, sir, right away, sir."

"You'd better believe it," Bob muttered.

The two men had never gotten along. Bob had been with the team for two years and had risen to Alpha, primary mission leader, within one. Krug had joined four years before him and had not taken well to his demotion to Gamma – or number two – by operations director Eddie Stone.

Bob figured the man should've been fired years earlier. He

had a mean streak and a temper. But he had a sense that Stone played politics, like most managers in Washington, and that he felt the two men kept each other in check, a weird balance of tensions.

They needed to contact the others. He tapped his earpiece, opening the channel. "Alpha to Delta. Come in, Delta."

"What's shaking, boss?" Richie Johnson was in an old delivery truck a few blocks west, with Michael Smalls, the tech whiz and recon specialist codenamed Epsilon. "I mean, Delta here. Over. Go ahead, Alpha."

Bob figured Smalls had given Richie an elbow and told him to stick with protocol. He knew they all thought he was a stickler for it. The team members had all served in different military branches, but few were known for their discipline. It was their skills and willingness to take risks that had led Stone and his predecessor Gerry Dahlen to their doors.

Richie was a math whiz and logistics genius, as well as a hell of a shot.

"What's the good word, Richie?" Bob asked. *Keep it light; keep everyone confident.*

"Intel was on the money, boss. The road crew has the day off for 'Khordad,'" Richie said, stressing the phlegmy softening of the Persian holiday's first two letters in his throat. "But they've left the concrete temporary dividers out on the roadside. They're as advertised, so about a hundred and forty pounds each."

There were six dividers. It was a lot of weight for the two men to move quickly. But it meant they'd have a route out of the area using Mohammadi Street that could then be closed off again.

"Perfect. Stay frosty until I call. Over."

"Roger and out."

The second team, including Kappa and Lambda – Jon

Rice and Ellery Azadi – were stationed in a second truck less than a kilometer south, along Hefdah Shahrivar Street, surrounded by a teeming mass of speech-goers. "Come in, Kappa," Bob called. "What's your status?"

"Kappa here. We're looking solid, boss. There are Asvaran patrolling this block and those close, but they're watching the folks on foot. Still thousands of folks walking to the square. It's humming down here."

The Asvaran were the city's mounted police unit, horses able to more easily get in and out of crowded streets and squares during public events. "Not seeing any stationary guard, but you can bet the square will be teeming with them. Over."

"Loud and clear," Bob said. "You ready, Lambda?"

"As ever." Ellery Azadi's family was from Tehran, but had fled during the 1977 Islamic revolution. He had more of a stake in the mission than anyone and had conceived the plan based on an intel leak two months earlier.

A junior secretary to the Iranian foreign minister who wanted to defect was being strung along for access to the intel. He had begun his assistance via coded information dead drops around Tehran. Azadi had convinced him to find out when the scientist was being moved.

"T-minus forty, gentlemen, keep it cool and traffic minimal. Over."

"Roger and out," Rice said.

"They sound like a fun pair," Krug said. "Rice is a queerbo, I think. Fucking Zonies, man... Yeah. Yeah, he's a fag. You think?"

Bob shot him a look of disgust.

"Hey, it's nothing to me," Krug protested. "But if the locals ever get a hold of him, they do not take kindly to that guy-on-guy action."

"Shouldn't you be moving by now?"

"Other roof won't be available until the top-floor office closes at noon, which is" – Krug checked his Timex – "still fifteen minutes away. But I could go mingle with the locals, keep an ear to the ground, if you'd like."

"Are you taking this seriously?"

Krug smiled wistfully, but it was clear he wasn't happy. "You know, Singleton, if you weren't my CO, you and I would have had words by now."

Bob knew what he meant by "words."

"Well, now... we'll be home in about ninety-six hours," Bob said. "Once we're Stateside, you're free to come take your best shot. I can spank your ass in the ring again, or we can do it up properly."

Bob knew it was stupid as soon as he said it, but it felt good to put the loudmouth in his place.

Krug eyed him bloodlessly, like a snake in long grass. "Be careful what you wish for, big man."

Bob ignored it, let him have the last word. They had bigger priorities. "Alpha to Zeta." The codenames were deliberately obscure, using Greek letters that were easily confused with typical military call signs. "Come in, Zeta."

"Zeta in position." Tyler Gaines was a quiet man, shorter than the rest of the team and more easily able to pass as a local due to his mother's Latin heritage. He'd grown up on a ranch in Texas and had been a sniper in the Marines.

"What are you seeing, Zeta?"

"As you figured, boss, they've got watchers on the farthest roof opposite your position. But they're looking for something big, an action against the crowd. There's a three-man team with shoulder-mounted SAMs across the square, and a spotter team on the building behind the stage. They're facing south, paranoid about the Israelis, as expected."

They'd known the event would be closely monitored due to the planned speech by Imam Suleyman Shokri. Shokri was wanted by the Israelis on a warrant for inciting terrorism. He'd made speeches in which he suggested Shia Muslims should attack Jews around the world, in response to the disabling of a nuclear facility two years earlier.

Andrew Kennedy had promised the Israelis ancillary cleanup of their problem if they strategically leaked word of a possible attempt to kidnap the imam using a chopper.

The Iranians would have air traffic blanketed with military coverage, confident of its impossibility given advance notice.

It would all be looking south.

In fact, it would be Zeta who took Shokri out. A smoke bomb had been planted under a concrete bench on the east side of the square. It wouldn't hurt anyone, but the flash and smoke would cause panic.

A second remote bomb armed with flash charges was located a half klick south of the square, to direct guards towards a potential source of the first "attack."

On the first detonation, the cleric would be ushered offstage, surrounded by his bodyguards... which would be of no use at all, Bob knew, given that Zeta's "blind" was more than a hundred feet above them.

The panic from the square would push fleeing crowds to one of two main exit roads. Both would be instantly blocked to traffic as thousands looked for safety.

As traffic on the surrounding streets ground to a halt, the trucks were to cut off the lead convoy vehicle carrying the physicist. Bob was confident his position was ideal for taking out the lead vehicle's tires, along with helping remove the guards.

He was less sure about Krug, who was tasked with suppressing the mounted Asvaran.

He heard the jets before he saw them, the low distant rumble familiar enough to make him turn around.

A trio of Iranian F-4 Phantoms soared overhead, and he breathed a sigh of relief at the local show of strength. The last thing they needed was for Israel or Iraqi forces to actually attack.

And that would be insanity.

Unlike what we're about to do, which is completely reasonable.

He'd had doubts since their arrival; so had Al. There had been word of a possible leak, a coded communique intercepted by Langley, a snippet of conversation between two sources, codenamed "Brighteyes" and "Excelsior," discussing Tehran urban logistics.

There was no reason to think they'd flushed the leakers somehow. They'd gone silent, and months had passed, with Stone convinced it was out of context, unrelated.

"Boss?"

Bob zoned back in. "Sorry, Zeta, just weighing some options. Keep it frosty; almost ready to rock and roll."

"Roger. Over and out."

He looked over at Krug. "Are you good to go?"

Krug checked his wristwatch. "Seven minutes until the office closes, five to get there." He rose to his feet. "See you on the other side, boss man."

He headed for the ladder down to the seventh floor.

Now it was a waiting game. Once they were all in place, it would be less than twenty minutes to the cleric's speech. Bob kept his breathing even. He tried to push down the nagging, probably paranoid feeling that something was off.

23

By the half hour, the crowd in the public square had swelled, a throng of bodies filling it from corner to corner, officials barely able to keep the exits to the streets and roads unclogged.

Bob looked down at it from his position in cover. There had to be ten thousand people crammed in, maybe more.

He was worried about the distraction, about people being trampled. But it couldn't be helped. There were going to be unworthy casualties, civilians hurt. There often were. They knew that was a possibility when they took the job.

"Talk to me, Alpha." Al wanted an update.

"Looking good so far, positions solid. Zeta says the security details haven't even bothered with top-down cover for the walk from the limos to the stage. What the hell was that flyby?"

"Reminding the locals that the government is protecting them from foreign devils. What about the Asvaran?"

"As we suspected, as many as sixteen within a ten-block radius, all carrying MP5s. Your boy Krug..."

"Eddie's boy, don't lump him with me, Bob..."

"Fine. He's got them covered. I don't trust him, Sarge."

Temple had been Bob's drill sergeant in the Marines before joining the Team as CIA liaison, replacing Stone after his promotion.

"Don't sweat Krug. He's an asshole, but he's damn good."

"What about the rendezvous?"

"Clear as day. The fiber optics Smalls installed have eyes on sixteen different angles of approach for a mile in every direction. It's abandoned, deserted. If all goes to plan..."

"They'll expect an immediate evac, shut down the airport, start surveillance on foreign embassy and relief workers, looking for anyone trying to get him onto a plane. But... four days, chief? I mean..."

"We know the risk, but we also know they're sure their local intel is so good he'll be gone long before then. The Azerbaijanis want our military help, and they want to keep the oil flowing, so bringing him across the border via the Caspian Sea by sub cuts transport time and risk dramatically. They're pissed off the Iranians keep showing diplomatic support for the Armenians, who they can't stand."

"Shocked," Bob deadpanned. "Shocked, I am, that oil is involved in all of this."

Krug keyed his mic from the rooftop two hundred meters south. "Gamma to Alpha, come in, Alpha."

"Go ahead, Gamma."

"I'm counting a dozen Asvaran officers, so we're on the low side. Like ducks in a barrel."

He took way too much pleasure in their work, Bob thought. It made him anxious, and he didn't get anxious.

"T-minus five, everyone, the current speech is wrapping up."

Bob raised his binoculars again, shields over each lens cutting efficiency by reducing light but also preventing them from reflecting glare. Onstage, a bearded, humpbacked elderly man in a hooded robe was hugging the taller presenter, a celebrated local playwright.

Behind the stage, a limousine pulled up twenty feet from the steps. Even from high above, the chanting was a deafening wave of sound. The crowd undulated like a single, breathing entity, arms raised in unison, fists clenched, bellowing, "SHOKRI! SHOKRI! SHOKRI!..."

"Target inbound," Zeta said perfunctorily. "Zeta is on target."

Bob checked his watch. In two minutes, the first smoker would go off and all hell would break loose. "Alpha to Delta. Ready to roll?"

"Roger, boss man," Richie Johnson said. "Barricades have been moved; egress is clear."

"Alpha to Kappa. Give me SA."

"Convoy is in sight, chief. Timing looks perfect. They're about a klick out."

"That distance will close real quick when we're go, so be ready. Silence until go. Alpha out."

He moved to the south side of the roof and lay down behind the SV Dragunov sniper's rifle. He checked the sight, adjusting direction until he had the convoy's lead vehicle sighted. Then he swung the barrel to the left, checking the trees beside the road for branch sway.

It wasn't his favorite long gun, but they were using all Russian equipment. It was staying behind and would confuse any ensuing investigation.

Minimal wind, less than five miles per hour. He swung his aim back to the truck's front tires and adjusted the scope for bullet drop.

He checked his watch just as Zeta chimed in, "Go in five... four... three... two... one..."

24

The robed and bearded cleric was old, his long face riveted with warts and acne pits, his frizzy hair a matte gray.

But as he spoke, he was enveloped in youthful passion. His hands accompanied each angry assertion, pointing, signaling, signing, saluting, a bony fist shaking with rage as the other hand propped him up against the lectern.

He was nearly eighty, but full of life, still. He'd talked for five minutes without referring to his notes. He had the square in a fervor, chanting back expressions in Persian to him in thundering unison.

The bench charge blew, a low bass hiccup, like gunpowder in a bathtub. Clouds of thick white smoke poured out from under the stone bench. The flash was larger than Bob expected.

The crowd in its vicinity began to panic, pushing away. A man was trampled, a woman screaming.

Onstage, bodyguards extended their weapons and surrounded the cleric.

They hurried him across the stage and down a set of stairs to the back area and towards his limousine.

One of the bodyguards went over backwards, shot through the chest. The others paused out of instinct, looking for the shooter. It brought them to a halt for just a few seconds, a fatal mistake.

The front of the cleric's skull took the second bullet, showering his guards in brains and blood.

Bob turned his head back to the rifle scope.

The convoy rolled onto the adjacent block. As it passed a side street, their first truck accelerated out and blocked those behind it.

Kappa and Lambda jumped out of the cab and blended in with the crowd on either side, leaving it stalled. Bob took careful aim and took out one of the two front tires, immobilizing the makeshift barricade, the rifle crack practically inaudible five hundred meters away from the cacophony below.

The lead convoy truck stopped, as they'd expected. Before they could change their minds, Bob sighted the driver's side of the windshield and pumped two 7.62 mm slugs through it. He saw frantic movement in the other half of the cab, the door opening.

He placed the crosshairs between the wide-swung door and the truck's frame. The moment the front passenger's head protruded but an inch, he took the second shot, the bullet knocking him backwards, dead before he hit the ground.

Around the truck, the mass of pedestrians began to scream and flee from it, some falling, others trampling over them, a woman in a light dress and head covering crouched and turtling.

He swung the scope over in time to see soldiers scrambling out of the truck's back end, from under the green canvas roof that disguised its cargo. He picked off a soldier as the man's feet hit the ground.

By then, three more had jumped down to the road, then a fourth. They began to set up a defensive perimeter around the vehicle. But they were barely settled and still moving in cautious crouches when Kappa and Lambda stepped out of the crowd, pulling the AK-47 assault rifles from under their robes.

They mowed the four men down efficiently, 7.62-caliber ammo blowing chunks of flesh and gore into a sidewalk spatter as their targets collapsed.

Bob spied two more trying to clamber out and away from the truck. He picked off one, but the other disappeared into the fleeing crowd.

Four blocks south of the square, the second charge blew. The crowd in the square was a panicked mass of undulating bodies, people pushing, trampling, scrambling to get out of there.

Kappa and Lambda moved towards the target truck. In the periphery, he could see the truck backing up until it was practically on top of the first. He checked behind the vehicle with his free eye. Fifty yards back, four Asvaran officers on horseback were closing quickly.

One went down. Then another. Then the third, each picked off cleanly by Krug. The fourth was clever, and seeing his colleagues die, he leaned in tight to the horse's neck to lower his target profile.

If Krug was trying for him, he was doing a lousy job, Bob thought.

The mounted officer was just ten yards away from the trucks and released the reins so he could search for the right target in the sights of an HK MP5 submachine gun.

Bob aimed for a spot less than three inches above the man's head and squeezed the trigger firmly. The bullet struck the man square in the face, knocking the officer off the horse.

He looked back towards the truck. Kappa and Lambda had hold of its sole occupant and were guiding him out of the vehicle with their hands under his armpits. From a distance he appeared tall and thin, in a white linen suit.

A flash of movement in the crowd to their left caught Bob's eye. Before he could resight the rifle, the guard they'd missed stepped out of the throng and opened fire with a handgun.

Shit, Bob thought. *This could go sideways.*

Ellery Azadi crumpled to the asphalt.

Kappa swung around, one arm around the scientist's back, his other hand still gripping the AK. He opened fire with a burst and cut the guard down, then began marching the scientist towards Johnson and Smalls's truck.

They were thirty yards away, the pair pushing through the crowd. Bob looked down the street behind them, the pedestrians in chaos, running in all directions like ants under a magnifying glass. Fifty yards back, four more mounted police were closing.

One went down, then another. Near a third, a glass lamp shattered. Bob took aim quickly and finished the task. By the time he'd swung his aim around to the fourth, Krug had already shot the officer, whose body was caught, one foot still in a stirrup, and being dragged away from the scene by his mount.

He shifted his line of sight back to Kappa, Jon Rice.

They were fifteen yards from the truck at most when the man in the linen suit pulled away from Rice, reached into his suit jacket and pulled a pistol, aiming it at Rice before he could turn.

Bob watched helplessly as the "scientist" shot Rice in the upper torso.

That's not Dr. Ahmadi.

It's a trap.

The shot knocked Rice off his feet, grip lost on the AK-47. The wound wasn't fatal, and he was struggling to his feet, reaching for his sidearm. The bait "scientist" walked over to him and levelled the weapon at the prone man's head.

Bob recognized that he'd frozen in the shock of the moment. He swung the scope to target and squeezed the trigger, praying his scope adjustments had been perfect.

The bullet cut the man down.

A fleeing passerby helped Rice to his feet. He stumbled into the crowd.

Bob tapped his earpiece. "Alpha to Delta, we are scratched; repeat, we are scratched. Target is bogus. Lambda is down. Get out of there now, and stay silent." The truck sprang ahead immediately, bowling over panicked passersby. "Alpha to Zeta, where are you?"

"Zeta heading due north on evac route, advise. Over."

"Kappa is cut off and surrounded, half a klick south of the square. Can you..."

"I can make it," Gaines said.

"Alpha to Gamma, what's your position?"

"Heading down the stairs to ground level now, boss."

"At exit, head due east to rendezvous with Zeta at the florist on Sarallah Street, just east of the target zone."

"Roger."

Bob clambered to his feet and headed towards the ladder that led to the apartment building's seventh floor.

"Base to Alpha, advise," Temple asked.

"We're scratched. We were sold out, Sarge. The target was bait, a dummy. Lambda is down, Kappa wounded. Zeta and Gamma are moving to help exfiltrate."

The sigh of exasperation was audible, an uncharacteristic

emotional display from his mentor. "Head directly to rendezvous; do not pass go; do not collect two hundred."

"Negative, base. Am heading due east to target zone."

"Negative, Alpha! Bob, do as I goddamned say! We're not losing more on this."

"Say again, base?" Bob lied. "I'm losing your signal."

"Goddamn it, Alpha, you've never disobeyed a direct order from me, and now is not the time to start."

"Sccttchh," Bob mouthed. "Too much static, base. Will advise when I can hear you. Out."

He tapped the earpiece to mute it. The plan had been his, and it was his responsibility to get them out. His boots pounded on concrete as he ran down the rear emergency exit staircase. He was goddamned if they were leaving anyone still breathing behind.

25

Bob pushed open the emergency exit... and emerged into chaos.

Sirens wailed as officials tried to clear the street, bodies fleeing in every direction, people screaming, children crying. Ambulance lights flashed two blocks north, the ambulance trapped. Knocked-over pedestrians were stamped, trampled, pulled out of the way by frantic family.

He could just make out the top of the truck carrying Richie Johnson and Michael Smalls towards the rendezvous point in the very north of the city.

He pushed and elbowed his way through the throng. He knew that if someone saw him key his earpiece to call the others, he could be in a world of trouble. But a perimeter check just confirmed there were too many panicking people to be sure. And without it, he had no idea where Kappa was.

Have to take that chance. He reached up as if brushing hair back behind his ear and tapped the call button, holding it down to lock it open. "Alpha to Kappa," he muttered. "Come in, Jon. Talk to me."

He heard just heavy breathing at first, a man panting.

"Kappa here. I'm... a half klick east of the target zone. Took a slug to my lower torso, think it missed anything important, but I'm bleeding heavily."

"Roger, Kappa, find cover near an identifiable landmark if you can. Over."

"Yeah..." He sounded exhausted. "Boss, the target was..."

"I saw. Save your strength. Over."

"Heading towards Babataher Park on Abuhoseyn Street. It's about three blocks southeast..."

"Roger, Zeta; Gamma and I are en route to assist. Out. Alpha to Zeta, are you catching all of this?"

"Zeta here. Roger that, boss, on my way."

"Copacetic. Out. Alpha to Gamma..."

There was silence in his ear, just a slight hiss from the open encrypted line. "Alpha to Gamma, come in, Gamma, do you read?"

But it remained silent.

Goddamn you, Krug, you chickenshit. You'd better be dead already, or when I find you, you'll wish they'd caught up to you. He shifted to a light jog, heading east, using his arms to ward off fleeing pedestrians.

There was another possibility, of course, which was that Krug wasn't nervous because Krug was the person who'd sold them out. And now he was going to leave Kappa's rescuers to their fate.

He'd covered two blocks by the time he saw it, a strip of green space along the street, separating it from the nearest buildings. It was still fifty yards away, but he began to scan the crowd nearby and the entrance area for Kappa.

He saw Zeta before Kappa, Gaines's short stature giving him away. He had a hand tucked into one side of his robe, likely holding a pistol. Bob scoured the area of sidewalk ahead of Gaines, trying to pick someone out of the teeming mass.

Rice was sitting on the edge of a stone flower box, clutching his side, a red splotch under his hand suggesting field dressing hadn't been enough. He was bent over, weary. Bob flashed back for a moment to meeting the kid, a gonzo, gung-ho Army Ranger out of Tucson, Arizona.

He looked back at Zeta. From the corner of his eye, a glint of light redirected his attention. An Asvaran officer with a pump shotgun was closing from behind. "Alpha to Zeta, you have trouble on your six... I repeat, you have..."

The shotgun blast echoed around them, more people screaming and fleeing. He saw Gaines go down hard. Bob reached for his pistol, but before he could draw it, the mounted officer spurred his horse, the beast galloping ahead. He slowed it to a canter, pumped the breach once, and shot Jon Rice through the chest.

Bob kept moving, hoping he'd just winged Zeta. Rice was done; there was no way he'd survive that blast. The crowd parted slightly, and he saw Gaines's prone body, the pool of blood around him growing.

Bob turned north, blending in with the crowd. He let the throng's movement carry him past the horse and rider, towards the sidewalk. When his right side was towards buildings, he reached up quickly and yanked out the earpiece, dropping it on the ground as he walked away.

26

CHICAGO

Bob craned his neck forward slightly, elbows on the cheap motel chair's armrests, a finger from each hand pursed to his lips as he recalled the chaotic scene.

He leaned back and let out a tense lungful of air. "We got out a day later, rather than four, and without Dr. Ahmadi. We lost three men: Tyler Gaines, who was twenty-seven and a new father; Jon Rice, who was twenty-five.

"It was even worse for Ellery Azadi. They seized his body from the scene. After they figured out his identity, they accused America of trying to foment a revolution and using locals to do it; they rounded up the remainder of Azadi's cousins, aunts and uncles..."

Dawn was on the edge of the motel bed, leaning in, her attention rapt. She couldn't believe what she was hearing. Suddenly, Bob's strange discordance, his alcoholism and choices seemed to make at least a little more sense. "And?"

"They lined them up, kneeling and blindfolded, in a public square. Nine people with no connection to our mistake whatsoever. Nine bullets."

"Jesus Christ," Marcus muttered.

"Don't blaspheme," Dawn said softly. She shook her head slowly, the thought of so much unnecessary pain and death clearly disturbing her. "Who was responsible?"

Bob looked at her with puzzlement. "Who...? I was, of course. I was the team leader, the one who was supposed to cover every eventuality."

"But... you were set up," Marcus suggested. "You can't take fault for that. What about the other guy... you know, the one you didn't like?"

"Gamma. Edson Krug. He claimed his earpiece had shorted, and he'd dumped it at street level to avoid detection. Given that I'd done the same, it was a hard case to argue."

"But you think..."

"I think he sold us out, yeah," Bob said. "When we got back, the recriminations were severe. But the only clues to the leaks were an encrypted message sent off a company server just after we returned. It referred to an official 'all clear' for 'Brighteyes.'"

"Then there *was* a leak. But... you said they blamed you..." Dawn frowned.

"Stone's theory. He'd already written off the notion of 'Brighteyes' being an Iranian source, so he stood to take some of the blame. He shifted it to me, blamed me for asking to bring Azadi into the team, suggesting I should've considered the fallout from including an Iranian American. He also intimated Ellery might have been the leak, shot once he was no longer of use to them."

"A double agent," Dawn said.

"That's what he conjured up, yeah. There was a review, took about a year. Then they fired all remaining five members of Team Seven, me included, and burned all of us."

"They BURNED you?" Dawn sounded shocked. "They literally..."

"No! No. In CIA terms, a 'burn' is a 'no contact' order passed between intelligence agencies. It meant we were out. We were all nervous as hell, because whoever was behind the betrayal would typically try to tie off loose ends in that kind of situation."

"And you're..." Marcus offered.

"A loose end, yeah."

"And my parents?"

"Same deal. Your mother wasn't involved, but given her relationship with Richie... I mean, your father..."

"But... that was more than fifteen years ago," Dawn said. "What happened...?"

"We all went into hiding. Al was clean, as he'd been in the embassy the entire time and was just advising. They let him stay on for another year and take early retirement. He suggested the rest of us go to ground, helped set us up with new legends. Your parents got plastic surgery to alter their appearances and changed their surname. Last I heard, Krug was working for some merc outfit based out of Georgia. Smalls was defiant, he told Temple he'd go overseas, but he told the rest of us he was staying in DC."

"And you?" Dawn asked. "What happened between then and... I believe you said it was ten years ago you decided to..." She made a wavy motion with her hand, the statement "to become a bum" obviously too harsh to put into words again.

He looked deeply hurt just then, like a mourner at a family funeral. "I'd met someone about a year before that. Maggie. We'd gotten engaged."

"She left you?" Marcus said bluntly. Dawn shot him a look.

"Yeah. While I was in Iran, she put a few pieces together and realized I was more than an 'overseas advisor' to the State Department. I'd made the mistake of telling her I'd be in the Middle East, and the fallout made the news in the form of

Ellery Azadi's body being paraded through the streets of Tehran on CNN and Al Jazeera. I don't know if she knew that I was directly involved or what... but I knew how much it wore on her. How much she wanted me out of the business."

Dawn felt a sense of dread, the unease of waiting for another shoe to drop. "What happened?"

"We... had a fight. It started off stupidly enough, with me leaving a plate on the kitchen counter. That devolved into me not listening to her, her telling me how much she hated what I did for a living. Me telling her she had to accept it."

"You didn't take her seriously."

"I... guess I didn't want to resolve the problem. I knew the end was coming for the team; we all suspected it after Tehran. But when she asked me to quit, I told her it wasn't her business."

"Bob..." Dawn shook her head disapprovingly.

"She was hurt. She grabbed her purse and her keys and headed for the door, said she'd stay at her friend's place in Gary for the night. I... I mean, I could have stopped her... But she was angry, hotheaded. So... I let her go. She was driving mad, not paying attention."

"Oh..." Dawn realized where it was headed. "Oh, Bob..."

"She ran a stop sign, and her car was T-boned by a semi. But... she shouldn't have even been there. If I hadn't chosen my work over her, if I'd even just promised to change..."

"You cannot possibly blame yourself..." she began to assert.

He shrugged. "I was an arrogant guy. I'd been an arrogant kid, too; I was sure that being a jock and a smart mouth was enough to get me through life. I was only eighteen when I signed up, and an immature eighteen at that. But... it is what it is. My sudden forced retirement came with solid severance, so I bought the townhouse in Chicago, my father's hometown."

"You weren't careful," Marcus said.

"I couldn't get over the feeling that most of what I'd done with Team Seven didn't do a lot of good. I should've been cautious, should've changed my name. But we were assured by Smalls that he had his ear to the ground in DC and no one was looking. And... I was in a bad place mentally."

"But no one pursued you?" Dawn asked.

"Temple kept his ear to the ground; from what he could figure out, the agency thought we'd been taken care of. None of us was looking a gift horse in the mouth, so we went to ground. My pension went to a family trust, which fit with me not being around anymore. I imagine your parents did something similar. I started poking around a little, calling old contacts, looking into the families and backgrounds of some of the people we'd taken out over the four years."

"It's only natural to try to find answers," the nurse suggested.

He looked up and stared at her pointedly. "I didn't like what I found, okay? Assignments that we'd taken on as being matters of national security and public safety wound up having purely political components, side beneficiaries, corporate interests more aligned with politicians and dealmakers like Andrew Kennedy than with doing good."

"So... you felt used," Marcus suggested.

He nodded. "I WAS used, as a deadly tool, against people who were sometimes just in the wrong place at the wrong time. I can't even calculate how many people I might be responsible for, people killed so that someone else could make a dollar or win political points. That was when I realized why she'd left me: because she realized I'm a monster."

He said it glumly, an accepted fact in his reality. He leaned forward again, elbows on knees, momentarily distant and pensive.

He seemed both hurt and embarrassed. Even with what he'd said and done, Dawn wanted to lean in and hug him.

"Bob... you were a soldier for your country. I mean... yeah, you can call it 'espionage' or whatever, but that doesn't change that you were trying to do the right thing..."

He shook his head vehemently and stood up, as if the sudden tension had jolted him. "Don't say that, please! Don't tell me anything about what we did was good, or that I deserve better! Maggie deserved better! Ellery Azadi and Tyler Gaines and Jon Rice all deserved better! Azadi's family... Nine people..." He licked his lips and tilted his head back, the stress weighing on him. "Christ. I need a drink."

"Don't blaspheme." She said it gently, though, and out of reflex. "You don't need to be doing yourself any more harm right now. Besides, we have this one to consider." She nodded Marcus's way. "You need to let go of all of this. If not permanently, then at least for now. There are people trying to kill us, Bob Singleton, and I am not doing this on my own."

He shook his head, this time more effusively. "No. No way. Now that you two are out of the line of fire, you need to go to ground, find somewhere secure to stay while I try to figure out who's hunting us and deal with it as best I can. You have family somewhere, I take it..."

"My sister is in Hawaii. My brothers are all on the west coast."

"They're named Ellis too?"

She shook her head. "Surname is Green. Half brothers. My sister's got her husband's name..."

"Married in Chicago?"

She shook her head. "No, sir. Honolulu."

"She's your best bet, then. You can go and stay with her until this blows over."

"What about me?" Marcus asked. "I don't have anywhere to go. I don't have anyone."

Bob wasn't sure what to suggest.

Dawn could read his anxiety over it.

He sighed. "You, we'll drop off with a social services outfit somewhere," he suggested. "You're underage, so they have to help you..."

"Uh-uh," Dawn said, shaking her head. "Who's to say that the men chasing us don't find him anyway? And what happens when his year is up? Besides, I can't afford a ticket to Hawaii. What if they figure out that's my sister? I mean, she took her husband's name and all, but there are public records. What if they decide to watch her in case I show up? Or my brothers? Then I've dragged them into this! No, sir: until you figure this nonsense out, Mr. Singleton, I'm afraid you're stuck with us."

He closed his eyes and scratched absently at his beard. "Sometimes, I think I should've just bought a tavern, listened to Otis Rush records on a jukebox, got old, drunk and fat on roast beef hoagies." He sighed. "We need to go to DC. The nearest surviving team member is Mike Smalls. If they came after us, he'll be next. He might even know who we're dealing with."

"Okay," she said, nodding. "Now you're talking about a plan. That's something."

It all seemed insane to Dawn, but he'd saved her life, and Marcus had confirmed how easily the men pursuing them had cleaned up his parents' murder. That seemed impossible without strong police ties. She had no idea whom else they could trust. "But... we have to do something first."

"What?" Her uncertain look caught him off guard.

"We need to risk a trip to the Walmart down the road. I looked when we passed, and it's open late. You need a shower, a shave, and a change of clothes."

Marcus nodded. "It's true, dude... I mean, I don't want to be rude or nothing... but you kind of stink."

Bob looked resigned to it. She noticed his hands were trembling. She wondered if he could hold it together, or if his first move outside the motel would be to find a bottle.

27

The shower was scalding hot, and Bob stood under its full force, facing the jet, letting it soak away the grime.

The water soaked through his thick, bushy beard, weighing it down. He hadn't had a proper shower in months, not since the shelter three blocks from his flop closed its doors. He'd tried hand washing in the El train station's bathrooms, using moist tissue.

But for the most part, his filth had become part of his identity, a fitting state for a life mired in the dirt. Now, it washed off him in sheets, following the contours of his fat-free body, running across muscle groups that had once been more powerful, over the myriad of knife, bullet, and interrogation scars.

Dawn had gone out, all three agreeing the men pursuing them would likely have a difficult time telling one middle-aged woman from another, particularly with her hair pushed up under Marcus's ball cap and the boy's jacket on.

They didn't have much money. Bob had advised against

her using her cash card or credit, insisting, to her shock, that the men hunting them could probably track them.

Instead, she'd taken the bus from in front of the motel to the nearest cash machine and used Marcus's card to withdraw the maximum five hundred dollars.

It was, Bob warned, likely the last time that card could be used. They'd gone after Marcus's parents, which gave them a small window on considering that a kid has his own finances.

But within a day, he'd suggested, even using the boy's account would be tantamount to waving a red flag on a flat road.

She'd come back with three pairs of slacks, one light tan, the other two dark gray and black; two dress shirts, in pale blue and black; two golf shirts; socks and underwear; and, at Bob's request, a black track suit. A cheap sport coat, a pair of soft-soled black shoes and a pair of black sneakers completed the collection.

He turned off the tap and got out of the shower. He toweled himself off roughly, realizing how much muscle he'd lost to hunger over the decade.

Dawn had cut his hair. Now he had to shear off the rest. Clipping the beard down with scissors was the easy part, great dark brown tufts tumbling into the sink. Shaving the remainder off was more difficult.

He watched himself in the giant motel bathroom mirror, trying to steady the hand holding the disposable safety razor with his other. Every few seconds, he'd nick himself, the sting familiar but forgotten, like the face of a long-lost cousin.

The shakes had started two hours earlier, but he'd tried to hold them in, stiffening muscles whenever possible to arrest his trembling. It had been so long, so long since he'd gone more than a few hours without getting alcohol into his system. His bowels were feeling it, too, as if the bacteria in his gut had been suppressed by hard liquor and vanilla extract. Now his head was aching.

He stopped shaving for a bare moment and stared at the half-groomed image in the mirror.

Acting like a human being. But you're not, are you, Bob? You're already dead. It's just a secret, is all. They can make excuses for you because you saved them. Because they're decent people. But they wouldn't be in trouble at all if you'd never existed. Neither would Maggie. She'd be enjoying the life you took away...

The strain felt overwhelming, a rush of depression and self-loathing he thought beaten down by booze and vagrancy. He looked down, unable to face himself, both hands on the sink counter as the weight of what he was doing settled in, surrounded by rising steam from the running tap.

He noticed the bottle of aftershave near the back of the sink. It would have a decent percentage of alcohol in it, he figured. He fixated on the little green, translucent container.

Would they even know if you just drank it? Would it matter if they didn't even notice you were a little drunk?

Then he wondered how Maggie would judge him from on high. *You don't get to do this, you useless piece of shit. You don't get to do to them what you did to her...*

He wanted to cry, could feel the tears welling. But he pushed it down. Self-pity wasn't just undeserved, it was unproductive. He wiped away the gathered moisture in the remnants of his beard and studied what he'd done so far.

You almost look human. When you can pass for one, you'll get a chance to do some good for a change.

He frowned. This time, his inner monologue sounded a lot more like Nurse Dawn. He hardly knew her, he realized, even though she'd treated him at least a dozen times over the prior four years.

The other doctors and nurses at the clinic averted their gaze to avoid looking him in the face. But never her. She'd not only met his stare, but she'd also engaged with him, talked to him like he mattered, like she had genuine interest in what he might tell her.

He wondered how it was that someone so different from himself, so utterly grounded in what was local and new and real – her community, her job, her life – could take pity on someone like him. Her heart had to be bigger than the clinic building.

And that was worth fighting for.

He took a deep breath and calmed himself. Then he got back to the business of scraping away his beard.

He dressed quickly once done, choosing the tan slacks and pale blue shirt. Eventually, he opened the door a crack. "Okay, all done. Now... don't laugh too hard, damn it. Sorry." He apologized before she could remind him that she considered it swearing.

He pushed the bathroom door open.

Marcus looked up from his phone, wide-eyed. "Oh, snap! Who's this dude!?"

Dawn stood and crossed her arms, studying him with talent-show-judge scrutiny. She nodded a few times. "Yeah... you look a lot better, Bob. But... fashion wise, you look like you manage the Walmart."

He shrugged. "I was going for the suburban dad look, so that's perfect, I guess."

The teenager snickered. "Dammnnn... you look proper academic. You look like my friend Parker's old man when he dresses up for church."

Dawn shot him an unimpressed look. "Your friend Parker's dad doesn't think much of the Lord if he dresses like an Apple repairman for Sunday service. He doesn't wear a tie, even?"

Marcus shrugged. "He's not real together, you know?"

Dawn studied her watch. "It's... eleven twenty! Oh my! No

wonder I'm so darn tired. Bob, you got cleaned up and dressed just in time for us to all get some shuteye!"

Bob nodded towards the bed. "You want the chair or the floor, kid?"

But Marcus had stopped listening. Instead, he was sobbing gently, trying to hold back more tears. Dawn moved over and put her arms around him, hugging him tight. "You have a good cry now, boy. You loved them, and they're gone, and the only thing that makes that easier to handle is time."

"I'll sleep on the floor," Bob said, trying to use the matter at hand to avoid his discomfort at the boy's grief.

The nurse rolled her eyes. "Don't be foolish, now. We all need rest. We share the bed... and you two use the top blanket only. We've all got clothes on, and we can all fit in there okay, but we ain't sharing sheets."

"And tomorrow?" Marcus asked, sniffling and wiping away the last tear. "They'll be looking for the Challenger. It's stolen, and... I mean... it's bright orange, Bob."

"Let me take care of that, okay? Get some sleep. We're gone at first light, and we have a few hours on the road ahead of us."

28

GARY, INDIANA

The tube lighting in his trailer "office" did him no favors, but there was no doubting that Ray Nichols – of East Gary Ray's Used Car Bonanza and Discount Deals – was weedy and thin, sickly even.

He looked undernourished, a bad salesman in a short-sleeved dress shirt, complete with pocket protector. Sweat trickled down his balding head, sandy hair plastered thinly from one side of his skull to the other for maximum coverage, a pencil-thin moustache completing the ensemble.

His blue eyes were watering, mouth slightly open as he panted from the pain.

He was reaching out to the desk just ahead of him, but it wasn't by choice.

His right arm was pinned to the wood, a four-inch-long steel nail protruding from both front and back of his impaled hand, a small puddle of blood beginning to form around it.

"Ohhh... Jesus Christ, that hurts so much..." he choked, half crying.

Across from him, Edson Krug sat patiently in the chair

normally reserved for suckers, the men and women cheated into buying his lousy, rebuilt used cars.

Next to the desk, Krug's number two stood with nail gun in hand. "You want me to hit him again?"

Krug arched his fingers as he watched the man squirm, then recoil from pain, then squirm and repeat the cycle. It reminded him of the fun he'd had as a kid, using his mother's pins to impale live insects and watch them wriggle.

He'd tried it with larger animals, too, but it hadn't felt as powerful or satisfying. But he could've had coffee and watched the salesman suffer for another hour or two, easily, as if bingeing a TV show.

"Please… no…" The salesman begged.

Krug removed his sunglasses and a handkerchief from his suit pocket. He used the square of cloth to polish the lenses, ignoring the man's protestations.

The trailer was untidy, they'd swept the folders and girly magazines off the man's desk onto the floor, but the rest of the room wasn't much better: just a desk, a couple of chairs, some cheap living room furniture against the back wall. A trash can was tipped over by the sofa, Kleenexes spilled onto the floor. The coffee table was piled with detritus, including a moldy sandwich that had begun to attract flies.

Krug weighed it all.

What a shithole...

On the table, a few feet from Ray's pinned hand, a white ceramic ashtray sat mostly unused, save for the wrapper of a Charleston Chew.

"Still with the bad habits in his downtime," Krug muttered. "What a waste of talent."

"Huh?" Ray stammered.

He turned his attention back to their subject. "The thing is, Raymond, we've already checked with our people in Indianapolis, and… believe me when I say this… we have people everywhere. And Bob's not in Indianapolis or St. Louis or Dubuque, Idaho."

"Iowa..." Ray corrected between gasps.

Krug didn't like to be corrected. He gave a curt side nod, and his man leaned over Ray's hand, pointing the nail gun down and yanking the trigger.

Another nail shot through him, the force of it driving the car salesman's palm into the desktop.

"OHJESUSFLIPPIN'CHRISTMARYANDJOSEPH!" he bellowed. He began to sob slightly.

"Let's try the question again: Where are they, Raymond? What did they tell you, from the beginning, and how do you know Bob Singleton?"

"I already said I don't, not really! Please... Goddamn... it hurts! Can you remove the nails, at least?"

Krug just stared at him.

"I told you: he helped me out a few years back with a repo job..."

"After an Alcoholics Anonymous meeting. Yes, you did mention that. But I meant useful information, you revolting little turd."

"That was it, I swear! He... unhh... got the guy to bring it back... and no one was the wiser."

"You sold a car that could've split in two and killed everyone in it... and he helped you? That seems strange if he has no other connection to you. What would he have to gain from getting a customer to return a dangerous vehicle?"

"I said... I said it already. We went off the wagon after the same AA meeting, and I'd had a few too many. I wasn't bragging or nothing, but I got full sticker for that piece of shit..."

"Even though it had been written off in an accident and you'd swapped the VIN with another car's? That doesn't sound like the do-gooder Bob that I remember. That sounds like you were on the fix together somehow, like he had a piece of the action."

The man shook his head, tears and sweat dripping down in equal measures. Near the back of the room, a radio on a shelf played an old blues song, Zuzu Bolin imploring his woman to "eat where you slept last night." The tube lights hummed an incessant, low drone, like sleepy cicadas.

"That's not it at all. I... I didn't tell him all the details; I just said it was an accident waiting to happen. Then he insisted I get it back."

That made more sense, Krug thought. It reminded him of Bob's holier-than-thou attitude. But... "So, this was..."

The man gulped and choked back phlegm and tears. "Four years ago, like I said."

"And he hasn't talked to you since? But he came to YOU this morning when he needed to get rid of a hot car..."

"It's true, I swear it." His labored breathing was becoming more pronounced, the constant pain from broken hand bones causing him to pant harder, as if he'd run a race. "He said, 'I... know you sell... hot garbage; I've got something... I need to get rid of.'"

"And you traded him the keys to his stolen Challenger for..."

"I told you... he... made me... turn around while he took a random... set of keys. I have three hundred cars... on the lot. I hadn't had time... to figure out which one..."

It had taken them seventeen hours to find the orange Dodge Challenger after it disappeared from downtown Chicago.

Most of that was waiting for their state police contact to get the word out to troopers to look for it, and for their contacts with Chicago Traffic to check intersection cameras.

But Krug figured the three had stayed in the city or close by for the night, as the trade had taken place at nine in the morning, and it was already five thirty in the afternoon.

That meant they'd been gone for nearly eight hours.

They would have to widen the search area, get more people involved. Dahlen wasn't going to be happy.

"Do you have a printed inventory list?" he asked the salesman.

Ray nodded quickly, perhaps sensing an end to his torment. "The clipboard... on top of the filing cabinet."

"You're a regular twenty-first-century trailblazer, Raymond," Krug suggested. He gestured towards his number two. "Take the clipboard, figure out which car they took. Have the men torch this place. I'm sure East Gary Ray here has an extensive and enviable criminal record, given his trade..."

"Nothing big..." Ray panted. "Wait... torch?"

"Yeah... I'm afraid your day is going to get worse before it gets better..."

Krug drew his Glock 17 pistol.

Ray's eyes widened. "NO!" he exclaimed. "Wait! Wait... I heard the woman say something about DC."

"DC? As in the capital?"

Ray nodded frantically, eyes wide with the realization that he'd just been helpful, that maybe his pain would soon end.

"Thank you, Ray. There! See," Krug proposed. "You're not a completely useless piece of shit after all."

He turned and shot the man through the head. The concussive force knocked Ray's body backwards slightly, but his hand remained pinned to the table. His chair rolled out from under him, and Ray slumped to his knees, dead, head down, nails holding his arm up on the tabletop.

"That's enough out of him." Krug rose. "Get it done and meet me back at the car. We need to get moving quickly."

"Yes, sir."

He'd have to call Dahlen, tell him they needed to expand

the coverage area. Bob had left town and taken the other two witnesses with him. But at least they had an idea of where he was heading.

His boss wouldn't be happy, but it wasn't as if Krug needed the extra motivation. He'd chided himself for his fear back at the warehouse.

Their tussles were long in the past. He was the biggest, strongest version of himself, he was sure. And he'd wanted to kill Bob Singleton for a very long time, indeed.

ALEXANDRIA, VIRGINIA
JUNE 19, 2006

THE BELL for the fourth round rang, and Bob sprang up from his corner stool, flexing his fists in fingerless gloves before raising them into a defensive posture.

Across the ring, Edson Krug struggled to his feet slowly. There was no referee to stop the fight, no crowd in the Team Seven training area to rouse some sort of miracle comeback.

Krug was already hurt, and it was obvious. One eye was almost closed by a purple welt, a smear of blood staining one nostril. He held his left hand low, as if too tired to raise it, although it was probably just a subconscious attempt at protecting his broken ribs.

Bob halted his own shuffle forward for a moment, the man's discomfort alarming. "We don't have to keep going," Bob said. "I've made my point; you've made yours. You're tough as cowhide, Krug, I get it. But this is the third time we've thrown down now in two years, and you have to get it. You have to understand you can't beat me."

Krug shuffled forward, sniffling, a few blood droplets spattering the ring surface. He raised his right hand, going into a boxing stance. "What... you... you chickening out... Bob? Can't take... another round?"

He staggered forward until within reach and threw an overhand right, his movements slow and lurching. Singleton bobbed backwards, and it sailed harmlessly by. He took a step back and to the left, creating space between them.

"Man... this is stupid, Krug. It doesn't matter how much we hate each other. Until they say otherwise – and we all know it's coming – we're still on the same team..."

Krug pivoted on his heel and threw a roundhouse right. Bob parried it with both hands, following the motion with a short right hand into Krug's lowered left guard. It smacked into his fractured ribs, and he grunted from pain despite the half-hearted effort. He stumbled backwards.

"Don't make me knock your ass out again..." Bob warned. "Like I said..."

"You... you know what I hate about you, Bob?" Krug panted. "Other than... other than stealing my job... as Alpha?"

"If I knew what was going on in that squirrel wheel you call a brain... No, Krug, I don't know what your deal is. That chip's been there since the day we met."

They circled each other slowly. "You remind me of my old man." As bruised and exhausted as he was, Krug managed to sneer as he said it. "He... hosted a kids show on local TV. A... paragon of the community, Uncle Davy. Until the cameras were off, and he needed to get his kicks with one of the kids who came to his tapings. Or... or to lay a beating on me."

He threw another overhand right. Singleton stepped aside, knocking his arm down with a double guard. "Krug, your past is none of my—"

"My mom liked beating on kids, too. But you know what? She was honest about who she was. She'd say, 'Sonny, I guess I'm just a mean bitch, and giving you the back of my hand feels damn good sometimes. I know you're my kid... but I just don't like you.'" He panted out a snicker of amusement. "Heh... I guess I came from her side of the family. But you? You're like my old man..."

He tried to rush into a short right. Singleton ducked it. Krug stumbled by him, then turned as quickly as he could, regaining his balance. He was panting less, trying to get his second wind.

"You're... you're willing to whip my ass... on a dare for three rounds, but then you pretend like you give a shit... if I'm hurt. You're a phony, Bob. You know why I keep coming back to try again?"

"No, Krug, like I said..."

"Because hitting people is what I like to do... and I guess I just don't like you."

He threw another overhand right, but this time it was a feint, Krug summoning the strength from some untapped reserve to load up and throw a follow-up left hand. It caught Bob in the temple... but the smaller man's strength was already gone, his legs weakened from body shots.

Bob reacted on instinct, snapping his head forward, raising his left to block any follow-up punch, throwing the right hand short and hard, from his shoulder, catching Krug on the side of the chin.

He went down hard, lying on his back on the canvas, his pupils dancing, arms spread wide, a mildly confused look on his face.

Bob looked down at him and shook his head. "Stay down, Krug, for crying out loud... Look, you got what you wanted. You got another shot. I'd rather you hadn't threatened poor Nicky Velasco to force the issue..."

Krug attempted to right himself, but the effort was too great. He fell onto his back, arms stretched out above his head, as if a champion had fallen over mid-coronation.

He began to giggle. "Poor Nicky. That's another reason your... your phony act pisses me off, Bob. It surfaces to protect weaklings like Nicky, geeks who think they belong in a mean business. He had his shot, and he got... he got weak at the knees. So Smalls took his spot. Survival of the fittest. He's lucky we even let him in the building."

"He's just a chiphead, a digital spook," Bob suggested. "He's not here by choice or selection, he was just assigned by Langley."

"He's a weakling, a waste of air." Krug rolled onto one side, trying to right himself.

"You need help, Krug. But you're not getting any more of my time. Challenge Nick or anyone else who can't take care of themselves, and the next time we do this, I won't be so forgiving." Bob headed towards the corner.

Krug snickered one more time, his senses less addled. He used the back of one glove to wipe spittle and blood from the corner of his mouth, then pushed himself up to a half-seated position.

"We'll do this again, Bob," he said as Singleton climbed out of the ring. "Even if the threats are true, and we're all in the wind a month from now. You and I will do this again."

29

WASHINGTON, DC

The eight-year-old SUV sat on the dimly lit street in Mount Pleasant, under the shadows from an oak tree. The tree's trunk and branches were backlit by the setting sun.

Bob rested his left elbow on the driver's door as he held Marcus's phone to his ear. It rang three times, and he hung up.

"I thought you were going to..." Dawn began to say.

He waved her off and redialed. "Call code."

It rang three more times before the other party answered. "Uh-huh."

"Sarge."

Al Temple sounded relieved. "Where in heck are you? Chi Town's crawling with suits, and I'm getting uncomfortable phone calls from old agency friends. I tried to catch you at the clinic, but you'd hightailed it out. Talk to me, Bob... You out of retirement or something?"

Temple's exasperation was loud enough to pick up over the tinny speaker.

"Nothing like that, Sarge. Just... old business. Look... don't worry, okay?" Bob insisted. "You're out of this loop."

"Nice to say and all. But the attention I'm getting says otherwise. This have anything to do with the Team?"

"Difficult to say. All I know is I'm hotter than an old Christmas tree bulb."

"Yeah? You didn't run into a kid named Marcus by any chance..."

"He's sitting three feet from me."

"Ah... hell. Why'd you go and do that? He's a boy, for Christ's sake..."

"Gee, Professor, I don't know... maybe because guys with forty calibers were chasing us halfway across the Loop. It wasn't by choice, believe me. I tried to get rid of them..."

"Them?"

"A friend we both ran into sort of got dragged into it."

"Anyone I know?"

"I don't think so; nurse at the clinic."

"So... what now?"

Temple was always about the business, Bob thought. His mentor had not changed. "Now? I need to figure out which of the many, many lousy things I did has come back to haunt us. Look... you might want to get out of Dodge for a week or three. These guys are relentless and don't seem to have a whole lot of worries about laying down fire in public..."

"I'm not going anywhere." Temple sounded indignant. "I've got a class to teach on Monday."

"You could be dead by Monday. Don't be stubborn, okay? These guys came after us hard and hot, with a team of eight, maybe ten guns. Anyone pulling that kind of operation on domestic soil is a little bit off their rocker. Your reputation and old friends aren't going to stop them if..." He caught himself before he finished the grim thought. "Do you still have that cabin in upstate New York? Take a few days off. Get out of town."

"You're a real pain in my ass, you know that?"

"Yeah, but you love me..." Bob suggested.

The line was silent for a moment while Temple composed his thoughts. Eventually, he said, "You know, the place hasn't been the same since you moved out and decided to... you know, drop out of everything. I mean, it was hard after Evie died, and it was nice for a while, having someone to talk to on the regular..."

"Yeah... yeah, I liked that, too, man..."

The professor's voice had softened. "She... she sure was something, wasn't she?" Temple said.

It had broken Bob's heart to see Al suffer, waiting for the inevitable to claim her. Evie was Temple's wife. She died a decade earlier of complications from multiple myeloma. He'd spent the ten years before that trying to save her; she'd been his high-school sweetheart and best friend for thirty-five years.

They'd tried everything: every drug, every experimental procedure. He'd sold their paid-off home to help foot the bill, and still it hadn't been enough. They'd moved into an old cabin in upstate New York, in the family for generations. If it hadn't been on leasehold land, they'd have sold it, too, and been homeless.

Temple had been a respected military man and handler, then an educator. Life didn't respect any of that when it came to doling out cruelty.

"She was the best, Sarge. The best of any of us."

"Best I ever knew, best I ever will know," Temple whispered.

When it was time, sometimes it was just time. He still had that emptiness, buried deep somewhere, that pain he felt whenever he thought about his folks. Or Maggie.

"I get that," he said. "Maggie and me... we weren't as lucky as you two, didn't have that long together..."

"I always hoped... you know, stupid stuff. We knew Evie couldn't have kids, but we had careers we focused on. I always figured maybe you two would have a family..."

Bob frowned and tugged nervously at the scrunchy on his wrist. "I promised myself I wouldn't be a dad unless I could be better at it than my old man."

"You would've been."

"I always figured if we had the chance to be parents... But that didn't happen. And then she was gone."

"And when they're gone, it's like you've lost a piece of your soul," Al said.

Bob could see Al in his mind's eye just then, looking at a picture of his late wife, his hope scarred like a burn victim's skin graft.

From the corner of his eye, he saw a bicyclist pass the parked car, and it snapped him out of his brooding.

Their mutual pain wasn't helping anyone, given the circumstances.

"I don't want to lose anyone else I care about, okay? Just do me a favor and keep your head down. Okay, Sarge?"

"Roger that. But don't worry about me; you know when the heavy shit hits..."

"You won't hesitate. Yeah, I know."

"Never did have your soft spot. He who hesitates is lost. You start worrying about collateral, collateral issues..."

"True. You know what's also true? You've been a professor for the last decade and then some, not a soldier."

"Point taken. So... what now?"

"My best guess is, this is exactly what we both think it is..."

"Some kind of cleanup for Tehran."

"I'm guessing we know who, also..."

"Maybe," Temple said. "You know I never agreed with you about Krug being 'Excelsior,' but you might have been right. You want I should make some calls…?"

Bob chuckled a little at that, but it was clearly exasperation. "What did we just talk about? Your fat was never in this fire. Don't get involved, okay? Stay clear until I tell you otherwise. Go to New York. Where's that cabin again?"

"Cayuga Lake. And you? What are you going to do?"

"We're going to track down Smalls, have a little talk. If they came for us, they might come for him."

"They might have already," Temple said. "How do you know he wasn't first in line? He lives in DC. I can't believe the little shit lied to me and said he'd go overseas. It's like thumbing his nose in the agency's face."

"True. But we have to start somewhere. Last I heard, he was doing some consulting with corporate espionage types, keeping away from the government stuff. If he wasn't making noise, maybe they weren't really looking; maybe he kept a low profile."

"Smalls?" Temple said. "That guy couldn't keep quiet in a library. But… like I said, if you need anything…"

"Yeah, will do."

They were silent for a moment, the professor composing his thoughts. "Son… you think you owe those guys left behind. But you don't. They made their own choices, and things went south. But that's not on you. It never was. Look out for number one, Bobby. Nobody else is going to. Okay?"

"Goodbye Sarge. Until later, anyway. Semper fi, buddy."

"Semper fi, kid."

Bob ended the call. He stared at the phone for a moment. He'd used the Marine slogan automatically with Al, as he had for so many years. But he hadn't felt worthy of it in a long time, and it was a strange, discordant sensation. He gestured towards the walk-up fourplex across the street. "Anything?"

"Not a peep," Dawn said from the passenger seat. "We've had two door-to-door salesmen, a young gentleman with a bicycle, and a mom with her baby, a husband-and-wife team. But no short, balding, chunky-looking white dude."

"Maybe he moved," Marcus said. "I mean... you said it yourself; it's been ten years since you talked to this guy."

Bob shook his head. "He had this place registered in his mom's name. As much as he put a brave face on staying in DC, he took steps to erase his past and his movements. His official address in Arlington is a storage locker. His phone number there is a cell plugged into a device that keeps it charged and redirects the calls to his phone. Smalls was a genius with computers and electronics. If he wanted to mislead people, he could keep them on one side of the city for days while he held a barbecue on the other."

Dawn looked unsure. "Well... that's great. Why am I not surprised it wasn't going to be as easy as parking here? How can you be sure he didn't do the same to you with this whole 'mom's address' thing?"

"I can't. But... we got along. I was his CO as head of the team. Smalls had a habit of getting himself into the soup, and I usually managed to get him out of it."

"Uh-huh. Also, not surprising. If he's not here..."

"We'll cross that bridge when we come to it. In the meantime, you've counted what sounds like the tenants of three out of four units. Maybe we'll get lucky soon enough..."

"And if we don't?" Marcus asked.

"We see if anyone in the building has a forwarding address. I'll door-knock a few..."

"It's not much of a plan..." Dawn said.

"... but we have to start somewhere."

Another half hour passed in relative silence, each alone with their thoughts. A tiny woman with short, bleached white hair walked up the front steps. She looked both ways before entering as if checking for attention. Bob could feel the anxiety building in the car's cab.

Keep it light; keep their minds off it all. "So... why'd you become a nurse?"

Dawn thought back and smiled wistfully. "My father was a surgeon. When I was little, he was still in school and doing his residency after that. We didn't see him much except late in the evening or at night. But my mother used to tell me he was a seriously gifted person, with a genius mind; hands so steady, he could draw perfect straight lines with his eyes closed. He felt he had a responsibility to use his gifts to help lesser people. Which, unfortunately, was sort of how he saw everyone."

"God complex," Bob said, realizing immediately that the story would be anything but light. *Good call, Bobby, you idiot.* "At least... I hear that's a thing with surgeons..."

She inhaled deeply, as if pondering the weight of it. "Well, I don't know about that. He was a faithful churchgoer, so I don't expect he'd have liked the comparison. But... yeah. I mean, he really did think a lot of himself. That was the trouble, too. As a surgeon in a public hospital, he'd work long shifts and see dozens of patients every week, a lot of them in pretty terrible shape: accidents, workplace disasters, gangsters with gunshot wounds. That kind of thing. And you know how it is in a situation like that: he just couldn't save as many as he needed to, as many as it would take to prove to him that he and he alone had the power over life and death."

"None of us do," Bob said.

"It caught up to him eventually, and he had a heart attack pretty young. My mother passed from cancer two years ago." She took another deep, cleansing breath. "Anyhow, I figured if I could make anything positive out of it, it would be that he wanted, ultimately, to save people. And I thought, I may not be a genius like him, but I can do the best I can to help people... maybe be a little bit happier about it, at that."

"He'd probably be real proud of you for that," Bob said.

"Maybe. More likely, he'd think I was a failure for not becoming a surgeon like him, and for not being able to save my boy, or my marriage. Doesn't matter now, I guess." She smiled. "I love being a nurse. Greatest thing that ever happened to me, other than Maurice, and I thank Jesus for that."

"Well, now, I imagine JC would definitely be okay with it," Marcus chimed in.

"Don't blaspheme!" she advised.

But Bob noticed she was smiling a little.

She looked at her watch. "It's six forty. Anyone working days is probably home by now. That might be it for the night."

Bob nodded. "We'll give it another half hour before I go check. Then we need to roll. The phone kiosk near here closes at eight, and we need another burner."

30

ARLINGTON, VIRGINIA

The man at the front counter was older, edging on retirement.

He was relaxed in his role, perhaps accustomed to decades of hardcases and sob stories. The storage units contained people's lives, their memories. That stuff meant a lot to them. He was the guy often in their way.

But it had been a long time since any of it fazed him, Krug figured. The old cardigan sweater and polyester short-sleeved shirt suited his casual, nonplussed expression. This was a man who had seen too much before most of them were born.

He probably had a shotgun under the front counter, but he'd also know that the five men in black suits standing ahead of him were more than he could handle.

Krug rested his pistol, flat side, on the counter. "We need to see a unit." It made a bizarre sort of sense that Smalls's last known address wasn't actually an apartment, but a repository of secrets.

"Got a number?" The man's expression barely registered life.

"3211."

"Got a name?"

"Lynette Welland or Michael Smalls."

The man shuffled over to the dusty, grubby, ancient PC on one corner of the counter. He stared at the monochrome screen and tapped the keys a few times.

"Welland, unit 3211."

Krug gestured towards the double side doors with the pistol. "Lead the way."

They filed out of the office. The vast paved lot next to the building was covered with rows of thirty-five-square-foot units, each with a corrugated roll-up door, padlocked at its base.

The old clerk led them to the seventh row, then past dozens of orange doors. He stopped at one and stooped low, unlocking the door.

He strolled over to Krug and handed him the padlock. "Close it up properly when you're done."

Then he ambled casually past Krug's team.

"Sensible man," Krug muttered.

The team entered the unit and began poking through boxes. In the back, against shelves, an old kitchen leaf table stood, one side folded down. A laptop sat atop it, its power cord attached to a yellow extension cable, which in turn snaked to the sole electrical outlet, by the door.

An old-fashioned digital answering machine was attached to the laptop via a jerry-rigged USB connector.

"Other than that, it's empty," his lieutenant said. "We'll pull it apart, go through the file history, and see what we can recover."

"You won't find anything. But this place is in his mother's name. Check with the old guy in the office, find out what ID was used to rent it, get an address off that."

"Okay. And the clerk?"

"Grab the security tapes. If he makes a fuss, shoot him;

otherwise... I wouldn't waste the bullet. He's not going to say shit."

"Affirmative."

His lieutenant strode back towards the main building as the team finished disconnecting the laptop. Smalls would have wiped it clean, but it was possible his mother had rented the box initially, and it was possible she'd left a real address.

If Bob and his friends were in DC, they'd gone on the offensive. That meant he would come into Dahlen's orbit sooner or later. And Krug planned to be there.

Soon, Bob. Soon.

WASHINGTON, DC

THE DORCHESTER CLUB'S patio balcony was eight stories up and looked out over DC at night, the rotunda on the Capitol building a glowing white dot from a mile away, the blackness spattered with the cherry glow of taillights and the haze of yellow streetlamps.

Andrew Kennedy drew deeply on the Cuban cigar, the embers glowing, tendrils of smoke drifting around his balding head and crown of white hair before flitting away in the light breeze.

The distant lights reflected off his spectacles as he studied the city. He liked to think everything he could see from the private patio was, in essence, his domain: not because he controlled it, or that any one person could; but because in the Beltway, he was a man of influence and power, someone to whom the nation's leaders would look for advice.

In his presence, bureaucrats trembled.

It had taken him fifty years to build that reputation, beginning with his graduation from officers' school and a tour as a lieutenant and commanding officer in Vietnam.

It had continued with four decades of service to the Central Intelligence Agency, first as a strategic analyst, a paper pusher. At his peak, he had been the agency's deputy director, its number two man after the politically appointed head. The real power behind the decisions the agency made.

It had lasted nearly a decade before the current director's predecessor decided he had grown too influential for the agency's benefit. His unwillingness to be crystal clear about his rapid growth in net worth hadn't helped.

He had been bumped down, first to chief operating officer and then, when he'd pulled strings to avoid mandatory retirement, to director of the Special Activities Centre.

It ran missions the Clandestine Operations division wouldn't touch, black-book stuff that would never be permitted or admitted. Stuff a lot of suits wouldn't touch, either.

He'd initially stewed at his declining political fortunes. Then he'd realized the free hand he'd been given: an agency with no oversight, an enormous budget, and a presumption that they would be breaking the rules.

As long as no one was caught doing so in America or brought to public account, it was a license to do just about anything he damned well pleased.

He blew out a series of smoke rings. The patio was eight stories up, and the wind quickly blew them apart.

"He's going to ruin everything," he muttered.

"Possibly." Eddie Stone stood at the corner of the balcony, looking northwest. "But unlikely. Dahlen is sneaky, and he has a rotten temper. But he's not very clever."

"Hmmm." *Ever the optimist, Edward.* "I could never read him."

"Gerry doesn't even get my pulse going."

Kennedy rotated the armchair towards him, the nonchalance irritating. "Maybe he should. You saw the reports from Chicago?"

"Yeah. He has Krug running around the Loop, burning down warehouses and scaring the shit out of clinic docs."

"Every guy he's hired in the last three years has been either former SEALs or former agency or former NSA. If they maintain their present penchant for public mayhem, one of them is going to get pinched by a cop we can't get to, and who knows what they talk about."

"Like black-book stuff..."

"For one."

"Or Team Seven."

"That would be the worst-case scenario, sure. He's also had Krug reach out to the current team, trying to poach. If any of them go over, or he decides political favoritism can save his neck..."

"Who knows what he'll say. I do see the problem, believe me. I don't understand what he's up to, though, so I can't really advise you on how we deal with it. Other than maybe directly."

Kennedy peered at him, unconvinced. "You want to wax Gerald Dahlen?"

"It's an option we have to consider."

"He runs the second-biggest merc outfit in the western hemisphere. I mean... Jesus H, Eddie... you think what he's up to now is bad? Imagine how vigorously he'd defend himself if he thought we were coming after him. And before you tell me you could do it quietly... I don't doubt it. Probably. But the margin of error is great enough, given the potential fallout, that we leave that as a last resort. Are we any closer to figuring out what he wants?"

Stone nodded. "I think it might be Tehran. He might have figured out who the leak was that led to the team losing their target... what?"

Kennedy had begun to chuckle. He took a sip of cognac and puffed on the cigar again. “We’re pretty damn sure HE was the leak, is what. In fact, we’re certain of it.”

“Get out! Can’t be...”

“Not long after he left, a lobbyist filing led us to a numbered company, which matched one associated with an account we believed was Dahlen, nearly $20 million, shortly after the mission’s failure. But we couldn’t pin it down. The coded message we intercepted to ‘Brighteyes’ and ‘Excelsior’ came from the same company, owned by Benjamin Usmanov, the political fixer.”

Stone’s brow furrowed. “Dahlen was already rich. Doesn’t make sense.”

Kennedy shrugged. “Maybe because his money came from his father. Maybe he thought Ahmadi was a wasted effort anyway. Who knows? Only Gerald Dahlen, I’d suggest. Wait a second... why Tehran now? It was dealt with, wasn’t it?”

“Every place his guys have visited so far matches a team member’s last known location.”

“I thought we’d had them removed from the board...”

“So did I. Apparently, promises made weren’t kept,” Stone explained. “We assigned a guy who had a perfect track record, and he pointed us to the bodies.”

“We checked against delivery?”

“As much as ever. I mean, he referred us towards the morgue in Chicago...”

Kennedy hung his head. “Eddie... did we actually go scope the bodies?” Then he shook it off. “Forget it. I already know the answer. I’m waiting for some autopsy details on a couple they took out in Hickory Hills, Illinois. We’ll know for certain then. Early suggestion is it’s Richie Johnson.”

“Johnson. Wait... the logistics specialist? But... even if he was still alive... why?”

"Maybe," Stone suggested, "he thinks someone on the mission found out something. Maybe he's trying to shut down the kind of leak that could ruin his reputation, put his firm out of business."

It raised the stakes considerably. If Dahlen thought he was cornered, the rules regarding discretion might go out the window. When guys of that stature got arrested or tied to heinous behavior, politicians paid attention.

The Tehran mission had been a fiasco, even getting media attention. The notion that they could create yet more trouble was vexing.

Stone sighed.

"What?" Kennedy asked. "You have scruples about something?"

He half shrugged and leaned against the balcony rail. "I mean... Sometimes? All of it. I wonder just what the fuck we're doing. Not the team per se, or assignments. But the backdrop. The politics. The double-dealing and deception. The endless rivers of scheming bullshit."

"Eddie... we're five decades in. It's a little late to be growing wary now..."

"I don't mean it like that. It's just... It's like it never ends. Every problem we solve, every time we come out ahead either for the country or ourselves, there's some tangential bullshit that needs covering up or protecting. When is it ever enough?"

Kennedy shrugged right back. "Where's the line, where too much of it is what we want, not what's needed? Too little of it is about the job and too much about the people in charge feathering their nests? Is that what you want to know? Because if I knew the answer to that, we could probably shut down half of Washington and go home early for the day."

"I guess."

"But we push on. And when you're in charge – and I very

much am, Eddie – well, then you have to make hard decisions. Better them than us. If Team Seven winds up at your door… you did something pretty goddamn awful to bring them there."

Team Seven was Kennedy's gem, the hammer he could call on when soft diplomacy failed.

"Find out who he's going after, specifically. You have a source within Dahlen's squad, I understand?"

"I do."

"Get to whoever he's hunting first, find out what he wants. If he tries to leave DC, arrange for a delay until we can decide whether he needs to be eliminated. We need to put our foot down on this, I think."

"Agreed." Eddie smiled slightly at that, which always made Kennedy shiver a little. He'd been a loyal soldier for decades, for sure. But Eddie took way too much pleasure in his work.

31

It had taken Bob another twenty minutes to concede defeat.

If Smalls was still living at the building on Lamont Street, he either hadn't gone out in hours, or he wasn't coming home that night.

He undid his seatbelt. "I'm going over." Bob opened the driver's door. "I'll be back shortly."

He crossed the street to the fourplex and climbed the front steps. There was an alarm panel with four buzzers, but none had names next to them.

Chances seemed good that, like most fourplexes, apartment one was at the front of the building. That meant two and four were probably overlooking the lane behind it. Smalls would want to stay away from the main road.

He rang buzzer four. "Yeah?" a woman's voice answered.

"Hi... I'm looking for Michael Smalls."

He waited a moment, but there was no answer. Had she not heard him, or...?

The speaker crackled. "I don't know anyone by that name."

"Okay, sorry to have bothered you, ma'am." He was about to ring apartment two, but it struck him that the pause had been awfully long for the answer given. He reached for button four again... then stopped, his finger hovering over it.

What would Smalls do in this situation if he thought the person at the door was a problem?

He turned his head and scanned the block. The end of the row was three doors down, a narrow gap – a gangway, in Chicagoese – suggesting a passage to the back alley. He trotted down the stairs and followed it. It opened into the back lane, a backyard fence directly to his left. He followed the fence line, around its corner, to the third wooden gate.

If I were Smalls, I'd be heading out the back way right about...

The gate swung open. The short woman with white hair who'd entered an hour earlier stuck her head past the gatepost. She looked left, then looked right, her gaze falling on Bob leaning against the fence. "If you were planning to sneak away undetected," he said, "I have disappointing news..."

The head popped back inside the gate. "Wait...!" Bob called out.

But she'd already sprinted to the back door and was frantically pawing at the lock with her key. Bob followed her. "Look, I'm not going to hurt you. I'm an old friend of Michael's..."

She stopped what she was doing for a moment. "Michael didn't have friends. At least not the kind who rang the front doorbell."

"Didn't?"

She shook her head. "He's dead."

Damn it. We're too late. "I'm sorry. How..."

She glanced around again, nervousness obvious. "Before I say anything else to you, how did you know about this place?"

"You mean as opposed to his storage-locker main

address? Because he told me. That's the only way anyone but his dead mother could know... right?"

"Maybe," she said. She checked both directions again, then said, "You want to come inside?"

He nodded.

She held open the door and swung an arm that way. "After you."

He did as requested, entering the building ahead of her.

"Stairs are to your right," she said.

He followed the staircase up. She followed, moving ahead of him at the second floor. She opened the door to number four and again waved for him to enter.

"Thank you," Bob said. "This is very—"

He didn't get a chance to finish the sentence, a five-thousand-volt jolt from her stun gun turning his muscles rigid from instant overproduction of lactic acid. He collapsed to the floorboards just inside the unit.

Bob couldn't move.

She crouched over him and searched for his wallet. When she found nothing, it made her that much more tense. She walked quickly to a nearby bookcase and pulled away a false book front, removing a nine-millimeter Sig Sauer P320 pistol from the cubbyhole.

"Okay, sweetheart, you're going to explain to me who you really are and why you're here. If you're lucky and tell me the truth, I might not kill you."

"C-l-tth!" Bob tried to say. His face began to turn bright red, his eyes bulging out. "C-lt-thh!" He struggled to lift his head slightly and his hand, waving a barely controllable index finger towards his throat.

"Oh shit, are you choking?!"

"Clltth-th!" he tried to mutter. He'd gone a shade of dark red, near purple.

She knelt beside him and reached down to unbutton his

shirt. His two hands came up before she could react, grabbing her lapels. Bob drove his forehead into the woman's nose; she fell backwards, the gun tumbling to the hardwood floor.

He rolled over and grabbed the stubby pistol before she could react. "For... future..." he panted, "... reference, you've... got five to ten... seconds, max, where the person can't move." He exhaled deeply and stood up creakily, keeping the gun on her. "Now, let's try this again... being civil this time."

She looked angry. She spat at him, the spittle falling short. She wiped a trickle of blood from her nostril with her sleeve.

Bob looked down for a moment. "Okay, so... you just spat on your own floor. Congratulations."

"I'm not telling you a goddamned thing," she said. "You bastards killed my husband, and I swear to God, if I make it past this, you're going to pay for it."

"Whoever you think I am, you're wrong. What happened?"

"You know what—"

"JUST... just humor me, okay? Humor the guy with the gun. What happened to Smalls?"

"Officially? He was hit by a bus two days ago, killed instantly."

"And unofficially?"

"Unofficially..." Her voice was tired, barely much above a wretched sob. "There wasn't enough left of his remains to ID him without dental records."

"That... sounds like a hell of a bus."

She looked more convinced that he really didn't know... or was a great actor. "Who are you? Seriously. Michael said nobody knew about our actual home..."

"I know this apartment was his mother's before she passed. You're his wife?"

She nodded. "His wife, Ginny... and you are?"

"I'm the one exception to his privacy rule."

"The one..." Her puzzled expression shifted quickly to wide-eyed surprise. "You're Alpha."

"Yeah, formerly known as. Or, you know... 'Bob' works pretty well."

"He never told me your name, just that you were his role model when he was off doing whatever it was you guys did. He never told me that, neither."

"We were all loaded down with secrets."

"I guess so. But... it's been more than ten years."

"Whoever killed him wants my head next, and I'd really like to know why that is."

"Ah... ah shit," she said. "He said everyone else from back then was probably dead..."

"Back then? Are we talking 2006 or thereabouts? An overseas mission?"

She nodded. Then she gestured with a head flick towards the living room. "We should sit down and talk about all of this."

"Okay." They marched over to the sofa and armchair. She took the latter. Singleton perched on the edge of the sofa, never taking his eyes off her.

"Okay, tell me: what did he do to trigger all of this?"

She smiled ruefully at that. "You did know him, then, I guess."

"Bailed him out a few times."

"He... he just wanted to make some problems go away, is all. For as long as I knew him – which was a good long while, I might add – he always loved the risk of gambling and the thrill of the occasional win. Anyway, he used to go down to Vegas, play some blackjack, see a show... Only, the last few times, he got into a high-stakes Texas Hold'em game. And he lost, big time."

"How much?"

"Everything. All our savings, our retirement funds, the value in his company. He was so sure he could turn the streak around. Instead, the hole got deeper and deeper. He tried to gamble his way out, so he borrowed money from a local bookie."

"Bad move. How much?"

"Yeah... you don't know the half. Turned out to be the first cousin of Albert Gabelli, the mobster, and Michael was into him for a half million. And they wanted their money or some equivalent. They were starting to talk about breaking things."

Bob felt a sudden disquiet, a sinking feeling in his gut. "What did he do, Ginny?"

Her head sank. "He... told me he had a plan. There was this guy he knew, from when he worked for the government. And everyone figured this guy had... I don't know the exact specifics... but he'd sold secrets or betrayed American interests or something. And he was rich. He is rich."

"Who...?"

"Have you ever heard of a man called Gerald Dahlen?"

The tension of the moment hit him, and Bob shut his eyes tight.

"So that would be a yes, then..." Ginny suggested.

"He tried to extort money from Gerald Dahlen?"

She looked embarrassed and hurt. "He told me there was no real risk. He didn't have anything, just a story about some mission this guy had helped plan, in Iran. So... if they called his bluff, he'd be up the creek, and we might have to get out of town for a while."

"And he called his bluff?"

"Worse... Michael actually found something on the guy."

Bob felt a flutter of nerves. That was the last possibility he'd considered, that Dahlen would be foolish enough to hang onto evidence. "Something, like...?"

She shook her head. "He said it was better if I didn't know

too much. About three years ago, he was doing subcontracting work for a home security firm that catered to rich Beltway types. He found out after taking the job that it was Dahlen and, knowing who this guy was, decided to put a back door into his system's software."

"He was snooping?"

"Basically. He thought he might get a stock or business tip off this guy. Instead, he recorded a conversation he had via an encrypted line. But at the end of the job, they decided to 'audit' Michael's equipment to ensure he hadn't violated privacy."

"He had to wipe the evidence?"

She shook her head again. "No, Michael was smarter than that. He left it in the one place he knew Dahlen would never look: buried in the folders of his own security network. The problem is, after the install, Dahlen changed the login interface so that only he or his right-hand guy could access the network. There's evidence there of some sort; Michael just had no way to collect it. So... he tried to bluff his way through."

Bob shook his head. "Smalls... what the hell were you thinking? He always did have a knack for missing the potential consequences, not seeing what was around the corner."

"The next thing I knew," she continued, "he didn't come home one night. That was Monday. I started calling around. The coroner's office put two and two together and figured I was the next-of-kin for their unidentified John Doe."

Maybe this is my fault, too, Bob thought. *Smalls had poor impulse control. I should never have let him join Team Seven. But he was so damn good with tech...*

He looked up. She was crying, tears tracing paths down her cheeks. She reached over to the side table and retrieved a pack of cigarettes, offered him one, then took one out for herself after he refused. She lit it with an orange Bic lighter.

She blew out a jet of smoke. “I really loved him, you know? We were both chip heads, both geeks. We went down to Hackathon in Vegas together. He was so talented – he was sure he’d be able to get back into the guy’s system, for one. We were going to have a kid...”

“I’m sorry. I really liked him,” Bob said. “I know he could be hotheaded and impulsive...”

“Like, crazy time...” She snorted.

“But he was a good soul. He thought what we were doing would make a difference. When it all fell apart, he was almost as bitter about it as I was...”

She nodded. “Yeah. He got some satisfaction by writing spyware and code, trying to buck the system by defeating government privacy, so to speak. Plus, he had a few corporate clients, so there was good money in it... well, until he gambled it away, anyway...”

Bob looked around the room, his tactical sense kicking in. “You need to pack and get out of here. I found you because he gave me your location. But Dahlen’s people are advanced, connected, and well supplied. They’ll get into that storage depot eventually and figure out he had another main address...”

She looked puzzled. “But... I’m just a software engineer.”

“Do they know that? You said you went to ‘Hackathon’?”

“I don’t do anything serious, just testing security for fun, seeing who’s not paying attention. I hacked into the city traffic control network once, and it scared the hell out of me having that kind of access, so I got out. I’m nowhere near as good as he was at... well, any of it, really. I didn’t work for the government.”

“That mission had bad fallout, and now Dahlen is killing anyone who might know about his connection. You were married to one example, and you have some experience in an area that could hurt him. Plus, Smalls might've told you something, which means..."

Her hands came up to her mouth involuntarily. "Oh shit... Oh shit, Michael, what did you do?"

"I'm sorry. Pack and go. Get out of town if you can."

"I... I can't! I have a job; I have a life. I can get, maybe, three days off..."

"Do you know anyone near DC..."

"Just family."

"Hang on..." A thought had occurred to Bob. "I... may have someone who owes me a favor. He might be able to help both of us. He's usually pretty low profile, outside the system. But I know the one way to find him."

"Outside the system? You mean, like, off any official records?"

"Yeah, very much so."

"Then that's where we should go."

"Do you have a phone?"

She nodded.

"Get rid of it. It can be used to locate you easily these days. Look... I know this is your home, but we should leave. I have associates waiting for me, and we can give you a ride..."

She folded her arms across herself. "I'm not giving up my freedom because..."

"You don't have to. You just can't be here, and time is pressing. Listen to me on this, okay? Pack your things, and let's get moving. You might not have much longer."

She nodded again. Ginny rose and walked through the far door to what he assumed was a bedroom. While he waited, Bob flexed his muscles repeatedly, trying to get the ache from the lactic acid to properly subside.

She reappeared with a soft-sided case, heavily stuffed.

He handed back the pistol, and she took it. "Okay, let's go meet the others."

They made their way back to the car. Ginny passed Marcus her case, then climbed into the back seat next to him.

"And... this is?" Dawn asked.

Ginny leaned over the partition. "Ginny Smalls."

"Smalls? The guy you came to see..." Dawn started to say.

"He's dead," Bob said. "And we're in deep, deep shit."

32

COLLEGE PARK, MARYLAND

The man in the collarless leather jacket was beaming from ear to ear. He had close-cropped brown hair and looked younger, he liked to think, than his thirty-nine years.

He stood on the sidewalk, under the evening streetlights, outside the unassuming, hundred-year-old two-story home. He gazed up at it with an expression that bordered on joy. It was quiet, with no traffic, wind gently buffeting the branches on a nearby elm tree.

In the home's top window, a small red light was just barely visible behind the cream-colored blinds.

She hadn't been available in nearly four years. But Lady Pain was back, and she'd emailed him to let him know she was ready for him.

He felt as if a small void in his life had suddenly been filled.

He made his way up to the front door and rang the buzzer.

"Who is it?" She sounded exactly the same, he thought, her voice almost husky.

"It's me. I got your message..."

The front door lock buzzed. He opened the door and ventured inside.

A cloakroom featured a wall of hooks, and he hung his coat on one. The home was period decorated, with dark wood wainscoting on the walls, dark green carpet, a replica of a Tiffany glass light fixture dangling above.

Ahead were the stairs, a beige silk runner creeping up them to the second floor. An opening to the right was cast in lamplight, betraying the stately interior of a drawing room.

"I'm upstairs, Naughty Nicky," the voice intoned.

He ran up the stairs, overeager, missing the third and almost falling on his face. "I thought I'd never see you again," he called back.

He felt a rush of excitement.

It had been too long, so many years without the exquisite pain, the sensation of her stiletto heels barely puncturing the skin as she strode up and down his naked body.

At the top of the stairs, a light was on in the first room, the other doors closed. He rushed inside.

Lady Pain was reclined on her four-poster bed, her six-foot-two frame a muscular picture of knots and curves under a blue silk gown.

"Mistress... I am your humble servant," he exclaimed as he approached the bed.

The voice came from behind him. It was a man's deep, familiar tone.

"Hello, Nicky."

He wheeled around and bolted for the door, but the figure hiding behind it was quicker, kicking it closed before he could reach it. A hand came up from the man's side, gripping a nine-millimeter Sig Sauer.

He stepped out of the corner.

"Holy shit..." Nicky muttered. "You're dead."

Bob's expression was stoic. "And you were supposed to do ten years for... what was it again? Wire fraud and industrial espionage?"

From behind Nick, the dominatrix on the four-poster bed held up a hand. "Excuse me, am I still required here? Because I've done what you asked. You're supposed to lose my address now..."

"You're free to go. Call the cops and I'll find you," Bob said. "Besides... we won't be long. Mr. Velasco and I go way back. Don't we, Nicky?"

Lady Pain scooted out of the room. "I don't want to know," she offered. She gave her former client a pointed stare. "You're a foolish, foolish man."

Nick looked around the room. "This place...?"

"Some family in Europe on vacation," Bob said. "They like posting their daily routine while overseas to social media. Not the smartest move, safety wise."

"You borrowed their house just to lure me here? I guess I should feel privileged. How did you know about...?" He nodded towards the door as the dominatrix disappeared through it.

"I followed you a couple of times back in the day, tracked down her real name. Long before Smalls replaced you, it was obvious you had... distractions from the Team."

"Now, the great Team Seven Alpha comes looking for me. You going to turn me in?"

"Nope. I just need to talk."

Velasco nodded slowly. "Uh-huh. For now. I assume there's more..."

"First, we talk."

He threw a glance at the pistol. "You going to hold that thing on me all night?"

"You have a habit of running. Give me an hour to buy you

a drink and explain myself, and then I won't bother you again if you're not interested."

"Okay. We'd better get out of here before a neighbor spots the activity."

"I know a place not far," Bob said.

"Uh-huh." But the other man didn't move.

"Nicky, if I wanted you dead..."

"I'd be on the floor by the door. Fine. Lead the way."

NICK VELASCO STARED across the vast, mostly empty confines of the Country Kitchen restaurant.

At eleven o'clock in the suburbs, it was a last resort for a greasy repast after too many beers, but on this night, even the college kids were giving it a wide berth.

A senior sat alone at one table, picking at peas with a fork, his other hand holding a paperback novel. In the back corner a small group sat together: two women, a teenaged boy.

"You really know how to party, Alpha," he said dryly.

"No one of any ilk we recognize would ever set foot in the place. So..."

"Okay then. You want to get a booth, or..."

"Follow me," Bob said.

He led him to the back corner booth and the trio.

"You're kidding me," Velasco said. He turned on his heel. "I'm out, Alpha."

Bob clasped his shoulder with one large hand. "Just... hear me out, Nicky, okay? Grab a seat, there. And it's just Bob now. I haven't been Alpha for a long time."

He looked up at Bob nervously as he clambered across the bench seat to the far side of the table.

Bob sat down. "This is Dawn, Ginny and Marcus. Guys, this is Nick."

"Well... I'm real pleased to make your acquaintances and all, but... Bob, can you tell me what the fuck is going on here, exactly?" Nick demanded. "Because I'm into some weird shit by any spook's standards, but this is..."

Dawn leaned forward slightly for emphasis. "Sir, please don't curse."

He stared at Bob, puzzled. "Is this... Is she for real? What the fuck, man...? These are civilians, right? That boy looks like he's not even shaving yet."

"They're friends. And they're in a hole. They've got no clout, and some bad actors are after them. You remember what that was like... right, Nicky?"

Velasco looked away for a split second, discomfort obvious. "Yeah... that was a long time ago. A different life."

"We only get one. And you owe me, as there's a real good chance Krug would have just kept picking at you, harassing you like his little plaything."

The memory of the fear he'd felt whenever Krug was in the room came flooding back. "I hated that fucker," Nicky whispered. "Still do, assuming he's still alive. I hate that fucker more than anything."

"I need your help taking him down."

Velasco looked up suddenly, the pain of bad memories replaced by an intensity. "You're kidding."

"I'm not. Last I heard, he's working for Gerry Dahlen. And Gerry Dahlen is trying to kill these folks because they knew people who knew people. That's about the extent of it."

"Huh." Velasco chewed subconsciously on his thumbnail as he thought back. "I remember the beating you laid on him right before the Team was let go. You whupped him six ways to Sunday. He left me alone after that."

"I did, and he did. I never asked for nothing in return, Nicky. You know it was just the right thing to do."

"Yeah... yeah, you always did have that soft spot." His eyes sank to the floor. "But... that's not my problem, not now. Not anymore."

Bob studied him back for a moment. The restaurant was quiet, the barest sound from the senior's fork scraping his plate across the room. "Nicky here was supposed to serve ten years in a federal pen," he told Dawn and Marcus. "Instead, I hear a year after I left the Team that he's angling for work from mercenary outfits, guys who want to expand their operations into the cyber realm."

"It was an attempt to reinvent myself," Velasco offered.

"Yeah... but we never figured out how you did it. By that point, you would've been three years into a dime stretch, and no alarms were raised, no one contacted the agency..."

"And one guy got wealthy, quickly."

Marcus interjected, "Someone served your sentence for you."

Nicky wagged his index finger in the kid's direction. "See, he's a smart one. He caught on quickly there. The dude had my prints in the system, my dental records; we looked similar. I'd made plans in case my little side venture went awry."

"Nicky got greedy," Bob explained. "He was the best hacker the agency had, able to take down entire branches of foreign government, to topple companies. But he got caught pilfering his targets..."

"Goddamned audit..." Velasco muttered.

"Still... a proxy prisoner. Ballsy move."

"There were a whole lot of Krugs waiting inside." He looked around the room again. He lowered his voice. "Look, you know I appreciate the fuck out of what you did for me, Alpha. You know that. But I stay really quiet these days, work a few income angles, a few fat cats who don't pay attention to their security. I keep my nose clean and my head down."

"If you don't help me, these people could die."

Marcus sensed his cue. "Please, mister... I don't want to die. I'm only seventeen."

Nick sucked on his tongue for a moment. He sounded frustrated. "Jesus H. You're not sparing any dramatics, are you? Really want me feeling bad about this, don't you, Alpha? I mean... Bob. I mean... Fuck!"

"Your conscience is your conscience, Nicky. But... give them a good look. Tell me you think they deserve to die for mere association."

Velasco slumped slightly. "Fine. Tell me what you need."

He listened while Ginny Smalls repeated her story. At the end, he nodded gently. "Okay, okay. All righty, then. I can work with that. Possibly."

"What do you need?" Bob asked.

"Get me Dahlen's security code," Nick said. "He's a suit, so chances are he's not tech savvy enough to use multiple passwords or secondary encryption."

"Even if I can pull that off," Bob said, "it'll be changed within hours."

"Doesn't matter. That should be enough for me," Nick said.

"And if whatever I'm looking for is hidden in the network security code itself?"

Nick crossed his arms. "Open book to me once I'm in. It'll stand out like a sore thumb."

"Uh-huh," Dawn said. "You sure don't lack for confidence."

Bob added, "He'll be in touch with Andrew Kennedy, potentially. Dahlen still works for Clandestine Ops, indirectly, by supplying mercs."

"Wow. Potential CIA server access if I can figure out a back door. That's some risky, enticing shit right there. That's a Holy Grail right there. What else?"

"Whatever help you can give us. We need new legends, a

gun, possibly some specific ID cards or security passes. Ginny needs a place to lie low. I'd ask you to take the other two as well, but they seem to have outvoted me."

"Still a soft touch, Bob..."

"Me, I just need access to Dahlen and anyone he might be dealing with..."

"And money," Marcus reminded him.

That seemed to strike the man as lowbrow. "Eh... money's not a problem, at least not temporarily," Nick said. "I've got access to other people's credit."

He took out his wallet and rummaged through it, then slid a card across the table. It was issued on a bank Bob didn't recognize. "There's unlimited credit on that one. The account it's tied to belongs to a gangster in Baltimore – a real scumbag, crack dealer type; but a rich one. He's the type who lends his cards to his girlfriends, so you've got probably a week of spending if you don't go crazy and do something stupid... What else?"

"Security?"

"Depends. Probably. Most buildings use one of three security protocols, nearly all involving swipe cards or prox cards, maybe the odd keypad, though those are less common now."

"How quickly can you turn something around?" Bob asked.

"Depends where and when, but... like I said, I'm still the best."

That much confidence was usually dangerous, Bob thought. Guys like Nick eventually made a mistake, and the fallout wouldn't be pretty. He'd made them before.

But they had bigger issues. "Okay. We'll make a deal. I'll get you Gerald Dahlen's password and deal with Krug if you get me the means to get close to him. Then you can... I don't know, hack his security or his agency, wreak havoc. Whatever it is you do."

Nick smiled wickedly.

THEY LEFT Ginny with his old associate and drove for twenty minutes before finding what Bob had been looking for.

He pulled the car up to the curb across the street.

Dawn stared past him and out the driver's side window. Her expression was withering. "Really? That place makes the motel in Chicago look like the Ritz."

Across the way, the accommodations were stark and grubby: a pale-yellow-brick building with a white glass shingle long since smashed past reading aside from the last line: Rooms by the Hour. Outside on the curb, a pair of winos leaned against the wall, passing a bottle in a paper bag back and forth.

Marcus had seen similar on TV. "Is that... I mean... is that a hooker hotel?"

Bob shrugged. "Basically, yeah. Residential, anyway."

"Residential?" That baffled the kid.

"It's so cheap people rent by the month," Dawn said. "Usually because nobody else will rent to them... and because no one else would ever stay there." She looked back at Bob. "I am not going in that dive. Uh-uh. No, sir."

"Look, any place even remotely respectable, they'll be checking. I need information on the guy who killed Smalls, along with finding out where he is and what his security is like. It'll only be for a few hours, a night at most."

Marcus chimed in, "I guess it's good they charge by the hour too, then, right?"

Dawn gave him a sour look. "No. No, it is not. Now, Bob, I know you've seen me deal with some down-on-their-luck folks at the clinic. But I am a lady..."

"One night, tops," Bob said. "It's that or sit in the car and hope it hasn't been ID'd yet."

Dawn looked both ways down the street. It was dirty, trash strewn. A car sat on blocks, the wheel hubs so rusted it must've taken root. A block up, two prostitutes were being propositioned through an open car window. On the block behind them, a pair of seedy-looking guys were having an argument. The old storefronts were rusty cages or boarded up.

"Oh Lord..." she muttered. "Fine." Then a thought occurred. "Wait just a minute, now; you're going looking for the guy behind all this? I thought you said you needed help from this Nick person..."

"I'm going to check out Dahlen's home, see if it's more vulnerable..."

"Uh-huh." She sounded doubtful. "You're not going to try to 'take this gentleman out' or any such crazy thing? I really wish you would tell me there's another way to deal with this than killing a man. There has to be."

"There probably isn't. But I'll look for one. Smalls left us something, at least. If we can get a hold of that recording, we have more choices."

"You promise?"

"I aim to please," he said.

"Longer we keep it that way, the happier I'll be."

He nodded towards the flophouse. "Come on. I'll get you guys a room... and you can stack furniture in front of the door until I get back."

She caught the little smile at the end. "Oh... Oh, very funny, Mr. Cold-as-ice or whatever. Know this, Bob Singleton: we're putting a lot of faith in you. You'd better not wind up dead and me stuck with..." She nodded towards the back seat.

Bob smiled grimly and didn't speak his first thought,

which was that nobody sane would put faith in him. "Let's go."

They climbed out of the car and made their way across the road. Even from outdoors, Dawn noticed, the crumbling building smelled like a sewer.

33

If Gerald Dahlen had one predictable flaw, Bob knew, it was his ego.

He could've left the agency, millions in the bank, and quietly disappeared. Instead, he'd practically set up a competing team, with none of the restrictions of government policies or agendas.

He could've bought a luxurious-but-low-profile condo near the Capitol building. Instead, he'd bought a mansion that backed onto Rock Creek Park, where most of his nearest neighbors were embassies and consulates from other nations.

At the intersection of Observatory Circle and Massachusetts Avenue, Bob parked the rented Nissan Leaf compact along the curb.

The forested park was open to the public and crisscrossed by dirt and paved roads. But it was also monitored on numerous closed-circuit camera systems and patrolled by Secret Service agents – a lower-grade, uniformed branch of the service, but with complete police powers of arrest in the capital, nonetheless.

That didn't stop the park from being popular with city walkers, joggers and cyclists. Bob hadn't been there in years, but it hadn't really changed.

Neither had the embassy locations. He followed the sidewalk along the edge of Massachusetts Avenue, past a string of modernist mansions on either side of the road. He kept his head down for all but the barest glances as he passed the South African embassy. Once past it, he stopped for a moment to orient himself.

According to a *Style* magazine layout featuring his since-divorced wife, Dahlen lived two properties away.

That meant he'd bought the closest private residence to the former Iranian Embassy next door.

The balls on the man.

The property had effectively been abandoned after the 1979 hostage crisis. But as a photo layout he'd found online by an "urban explorer" demonstrated, it was also relatively insecure, just patrolled a few times a day by a security company doing rounds.

He crossed the street.

The difficulty was making sure he wasn't spotted by one of the South Africans. They were using the Iranian Embassy's vast side cul-de-sac for overflow parking. Some of the cars probably belonged to agents in the park, as well.

Would there be an easier approach on the other side of the properties, where Thirtieth Street cut north through another cluster of homes?

Possibly. More trees, anyway.

As the trees along the road gave way to the left entrance of the Iranian Embassy's semicircular driveway, he spotted a van parked near its front steps.

It was black, the windows tinted; a sign on the side read "Capital Heat and Pipe." The front passenger window was rolled down, a head of blond slicked-back hair poking out as an occupant checked the street.

Bob pretended not to notice, keeping his head down. The earpiece had been obvious. A half block up, near the corner of Thirtieth Street, a man in a light jacket was standing as if waiting to cross but showing no signs of actually doing so. He had a rolled-up newspaper under one arm.

Earpiece number two.

On a hunch, he waited until he'd passed the corner opposite the man, then turned abruptly left to cross. The man looked up suddenly, saw him coming, cupped one hand to his ear for a split second, then crossed the road. He didn't look up as he passed Bob.

Before reaching the other side, he glanced over at Dahlen's house. Two guards were outside the front driveway.

Probably more in back.

But if they're watching the house, why is a van and a guy on the street watching them?

Someone was keeping tabs on Dahlen. Someone with serious pull.

Agency? Probably. And that probably means... old business rearing its head again. How the hell do I flush Dahlen out of there, or get inside?

He turned and walked backwards a few steps, keeping an eye on the van. He was about to cross the street, to a view of the back of the house, when a black Mercedes pulled up next to the van and stopped.

The driver's window rolled down, and the blond agent chatted with the driver. Bob couldn't see who it was because of the angle. But the conversation was taking a while, suggesting it wasn't someone stopping for directions.

Come on, show me who you are. The car was expensive, out of a rank-and-file agent's price range. That meant it was someone official, maybe whoever was in charge. It had been more than a decade; major players had changed. But there was always a chance he'd know the face and therefore the agency running the surveillance operation.

He couldn't afford to linger in one spot for too long, he realized. Cross-corner to his block, the agent with the newspaper under his arm was looking his way, murmuring something quietly, probably to whoever was on the other end of the line.

Time to go, Bob decided. *Come on, damn it, lean out just a little. Give me a view of...*

The head poked out of the car window just slightly, made a few remarks and nodded. It ducked back inside, and the car pulled out of the driveway and back onto the avenue seconds later.

Bob smiled.

Eddie Stone, as I live and breathe.

You're still in the game.

If Stone was running teams on Dahlen, Stone knew Dahlen was up to something, something that troubled Eddie's boss, Andrew Kennedy. The two were joined at the hip.

If Eddie was still running Team Seven, Kennedy was probably still running the Strategic Activities Centre, assuming old age hadn't caught up to him first.

They must know what he's up to. Which means Eddie is going to help me out, for old times' sake.

He crossed back to the other side and continued north for a block on foot before turning east, then south again to backtrack to Massachusetts Avenue. He checked his watch; it was eleven thirty at night, traffic down to the odd passing car, the city's constant din reduced. For the boss to be out checking the troops, he had to be nervous, perhaps that Dahlen would need to get out of town quickly.

They had an advantage, finally: Dahlen was in trouble with the CIA, which meant the agency had either gathered evidence on him... or his actions to cover his tracks were making Kennedy and Stone very, very nervous.

We can use that. Time to get back and make plans.

34

Dawn sat in the rickety wooden chair by the flophouse room door, her arms folded; the .38 Colt borrowed from Nick Velasco rested on her lap, the romance novel she'd had in her purse spread out on top of it.

She wasn't trying to hide the gun so much as not see it. The first thing she'd done, once Bob was gone, was to demand the boy hand it over, as he was too young for that kind of responsibility.

Her doubt about what they were doing had been allayed, briefly, by being introduced to potential allies. It had returned in full force when Bob had admitted the only way to deal with Dahlen might be to kill him.

She'd felt like walking away right then. Dawn had grown up with violence in her life, from her father, from the gangsters who'd killed her son.

It occurred to her in the moment that, when push came to shove, most folks were just vulnerable. They didn't have the hatred or anger needed to hurt others, and they didn't have sufficient fear to do anything stupid. They just avoided trouble, which was probably how it should be.

But trouble had come looking for her. For all of them. It wasn't like Bob deserved to be killed any more than she did, no matter what he'd done in the past. That was God's business, life and death, not men's. But it also wasn't like he had a right to mete out justice.

Yet... she understood his position. Like a surgeon who has to let one patient die to save another, he saw it as "kill or be killed." Given how much money this Mr. Dahlen had, she wasn't sure he was wrong.

It unsettled her greatly.

The lock to the room door began to slowly turn. She knew it was probably him but felt herself quaver slightly from nerves, her hand finding the pistol grip.

The door opened, and Bob poked his head through. "It's me."

"Shhh!" She nodded towards the lumpy double bed, where Marcus was sprawled out, still fully dressed, on the stained bed cover. "Boy's had a heck of a couple of days. Fell asleep as soon as he lay down."

"It's after midnight. I thought you'd both be out cold."

"Humph," she said, rising from the chair and shaking her legs to get the circulation going again. She gestured towards the TV, where a local station was playing a late-night music show, something from the eighties. "They've got reruns of *Soul Train* on at this time of night. Besides, someone had to keep an eye on him. If you didn't notice, this is not exactly the Ritz. Did you find what you were looking for?"

"Better. I spotted someone I know, someone who can tell us what's going on."

"And?"

"He's not the kind of guy you just walk up to. He's... not what you'd call a fan of mine."

"Uh-huh. Does that mean he's also trying to kill you, Bob? Is there anyone in DC who isn't?"

"Well... there's Nick. And Marcus. And you."

"Uh-huh. Don't be too sure on that last one. We're not out of the woods yet, far as I can tell."

"Not yet, no."

"So who is this dude?"

"Someone I used to work for. He's running a watch team on Dahlen's house, probably on his business as well. Now I just need to know why."

"And..."

"And... tomorrow's Sunday. The guy is really private and really careful. But I know one thing that won't have changed since back in the day: he's also really Catholic."

She looked horrified. "You're going to confront him at CHURCH?"

On the bed, Marcus stirred.

"Just... calm down, okay?" Bob whispered. "No, I'm not going to confront him at church."

"Good."

"I'm going to confront him outside the church, in a nice, quiet spot."

She closed her eyes and held a hand to one cheek as if warding off a flushed feeling. "Oh, my sweet Lord... that can't be right. Can it?"

Bob looked a little chagrined. "I knew it would bother you. If you've got a better idea..."

"Can't you just go to the man's house?"

He shook his head. "Nope. Closely guarded secret. Stone has a lot of enemies but probably still refuses a security detail, on account of being such a corrupt bastard that he needs as much privacy as possible."

"Don't swear!" she demanded tersely.

"Sorry."

"But you know where he goes to church because..."

"I went to his wife's funeral fifteen years ago, when our

version of the team was new. As long as he wants to be near her, he's probably going to the same church."

"Oh! What about us?"

Bob didn't follow. "I... What about us?"

"Well, where are we going to go?"

"You're not coming. This could be dangerous. You two will..."

"To church, genius! I'm not missing Sunday service! People may want me dead, but that worries me a whole lot less when I'm sure I'm right with the Lord."

He sounded defeated. "Not even once?"

"Not even once."

He gestured towards the door. "I noticed a relief mission down the street. It won't be the most upwardly mobile company, given the neighborhood."

"It is easier for a camel to pass through the eye of a needle than for a rich man to enter the Kingdom of Heaven. Matthew, chapter 19, verse 26. I don't have any problem with folks who are struggling. You of all people should know that." Then she caught her own tone. "Oh! Oh... I'm sorry. That was rude."

"No, that was honest."

"Sometimes, Bob, honest is rude. It probably wouldn't hurt any of us to try to be a little softer, so take the apology, you big... man." She said the last word with just a hint of frustration. He pretty much summed up how she felt about most of them, most of the time.

"Okay, apology accepted." But he blushed when he said it, which she thought was kind of sweet.

"Are you going to hurt this man?"

"Probably."

She gave him a withering look.

"I'll try to avoid it. I'll always try to avoid it, okay? But I'll defend myself if I have to. And not you, nor any book, is going to tell me that's not okay."

"Bible doesn't say you can't defend yourself. It doesn't even say you can't earn and have money. It just says you should use your dependencies and your actions for good deeds, to help others. If you weren't doing that, Bob... You remember what I said to you after those kids hurt you at the corner store?"

"After one of them shot me, you mean?"

"Uh-huh."

"You said something like 'anyone who'd try to help save that store clerk is a good person.' More or less that."

"More or less. Still applies." She reached up and pinched his cheek like a proud aunt. "I know you don't believe it, but God loves you, Bob. And anyone can be redeemed, even when they don't think they deserve it. Maybe especially then."

She turned and walked over to their single suitcase, picking it up and putting it on the bed beside the sleeping youth. She unzipped it and began to take out the clothes they'd bought him.

"What...?" he began to ask.

"I'm taking out the jacket and tie now. You leave them out overnight, they won't be all creased for church. You need to look your best."

35

The Sunday service was always the same, Eddie Stone concluded.

The congregation filed out of the pews to the muted organ strains of "How Great Thou Art."

He'd ignored most of the service, as usual. He knew that whatever the priest demanded of the flock, he'd have broken any rules a thousand times. He knew the only way he'd avoid going to hell was to be absolved on his death bed.

But it was better than nothing, an ending he looked forward to, a sort of otherworldly corrective surgery for his tattered soul.

A few well-dressed congregation members politely said hello as they streamed out of the building. He avoided conversations by keeping moving, nodding back politely, and giving a firm, slightly grim smile to each.

He didn't know his neighbors. They were just statistics, numbers for someone else to annotate, manipulate and control. If they mattered to the agency, and his mission of making the American way of life a dominant force around the globe, then they mattered to him.

But otherwise, they might as well have been ghosts. Or maybe calling them a flock had always made sense. *They're just sheep, fodder for the wolves, a drawback for the shepherds.*

He stood outside the church and took out his cigarettes. It was sunny, a light breeze pushing the smoke away. He'd quit and restarted so many times over the decades, but his heart had never been in really trying to give them up.

After his wife had died, the parish priest had made unsubtle noises, grunting about how suicide was a mortal sin, a venal act to shed the indignities of this life and so unrewarded by God. Eddie had had to set him straight, to make sure she'd been given a dignified and sanctified Catholic burial. The priest had transferred parishes not long after, which was just as well.

He waited until the crowd had thinned before walking towards the adjoining cemetery, its parklike atmosphere as much a comfort as going to see her. He knew she'd loved him, despite how it had ended. He also knew he was probably why she chose that way out, her depression growing annually with his refusal to allow them to have children.

Or perhaps it had just been neurochemistry. Perhaps she'd just had an inglorious destiny. The big man upstairs truly worked in mysterious ways, he figured, if a murderous, brooding, angry man like himself was spared and she was taken.

But that was life, Stone figured: inexplicable and seemingly more meaningless with each attempt to ascribe meaning to it.

The wind gusted, rustling leaves on the tall aspen trees by the road.

The walk only took about three minutes.

He was halfway there when the hairs on his neck stood up. Something felt off. Usually, on a project or mission, it meant he'd noticed something out of place.

But he was seventy, despite looking a decade younger. If he'd seen something, he hadn't registered it enough to defeat his fading short-term memory.

He stopped and looked around, but saw no one aside from a pair of other families halfway across the property and a lone woman in black, a few hundred feet away, standing before a plot in the cemetery's newer section.

He reached his wife's plot. Her gravestone was clean, as he'd left it, the preserved rose in glass still perched atop the headstone reading "Sophie Jessica Stone, January 22, 1965 – August 18, 2005. Beloved wife and daughter."

"Hey, sweetie," he said. "It's been a while."

"It certainly has, gorgeous."

Stone was already lashing out as he turned, shifting into a spinning side kick towards the man's voice. The figure jumped back, out of reach, taking a sideways defensive posture.

Stone raised his hands in a guard, then realized who it was. "Jesus Christ!"

"Given the surroundings, not the worst guess you could've made," Singleton offered. "But… no."

Stone stepped in and threw a punch, a short, sharp jab that caught Singleton off guard. But it missed his chin and caught him in the mouth instead. The younger man staggered backwards a step, and Stone allowed no time for recovery, ignoring his joint pain, dropping low to swing his leg in a semicircle, sweeping Singleton's out from under him.

Singleton crashed to the ground.

Stone pounced forward from his crouch, trying to get a dominant position on top of the other man, where he could pound him unconscious. But this time, Singleton was too fast, rolling to one side, coming up on his feet. Stone turned that way and stood in one motion, taking a one-step hop into a side kick.

Singleton caught his foot, twisting it and using Stone's momentum to slam him, face forward, to the ground.

When he was a younger man, Stone would've rolled and recovered, used his hands from a backspring position to regain his feet. But the years had caught up with him, and the drop to the ground felt more like tumbling from a roof onto concrete, pain shooting through every joint.

He tried to roll back over, but the shoe came out of nowhere, catching him flush in the chin, the world suddenly going black.

Well... shit, it was the rental car. You saw a rental, he thought as he lost consciousness. *Is this how it ends...?*

36

Eddie Stone dreamed in abstract images of flame and death: a fire in a mosque, people screaming; a woman beckoned, blood dripping from her pale white skin, her wrists cut.

Then she was gone, fading to white. His hearing kicked in first, a squelching sound in his ears as he returned to the land of the conscious, followed by a strange tic in his right leg.

It jerked several times spasmodically before he opened his eyes. He looked around, his bearings having to be reoriented in an instant. He was on his backside, leaning against a wall. Or...

Not a wall. A tombstone. His hands were tied behind his back with something soft. He felt the warm autumn breeze against his chest and realized his tie was missing and his shirt collar unbuttoned.

"Wakey, wakey," Singleton intoned. He was standing just ahead of him, blocking any direct line of sight. He had a cheap sports coat on over a white shirt and knit tie.

Stone looked around. The cemetery appeared empty. "You look like an insurance salesman."

"Good. Apart from the fashion advice, which I could take or leave, I was afraid from your lousy defense that you'd gone senile and forgotten all about me."

He couldn't hide his surprise. "You're also supposed to be dead."

Singleton smiled at that. "In the twenty-one years I've known you, Eddie – on and off, of course – I don't think I ever saw you surprised by anything. This was worth it just for that."

"As I said... you're supposed to be dead."

"But I'm not. No thanks to your buddy Gerry Dahlen."

"He's no friend of mine. A friend of the agency, maybe..."

"Why is he trying to kill me, Eddie? And worse, why is he trying to kill a seventeen-year-old kid?"

Stone had seen his group's report on Hickory Hills. "The son. You have him?"

"He's safe."

"Singleton. As I live and freaking breathe..."

"For now. I confiscated the .357 from your shoulder holster."

Stone's gaze narrowed. "You're not going to shoot me, and we both know it. If you think you're facing heat now..."

"Don't tempt me." Bob let it hang there. He wanted Stone to read his face. "Tell me, Eddie... Do I look like someone who won't shoot you? Given our shared history, do you really think I'd hesitate for even a moment?"

Stone gestured to their surroundings. "Why pull this, at my wife's gravesite, no less? Why not just call me? You're a resourceful guy; you could've pulled that off without us tracking you down."

"Maybe. But you wouldn't have helped me."

"And you think this stunt is going to make that happen? I've got news for you, my friend..."

"Ah... but we're not friends. And if there's one thing I

know about you, you value yourself over everything: over your country, over Andrew Kennedy, and most certainly over your agents. Nobody as venal and self-interested as you will accept prolonged interrogation over giving up a worm like Gerry Dahlen."

"So that's the plan? To interrogate me? Not here, I'm guessing."

"Nope. There's a strip of old, abandoned commercial buildings less than two miles west of here."

"In Congress Heights. I know it."

"If I know you the way I think I do, you have some sort of RFID tracker carefully hidden on you. I imagine if you stray too far off your normal path, alarms will go off, and someone will come looking. So instead, we're going to take your car and head down there."

Singleton walked over to him and helped him up with a free left hand. His other hand was inside his coat, presumably holding the gun.

"So that's your plan? To go after him before he kills you?"

"Wouldn't you?"

"Huh. Yeah… Yeah, I guess I would. But then, I never failed in the field so badly as to be cast out and left friendless, so your problems would never happen to me."

Stone was uniquely talented at getting under people's skin, Bob remembered. "You haven't gotten any less arrogant with age. In case you didn't notice, I'm the dude with the big gun, so my problems are your problems. Also, everyone seems to think I'm dead already, so I don't have a whole hell of a lot to lose."

"What do you want, Bob?"

"Answers, to begin with. But not here. When we get to the car, you're going in the trunk."

"I'm seventy-nine-years old…"

"Even that you lie about, looking for sympathy. You're

seventy. Which means you've had that much longer alive to figure out ways to escape. If I stick you in the back seat, you'll force a crash or something stupid like that. I'd rather not shoot you if I don't have to."

They began the walk. The parking lot was a few hundred feet away.

"You're making a big mistake, Bob. When Andrew finds out..."

"What? He'll scour heaven and earth to rescue you and find me? If it suits him. Don't kid yourself into thinking he wouldn't hang you out to dry like the rest of us."

Stone shrugged. "I'd do the same to him if I had to. That's why I respect the man: he's honest about who he is. You, on the other hand, always had some white knight delusional bullshit kicking around in your head..."

"Huh. You sound like someone else we both know..."

They neared the lot. Another family was just arriving, piling out of a station wagon.

"Don't get any ideas," Bob advised. "The last decade of my life has been kind of rough, and while I'd hate to shoot a bunch of witnesses, I'll do what I have to do to survive."

"The most honest thing you've ever said to me," Stone spat.

They reached the car. Singleton fished Stone's keys from his jacket pocket and opened the trunk. It was clean and neat inside. "Get in."

Stone delayed. "What do you really think you're going to get out of me? You can't possibly think you're the first guy with a gun to try to make me talk..."

"Why is Gerry Dahlen trying to kill me?"

Stone shook his head. "We don't know. He told us sweet FA before the thing in Chicago, not much since. He's scared of something though, something he thinks you know."

It had to be the code Smalls had saved. "About Tehran?"

"Based on who he's taking out."

"But... he was already gone by then. That was your baby."

"No, that was YOUR baby. I was Stateside when you ditched, remember?"

His captor looked unimpressed. "You never were big on taking responsibility for the people under you."

"Nobody's 'big' on wearing someone else's fuckups, Bob."

"If he's clearing the decks on Tehran, that suggests he has something pretty terrible to hide. Like, maybe that he was one of the Iranians' sources. Maybe he was 'Brighteyes,' the initial leak."

"You were never Einstein, but you're smart enough to put the pieces together yourself. So... what good am I?"

"Let's go find out, shall we?" He gave the older man a firm shove, Stone wincing as his shins banged into the back bumper. He tumbled over the edge, Singleton lifting and shoving his legs in after him.

The trunk slammed closed; the compartment was pitched into darkness.

37

The old warehouse was falling to ruin, floors rotted, glass broken, doors boarded.

Bob led Stone to its rear alley and a back door he'd pried open.

Inside, he guided the older man through a dingy, empty back room to a front office. A Coleman lantern had been set up on a crate, allowing them some visibility. The place was deserted save for debris: a small mountain of old crates and boxes near the front wall, a couple of typing chairs, the seat ripped open on one.

"Again, what are we doing here, Bob? I already told you I'm not working with Gerald Dahlen."

"I know the way you think, Eddie. You and your lizard of a boss. Kennedy never cared about who was making money on the side, and Dahlen's been working for the agency as a private contractor for a decade. If he planned on taking Dahlen out, he'd have arranged it long ago. But now that Dahlen's riled up and making a ton of noise, I figure he's ordered you to keep an eye on him."

"Smart boy."

"That means you've got a team watching him, and you've probably got his offices tapped somehow. You'll know where he is twenty-four seven. And when he's vulnerable."

"And I ain't telling you shit, son..."

Bob showed a hint of a smile at that, too. It irked Stone that he was alive, but it bothered him even more that Bob seemed a step ahead.

"You won't need to. I have your phone. Hell of an age that we live in."

"Won't help you. Locked and encrypted."

"Uh-huh. Probably something fancy, too. Retinal scan?"

"Yup."

"Would you like me to remove one of your eyeballs to make my life easier on a more permanent basis? Or you can just co-operate and keep your left eyelid open while we do this."

Stone's blood was beginning to boil a little. "When this is done, you'd better kill me, Bob, because the shit Dahlen is pulling is going to seem like an Easter egg hunt compared to what we'll bring to bear."

Bob ignored him. With gritted teeth, Stone did as demanded.

Bob looked at the screen. "Which app?"

"DuoScreen. Lower right."

Bob tapped it, and texting software booted. He had three new messages. He tapped the first.

You've got a team on his home, which I already knew. Where else?

"His person, his limo, his office, his place on the West Coast."

Bob scrolled back, but there were no earlier messages. "There's nothing older than an hour."

"It wipes itself. It's peer-to-peer, so there's nothing held on a server. That's the whole point."

"What about his schedule?"

"We have it. It's in my email."

Bob scrolled through the headings. "They're encoded."

"It's about four down, GL87-something."

He found the message. "He's at a charity lunch in Georgetown, slated to end in just under two hours from now. Then he's heading straight home. This afternoon... Huh. Well, THAT might work."

"If you leave now, you can make it in time to be shot dead by his bodyguards," Stone said dryly. "You're not seriously thinking of..."

"Give me options, Eddie."

Stone shrugged. "Give up? You're a dead man walking. If he doesn't kill you, Andrew will put the word out. He won't even bother sending the team after you, I don't expect. He has enough juice and resources to make sure every contractor, merc and hitman from here to Singapore goes after you..."

"That's not an option."

"Maybe it is. Maybe if you turn yourself in now, I can convince Andrew to let the kid go. That's something, right? What do you care? You've been off the table for a decade. But the kid might have a life ahead of him. You want to make the same mistakes you made in the past, get more people hurt?"

Stone felt a surge of confidence. For a split second, Singleton's expression had shifted to one of doubt.

"That's it... isn't it? That's why you disappeared off the map. You knew that everything that went down was your responsibility. You knew you were the reason Azadi's family were butchered. Well... this is your chance, Bob. This is your chance to make it right." He rose to one knee and leaned forward. "Give me the gun."

Bob tilted his head and studied him. "You're just awful, Eddie, you know that, right? Always have been."

38

It had been three hours since Bob left, and Dawn's stomach was fluttering from nerves.

She'd done as he'd asked and kept an eye on Marcus while they attended the ramshackle storefront church down the street. They'd sat on the back bench, by the door. Dawn wrinkled her nose in disgust at the walking urine stain a row ahead, who kept trying to flirt with her.

Her instinct to help Bob was gnawing at her.

By the time they got back to the hotel, she was in the throes of self-doubt.

She sat in the old chair by the chest of drawers and watched Marcus staring at his phone. He'd been eating up its minutes watching videos, despite her advice. But it was generic, safe entertainment that kept him from dwelling on his parents, as well as off social media or contacting his friends.

What are you doing here, Dawn Marie? That boy has lost his family, just like you lost Maurice. And your answer to that is running around with a man who, three days ago, was living in an alley off North Peoria.

You don't know him, yet you're trusting him.

With everything.

She thought back to the day before it had kicked off, when Bob had shown up with a chest wound from rock salt. The police said he'd saved that boy at the convenience store. But maybe the incident at the store would never have happened if Bob hadn't been there. Maybe he was the reason, the catalyst to gunfire.

Maybe he is the bad news he claims to be.

Marcus looked up from his phone and stared at her for a few seconds.

"What?" she asked. "Do I have something..." She motioned towards her face.

"No. You just look so worried."

"Oh! Oh... don't worry about me, child! I'm fine, believe me. I've been through difficult times before."

"Yeah... but nothing like this."

She nodded. "Before he left, Mr. Singleton seemed... well, I wouldn't want to say happier, but..." She looked his way. "Am I crazy?"

"No," he confirmed, "I got that, too. It wasn't happy or, like, thrilled or anything. But he had a weird kind of... I don't know... focus or something. Like the girl in chemistry class who always has the best lab..."

"Or an athlete. My eldest brother, Phil, he played high school football. Pretty good running back in his day. He had that game face he'd put on. Same thing, kind of."

"That's what has you worried?" Marcus asked. "That he's off doing something crazy?"

"Uh-huh. Neither of us knows him. Let's be real honest on that."

"But he saved both of our lives."

"My life didn't need saving until he showed up," Dawn said. "Point of fact, I was the one who got to help save people.

And… it's just hard, you know? To separate this version of Bob from the one who used to stagger into the clinic so drunk he could barely see straight. It's like… it's like he's a different person."

"But that's a good thing, isn't it? You said yourself you used to tell him how much he had to live for. Maybe all of this has given him a reason to fight," Marcus reasoned. "You heard what he said about his old job, his fiancée dying… I mean… maybe I just don't know enough yet, but that seems like a hard life to me. If he's not real… um, stable and all, that doesn't change what he did for us."

It was true. But she felt a need for reassurance. She felt like giving in, trusting that no matter how powerful this dude after them was, he couldn't have his hand in every police officer's pocket.

There had to be someone official who would listen to their plea for help. "Maybe we should call Mr. Temple and ask him what he thinks. He knows Mr. Singleton better than anybody, I guess…"

Marcus frowned. "He told us not to contact anybody. I mean… he may have been a bum for a while, or whatever, but he still seems pretty smart to me. If he says we shouldn't call anybody, I vote we listen to Bob."

She nodded. "Okay, then. But I sure hope he knows what he's—"

Marcus's phone began to vibrate.

"Give it to me," she demanded. He handed it over.

She answered it. "Hello?"

"It's me."

"Where ARE you?" she snapped. "It's been nearly three hours."

"I got sidetracked gathering intel. Grab the boy, call a car, head to the following address, and pick up the rental. Then I need you to meet me—"

"Hang on, hang on, I need a pencil or something..." She rummaged through her purse and found a pen. "Okay, go ahead." She copied down the addresses. "Uh-huh... so where are these?"

"The first is his church. I left the car there and borrowed his. The second is a derelict building. Come around back; I'll explain when you get here, okay?"

"I guess..."

"I'll see you in twenty." He hung up.

Marcus nodded towards the phone. "He's coming back?"

"No, he needs us to meet him." She wondered again if she shouldn't call Professor Temple. But the boy was right; Bob had saved them both and put his trust in her.

"Meet him? Why?"

"Well, I won't pretend I have the slightest clue," Dawn said nervously. "Just that I need to call us a car, and we need to be moving."

39

If Dawn had been nervous before they left, the scene at the warehouse made her stomach leap into her throat.

The man was seated on an old wooden office chair, his hands bound behind him with what looked like a tie, his feet secured to the chair legs with his socks, his shoes removed and fifteen feet away.

Bob stood nearby, arms crossed.

"Oh, my goodness, Bob... what have you done?"

"Long story short? I figured out what's happening to us, and why. And now, I'm going to use some information from the gentleman seated to solve our problem."

She glared at him. "You know, when people say 'long story short,' they're usually trying to be polite. They don't actually mean 'I'll leave out all the pertinent details about how I kidnapped a dude and tied him to a chair.'"

"I didn't have a lot of choice. I tried talking to him, but he attacked me."

Stone piped up, "What did you expect? He ambushed me at my wife's gravesite."

"Bob..." Dawn said, frowning.

"Just... have a little faith, okay? I know you can do that, so... trust me that this guy is a major-league scumbag. Don't believe anything he says."

"Who is he?" Marcus asked.

"You don't want to know, kid." Stone cackled. "Or else I'll have to kill you."

"Ignore him," Bob said. "He's going to try messing with your head."

What is Bob playing at? Dawn wondered. "What do you mean, 'going to'? What are you up to?"

"I have to go out again for a while. Thanks to his decision to run surveillance teams on the man who's trying to kill us, I now have a constant flow of information about his location and movements. Oh... and six hundred bucks in cash, which never hurts. Nice job, Eddie. I'm borrowing the Mercedes, too."

"I am so going to enjoy killing you, Singleton," Stone muttered through gritted teeth.

"This doesn't sound like much of a plan," Dawn suggested. "We're being chased by a guy powerful enough to send a team of men after you in Chicago, and for this guy to use what I'm going to assume is government resources to spy on him. And you're going to... what, sneak into his house as the cleaning lady? This is not *Mission: Impossible*, Bob, and you are not Tom Cruise."

"Bob doesn't need to be," Stone interjected. "Bob's a killing machine. Like, a real-life, honest-to-goodness living weapon."

"Shut up, Eddie," Bob barked.

"Hasn't he told you yet?"

"We know what he used to do," Dawn offered solemnly. "If you're expecting we'd be surprised..."

"Oh, but how much has he told you?" Stone asked. "Have

you told them about the Thai hooker, Bob? How you sent her into a den of opium drug lords with a remote bomb in her purse? How about the former French foreign minister you strangled in Mauritius using... what was it again? A bicycle chain?"

"Motorcycle, and it was Madagascar," Bob said. He noticed Dawn's and Marcus's worried stares. "And he was a pedophile who'd sold French nuclear technology to terrorists, okay? We're not talking *Springtime in Paris*, here..."

"And the hooker?" Marcus sounded hopeful that was something better, at least.

"The 'hooker' was the number one girl of one of Southeast Asia's most murderous criminals, and on his orders, she'd executed a man who didn't pay his bills, at point-blank range, barely a day earlier."

"He always has an excuse," Stone said. "You'll get used to that."

Bob ignored him. He ushered them over to the far wall and lowered his voice. "We need to keep him here. Now that he knows I'm alive, he's as likely to kill all three of us as Gerald Dahlen is. And he has even greater resources. If he so much as reaches a phone, we're sunk."

"Are you asking us to guard this guy while you're out getting your head shot off?" Dawn asked.

"Can you give me another suggestion?" Bob said. "If we leave him unguarded, he'll figure out a way to free himself within an hour, I guarantee you. Don't let his age fool you; Eddie's been doing this kind of thing since before any of us were born. He's a spook's spook, as cold as they come." He turned to Marcus. "You have the Colt?"

"I do," Dawn said.

He handed Marcus the .357 Magnum. "You ever fire one of these?"

"Nope." Marcus sprang the cylinder, rotated it to check

the load, then flipped it closed. "But something near enough. Damn... that's heavy."

"That's because it'll blow a hole through an elephant. If he gets loose and comes at you—"

"Aim center mass, I know," Marcus said. "I told you, my father made me take survival training."

Dawn grabbed Bob's elbow. "May I speak with you privately for a moment?" She gave Marcus a sympathetic smile. "Adult stuff."

He rolled his eyes. "Really?"

"Really. Bob?"

Bob stepped aside with her. "Look, I already know what you're going to say—"

"ARE YOU OUT OF YOUR MIND?!" she hissed, trying to keep her temper inaudible. "He's seventeen years old! You can't ask him to shoot a grown man! You shouldn't have let him have the pistol, neither!"

"I'm not asking him to shoot anyone," Bob said. "I'm just telling him not to be afraid if he has to defend the two of you..."

"That kind of thing, that's messing with the boy..."

"What... more than watching his parents be murdered? Believe me, Nurse Dawn, he already has a lifetime of therapy ahead of him. And I hate to break it to you, but we're running short on other options. Eddie doesn't give a crap about the two of you, I guarantee you. Once this is done and Dahlen is jailed or dead..."

She turned on her heel, both palms held out from her sides. "Nope. Don't want to hear it. Don't want to hear another word..." She walked across the room, her back to him.

"Don't worry about Nurse Dawn, okay?" Marcus interjected. "I'll be fine." Then he frowned. "You really have to kill somebody...?"

"Probably, yeah. If there really was proof that this guy betrayed the country, then – as much as I can't stand the guy – Eddie or his boss, Andrew Kennedy, probably would've arrested him at the time. I can't count on getting Smalls's code, so..."

"But I thought you said this guy still works with the CIA?" The boy looked confused.

"He does. Or his company does. They'll still do business with him as long as he isn't legally compromised. Moral compromises... those don't faze the agency nearly as much."

Stone was craning out of the chair, trying to catch the gist. "Is he crapping all over me, kid? Ask him about the time he killed a pregnant woman..."

Bob looked irritated, but he ignored the taunts. "Like I said, he's going to try to fill your head with all sorts of garbage. Just assume anything out of his mouth is a lie. Okay?"

Marcus frowned. "But... did you?"

"Do I seem to you like the kind of person who would do that? We had a mission to take down a cell of Indonesian fundamentalists. During the crossfire, one of them shot a pregnant woman who wasn't supposed to be there, according to the intel HIS analysts provided."

Marcus nodded, but he didn't look happy. Then, puzzled, he stared at the revolver. "Where'd you get this?"

Bob looked over at Stone.

"But... if I have this gun, what are you going to use if you have to... you know...?"

"Let me worry about that."

"Bob doesn't need a gun," Stone offered. "Like I said, he's a killing machine. Right, Bob? Remember that Libyan bomb-maker you iced with... what was it again? Your thumbs, if I recall, through each eye socket..."

"Oh, my Lord," Dawn muttered. "This is going to be a

long night."

40

COLLEGE PARK, MARYLAND

At six thirty, Dahlen was scheduled to cut the ribbon on the Kenneth Dahlen Memorial Hangar at Dulles International Airport, a half hour from the city.

They had six hours to get ready.

Bob stood over the map he'd laid out on Nick Velasco's central desk arrangement, much to the coder's amusement. He'd wanted to just "bring it up on Google Maps," which irked the former spy. He was accustomed to working out mission details on paper, not a seventeen-inch monitor.

"Somewhere to take him is easy," Velasco said. "See this Quonset just off Glide Slope Drive? It's being used for heavy equipment storage. These are commercial lots the airport owns and leases. They've been trying to sell them for years, but they're so out of the way that no one's interested. Anyway, it's always quiet there. One of my... associates, we'll say... has done some war driving based out of there, because with a range booster, he can swipe packets as far away as the airport terminal."

Bob turned slowly and gave him a long, hard look. "Okay, now repeat that in English for us mere mortals."

Velasco rolled his eyes, as if he'd been forced to explain astronomy to a chimpanzee. "War driving means using capture software to snag packets of data out of the air while they're being transmitted wirelessly. Sometimes wired, too, if the person is dense enough to not protect their router."

"So... stealing Wi-Fi signals?"

"No, the actual data the Wi-Fi is being used to send."

"You can do that?"

"People have been able to do that for about fifteen, twenty years."

Bob felt a sting of embarrassment. *That was something I should already know. But that was why we had Smalls...*

"The point is," Velasco continued, "the Quonset is always empty. You won't be bothered there while you do whatever it is you have to do."

"First, however, I have to grab him somehow."

"I've got that covered." He reached under the desk and pulled out the main drawer. "The ID I've made you is letter-perfect. I've tapped into the airport security database and added you in, under the name Robert Plant."

Bob squinted at him. "Why?"

Nick's eyes danced nervously. "Why... did I give you a pseudonym? I don't..."

"No, not why did you give me a pseudonym. Why use the name of someone so famous? Won't that attract attention?"

"Huh?"

Bob looked at him forlornly. "Are you serious?" He glanced over to the corner of the room, where Ginny Smalls sat on a sofa, watching TV. "Is he serious?"

"You've got me," she said. "I don't know who you're talking about either."

Bob sighed. "How old are the two of you?"

"Thirty-eight," Velasco said.

"Thirty-one," Ginny said. "This is some old shit, then..."

"He's the lead singer of Led Zeppelin."

"Oh. Huh..." Ginny weighed the information. "I mean, I'm guessing most people won't know that, but if they do, at least you have an anecdote. Is anyone else there going to be old?"

"Probably," Bob said, ignoring the jab. "More likely, someone who's been there a long time wonders why he's never met this 'Robert Plant.' I mean, it's not like they're going to forget..." They were both staring at him blankly. "Never mind. Can you change it?"

"I could, but the back door I was using appears to be closed now," Velasco said. "It's important?"

"Probably not. Forget it. What about security doors?"

"Ah!" He rummaged around the empty chip bag and candy wrappers next to the monitor until he found his handiwork.

"Here." He walked over and handed Bob a laminated airport ID card, as well as a gray plastic rectangle the size and thickness of a credit card. "Proximity detection card. It gives you access to every secure part of the facility. It's tied to your name in the database, so as long as Robert Plant has clearance, you can come and go."

Bob clipped the ID card to his breast pocket and stashed the prox card in his wallet.

Velasco opened a lower drawer and pulled out a cheap plastic chain. "You hang it around your neck, or at least the pictures I found online of terminal staff suggested most do..."

He took the proffered chain and did as suggested. "You're sure this'll work?"

The former agent shrugged. "We won't know until you try."

"What about metal detectors, weapons sniffers?"

Velasco shook his head. "You're on your own on that front.

And you can bet there will be both, in the terminals anyway. I don't know if the sniffers are sensitive to the amount of gunpowder in a bullet, but my reading suggests they pick the stuff up, as well as any common form of explosive."

"How do security get around it? I wonder," Bob asked.

"Just guessing, but the sniffers are in gates, along with the metal detectors. Security officers are probably allowed to go around them."

"And am I officially a security officer?"

Velasco shook his head sheepishly. "Senior communications staff. I'm sorry, okay! You said it was a press event, so I made you something to do with the press."

"Shit. Now THAT might be a problem."

Velasco looked irritated. "Hey... we're going out of our way here for you already, okay? A little gratitude..."

"Like you said earlier, this is a tit-for-tat, right? I get you Dahlen's password; you get me access..."

"Which I've done. You didn't say you had to be armed. And you don't have access yet. I'm not sure how you're planning on pulling that off..."

"I need to isolate him. He'll have at least a couple of bodyguards, possibly federal agents watching him. It's doable."

"What did Dahlen do to make killing so many people so necessary?"

"You don't want to know."

"Oh, but I do."

"He betrayed his country."

"Huh." Velasco sounded unimpressed. "Well... I'm not so big on nationalism. But nobody likes a backstabber."

Bob gathered up the map. "I should get going."

"Good luck, I guess," Velasco said. "If this is a ceremony, there are going to be a lot of people there, and you're going to need it."

41

LANGLEY, VIRGINIA

The office of the director was twice as large as Andrew Kennedy's own, with teak bookshelves and an expansive picture window across most of the rear wall. It looked down on the Virginia countryside, as if separated somehow from the bureaucratic reek that permeated the rest of CIA Headquarters.

He'd been there many times, particularly during his stint as deputy director of the agency. It always made him uncomfortable.

Inevitably, the man behind the desk was there by virtue of a politician's whim. He hadn't worked his way up through the ranks; he wasn't a former analyst or field handler.

He hadn't taken the risks. Not to life and limb, anyhow.

On one level, as he'd aged and felt less nostalgia for the bad old days with each passing year and aching joint, Kennedy had come to admire anyone who could pull off that level of ambition. On another, he wanted to kick the man in the teeth.

The current man in the job irked him more than most of his predecessors. Though his father had been military, the director himself had chosen the route of diplomacy, going into the foreign service right out of college and steadily progressing until he was an ambassador. He was a purely political animal and deserved no sympathy, Kennedy had concluded.

Now the director was leaning forward on his teak-and-rosewood desk, elbows down, fingers arched like a priest giving a brief lecture to a penitent during communion. "Andrew, as much as we'd like the old days and the old ways to stick around forever, we just can't have these kinds of shenanigans disrupting the day-to-day."

"Of course, Director."

"And I'm concerned. I'm concerned I didn't receive word that something domestic was going down from you. You want me to rest assured that this is essential, but it sounds like you're not even sure if this is a genuine domestic terror threat. Meanwhile, I've got the mayor of Chicago calling my people, asking why what appear to be government agents are burning down warehouses. Can you understand what it makes me look like to have some asshole in local government ringing me up? It's beneath us, Andrew, and it's annoying. It makes the suits on Pennsylvania Avenue wonder if our house is in order. Am I clear?"

"Crystal, sir."

"Not good enough. I want this to be so transparent, it's invisible. If you can't do that, end the operation now and make it go away. We don't ask you too many questions about the SAC, because we know the kind of work you fellas need to do to protect the nation. But the deal, as a consequence, is that your teams don't officially exist. If need be, that will become as much reality as convenience, especially if anything on our home turf turns out to be... below board."

"Completely understandable, sir. We'll get on the horn to the guys and tell them to wrap it up as soon as possible. Of course…" He hesitated as a deliberate tactic, letting the other man fill the silence and remain invested.

"Of course what?"

"If it turns out we do have domestic terrorists planning something in Chicago or DC and we ignore it, the fallout won't drift the SAC's way… because our teams don't exist. Naturally, internally, we'd expect to pay the price. But that won't help the agency explain things to Congress without admitting our presence. That, in turn, opens up the door to questions about other projects overseas that have been… extralegal."

The political appointee pondered that for a few seconds. "Point duly taken. Deal with this, okay, Andrew? I know there's been some heat about you staying on because of your age, and I'd really like to be able to give you my endorsement in that regard. The more I trust in your efficient management of a crisis…"

Kennedy rose and held up a palm casually. "Say no more. It's dealt with."

"Good man."

Kennedy was on the phone to Stone before his driver had opened his limousine door. He climbed into the back seat as the call rang through.

But after four rings, it went to voicemail that hadn't been set up. He ended it and stared at the phone as the driver closed the door.

Stone never missed a call. He couldn't remember the last time he had, anyway.

He tried the phone again. It went to voicemail immediately, as if in use.

Damn it.

He waited a few moments while the driver got behind the wheel. "Take me to the club, Tom, and don't spare the horses," he commanded.

The limo pulled out of its spot in front of the doors.

He tried Stone's line again. Four rings.

Voicemail.

What the hell is going on? He'd always considered Eddie a necessary ally, even if they didn't completely trust each other. They'd made enemies together, sometimes warriors. They'd cheated death together more than once.

He had a sinking feeling that perhaps time had caught up to his old colleague.

He speed-dialed the Special Activities Center watch officer's line. "It's Kennedy; who's on?"

"Jody Henry, sir."

He avoided changing his tone to give away what he thought of leaving a woman in a potential high-stress position. He didn't even like them as field agents, let alone keeping an eye on the world's trouble spots. "Get me Stone's location," he said. "I've tried his cell and nothing."

"Yes, sir!" she said crisply. He heard muffled conversation as she ordered an analyst to run a track-and-trace. "It'll be momentary, sir; he has a subcutaneous emergency RFID."

"I don't need to be told that, Henry; it was my idea."

"Of course, sir, my apologies... He's back. Just a moment..."

If it was old age, it was old age. But if he was off the board, Kennedy suspected, it would be tied to Gerald Dahlen's problems.

She came back onto the line. "Sir, we have a hit on his RFID two klicks north of his house, in Congress Heights. It looks like he's either gone home, or is on his way there and stopped for something."

That didn't jibe. "In Congress Heights? What the hell would he be stopping there for?"

"Ah... good question, sir, of course. Would you like me to have someone stop by...?"

"Stop by his..." He stopped short of screaming at her. He could think of a creative way to fire her later. "Does he still have a team on Gerald Dahlen?"

"Yes, sir, a spotter on the ground, and three nearby from Team Seven."

"A spotter? There's restricted access?"

"He's at a public event this afternoon, sir, some sort of dedication at Dulles to his father. Should I recall them?"

Dahlen clearly had no intention of fleeing. "Yes, pull them immediately. Send the full team. Something's wrong, and until we find Stone and determine what, we have to assume Dahlen might be responsible."

"Yes, sir."

"Where are the other four team members?"

"They're on standby at the training center, sir. Should I send them to Dulles?"

"Send them to... Did you not get the part where I said 'the full team'!? Agent Henry, your operations director isn't where he should be, and he's not answering his phone. Where do you think I would like you to send the rest of the team, given that information?"

"To the tracker hit, sir?"

"Immediately. Let me know when they're on scene."

"Of course, sir, I'll—"

He ended the call before she could finish. *What's going on, Eddie? Why are my hackles up on this one? And where the hell are you?*

42

An hour had passed since Bob's departure, and Dawn's unease was growing by the minute.

From outside, through the boarded-over windows, a loud, metallic squeak made her jump slightly. But it was just a truck braking hard.

The old warehouse off Sixth Street East wasn't in an area that got much vehicle traffic despite the signs promising imminent gentrification and new condo apartments. But every road noise played at her nerves.

Stone had been talking just about nonstop, to the point where Marcus had turned up the YouTube videos he was watching, trying to drown out the endless drone of negative comments about Bob with help from its pitiful speaker.

He turned his attention her way. "How about you, 'Nurse Dawn'? How'd you wind up tagging along with a sociopathic killer like Bob Singleton?"

She ignored him, pretending instead to read her book. But she couldn't concentrate; the half-light shed by the Coleman lantern wasn't helping. Mostly, however, she couldn't help but be distracted by his patter.

"He isn't who you think he is. Don't you get that?" Stone said, switching from folksy to almost frustrated. "I'm a law enforcement officer with the government. He's a former assassin who has dragged you into a terrible situation that he created. I'm trying to get you out of it..."

It was like he thought she was an idiot. She put the book down momentarily, peeved. "That man saved my life and that boy's life. And he told us you'd do this, that you'd cast aspersions all day and night. You should be ashamed." She went back to her book. He didn't deserve any more than that.

"Manipulation is what Bob does to get to his target, to get his way. Good people like you are easier prey for him because he knows you'll feel indebted. He probably set up whatever situation he saved you from! Let me guess: some ambush with guys who seemed official, maybe agent types with sunglasses and earpieces..."

That gave her pause. That was dead-on. But... he'd almost killed those men rescuing her. That couldn't have been staged... could it?

Girl, what are you thinking!? When would he have planned that and how, considering he was a bum for years before that?! You're the one who treated him!

She looked up from the book. "I've known him a lot longer than you think, so that bull will not cut it with me, sir. And the more you lie, the more obvious it is that he was telling the truth about you."

He sniffed, nostrils flaring, as if that had caught him out a little. "Everybody has their own version of the truth, Nurse Dawn. You don't have to believe any of that. But believe me when I say he told you the truth about what he used to do. He was a killer, and once a killer, always a killer."

"Says you. I've met plenty of men who went to prison for things as bad, and they changed their ways." She nodded towards Marcus. "His parents used to be in the same Team, right? They became an accountant and a librarian and raised that boy up right. He's polite; he's kind. There wasn't any evil manipulation involved in that."

She regretted the example as soon as she said it. She could read his reaction, his gaze narrowing slightly as he turned his attention back to the boy. "Hey, kid!" he yelled. "I'm guessing he didn't tell you the truth about your parents, either."

Marcus tapped the phone's screen to pause the video and looked up. "Like what?"

"Don't listen to him, Marcus; remember what Bob said," she counselled. "He's a trickster."

"To start with," Stone told him, "they're not your real parents. You were adopted."

Marcus's mouth dropped open.

"Marcus—" Dawn began to say.

But the young man cut her off. "I knew it. I always knew it wasn't right."

"I was their boss. I know everything about them. You probably never felt quite like you belonged, did you?" Stone confirmed Marcus's thoughts as if it were without question. "That's because they were doing Bob a favor."

"He's lying, child..."

Marcus shook his head. "No, he's not. It's just like he said. I always knew I didn't fit in there. They never wanted to be called Mom and Dad; they never wanted to talk about other family. And we're so different. We... we *were* so different." A tear traced his cheekbone.

"Bob didn't want you after his fiancée died. She ran her car into a railway crossing marker because he forced her to give you up. He's the reason your mother is dead."

Dawn took in a sharp intake of breath. The boy was

certain about his folks. And Stone's story matched with what Bob had told them, sort of. "He said she got T-boned by another driver."

"He's good at that," Stone insisted. "He's good at telling you just enough that's true to think you can trust it."

Marcus looked aghast. "Bob's... Bob's my father?"

She could see the boy's confusion, but... Stone didn't know about Bob's time on the street, or he'd have raised it at some point during the hour. He couldn't know how long she'd been helping the man.

"You just gave yourself away again. Marcus, don't listen to this man. What he said about you being adopted... I don't know, maybe. Lots of folks are. Doesn't mean their parents don't love them. But the rest..."

"If he wasn't your father, why didn't he tell you about being adopted?" Stone asked Marcus. "Why didn't he come clean when they died, spare you some of your grief?"

Marcus looked confused. He looked up at Dawn. "I always knew something was different with us. I always knew my parents... I mean... I guess they weren't ever, really... He could've told me. He would've told me if he knew how much it hurt..."

"But he didn't," Stone spat. "Look at me! Look. At. Me, boy... I'm eighty years old. You think I pose any threat to a guy like Bob, a guy who has admitted he's a trained murderer? He had no compunction about beating the hell out of me just to get access to sensitive government records."

"He was a soldier..." Dawn tried to interrupt.

"He was a killing machine!" Stone barked. "A remorseless, relentless assassin who spread carnage around the globe. Look at this place: why do you think he picked this abandoned warehouse to hold me?"

She shrugged. "It's isolated. No one comes here..."

"It's concrete. It's an old building with thick walls, making cover easier to find. A modern building is made of two-by-four frames, plywood, and drywall. It can be perforated by machine-gun fire. All the attacking squad has to do is get me separated from the rest of you. In this place, they need clear sight lines, which are hard to find. A single gunman could hole up for a long time, do a lot of damage. A team loses its advantage in confined spaces with limited movement."

"So?"

"The point is, he's thought of that. He's thought ahead. He's probably planned the next five days down to the minute. He's meticulous, cautious. And yet, he dragged you here with him. Do you really think he plans to let any of us here leave alive? Square that circle, 'Nurse Dawn.'"

He turned his attention back to her, the words laced with contempt. "Let me guess... he went undercover for a while, played like he was down on his luck to get you to trust him. And you fell for it. And you dragged this kid into it, too."

"Marcus, you trust me, right?" Nurse Dawn said. "You know what I'm about, that I respect the Good Lord too much to give you any of the nonsense this man is feeding you?"

"I... Yeah. But... we don't know Bob, hardly. I mean, everything he said could be..."

"Did he save you?" she asked. "When he did, were the men shooting at you using blanks?"

He shook his head.

"Then they could have just as easily shot him!" she said. "You think he'd take that risk just to trick a seventeen-year-old into... what? Following him around just to inconvenience him? What sense does that make?"

"You're leverage," Stone said. "Hostages who don't know they're hostages. Is he that good at deceiving? HELL YES! He was the most dangerous agent we could produce..."

Dawn could see the youth's doubt growing, her hold slipping. She needed an ally, someone to make it clear Stone was a snake in the grass. "I haven't lied to you, have I, Marcus?"

He shook his head. "No. I mean... I don't think so..."

"And Professor Temple tried to help you, right?"

He nodded. "Yeah..."

"Allan Temple?" Stone interrupted. "He was Bob's Marine drill sergeant, for Christ's sake—"

"DON'T YOU BLASPHEME!" she snapped at him. "Did Professor Temple try to hurt you in any way?"

"No..."

"Then let's call him. If anyone knows what the exact truth is, maybe it's him."

Marcus nodded enthusiastically.

Dawn walked over and took his phone, keeping her eye on Stone throughout.

She hit redial on Temple's number. It rang twice.

"Hello?"

"Professor Temple? It's Dawn Ellis. Nurse Dawn?"

"Where are you?" he demanded. "I haven't heard anything in two days..."

"It's complicated, but we're still in DC," she said.

"Where? With Smalls?"

"No... no, that went badly. We're at an old warehouse in the south somewhere. We need your help settling some things. Things about Bob and his background..."

"Is he there?"

"Uh-uh. He had to go... you know, deal with things. With the man who's after us... Look... is Bob Marcus's father? This gentleman is trying to convince Marcus it's true..."

There was a pause. "It's creative, I'll give him that," the professor said. "Are you sure the kid wants the truth?"

She gazed over at Marcus, who was anxiously awaiting news. "Oh, yeah, pretty sure on that front."

"Then... no, he's not. But Marcus was adopted. His real parents were in the trade at the same time we were. But they died when he was an infant. I can explain this all better in person."

"We're in DC, though..."

"So am I," he said. "Came down on college business this morning. Where are you?"

She felt a surge of confidence. Whatever tall tale Stone was trying to sell the boy, it wasn't going to work. She gave him the address. "It's an old warehouse or something. You'll understand when you get here. We came in through the back."

"Give me ninety minutes," he said.

"Okay, just..." But he ended the call before she could finish the thought. "Hurry."

She put the phone away. "He's lying, Marcus, as I told you. He's playing on your feelings, on the need we all have for family and people who care about us."

Across the room, Stone was grinning, almost as if he wanted to break out laughing.

She shook her head. "My pastor teaches me that everyone has something worthy about them. But you..."

That snapped him out of it. Clearly, the man did not like to be judged in return. "HEY! I spent fifty years of my goddamn life protecting simpletons like you and that kid from the Bob Singletons of the world, the killers, the bad guys. From communists and terrorists. From gooks and chinks and the Russkies and just plain bad motherfuckers. You don't have the agency, the right, to judge me! YOU'RE A FUCKING AMOEBA when it comes to the things that really count in this world! A fucking speck of dirt on the universe's front bumper. They vest the power and authority with people like me because people like you are too goddamn simple to understand that you need protecting. Half the time, it's from yourselves. You judge me? It means nothing. Tomorrow you'll both be dead... and I'll be on the seventh tee, trying to lower my lousy handicap."

43

The black stretch Lincoln limousine followed the side access road the length of Dulles Airport's massive rural property. It drove past the boxy white main terminal, past the two long, rectangular departure lounges that sat adjacent to the runways.

Dahlen hated the perfunctory niceties associated with public relations, the handshaking and bragging, the insincerity of it all. He watched a Boeing 747 taxiing. If they were lucky, he thought, it would all be over in less than two hours.

Across the back seat from him, on a jump seat, Edson Krug looked glum. "I just want to reiterate that doing something public right now is not the smart tactical move," he muttered. "We were close. We know he visited the apartment block in Mount Pleasant. If you just let me put some squeeze on that scrawny fucker in the first unit—"

"You've already made the point, Mr. Krug. And I continue to be of the opinion that public gunfights in DC are a bad idea. Equally, a restricted-access press event at a well-guarded public facility is not Bob Singleton's style. He'll try to hit the house, keep the public out of it. Mark my words. He'll try to breach the home's security within forty-eight hours, and find your men waiting for him."

"I still think bringing more would have been wise..."

"Every media outlet in DC is here, Mr. Krug. How would it look if I showed up for a ribbon cutting with a phalanx of armed guards? Hmm? Stop worrying so much. We'll get this done and be back in time to catch it on the evening news."

Bob spun the car's wheel, turning it off the access road and onto Windsock Drive. It bypassed the giant parking lot that fronted Dulles International Airport's main terminal, then connected to Compass Court and the East Service Road.

To his right, through the passenger seat window, he could see the twin departure buildings, where planes taxied right up to the gates. Just past the second, the service road crossed a taxi apron before reaching the end of the property and a series of storage buildings. Behind them, Dulles gave way to marshy green fields.

A security gate barred the access road with an orange-and-white swing arm, just past the second departure hub. A guard in a white shirt and dark ball cap manned a small booth next to it.

Bob pulled the Mercedes up. According to the press release from the airport, the ceremony was taking place at the new hangar building.

The guard walked over.

He rolled down his window, flashing his ID badge. "Bob Plant, with corporate communications. Here for the hangar presser..."

The guard looked at his ID tag. He'd taken Nick's advice and had his proximity security card hanging around his neck. The guard appeared convinced. "You know the way?"

He didn't... but could see a handful of buildings about a

half kilometer away. "Yeah, straight ahead and look for the sleepy group of journalists..."

The guard smiled at that. "Yeah, ribbon cutting. Better you than me, Bob..."

It was like they were old friends. Bob noted his name tag. "Thanks, Vince, have a good one."

The gate lifted, and he drove on.

The hangar was the size of a department store and the height of a cathedral spire. Twenty or so vehicles were parked on its left-hand side. Its thirty-foot-wide front roll-up doors were fully retracted so that people could see the interior, access limited only by the giant red ribbon and bow strung across them.

The group milling in front of the building was twenty or thirty people deep. A cordon rope had been set up to keep people clear of the podium and temporary stage, ahead of the doors.

He slowed the car, rolling in idle towards the empty parking spaces. Through the passenger-side window and ten feet past the podium, he could make out Gerald Dahlen. The man next to him had a neck as thick as Bob's thigh.

That'll be a bodyguard. But only one? With everything that's going on?

It didn't seem likely.

He parked the Mercedes next to a Toyota that looked old and cheap enough to be a reporter's car.

Bob kept his eyes on Dahlen. The businessman's thick-necked protector nodded to acknowledge something, then turned and headed towards the right side of the building, where the first row of VIP vehicles was just visible.

He felt a pang of regret about not bringing a gun. In the end, security had been minimal, the event too dull to attract trouble, too far from public buildings. He'd wanted to bring the Colt, but had worried about leaving one of his friends unarmed with Stone.

As he got closer to the small crowd, he realized the cordon extended to the near corner of the building, cutting off access inside. But a group of reporters were behind the ribbon, cameras and phones pointed back towards the podium a dozen feet away.

Maybe they just ducked under the cordon...

He took a few steps back from the group of onlookers and checked the side of the building.

Side entrance. They were probably let in by a PR person before the audience filled up.

He looked back, toward the row of parked cars just opposite his own. *No limo.*

He's parked somewhere else. But where? Around the right side of the building, most likely, where the angle is cut off.

Knowing Dahlen's egress point in case things got out of hand could provide an edge.

There had to be another exit from the building, assuming Dahlen didn't want to wade back through the media blocking the front entrances. He looked around for a moment, taking a few seconds longer than necessary to make it appear as if he were looking for something or someone specific.

By the door, a black panel was mounted on the hangar wall. It had a red light on it, but no other markings.

Moment of truth, Bob...

He leaned in slightly and flashed the gray prox card in front of the panel.

Nothing happened.

His stomach turned slightly, and he felt nerves kick in; but old training took over. He evened his breathing out and took off the prox card chain, then held the card right up to the panel. *For pity's sake, work, you piece of...*

The light turned green.

Bob yanked on the door handle, and the side entrance opened. He stepped inside. The back of the reporters' scrum was ten feet ahead of him.

He checked his surroundings.

Beyond the scrum of press, the hangar was empty. But it was vast, perhaps sixty feet wide. On the far wall, a mural had been painted depicting a 1940s-style passenger prop plane zooming across a ribbon. Underneath it were the words "Kenneth J. Dahlen Memorial Hangar" in ornate script.

Movement along the far wall caught his eye. There was another door, near the back rear corner, and a man standing next to it had shifted in place slightly as he lit a cigarette.

Bob's nervousness momentarily returned.

Edson Krug.

He turned the other way – perhaps too quickly, he immediately realized.

Krug was probably there to keep an eye out for him. He was working for Dahlen, and that meant maybe he had all along. It fit the theory that Krug had been the second leak on the Tehran mission.

Now they were clearing up their mutual problem.

But has he seen me?

44

Gerald Dahlen waited patiently in a guest-of-honor seat a few feet to the right of the lectern.

He had a half smirk plastered on and was trying to hold it in place despite the seething, bubbling contempt he felt for those in attendance.

"… a pinnacle of the DC business community's charitable efforts…" The emcee droned on. Dahlen had a brief notion that it might be nice to crack the man's head off the edge of that lectern, watch him slump to the ground as the crowd screamed.

But reality intruded. He crossed one leg over the other and straightened his tie. The crimson worked well with the suit's blue-gray pattern.

The crowd there was half media, half airport staff, a smattering of business leaders in the seats adjacent to him and one row back. It was all for the cameras, nothing personal to any of it.

They'd invoked his father's name multiple times, even though Dahlen knew Kenneth would've gladly drowned the lot like unwanted farm cats if he could've made a dollar off it.

He was that kind of man.

Dahlen was under no illusions as to how much he himself cared for others. He knew his father's emotional indifference had been inherited.

But he liked to think that what separated him from – and elevated him above – his father was his ability to keep his temper. There was nothing to be gained from letting the crowd of cud-grazing sycophants know how he felt.

He was smarter than his father. Of that, he was sure. His father would've panicked, sent an army after Singleton, crushing a fly with a tactical nuke and further sullying his image. In the modern era of instant information, that was no longer an option.

He knew how men like Singleton worked, in the shadows, dangers minimized, away from prying eyes. Despite Krug's mewling, there was no danger to be feared in the land of the insipid and the weak.

"... and a great man in his own right. His donation has helped to make this all possible." The emcee took a quarter-turn in his direction. "Ladies and gentlemen, I give you Gerald Dahlen..."

Dahlen rose to applause, his plastered-on smile rigid, unyielding.

Bob strolled into the middle of the gaggle of press, most watching the proceedings or taping, a few taking old-fashioned notes with a pen and pad.

He chanced a glance backwards once he had a few bodies behind him. Krug hadn't moved and was smoking a cigarette, leaning against the wall.

That complicated matters.

The door was another exit, without a doubt. Beyond it was likely nothing but asphalt and Dahlen's limo. They would usher him out that way when the speeches were done. That was Bob's best window, when they were past the door. But it would be three against one, at best.

He looked back towards the other side entrance. He hadn't seen anything or anyone behind the building, just asphalt stretching back a few hundred meters to the property line. That meant it might be possible to walk around the back...

Around him, the media's murmuring conversations were suddenly slightly louder. "Here we go," one of them said. "They're getting to the speeches. We can get out of here soon."

"Yeah, if by 'soon' you mean after twenty minutes of hot air," another replied.

If he could make it around the back side of the building, he could be waiting for them, ambush them and reduce the numbers advantage. But that meant walking out of the crowd of reporters, which might catch Krug's eye.

He began to shuffle sideways through the crowd, to its edge.

I just need the right moment, when he's not paying attention.

He chanced a quick glance that way. Krug was still smoking the cigarette, still staring at the proceedings.

The second I move, he's going to spot me. But if I can't get out of here, Dahlen has an easy path out, and I'll have blown our only chance.

The door was perhaps fifteen feet away. He stood at a slight angle, to keep Krug visible out of the corner of his eye, waiting for the opportunity.

At the main podium, the airport authority CEO was introducing Dahlen as a "pinnacle of self-made success," which Bob figured was probably easier when a guy's father had billions of dollars.

"We're going to have a couple of speeches, and then Mr.

Dahlen will cut the ribbon, followed by a brief talk from our own Karen Breland, of Airport Communications. And now... it gives me great pleasure to present the son of today's honoree, and a great man in his own right. His donation has helped to make this all possible. Ladies and gentlemen, I give you Gerald Dahlen." He finished the introduction and turned to his right to shake Dahlen's hand as the tycoon rose to his feet.

An object flew at him, something small, and the CEO ducked. The egg shattered on the concrete behind the stage.

"Warmonger out!" a man in the audience yelled, standing to reveal he'd smuggled in an entire carton. "No more blood for oil!" He selected another egg and drew his hand back, but security acted quickly, the officer beside the stage striding forward and grabbing his arm before he could fling it, pinning it behind the man's back in one smooth motion.

"Get off me, you fascist pig!" the protestor squealed.

The audience was murmuring and chuckling at the disturbance.

Bob head-checked Krug. He was taking in the spectacle with everyone else. Bob turned quickly and maneuvered through the crowd to the door. He didn't pause to see if he'd been noticed; if he had, he was going to find out soon enough.

The speeches and crowd were reduced to a muffled murmuring once the door closed behind him. It was still warm despite being early evening, the sun still firmly above the horizon.

He walked briskly to the back right corner of the building and poked his head around quickly to check that it was clear. He took a few more steps to his left, to get a better look around.

On the far side, set back twenty feet from the hangar, he could make out the back end of Dahlen's limousine parked in the VIP section. He hadn't seen the driver onstage. That meant he was probably the wide-necked second protector, waiting in it or nearby.

He headed towards it, walking quickly but calmly.

"Sir! Sir, stop right there, please..."

The voice came from not far behind him. Bob allowed himself an exasperated breath. "I have a press pass," he said as he turned, ten feet short of the corner.

It was a security guard.

He had his hand on a hip holster, but it looked too small for a pistol. "ID, please," the guard asked. Bob took a half step forward, and the guard's other hand came up in protest. "Ah! Just... slowly, please, sir. This is a restricted area..."

Bob took the ID tag off his shirt and proffered it at arm's length. "See? Communications."

"Uh-huh," the guard said, looking down his nose slightly at the card, as if adjusting focal distance. "And would you be... yep, that's the one... Mr. Plant, I'm going to ask you to come back to my service car over on the east side, here, and accompany me back to the security center while I check this..."

"I can't do that," Bob said. "My role requires me to be here for this important event. Now, I'm sorry if they haven't given you a proper sheet on who is and who isn't..."

"We have a full registry of participants, sir, and there are indications you are not on it. So if you'd just come this way..." The man turned slightly to one side and ushered with his free arm. Bob knew he had no choice; he didn't want to hit a senior citizen, but...

He shuffled forward slightly to close the reach distance. But the guard's head bobbed, as if he'd noticed the subtle change in position, his hand flying up from the side holster before Bob could see what he was holding.

Bob reacted on instinct, turning his left shoulder in, snapping a backhand up from the elbow, the back of his knuckles catching the object square.

The stun gun flew from the man's hand.

The guard swung a meaty fist at him, but he saw it coming, time slowing down. He used the guard's passing arm for leverage, catching him under the armpit and slamming him to the ground, back first.

The guard scrambled to recover. Bob leaned down and hit him on the side of the chin with a sharp jab, flush to the mental nerve. The man's eyes rolled back in his head for a moment, and his eyelids slammed shut, fluttering as the man fell into rapid-eye-movement sleep.

Bob knew he had less than thirty seconds before the man awoke and things once again got out of hand. He took off his tie and used it to bind the man's wrists, then took off one of the man's shoes and a sock, jamming it into his mouth just as he began to stir back to consciousness. His eyes fluttered open, and he realized he'd been restrained and gagged. He began to struggle.

Bob reached over and picked up the stun gun. "I don't want to use this on you. But I will if I have to. Understood?"

The guard peered at him, his anger obvious. Then he nodded.

Bob crouched and removed the man's other shoe, then his athletic sock. He used the sock to tie the man's ankles together. None of it would hold for more than a few minutes of struggle. But that was probably all he would need.

The guard's cap had fallen off. Bob picked it up and put it on. It was a little loose, but coupled with his white shirt and dress slacks, he looked at least a little official. "I'm borrowing your stun gun. I'll leave it behind if I get a chance."

He returned his ID clip to his breast pocket. "Again, my apologies. I know you're just doing your job."

The man muttered something indistinct, but from the

tone, it was scathing. He was still muttering as Bob made his way to the far corner.

He checked to see if it was clear sailing to the limo. A man was leaning against the driver's side door, smoking a cigarette and reading something on a phone.

Bob kept his footsteps light as he walked over to him. He caught the man's peripheral vision as soon as he passed the back end of the car. The driver saw him and frowned; he was even stockier up close, shoulders seemingly door width.

Bob darted towards him, one eye on the northwest corner of the building until he was sure the crowd outside was cut off and couldn't see them.

The driver wasn't fazed, his free hand going for his shoulder holster. Bob saw the pistol come clear of the man's jacket. He pointed the stun gun and fired, four electrode leads shooting from its tip and embedding themselves in the driver's torso.

The man tried to aim and shoot anyway, even as he convulsed from the strong current, but his limbs had stiffened. He battled the current, trying a half step forward. But the effect was too powerful, and instead, he collapsed onto his side, the phone clattering with glass-shattering force onto the ground.

The pistol flew out of the man's hand and slid under the limo.

In the background, the air was filled by a shimmer of applause, slightly prolonged.

Speech is ending. Shit.

Bob wasn't sure if he had time to fish around under the car for the gun.

First things first... He heaved with all his strength to roll the driver over onto his stomach. He pulled off his own belt and used it to tie the man's wrists, then pulled down the shoulders of his jacket until they were restraining the man from reaching out. He took off the man's tie and used it as a gag.

Bob crouched on his knees and stared under the limo. The pistol had managed to make its way to the center of the vehicle. That would mean sliding himself under it, and from the sounds of the audience, he knew he might not have time...

The side exit began to swing open.

45

Bob rose to his haunches, his back against the lower-front wheel of the car. He peeked around the corner of the limo.

Dahlen was heading straight towards him, Krug right behind him.

He broke cover as soon as both men were within ten feet, arm levelled towards the former agency man, index finger yanking the trigger of the stun gun. The leads flew towards their intended target.

But Krug was faster. He'd broken into a run as soon as Bob had appeared, and hurled himself, like a football line-backer, at his boss. Both men went down hard, the leads missing.

Bob had no time to withdraw them and try again, and he tossed the stun gun aside as he sprinted towards them.

Krug got Dahlen to his feet just in time. "Go, take the car and get clear!" he instructed, shoving Dahlen towards the car's front end just as Bob threw himself at his former colleague, elbow coming around with whip speed, bone catching Krug flush and knocking him to one knee.

He followed with an uppercut, but Krug clasped his forearms together, the split-second defense sparing a knockout blow. The force made him stagger backwards, but instead of trying to maintain balance, Krug let himself go down easily, then rolled to one side and used a handspring to leap back upright.

Bob tried to anticipate the move, spinning into a reverse kick. Krug caught the foot and turned it sharply, trying to snap his ankle and end the brawl quickly. Bob went with the motion, allowing his torso to spin, the broken bone avoided, but the crunching fall to the hard asphalt inevitable.

Krug stepped in and swung a kick at his head. Bob rolled over at the last moment. He scrambled upright in time to see Krug reach down, withdrawing an eight-inch blade from a sheath around his lower leg, blade down in a stabbing grip.

"Oh, I've been looking forward to this for a long, long time..."

He swiped quickly at his former team leader, once with a backhand, then again in the reverse direction. Bob skipped a few steps back with each slash to avoid having his throat cut.

A few feet away, the engine of the limo roared to life. "Assignment blown yet again, huh, Bob?" Krug sneered, squaring off with him. "By the time we're done, he'll be long gone, just another fuckup in your long history of them."

The limo pulled away, and from the sound of it, Bob figured, Dahlen was standing on the gas pedal.

"He got some help in Tehran," Bob said, looking for an opening, a quickly exploitable weakness in Krug's posture or defense. "You sold us out."

The comment caught Krug by surprise. "What bullshit are you playing at now? I didn't have a goddamned thing to do with that." As he finished speaking, he reached in quickly and slashed at Bob's torso.

Bob threw himself out of the way, bones rattling as his

bulk met asphalt. He rolled back and to the side, coming up on his feet as Krug rushed in with a series of short, sharp slashes on both backhand and forehand. Bob took advantage of the lack of distance, using his forearms to intercept Krug's, the blocks preventing the blade from reaching him.

He leaned in and head-butted Krug in the bridge of the nose, the man's grip on the blade lost. It clattered to the asphalt.

Krug's hand flashed towards the speed holster at the small of his back, but Bob kicked out hard, nailing the other man's wrist as the gun appeared from behind him, the pistol bouncing off the hard ground with a metallic *thunk*.

Krug leaped a step back, the pair in fighting stances, Bob falling back into old methods, mechanical precision from years of White Crane training as he balanced on the arches of his feet. "Then why are you helping Dahlen cover up what happened?"

The former Team Seven Gamma chuckled mirthlessly. "He's paying me."

"Bullshit!" Bob spat. "You betrayed the team. You were 'Excelsior.' That's why you left Gaines and Rice to die..."

Krug fairly sneered his response. "I left them because our handler called us in. The mission was scrubbed. You just chose to disobey, like the fuckup you are..."

Both men's eyes flitted to the right, to where the gun lay less than ten feet away. They reacted in unison, turning towards it and diving for the pistol.

Krug got there first.

He rolled over onto his back and aimed upwards just in time to stop Bob from pouncing on him. "Ah! Ah, ah, ah, Bobby boy! Back off and keep your hands high."

Bob took a step back as ordered.

"On your knees. NOW!"

Bob bent down on both knees. "You can't just shoot me. There are people all over this place."

"Self-defense." Krug nodded to the knife on the ground, a few feet to Bob's left. "You came at Gerry with a knife. I had no choice." He smiled wickedly. "After all these years, I finally get to fucking end you, Bob Singleton, you enormous pain in my ass."

"Just shut up and do it," Bob said. "Nobody ever liked hearing you talk."

It had been years coming, Bob knew, and he had no intention of closing his eyes. Perhaps it was the best ending, paying for his folly at the hands of the man who ruined them all.

Krug yanked the trigger.

The gun clicked hard.

Bob knew the sound of a jam, the pistol's slide catching before the hammer could come down. He threw himself sideways as Krug tried to work the slide in vain. Bob's hand found the blade of the knife. He threw it sidearm, making sure to keep his wrist locked, the knife's balance working in his favor. It flipped end over end twice before burying itself in Krug's stomach.

Krug dropped the pistol and collapsed to his knees. He tried to pull out the knife, but the damage was too deep, his eyes already swimming around as the pain set in.

"Shit," he said as he collapsed onto one side. He was gritting his teeth, wincing. Bob covered the distance between them and leaned down, then yanked up on the blade with all his might, the serrated edge tearing through Krug's innards like they were tissue.

Bob looked back over his shoulder. The limo was a dot, if it was the right car at all, taillights barely visible as it turned onto the main road outside the airport.

He could hear someone speaking, the official ribbon

cutting evidently not ending the press briefing around the corner.

He reached into Krug's pockets. "He wouldn't have let you ride with him. That's not Gerry's style, accommodating the help. So... what did you..." His hand withdrew a key emblazoned with a Ford logo.

He looked around as Krug moaned through his last moments.

There. A burgundy Mustang sat in the last VIP parking spot, about ten feet past the squirming-but-restrained driver.

"Didn't... betray anyone," Krug muttered. "Just... hate your punk ass, Singleton."

Bob rose, ignoring him, and headed towards the car. He stooped to pick up the driver's pistol. The driver was struggling with his bonds, trying to yell through the sock ball-gag. "It doesn't matter anymore. You're done."

Krug barked a guttural, wheezing denial through clenched teeth. "Wasn't me. Swear it. Figured... figured it was you." He could no longer hold himself up, and he lay back down, consciousness ebbing.

The gut wound would kill him, Bob knew. Chances that the emergency techs would find him in time were slim, and those of stopping both the bleeding and the septic infection from organ damage next to none. He climbed into the car, starting it with his right hand, taking out his phone with his left.

He threw the car into gear and backed out, then into first as he punched the gas. He hit redial on the phone as he sped past the end of the hangar, where the rest of the crowd was just dispersing. In a few seconds, they would discover Krug and panic, but he would already be gone.

The call rang through. "Hello?"

"Ginny, it's Bob. No time to talk. You have my location?"

"I... do now. Go ahead."

"I'm going after someone's limo. They're out of sight, but I know where he's headed. Remember that other favor?"

"Sure. But I don't know how long I can get into the system for..."

"Then stand by. This is going to get hairy pretty quickly."

"Like... how quickly? I need to leave my entry until the last moment, as they have alarms up the wazoo..."

"Fifteen, twenty minutes tops. And I may need your help finding his car."

"Okay. Are we expecting our friends in law enforcement?"

"One way or another, yeah. Even if my target didn't call them, my driving through the fence at the airport in about twenty seconds will demand a response. That and... *other* circumstances sort of guarantee it."

"Okay."

Bob ended the call.

He shifted the Mustang into fourth gear, the car barreling along the old jetway parallel to the property, speedometer pushing sixty miles per hour, then sixty-five, then seventy.

Dahlen would be desperate to avoid police involvement, given his own crimes and his reputation. But chances were high he'd see no other alternative once Bob was on his tail. The tycoon's protected compound, in the northwest part of the city, was nearly thirty miles away, and the limousine couldn't outrun the muscle car on a three-minute head start.

He cut a corner where the jetway reached the private jet hangars near the access road exit, then stomped on the gas as the car reached the chain-link fence surrounding the airport's north perimeter, smashing through it.

The car bounced as it reached the strip of grass separating the hangars from the turnoff to the highway.

Bob knew he had to stop Dahlen before he reached his house.

46

Gerald Dahlen's foot was to the floor, but the limousine was barely pushing seventy miles per hour. He slammed a palm angrily against the wheel, frustrated that his escape vehicle was a lumbering beast.

His orders to Krug and Gustav had been longstanding: if they were separated at any point, they were to check in every five minutes until contact was re-established.

It had been nearly ten minutes since he'd left the airport, the freeway a broad ribbon of asphalt, suburban office blocks and residential exits flying by, all set well away from the eight lanes of traffic.

If both men were down, he suspected, then Bob Singleton was probably still alive and on his heels. He cursed his own shortsightedness for thinking a public event would be safe.

It had been a mistake, he knew now, to trust that money was enough to buy his peace of mind. He'd left the wrong people responsible for the cleanup after Tehran. It was clearly their fault, not his. Now there was a chance he would pay for it.

The obvious move was to head directly to the compound. He had at least eight men on the property, all armed, as well as whatever surveillance Andrew Kennedy's people were pathetically maintaining. Singleton wouldn't stand a chance.

He swung the limo into the other lane to get around a slower driver. He felt his anger swell towards Edson Krug. Yes, Krug had warned him about such public events, given the circumstances. But he'd backed down easily when Dahlen had suggested he was being paranoid. That failed attempt at foresight made any failure on Krug's part to defeat his former colleague that much more galling.

Dahlen checked his watch. It was just after seven o'clock on a Sunday, which meant no tolls required to enter the city on Interstate 66. If he was lucky, he could be across the Roosevelt Bridge in ten minutes, and in Kalorama ten minutes after that.

He looked at the "phone" button on the car's wheel. He was tempted to punch it, ask the system to call Krug, find out what happened. But that would be a show of weakness.

Dahlen hadn't been afraid in a very long time, not since his father's correctional beatings during childhood. He'd always had someone to handle a problem, someone who could be paid with either his father's money or his own.

But Singleton wouldn't be bought.

It gave him an idea. He hit the phone button. "Call home two," he said.

The call rang through. "Carter here, sir."

"Carter! I'm being pursued in the limo. Don't ask questions; we don't have time. We have some decent DC police contacts still, yes? Yes?"

"Yes, sir."

"Have one of them track me down. Can you locate my limo on the system?"

A pause.

"Sir, I've got you on I-66, heading into the Ashton Heights neighborhood of Arlington."

"Send my satnav co-ordinates to one of our police friends. I need an escort. I believe I'm being followed, but I haven't seen the car yet."

"Right away, sir."

"Have the men ready in case I can't shake him." As an afterthought, he added, "Do you have a location on Krug's vehicle?"

"Yes, sir... He appears to be less than two miles behind you, closing distance steadily."

Closing distance? Krug was no wilting flower, but Dahlen had had the speedometer needle over eighty for parts of the trip. Either Krug was trying to catch up in a panic, or...

Or Singleton took his car.

"Have our friends look out for Krug's Mustang. Give them his satnav co-ordinates as well."

If Krug was right behind him, he'd have called. It had to be Singleton. He subconsciously tapped his left suit jacket breast, where the lump from his holster was carefully disguised by perfect tailoring.

He'd never been a full field agent, never taken the risks that Singleton, Krug and the others had taken. He'd played the political game, been promoted rapidly. And then he'd betrayed them, in exchange for the $20 million in seed money to start Critical Safety, a chance to build something without his father's help, to outdo the man.

The idea of battling Singleton was not remotely appealing. He'd barely qualified at the agency to carry a sidearm.

Hopefully, it wouldn't come to that.

47

Traffic on the eight-lane interstate was steady despite being Sunday. Bob didn't spare the horses, the pedal down as the Mustang cut in and out of lanes, zipping by families in minivans, high rollers' German sedans and rural residents' pickup trucks.

He thought he'd seen the limo just before Arlington; but if he had, it had been lost by the delays when a semi cut off one lane, a slow driver in another. He hit redial on his phone.

A familiar voice answered. "Go for Nick..."

"Nick, I need a location on him. I need to know where he's—"

"Straight ahead of you. He's the only limo I can spot via the traffic cams anywhere near your current location. You're just a couple of miles back. Do you want Ginny to shut down the bridge lights? Once we go from being passive to active, they'll know we're in the system."

"No, that'll leave me a sitting duck if he has police watching his back. Even if you change the lights quickly enough to slow them down, DC cops have air support."

"Police chopper."

"Exactly. I need to account for that. I'm going to push it hard, try to get into visual range of him before we cross the bridge. Once we're over, I need an immediate delay or diversion at the Potomac River Freeway, okay? Something significant. I need to push him just south, onto E Street."

"Gotcha. Then what?"

Then, Bob thought, *we find out how well Dahlen knows DC.*

48

There was no sign yet of a limousine or a car chasing it. But Sgt. Teddy Purcell of the DC Metropolitan Police was getting nervous.

It was beyond any request in the past.

He stood beside his unmarked cruiser, parked just ahead of the Roosevelt Bridge, and stared at the scattered parade of traffic heading that way.

Fixing tickets was one thing. Arresting someone on a trumped-up charge was a full step up in seriousness. But they'd no doubt pay him the same monthly "gift." Now there were radio calls out for a maroon Mustang for an incident at Dulles Airport. It couldn't be a coincidence.

Better to be safe than sorry. He took out his phone and hit speed dial.

"GO FOR MAGNUSSON," the other party yelled, the sound of chopper blades smearing the background with wind-whipped white noise.

"Mike! Teddy P."

"WHAT'S UP, BUD? I'M IN THE MIDDLE OF MY WESTERN SWEEP..."

"I need a favor," he said. "I think the County Mounties are looking for the same car I am, a stolen maroon Mustang. Plates are TOR-133, registered to an Edson David Krug. I got a tip he's heading towards the Roosevelt Bridge, but the guy driving is a key source of mine. I don't want to lose him, but I need this on the QT. Can you log out for a few minutes, take a lunch break or something?"

"YOU WANT ME TO TAKE A RUN OVER THERE?"

"If you don't mind. See if you can get eyes on him before he gets here. I'm going to shut him down before he gets to the bridge, block the lanes. But just in case he gets any weird ideas..."

"ROGER THAT. POKER FRIDAY NIGHT?"

"Wouldn't miss it," Purcell promised.

They ended the call. He climbed back into the car and checked his display terminal for the satnav locations already pinged. The lead car was just a mile away.

Time to get the show on the road.

He looked through the cruiser's rear window. The east lanes were busy on the bridge. No reason to think he'd try to go around the cruiser. If the GPS was right, the limo still had a few hundred yards of lead. He just needed to let it pass first, and then...

He spotted the limo. With his years of experience, he was sure it was well above the speed limit. *That should cost them extra*, he thought. He wondered what its passenger had done to draw the other driver's ire.

The limo approached the bridge. He threw the car into gear. *The moment it passes...*

A few seconds later, it zoomed past his spot. Purcell depressed the accelerator, the cruiser rolling as he turned the wheel left until it had made a quarter turn, across the east-bound road, covering the middle lane and butting into the outside and inside lanes. He turned on its flashing lights and got out of the sedan.

He walked around to the back door and opened it, taking out a pair of orange traffic cones. He placed them in the unblocked portions of the other lanes.

At least it looks official.

He peered over the car's roof. The Mustang came into view, eating up ground rapidly.

He should see the lights now, start slowing down.

Above, he heard the high-pitched whine of the Eurocopter's muffled propellers. He craned his neck slightly, catching sight of its running lights as it swooped in an arc to a position behind the approaching sports car.

Slowing down, any second now...

The Mustang was closing rapidly. Behind it, a few other cars came into view.

If he didn't brake soon, he'd risk clipping the cruiser or possibly cars in the oncoming lane. There was probably enough space to swerve around him, assuming the driver didn't leave it too late to judge the gap...

He's not stupid enough to bolt, is he?

Purcell felt his stomach turn slightly. If he didn't know better, he told himself, he'd swear the Mustang was actually picking up speed. He tapped redial on his phone. "Ronnie, keep an eye on this guy. I think... Oh shit... here he comes!"

The Mustang's engine growled as the driver milked it for every drop of speed.

Purcell turned and ran, clambering over the concrete guardrail separating the road from the sidewalk. The Mustang swerved towards him at the last second, aiming for the gap between the nose of his squad car and the rail. "No! Jesus Christ, don't...!" the officer managed to blurt before it blew past, smashing through the traffic cones, catching the very tip of the car's bumper, hard plastic shattering around reinforced steel.

The Mustang fishtailed slightly as it regained the center lane.

"MY FUCKING CAR!" Purcell yelled. He ran back towards the damaged cruiser, plastic from the bumper and glass from the light assembly strewn around it.

He climbed back behind the wheel. It had stalled, but he restarted it as he dialed his friend in the chopper. "You catch that shit, Ronnie?"

"Yeah, but I've got him. Look, Teddy, I have to call this in..."

His paymasters wanted it on the downlow, but Purcell now had a dozen good reasons to arrest the driver. More help was always better than less. "Do it. I owe this guy now..."

"You might get a chance sooner than later. Two of the three exits are jammed solid. Nobody's getting onto Constitution or Independence."

That meant he'd have to follow I-66 up to the E Street exit, Purcell figured.

After the off-ramp, a massive circular junction would force the driver to slow down or go off the road.

And then he's mine.

49

The bridge was just a couple of miles away. Bob called Nick Velasco's line.

"Nick, Bob. Pass me to Ginny."

He waited.

"Ginny here."

"Do you have me on camera?"

"I do. Traffic cams have been catching you every half mile since you entered Alexandria."

"There are intersections just beyond the exits to Constitution and Independence. I need you to shut down the lights there. Put them on blinking red so that people are treating them like four-way stops." Bob kept his eyes on the three lanes of traffic, swerving the Mustang adroitly around slower cars until the road ahead was empty again.

"That'll back traffic up towards you..."

"That's the idea, yeah."

"Anything else? Chances are as soon as I make the switch, alarms are going to go off at traffic control's IT department, and I could get locked out."

"Yeah. Once you see where we're headed, wait for the

limo to get past the Twenty-Second Street intersection, and shut down the traffic lights on E Street as far as you can."

"You mean once you're in..."

"Exactly. I have a police chopper circling due east. I expect he'll be right behind me. Can you knock out the traffic cams there, too?"

"If I still have access. After today, they'll be ramping up their security."

The Mustang negotiated the last sweeping bend before the bridge. Ahead a few hundred yards, a set of police cruiser lights flashed into life. The vehicle was parked horizontally across the eastbound lane, but the gaps on either side were passable. Technically.

Don't pretend you didn't miss this, he thought. *Don't pretend you're not enjoying this.*

He stepped on the gas and twitched the wheel to the right, aiming for the traffic cones the policeman had placed in the outside lane. The cruiser was butting a couple of feet into his way.

But if I steer this just right...

A shadowy figure jumped over the side guardrail. The Mustang blew through the gap, the traffic cones sent flying, the barest contact with the cruiser's bumper nearly slamming him into the steering wheel column, the sports car fishtailing slightly as he jerked the wheel back and forth to regain control.

Ahead, two lanes were already beginning to back up onto the bridge. If he'd been late and the limo had already crossed...

There was no point worrying about it. He eased off the gas slightly, swerving around a pair of vehicles as the drivers tried to alter their routes to avoid the snarl. The exit turned into a long, steady curve, and he had to be careful as he negotiated the Mustang around other drivers.

The road exited onto E Street. Bob could hear horns blaring ahead, the cars in front of him quickly slowing down. In his rearview mirror, he caught a flash of the chopper attempting to follow.

But he'd thought ahead, prepared for that eventuality.

Just past Twenty-Second Street, the road dipped into the tunnel at Bernardo de Galvez Memorial Park. The two lanes weren't full but had screeched to a halt, nonetheless.

Ginny had done her job too well. The lights were solid red instead of blinking, traffic utterly immobile. The limo was trapped in the tunnel, likely a dozen or more vehicles ahead blocking both lanes. The Mustang followed it in, but was halted immediately by the jam. Bob put it into park and got out, retrieving the pistol from his waistband and secreting it in his coat pocket as he sprinted alongside the row of cars, looking for Dahlen's ride.

There. It was at least five cars back from the tunnel exit, too wide to get past the guardrail to its left or to use the other lane for escape. Two of the vehicles in front of it were semi-trucks, the drivers unwilling to buck the red lights, which clearly weren't changing as expected.

He was twenty yards back when the limo's driver-side door opened slowly, Dahlen poking his head out and looking around. He spotted Bob and scrambled to get out. He ran a few feet, then turned.

Bob threw himself against the left retaining wall, trying to narrow his profile as Dahlen squeezed off two rounds, the gunfire booming from the tunnel's echo. Bob heard someone scream. A driver in the other lane who'd poked his head out of his car quickly rushed to re-enter his vehicle.

Dahlen turned to run again. Before he could make headway, Bob squared up and took aim towards the top of his torso, trying to account for his own nerves. He fired two shots.

On the second, Dahlen squealed in pain, grabbing at the back of his thigh as he collapsed to the ground.

Bob ran to close the distance, but Dahlen pivoted from his half-lying, half-sitting position and opened fire, emptying half the magazine in a furious burst.

Bob threw himself behind the back end of a Nissan pickup for cover. He peeked around its left back bumper. Dahlen was trying to rise, to run on, dragging his wounded leg.

Bob stayed in his crouched position and fired another shot, the bullet catching the tycoon in the left arm. Dahlen stumbled and fell face-first onto the asphalt, the gun skittering from his grasp. Ahead, one of the semis started to slowly roll again, running the red light as horns blared, obviously more willing to chance a ticket than being caught in a gun battle.

Dahlen had just about reached the pistol when Bob caught up to him. He planted a shoe on Dahlen's arm and pinned it for a moment, until the other man stopped fighting. He trotted ahead a few feet and kicked the other pistol to the side of the road.

His target tried to right himself, then looked around frantically.

"None of these drivers is going to risk being a statistic by helping you," Bob calmly told the former agency man. "The police chopper is cut off by the tunnel. Any help they can offer you is stuck behind dual traffic jams. You're done, Gerry."

Dahlen was breathing hard, excited by fear. "I'll give you whatever you want," he begged. "Anything, Singleton. It's yours..."

"I don't want your money. I want answers. Why? Why, after all this time...?"

"You know why. Smalls—"

"Smalls was fishing for leverage." Bob switched magazines on the pistol, pocketing the empty one.

"I couldn't take that chance."

"Then you were behind Tehran."

Dahlen smiled thinly, panting at the pain from the gunshot wounds. "Ah... but technically I was already gone, remember? Replaced by Edward Stone before the mission launched. Are you suggesting I leaked an assignment I wasn't even supposed to know about? That seems unlikely."

"You were Brighteyes. Everyone figured that. The second leak, Excelsior, was your source inside the operation. That was Krug."

Dahlen shook his head gently, chuckling slightly through grimaces. "You are so naïve, Singleton. You always were."

"TELL ME!" Bob insisted. "Tell me the truth about what happened. Tell me you didn't just do it for the money."

"Go... go fuck yourself..."

Bob ignored his swelling anger. "I need access to your network. Password? Tell me quickly, or I'll step on that femur wound and see if we can rupture an artery or two. You *do* know what happens with a femoral rupture, right, Gerry?"

"Like I said... go fuck yourself. You're going to kill me anyway..."

"I'll kill you if you don't give it to me. If you do, I want you to live to see your world come down."

Dahlen sighed, but whether it was loss of blood or exasperation wasn't clear. "Eight digits, G328164!"

Bob took out his phone. He dialed Nick.

"What's the good word, Alpha?"

Bob relayed the password. "Make sure it works. Once I've restrained him, I'll find us an exit vehicle. We can hold him until the press has whatever Smalls hid away."

He waited a few moments.

"We're good," Nick said.

"See you shortly," Bob replied as he ended the call.

He saw Dahlen's hand shoot back into the inside pocket, then come clear.

The world slowed down. The onset of danger fired his adrenaline, a hard focus taking over as he saw the butt of the Derringer clear the jacket. But instead of pointing the pocket breech loader at him, Dahlen's arm was pointed at the inside lane.

A woman had begun to climb out of her car, phone in hand, to record the confrontation.

"Halt!" Dahlen yelled at her. "Move and I'll shoot you. You too, Bob. Move, and the woman is dead."

THE EXIT RAMP hadn't been slow enough. By the time Sgt. Purcell had re-entered his cruiser, turned it around and rejoined traffic, the Mustang had disappeared into traffic again.

Instead, he turned on his cruiser's siren and followed it towards E Street, forcing the near-inert other drivers to pull to one side – albeit slowly – so that he could crawl through them to the tunnel.

At the top of the street, he saw a throng of traffic blocking the tunnel entrance. He looked up to see the chopper hovering nearby.

If he loses eyes on this guy, we could lose him for good.

How am I going to explain all this?

How am I going to tell my captain this started as doing a favor, not a routine traffic stop?

He needed a plausible excuse.

But it would help if I caught him.

He pulled over, flashing lights still revolving, and got out of the cruiser. He kept his gun holstered as he trotted towards the tunnel entrance on foot, vowing that if he didn't get fired, he'd finally take his wife's advice and go on a diet.

Purcell stayed close to the vehicles. Nobody was outside their car despite the jam, which seemed weird.

He'd passed a dozen cars by the time he realized why. Twenty yards ahead, two men were in some kind of standoff. One of them was holding a woman around her midsection, using her as a shield or hostage.

Ah, shit. It's a domestic of some kind. That's probably his wife, and the other guy is... what, the boyfriend? Maybe.

The hostage would complicate things unless he could talk the guy down. Protocol suggested keeping them covered until backup could arrive. But he had no story to give them, no excuse for his conduct up until then.

If you bust him before the others arrive, you can say whatever you damn well please, Teddy.

He waited until he was a few dozen feet away, then moved closer to the inside wall so that any risk of gunfire hitting a driver was minimized. He went down on one knee in a braced position and took aim at the smaller of the two men.

"Metro Police!" Purcell bellowed. "Sir, release the hostage immediately. I won't give you a second warning!"

50

Bob raised his pistol, aiming it at Dahlen's head. He was partially covered by the woman, and even the slightest twitch in either direction could mean shooting the wrong person.

"Let her go, Gerry! This is between us."

"Why don't you put the pistol down and save us the time of this playing out, Singleton? I know your history. You're the do-gooder, the killer who thinks he has a conscience. You aren't going to take the chance against a human shield."

"We're more than ten feet apart. That Derringer is as likely to miss as hit, and then you're dead to rights," Bob warned. "Don't do it. Don't be stupid."

Dahlen snuck a backward glance at the still-snarled tunnel exit. He moved back slightly, towards the woman's open car door. "What do you think, Singleton? Could her little subcompact make the gap between the wall and the other cars?" He pulled her towards it.

"You're not going anywhere," Bob said. "You're done. You just don't know it yet."

Dahlen peered at him, then sideways at his blubbering

hostage, then at Singleton again. "I don't need to hit you," he said. He thrust the short-barreled gun against her temple. "Think I'll miss her from here? Now... put it down."

"If I put it down, you'll shoot me. So... no."

"If you don't, I'll definitely shoot her. I'm willing to bet that with your history, you don't want that... and this little gun has a hair trigger. Just making me any more nervous might be enough."

He looked wide-eyed and frantic, the pain from his wounds doubtless playing a part. Bob knew he was stuck. He reached down to the pavement. "Okay, pistol down. Now let her go."

Dahlen turned the Derringer back towards him. "You always were a feeble-hearted fool, Singleton. You were too weak to be Alpha. Now? Now you're dead, as you should have been ten years ago."

Beyond Singleton, a voice bellowed through the tunnel's echo, "Metro Police..."

Bob ducked and turned at the sound, the tiny two-shot pistol booming as Dahlen yanked the trigger. Behind him, he saw the police officer fall over backwards from his crouch.

Bob shot a look back towards Dahlen. A look of sheer horror crossed the tycoon's face. He'd realized his mistake and was clambering into the woman's subcompact via the back door, forcing her into the driver's seat. "GO!" he screamed at her.

There would be no way to catch him once he was out of the tunnel, Bob knew. The car was small enough to squeeze by the jam. But it might be slowed enough for him to keep up in a sprint.

Or...

He gazed back at the policeman as the subcompact wrenched its way clear of the line and into the small gap between it and the interior wall.

The man might not be badly hurt, or he could be bleeding out. His colleagues wouldn't make it there in time.

Bob ran twenty feet back to the prone figure, the line of traffic all trying to pull ahead, drivers worsening the snarl by trying to get around each other and away from the gunfight.

The policeman's name badge said "Purcell." He was gasping for air. The bullet had caught him in the chest. Bob leaned down to assess the damage, but before he could pull the cop's shirt open, the man coughed, bright rivulets of blood streaming out of both sides of his mouth.

His lungs are filling up with blood. You have no way of removing the slug, no bandages.

The policeman stared at him, his eyes filled with fear and panic. He was trying to move his head and speak. "Shhh..." Bob said. "Save your strength."

He looked back down the tunnel, frantic, hoping to see flashing lights close enough to make a difference. But he knew there would be no help.

The man had little chance.

Bob laid Purcell's head back against the road, trying to ignore the look of confusion in dancing, desperate eyes.

He rose and ran back to where Dahlen had initially fallen. The subcompact was already out of the tunnel and gone.

No time for pain or guilt right now. No time for anything but the job.

If Ginny had performed to expectations, E Street was a snarled mess; Dahlen would likely turn immediately at Twentieth Street, try to put distance between himself and police. Chances were that either the wounded officer or the man in the chopper had been after him, so they'd be looking for a burgundy Mustang.

He studied the line of traffic. Near the front, thirty or forty feet ahead, a man on a motorcycle was half turned. He'd either not seen the woman taken hostage or learned nothing, as he had a phone out, held horizontally so that he could take video of the crime scene in action.

Bob ran towards him. At the last moment, the rider realized what was about to happen, and he tried to turn away and store the phone in his pocket.

Bob slapped it out of his hands, the device clattering to the ground.

He stepped down hard on its glass screen, then ground his heel in as hard as he could.

The motorcyclist tried to pop the bike into gear, but he had nowhere to go. Bob grabbed him by the collar and pulled him off the Kawasaki, then took his place. He turned the handlebars as far right as they'd go, pushing it in a semicircle so that he could go backwards, around the adjacent car's tail end.

He threw the motorcycle into gear and twisted the throttle, the bike picking up speed quickly, his left foot ticking through the gears.

It zoomed out of the tunnel, police lights near blinding as they tried to parse the jammed intersection. He leaned hard left, turning at ninety degrees to flee up Twentieth Street.

51

Nick was waiting, six blocks north, in a green SUV.

Bob ditched the bike in an adjacent alley. The proximity to the White House probably meant a massive response to the tunnel. Even from nearly a mile away, he could hear the droning of dozens of sirens.

He walked over to the SUV and climbed in the passenger side. He realized his hands had begun to tremble, waning adrenaline making his brain crave a hit of booze, something to dull the tension. He felt shaky, as if his blood sugar had dropped precipitously.

"That's it?" Bob asked.

"That's it. Unless this guy has his entire security network shut down already, I've already cloned the operating system and your friend's code. Now I just need to go through it." Nick frowned. "You look terrible, Alpha. What happened back there?"

Bob tried to slow his breathing, calm down. "The man I was chasing shot a policeman. If Ginny did her job, the tunnel cameras were down, so we're clear, but..."

"But..."

"I don't think he was going to make it."

Nick blanched. "Ah… hell."

"I don't know how I would've avoided it. Things were moving really fast. It wasn't my fault," Bob offered.

"It doesn't sound like it was."

Bob stole a quick glance at the younger man, trying to gauge what he felt about it. But his expression was earnest, understanding. It didn't help the sensation already building, that his master plan had gone awry, and another innocent bystander had been killed. It wasn't Azadi's family all over again, but it didn't feel any better.

"We need to go," Nick offered, his tone slightly hushed out of respect for his passenger's distress. "If you left your wheels, they probably have your prints."

Bob shook his head and held up his left hand, palm first. "Don't have any."

They drove across the city in silence. At one point, Nick reached over to turn on the radio, probably curious about the scene. But Bob stayed his hand and emphasized it with a small shake of his head.

They were about a mile from the warehouse when Bob saw the neon sign. His hands were still trembling, his nerves shot. "Pull over here," he said.

Nick sounded anxious. "We're on MLK. It doesn't have the safest rep at night…"

"Just… just drop me here, okay? I got you what you needed. This is near my stop anyway."

"O-okay…" Nick stammered. He steered the car over to the curb. "You want me to wait…"

"No. Just leave me for now, okay? Tell Ginny I'll call her tomorrow, figure out where we go from here."

The hacker nodded. Bob climbed out of the car. A few moments later, it had completed a U-turn and disappeared back towards downtown.

Bob held both hands in front of him, palms up. They were shaking as if in an earthquake.

I'm a mess. I'm a raw nerve running on fumes. My hands are trembling; my mouth is like sawdust. Even if I could avoid having a drink, what state would I be in to help anyone? And what harm will a few swallows do?

He stared at the liquor store's neon Open sign. He'd been good for three days, behaved himself. He hadn't asked these people to insert themselves into his life. He hadn't walked back into the business willingly, he told himself.

I don't have to get completely shitfaced. Just a pint, a few swallows before I return and have to deal with Stone, as well as telling them what I did. Just a taste to deal with the deadly reality of it.

He hadn't anticipated the Derringer. If he had, maybe...

I led an armed man into a tunnel filled with civilians. It was my plan. That's why I had Ginny block traffic. That's why I diverted him into the tunnel, so there were no prying eyes from the chopper. That's why I had Ginny shut down the cameras.

There was no escaping the fact that he'd been running on autopilot since arriving at the airport, just looking for advantages and taking them. But an innocent man was dead, more than a decade after Bob had sworn never to kill for his country again.

But this wasn't for America, or even for me. This was for that boy and the nurse who's helping both of us.

None of this is on me. It's on Dahlen, for Tehran, and it's on Krug, too. They made their own beds. They're why that officer is dead.

He got out of the car, entered the store, and walked past the bored-looking clerk to the vodka aisle. He bought a pint of Finlandia for nine dollars, using the credit card Velasco had provided.

He left the store carrying it in a brown paper bag.

He peered down Martin Luther King Jr. Boulevard. Traffic

was busy in the evening. A few doors down, kids were hanging out at the end of an alley, laughing and joking. It was only a half-dozen blocks to the warehouse, a ten- or fifteen-minute walk.

It would give him time for a few swallows from the pint. He looked around for anyone paying attention. Seeing no one, he cracked the seal on the bottle and took a swallow.

The warming sensation from the booze felt as welcome as a family home.

He let out a sigh of relief, then stashed it in his side pocket.

A few more sniffs before we deal with the issue of Eddie and Dahlen escaping. That can't hurt anyone. Just enough to stop the shaking, get some control.

He began to make his way south, towards Sixth Street. Every half block or so, he pulled out the pint and had a quick swallow. After three blocks, the warmth had spread throughout his body. His thoughts were distracted, taken away from the tension of the day.

This isn't wrong. I deserve this. It's not straight vanilla while lying in the flop. It's just having a couple of drinks after some difficult decisions. I'm not the one who should feel guilty.

But he did, so he took another swallow. By the time he'd covered two-thirds of the remaining walk, most of the pint was gone, and the happiness had turned to a fog, which still beat thinking about what had happened to the police officer. What he'd done.

I was doing what I had to do. That's... that's what matters.

His phone began to buzz. He'd forgotten it, forgotten Dawn and the boy, at least for a few minutes. He retrieved it from his left pocket. It was the other burner's number.

"Hey," he answered, knowing it would be one of them.

"Hey?!" Dawn asked. "As in 'Hey, where the heck are you?' That kind of 'hey'?"

That was funny. He giggled a little at the image of her with one hand on a hip, lecturing the phone speaker. "Exactly. Exactly that kind of 'hey.'"

"Are you okay?" she asked, at least a little seriously. "Is that... do I hear road noise? Are you walking?"

"Had to ditch the wheels. Be there in... like, five minutes, tops."

"Things have gotten a little strange here. So the sooner—"

"Yeah, yeah," he said, cutting her off. He ended the call. She could bitch at him in person in a few minutes anyway. Seemed sensible.

52

Bob felt warm and fuzzy.

Beyond that, he felt little at all.

He drained the last few drops of vodka from the pint, shaking the bottle to coax them out before tossing it, overhand, into an already stuffed trash can nearby. It bounced off the mound of refuse and shattered.

That's government for you. People pay taxes; nobody picks up the trash; politicians and senior bureaucrats walk away rich.

Wait... I'm drunk.

I'm a little drunk, anyway. Finished that pint too quickly.

He approached the building at a slow, cautious walk.

He checked the street again, then drew the pistol from his waistband and chambered a shell. He stored it in his right-side pocket. He crossed Sixth Street once more and walked behind the building.

He peeled back the particleboard over the door and crouched to get inside. A few seconds later, he was at the open entrance to the back room.

"Bob!" Dawn sounded relieved to see him.

He turned, and his eyes began to adjust to the lower light

inside, the Coleman lantern not doing much to brighten the place.

He covered half the room, to where the stacks of crates divided it, towering ten feet above them. Behind them, Stone was leaning, seated, against the far wall.

Marcus was perched on a small wooden crate. "You don't look so good," he said. "We took away his chair, figuring he might shut up. But it didn't work."

Dawn approached him, then wrinkled her nose. "Have you... Lord, Bob, your breath... have you been drinking?"

"I had a few shots to calm my nerves. I'm fine." He didn't take his eyes off Stone. "What about you, Eddie? You feeling okay?"

"Let me guess: if you're boozing, something's bothering you. Did you track down Gerald Dahlen and make all of our lives easier?"

"Oh, I tracked him down, sure."

Dawn looked worried. "Did you... you know...?"

He shook his head. "I didn't kill him, no. But I got his security access to our friends. If Smalls left any evidence in Dahlen's network, chances are good we have it now."

"You've got... Wait a second: are you saying you have proof that Dahlen was 'Brighteyes'?" Stone asked incredulously.

"It seems likely, yeah. Doing your job for you."

Bob took a few steps toward the front window and began to peel back the particleboard in the same spot Dawn had loosened earlier. They needed an emergency exit. Dealing with Stone was just one of their worries.

There would be physical descriptions of him from the chase, possibly footage of him at the airport.

He managed to shake off the blurriness for a moment, but the booze was definitely dulling his senses. He felt a little sad, the giddiness beginning to pass.

"Can that wait while we talk?" she asked.

He let the still-attached board snap back into place and turned her way. *Maintain, Bobby. Let her know you're in charge.* "Did you check my perimeter alarms?"

She nodded. "Still intact, assuming you didn't stumble over them. What happened, Bob? Talk to me."

"Just... leave it for now, okay? I'm just concerned. Until I hear the feds have picked up Gerry Dahlen, I'm going to worry. Again, no thanks to your efforts, Eddie."

"If you think any of that is going to get you any credit with Kennedy, you're kidding yourself," Stone scoffed. "Eventually they'll find me. You'd just better hope it's long after your departure."

"He's been like this for hours," Dawn said. "Had Marcus all riled up, told him he was your adopted son."

Bob shot him a foul look. "What a piece of work you are! Gaslighting a child. Jesus Christ. And I thought I was pathetic..."

"Aw, shucks, you poor li'l things." Stone's tone was straight mockery. "Don't worry. The professor set him straight. Besides, I didn't lie entirely, right?"

"You owe me an explanation," Marcus said, rising from his crate. "Why didn't you tell me about my parents?"

"Yeah, Bob, why didn't you?" Stone said.

"It's complicated," Bob told Marcus. "I'll explain it to you when this is over and done, okay?"

"Sure you will, Bob!" Stone said. "You're a pathological liar. You'll say whatever the kid needs to hear to get rid of him. Right?"

Dawn shook her head and looked angry. "How did you ever work with him, Bob? He's a monster."

"He's... yeah, well... that's not far off. There are a few of us out there."

That gave her pause. She leaned in close and lowered her

voice. "I'm serious; tell me what happened so that I can help, okay? It's obvious something really shook you..."

Outside the building, a bottle smashed to the ground. Bob's head swiveled that way for a moment. "We need to go, now!" he hissed. "That was the back line. We take the front door..."

The creak of the front-door boards stopped him in his tracks. Closer, just beyond it, another bottle broke.

"We've got at least one out front as well," Bob whispered. He jogged over to Eddie Stone and grabbed him by the collar with both hands, dragging the sitting man over behind the main crates, next to Marcus. "Marcus, get off that crate and on the floor."

"What are we doing?" Dawn hissed.

"They'll use infrared to locate us. But if we're all seated, they won't be able to tell which is Stone. Otherwise, they'd simply perforate these crates until we were all dead."

"Oh! Oh God... Oh God! We're trapped here!" Dawn gasped, putting the pieces together. "What... what about running out the front door with him, you know, so they don't shoot?"

Bob shook his head quickly. "They have guys who can knock a quarter off your head at fifty paces. They'd shoot, believe me. I just need..." The booze was fogging his mind, distracting him, thinking of Stone and the Team again when he should've been doing SA... "I just need to think a minute..."

In the back entryway, the boards creaked, then tore, a crash of splinters as they were ripped away from the hole covering the back wall.

They collectively peered around the crates and through the door on the other side of the office, in time to see a small object roll into the back room.

53

The two teams of men climbed swiftly and quietly out of the two vans, a block from the old warehouse. The team leader, designated Alpha, looked back at his colleague. "Epsilon, anything yet?"

Epsilon was carrying a hand-sized scanner, staring at the bright screen in the street's relative darkness. "Nothing, chief. The ping was definitely within two blocks of here."

"Give me a FLIR check," he ordered.

Epsilon pulled down his night-vision goggles. "Nothing immediate, no indoor heat signatures."

"Fan out, four of us on each block north and south," Alpha commanded. "We're likely looking for someone in a derelict building, seated but not moving, possibly prone. Radio in as soon as you see anything." He waved a forefinger in a semicircle, and the team began to move out.

They'd covered two blocks when Theta radioed in. "Sir, I've got a group inside the boarded-up warehouse at the end of the north block. I'm counting... four signatures, one seated..."

"Hold position, Theta; we're on our way."

It took the eight men less than a minute to reconvene. The alley behind the building was pitch black, and they kept their goggles down. "Stand by, gentlemen," Alpha said. He keyed his earpiece. "Alpha to Homemaker, come in."

"Go ahead, Alpha."

"We have eyes on a potential target but require a breach, an old warehouse in Congress Heights... please advise."

There was a pause for fifteen seconds. "Alpha, Papa advises to dust everyone who isn't the package, then torch whatever's left. Bring the package home for debrief. Over."

Alpha took the news without pause. He knew the targets likely included a civilian woman and a boy. But he'd participated in much worse in Central America, and any moral scruples that might have stopped them were long gone. "Roger that. Over and out."

He turned back to his team. "Okay, gents, we're going to go in hard. The front is completely boarded over." He gestured at Kappa. "Taylor, you watch the front in case they're flushed that way somehow. We'll use flashbangs through the partially open rear exit, then follow, laying down suppressing fire. Odds are Stone is bound and gagged, so look out for him and don't hit the immobile target. Positions to breach, gentlemen."

They waited thirty seconds for Kappa to make it around the building. Then they moved to either side of the rear exit. Epsilon removed a flashbang from his web belt. He crouched by the door... his shin hitting a hair-thin line of fishing wire. A bottle was balanced on it, behind a weed, along the bottom edge of the wall. It fell immediately, shattering.

"Primitive alarm," Alpha said. "Not much point in subtlety now."

Alpha knew that if Stone was hurt or they returned empty-handed for other reasons, he would pay the price. He reached up and grabbed the edge of the particle board cover, pulling it away from the wall with a mighty rip.

Towards the front of the building, they heard the fainter sound of another bottle shattering.

"Go!" he commanded.

Epsilon rolled the flashbang through the opening.

54

Bob's subconscious was working faster than his alcohol-addled mind could keep up.

He saw the flashbang roll into the next room and was turning well before it blew, grabbing Dawn by the scruff of her coat and Marcus by his collar, dragging them both down and away, averting his tightly shut eyes by trying to bury his face in his shoulder.

Even then, the flash was powerful enough to blast through the doorless entry to the office, blinding him momentarily. He heard the back entry being kicked in as he dragged them both behind the stack of crates.

The particle board gone, men began to stream through and inside. He could hear boots hitting hardwood.

Stone yelled, "They're in cover, back room!"

Bob leaned around the crates. "Gun!" someone screamed. He had to press their one small advantage while the men were in the open. He opened fire wildly with the pistol as the white flash began to fade from his vision.

He heard them scurrying, finding cover positions, likely on either side of the entrance to the back room. He glanced over at Dawn. Her eyes were streaming tears, and she was rubbing them. “I can’t see,” she said.

Marcus had already shaken off the double vision, both eyes watering.

He had to buy them a few seconds. He couldn’t carry her out, and the only other exit, the boarded-over front door, was in line with the open room entry... and in direct line of sight of the men covering them. They wouldn’t make it the fifteen feet, let alone get the two boards down.

He felt a sense of hopelessness kicking in, the booze dulling his reactions, confusing his thought patterns.

There would be multiple team members, if they were there for Stone, heavily armed. Out of instinct more than desire, he leaned around the box and fired two more shots.

“You’re fucked, Bob,” Stone yelled, his hearing damaged by the gunshots. “Better to give in now, make it quick and merciful for them...”

Dawn ground her forearm against her face, trying to expunge the stinging sensation and tears. “I can sort of see, but it’s clouded over...”

He leaned around the box in time to see a team member attempting to creep around the doorjamb. He fired twice, the man ducking out of sight. “We don’t have long to figure out what to do. They’ll figure out the front door is passable quickly enough and then send a team around to flank us...”

He slumped back into cover, his back against the crate. He popped the magazine from the pistol and swiftly replaced it with a spare from his pocket. “If you want, I can surrender. You’re civilians. They’ll probably go easy...”

“Like they did with Marcus’s parents?” Dawn didn’t like the option; that was clear. “Are you crazy?!”

“It’s useless,” Bob said. “We’re pinned down. If we bolt for the front exit, they’ve got us dead to rights, and we certainly won’t survive getting it open. If we stay in cover, they’ll eventually either flank us or just tear the crates to shreds with submachine-gun fire. The only thing stopping that now is the fear of hitting Stone or me hitting them. We're done."

She punched his shoulder with surprising force. "We're NOT done! I'm not done! You have to think of something!"

His eyes danced from side to side as he tried to develop an option, his brain in a fog. "I... I can cover you. You run for the front window, hit it hard with your shoulder to take down the loose particle board. I'll start shooting. By the time I empty the magazine, or they fire back, you should be clear," he muttered.

"I am NOT leaving you here, Bob," she stressed.

"Not an option," Marcus agreed.

"It doesn't matter," he said softly. The ebullient buzz of the booze was gone, the morose reality setting in, a depressing sink. For all his efforts, an innocent man was dead, Gerald Dahlen remained free, and his friends faced imminent peril. "Just go. Leave me to face this."

From the doorway, a pair of torsos leaned into the open and returned fire, bullets chewing through the end of the stack of crates, the smaller one that had been Marcus's seat quickly splintered to ruin.

Dawn stood up behind the stack of crates. "I am NOT going out like that!" she declared.

Then she ran straight backwards towards the covered-over window, grabbing each of their jackets, one in each hand, forcing them along with her, leaving Stone prone on the floor.

Bob almost tripped as he tried to keep up. "JUMP!" she screamed as she threw their combined weight at the particle board over the wide picture window, the rotten wood snapping and collapsing, the small amount of remaining glass beyond it crashing to the ground alongside them.

Bob landed outside. He righted himself and helped pull

Dawn to her feet. He saw a flash of movement to his right, nearer the front door, and swung his leg out in a "coffee grinder" sweep.

His foot caught ankle bone; the moving target upended, a black-clad operative slamming to the ground, back first. On instinct, Bob remained crouching, shifting his weight to his left leg as he leaned over the man and hit him on the side of the chin with a short right cross. The man's eyes rolled around as he lost consciousness.

He rose as the other two sprinted across the road, towards the rented Nissan, Marcus clambering into the back.

Bob turned as he ran, opening fire in time to see a man's head duck away from the hole they'd just created. Dawn opened the driver's side door and climbed in. She pulled splinters from her hand, then punched the ignition button.

Bob opened the passenger door, then paused, looking back across the road. He fired two more rounds at the opening, bracing the gun butt on the car roof, heads ducking back into cover.

"They'll never stop," he said. "Unless I stay and you two go, they'll keep coming for us." He fired at the window again. He gazed at the pistol absently, swaying slightly in place from the combination of drink and fatigue. "Last round. That fits."

"Get in the car, Bob," Dawn demanded sternly. She flicked a look back towards the impromptu exit. A man dressed completely in black fatigues was clambering over the broken frame. He stopped to wake his unconscious friend, pulling the man to his feet.

"There's no point in trying to help me," Bob said dourly. "I'm beyond help."

"We're out of time! GET IN THE CAR!" she barked.

"I'll just hurt you," he said, shaking his head. "I'm a fool."

Dawn looked back. The first man was on his feet, and they were being joined by others. One began to jog towards the road, raising his gun with steady precision. "BOB, FOR THE LOVE OF GOD, GET IN THE FUCKING CAR!" she screamed.

Dawn slapped her hand over her own mouth. "Oh my!" Then she turned back to him. "Get in the car," she said calmly, "… or I'll turn off the engine and stay."

A burst of gunfire rang out, bullets strafing the building beyond them.

She'll stay…

That couldn't happen, he knew. He climbed in and closed the door. Dawn stepped on the gas, the electric vehicle's acceleration surprising her, the wheels peeling rubber as it darted onto the road, a final volley of machine-gun fire missing its mark.

55

In the first half hour of driving, they only spoke once, and briefly.

About ten minutes in, Dawn asked for directions, and Bob just muttered, "Head north, towards Baltimore," without taking his eyes off the road ahead.

"What happened back there at the airport?"

He just shook his head. "The airport wasn't the problem. Dahlen shot a policeman and killed him in the E Street tunnel."

"Oh, shit," Marcus said.

Dawn let it slide. "How...? Why?"

"He was aiming at me." He went silent again.

Twenty more minutes had passed by the time Bob's phone rang. He checked the number.

"Ginny."

"Hey. We... heard what happened at the tunnel. It made the evening news."

"Yeah. Not good."

"No shit," she said. "But... I do have something positive. We extracted Michael's file from the network operating system. It's a recording of Dahlen. It's audio of him speaking with another man."

"What?!" Bob asked, suddenly focused again. "What did he..."

"He was discussing the Tehran mission. He says, 'If the agency ever determines I'm Brighteyes, you and I are both going to jail, if they don't execute us on the spot.'"

You and I...? "Who was the conversation with?" It had to be Krug.

"It's not clear from the recording. You don't hear the other man's voice, and there's no record attached of the number he was calling at the time."

"Can you figure that out somehow?"

"Possibly. Nick was in his network for nearly an hour. By the time they shut it down, he had a lot of material to sift through..."

"Look and listen for any references to the codename Excelsior," Bob suggested. "This is the closest we've ever been."

"Nick said Dahlen got away."

"He did. But it won't help him. There's a reporter at the *Washington Post*, Terry Phillips. I mean, assuming he's still there. He's their expert on the intelligence community and knows some of the background. Get the recording to him tonight."

"You're going to burn him publicly."

"The *Post* will do it for us. But... yeah, basically that's it."

"He's got a shit-ton of money. He might fight it, try to clear himself."

"He can't, and I suspect he won't. If the authorities aren't at his door asking him to surrender his passport tonight pending charges, he'll be on an earlier flight to somewhere without an extradition treaty, once the story comes out. But until then, he has no idea what we have. He's too proud to flee on a chance of exposure."

"This will ruin him," Ginny suggested. "It won't bring Michael back, but..."

"Until the story runs, he's as dangerous as whatever protection hundreds of millions will buy. Even then, he's going to try to find you, because you're a material witness to the recording's authenticity."

"So... it's not over."

"Not yet, no. He'll fight to clear his name. But if he finds you, he'll kill you."

"What are you going to do?"

"We're getting out of town, at least for a few days. If he gets wind of my location, he'll try to use me to get to you. The farther apart we are, the better, for now."

She sniffed a little, and Bob could tell she was crying. "I heard about the policeman. I know it's not going to help right now, but I don't believe that was you..."

"It was Dahlen."

"Thank you for what you've done for Michael. That man dying... that's not your fault, Bob."

He took a sharp intake of breath. "I keep hearing that. But it doesn't ring true. Look... I have to go, Ginny. I'll call you tomorrow, okay?"

"Okay, but—"

He ended the call before she could offer up another platitude or raise the matter of the airport. He didn't feel all right with the officer's death, not even slightly, and he didn't want to explain Krug to the others.

Dawn slowed the car. Ahead, on the right-hand side of the road, sat a motel. The "no" portion of the No Vacancy sign was unlit. "This looks good," she suggested.

Bob studied it for a few moments. "No. Not ideal. Map says there's another in two miles, if we take the exit..."

Dawn glared at him. "That's four places you've said no to already. We're going to wind up in Baltimore before we find anywhere..."

"Just... don't worry about it, okay?" Bob requested. "Just do me a favor and check out the next place..."

She reverted her attention to the road, but clearly wasn't happy.

The next motel was no more suitable, Bob decided. They passed Baltimore, going around the city by staying on I-95 towards Philadelphia. Marcus had been quiet throughout. But after forty minutes of driving, the young man spoke up nervously. "Mr. Singleton..."

"You can probably just go with 'Bob' at this point."

"Mr. Singleton, who were my real parents?"

Bob had tried to keep to himself and minimize questions since leaving the city. He felt trapped; he was responsible for the safe passage of two people he hardly knew, at the same time knowing his decisions had led to another innocent man's death. He felt like a fraud, a Bad Samaritan, offering a hand, then leading the faithful into the wilderness, lost and alone.

"Are you sure you want to know any of that?" he asked. "Your parents – Richie and Janet – they raised you. They loved you. They didn't take you because they were forced or anything. They couldn't conceive on their own; they were starting a new life..."

"I know. I mean, I guess I get all of that," he said. "I don't love them any less, Mr. Singleton, and I miss them so much. But... there was always a separation. From them, from me. And... I mean, I deserve to know. I think every person has a right to know their own parents. Where they came from."

Might as well tell him.

"You remember that story I told you about the mission in Tehran?"

"Of course, yeah."

"You might recall our sniper, Tyler Gaines, was Zeta. He abandoned his own evac to try to rescue Jon Rice."

"The first guy who was shot by the policeman."

"Yeah. Tyler was your father. He was killed trying to save a friend. He made something noble out of an ignoble mission and an ignoble betrayal. He was a good man."

Marcus mulled the information over. Then he said, "And my mom?"

"Susanne, his childhood sweetheart. She died of septic shock after a mistake during surgery to remove her gallbladder. Tyler was overseas at the time and didn't even know she'd gone into the hospital. They were both good people." Bob felt awkward, trying to paint a picture for the boy of a life he'd never know. "They were from Midland, Texas. They didn't have surviving parents or siblings other than Tyler's stepfather, who he couldn't stand. So we found a better option."

"And you arranged for me to—"

"No," Bob said quickly. "Believe it or not, with all the terrible things he's done in his life, you can thank Eddie Stone for that one."

Dawn's befuddlement was obvious. "You cannot be serious?! That man showed empathy towards an orphan?"

"Aren't you the one always reminding me how complicated people can be?" Bob said. "You know, all that stuff about trying to do the right thing? He arranged it right after we got back, before the kill order was issued."

"So... he helped Marcus find a new home... then issued an order to kill his parents!?"

"That was his boss, Andrew Kennedy. Kennedy farmed it out, but something went wrong."

"Eddie Stone was trying to do the right thing!?" Dawn

exclaimed. "He seemed awful. And with everything you've told us..."

"I know, he's a murdering son of a bitch, believe me. He's everything I used to be, with a dose of self-interest on top. But... he's also crazy enough to think he's right most of the time, or doing things for the right reasons. He served two tours in Vietnam, thirty years overseas as a CIA operative and section head."

"I guess," she said. "But when I think of folk like him, it seems all about the power, being addicted to it."

"It is. But that's just part of the persona he's developed. He sees the power as enabling his own goals, which he pretty much always justifies as being righteous in some manner, no matter how shitty the behavior... pardon my language. The bigger the goal, the more power he needs."

"Humph. I guess. Sounds like a recipe for a dangerous individual to me."

"He is that; don't doubt it!" Bob assured her. "His boss is the same way, but with more tact and less principle."

"So... like a politician," Marcus suggested.

Dawn pointed a thumb towards the rear seat. "Bright boy, that one." Her mood changed quickly to serious concentration. "I believe the exit is coming up over the ridge, here..."

The car crested a small hill. Below, exit 74 towards the towns of Fallston, Joppa and Clayton, Maryland, was quiet in the evening, the turn lane empty, a blue-and-white lodging sign indicating a motel a mile away.

They covered half the distance before Dawn turned to Bob. "Well?"

Bob peered out the passenger window, squinting a little to adjust to less-than-perfect visibility. "This will do."

"What was he like?" Marcus asked. "My father, I mean..."

Bob nodded his head a few times, trying to give the question some real thought. "Uh-huh, uh-huh... Yeah... Well... he wasn't a gentle soul, exactly. He wasn't a dick or insensitive or anything, but he was sort of rough-and-tumble. He'd worked on the West Texas oil rigs before joining the Navy to see the world, and, eventually, joining the SEALs. In his late teens, early twenties, he'd been a rodeo bull rider, and an honest-to-goodness cowboy during the summers, roping cattle, running cattle drives, breaking horses."

"It sounds like his life was exciting."

Marcus sounded forlorn, Bob thought. "Restless, mostly. He was into that stuff, but he also didn't mind leaving it behind, travelling the world, experiencing new cultures."

"Meeting new friends and killing interesting people," Dawn interjected bluntly.

It was clear the showdown at the warehouse had embittered her at least a little, Bob thought. "You know, I can understand if you're mad at me..." he suggested.

"I am."

"But I was the one who froze when you needed me, not Marcus."

She looked a little ashamed of that. She glanced over her shoulder quickly and smiled gently at him. "He's right. My apologies. He sounds like a fine man."

"Why did he do it, Mr. Singleton? Why was he a sniper for Team Seven? If he was a good guy, why choose that life?"

It was difficult to explain to a kid, Bob thought. "Things are more complicated when you get older. Things you were certain were true become less certain. Sometimes, we give up on our beliefs and opinions too easily. But most people hang onto them for too long. It's arrogant, because we're easily misled as a species, particularly by people we like and trust, often just because they have bad information, not bad intentions."

"Uh-huh," Dawn muttered dryly.

"We all thought we were vanguards for a better way of

life, Marcus. We figured we were making it possible for people trapped in undemocratic nations to make their own choices. To choose a destiny that would allow them to have the best of what we have here in America."

"That doesn't sound naïve," Dawn said.

"It doesn't," Bob said, "until you consider how complicated that statement is to unpack. How hard it is to get from the worst a society has to the best it can be."

They reached the motel. The lot was nearly empty, just three cars parked in front of a dozen or so units. Next door, a bar's neon sign was lit and its parking lot nearly full.

Dawn parked the SUV next to the motel office.

"At least... I mean... I guess he was trying to do the right thing, to be a good person," Marcus suggested.

"The same as Richie and Janet," Bob added. "Which is why they taught it to you."

The youth began crying again, then wiped away tears with his jacket sleeve. "They gave me so much."

"That they did, son, that they did. Now let's go get a room and get some rest. I figure at this point we deserve it."

56

Gerald Dahlen paced the floor of his palatial bedroom, shoes off, the red-and-gold pile carpet soft under his socked feet, his left leg limping from pain, his left arm in a sling.

The flat-screen TV on the wall had CNN on. It had been showing an artist's renditions of Singleton's face, drawn from a security guard's description, for two hours.

He was the unknown "prime suspect" in the murder of Edson Krug, after all. But the story had made it plain that police thought Krug's employer knew more than he was letting on.

Pacing the carpet was a nervous habit he'd picked up in years of business, to retreat to the safe space and silence so that he could think everything through. It had gotten him out of trouble more than once, with the agency, with the Securities Exchange Commission, with his now ex-wife.

An answer or next option always presented itself.

But this time, nothing was coming to mind.

Despite his private physician removing the slugs without reporting he'd been shot, he'd still spent three hours in the hospital. They'd had to compensate and re-traumatize the woman he'd taken hostage, as well, to ensure she'd shut up.

When he got home, he'd spent another two hours talking to police, trying to assuage their vitriol that he would offer no information of value on Krug.

It was only by the good fortune of the hangar being a new building, and the last on the airport property, that they'd avoided the fight behind it being caught on a security camera or phone.

But the police weren't satisfied; they wanted to interview him further the following morning. His idiot lawyer thought it was a good idea, to make it clear right off the top that he couldn't help them.

Dahlen supposed they would work the case until they could blame him somehow.

The day had gone from bad to worse. On arriving home, he'd been informed that his computer network and home security had been breached. They had no idea what might have been seen or taken from the system.

And then there was the matter of the dead cop.

He forced his way into the situation.

He distracted an armed man holding a hostage. He doesn't deserve pity; he deserves contempt for being bad at his job.

But he could fix everything. He just didn't know how. Yet.

His phone rang. He looked down at the number, ready to hit "ignore."

It was a call he couldn't ghost.

"Andrew! Hearing from you again so soon! And you have my new number already, even though it's... less than two hours old. What a surprise!"

The painkillers were at least making his attempt to sound charming and carefree a less absurd proposition.

"I think we can skip the pleasantries tonight, Gerald. I thought I'd call and let you know I'll be cancelling your company's personnel supply contract with the Special Activities Center first thing in the morning."

"What?" It was a bolt from the blue, which caught him flat-footed. The contract was worth forty million dollars in future business, at a minimum. "You can't do that!"

"I can and I will."

No, no, no, no. This cannot happen. I won't allow it. "Andrew, I have shareholders, a board to answer to. You can't flush a fifth of our value down the toilet over... what? Today?"

"The incident at the airport? Hardly. I hear the man who died used to be one of ours..."

"He was. But if not..."

"Tomorrow's news, Gerald. The *Post* is set to report that you were paid by a foreign lobbyist to leak the time and place of Tehran. As you're aware, I'll have an obligation at that point to ask the Justice Department and Homeland Security to consider federal charges against you for espionage. Don't even think about trying to leave the country. We'll be keeping an eye out."

Dahlen could feel his world falling in. He steeled himself. "I'll fight it, of course. Not just the ridiculous charge, which you can never prove, but the contract as well. And I'll win."

Kennedy sounded unconvinced. "We shall see. We have a recording; we have a material witness from the day it was recorded willing to endorse it. Good night, Gerry, although it seems unlikely to be good given the circumstances."

He ended the call.

Dahlen stared at the phone for a moment, dumbstruck.

A recording? What on earth could that mean? He'd never, to his knowledge, discussed Tehran outside of his home other than during the interrogation of...

Michael Smalls.

He'd lied. He had something that was incriminating. He'd been willing to die rather than give it up.

Or he knew he was dead either way. Damn it.

They'd still been unable to track down Smalls's wife when Singleton arrived.

Somehow, he'd found her.

Singleton was a veteran intelligence officer. If she'd gone to ground, he might be the only person who knew where she was hiding.

Dahlen knew he had to find her. If his men couldn't find her, he needed to find Singleton, capture and interrogate him, then kill the witness once Singleton disclosed her location. A recording? If it was just audio, it could be suppressed, or at least have its evidentiary value minimized... as long as the witness was dead.

But first, he needed to leave before they arrived in the morning to arrest him.

The airport would be out of the question, as would his private jet; they'd have flagged his information in the system, and it would be considered an attempt to avoid prosecution.

He hit speed dial on his phone. "Gustav, have the chopper fueled up and ready to go in one hour. We need to get out of town for a while."

57

They hadn't eaten in hours.

There was a fast-food joint just down the access road, a few hundred yards past the motel. Dawn volunteered because she was hungry, Marcus was starving, and Bob seemed indifferent.

She walked back to the room carrying two brown paper sacks, with midnight approaching as she passed the bar next door.

It seemed popular with locals; it was still a hive of activity despite the late hour. A man walked out, staggering slightly, music and voices blaring out the front door for a brief moment before it swung closed.

When she reached the room, Marcus was sitting on the end of the bed, watching a talk show. She passed him a bag. "One giant burger, extra cheese, fries and an apple pie."

The youth looked up and said a silent prayer of thanks. "You have no idea how much I appreciate this. I'm starving."

"Bob's had us moving pretty much nonstop," she said. Then she frowned. He wasn't anywhere in sight, and the bathroom door was open. "Where'd he go, anyhow?"

"He walked out right after you did. He said he had something to take care of."

"Uh-huh." After the incident at the warehouse, she had a good idea of what. Dawn had been working with addicts for years at the clinic. "Stay here, okay? I'm just going to make sure he doesn't need a hand."

She set the bag down on the end of the chest of drawers, a foot from the TV.

"Is he okay?" Marcus asked, sensing her unease.

"Oh... I imagine he'll be fine. Don't worry about Bob; he's gotten us this far, right? Not that I have any idea where we are or where we're going. But... details."

She left the room and closed the door behind her. It was quiet, just the wind to greet her and the faint strains of the jukebox from the adjacent business.

Her flats crunched on the lightly graveled dirt lot as she made her way across the length of the parking lot to the lounge.

Dawn pushed the door open. She was greeted by ear-pounding music, the stereo jacked way up to account for the two dozen or so drinkers, blaring Alan Jackson's "Chattahoochee."

A few turned on noticing a new arrival, their eyes following her as she crossed the room to the bar. The regulars seemed uneasy, at best. She smiled politely, hoping it was just an unfamiliar face that had set them on edge.

"Good evening," she said to a man drinking at the bar, giving him a polite nod.

He went back to his beer without comment.

Ooo-kay then.

At the far end of the bar, where it curved into a narrow C shape near the bathroom doors, Bob was hunched over the polished wood countertop. He had a near-empty glass of draft beer in front of him, as well as an empty shot glass.

She took the stool next to him.

"Couldn't resist lecturing me, I guess," he muttered. "Had to come say something. Remind me how irresponsible I am."

She shrugged. "Something like that. I was going to go for a less judgmental approach, remind you that there are people who care about you, that worry isn't the same as antipathy. But if judgment is the narrative that'll work for you..."

"Has it ever?" He drained the beer. "Barkeep!" He held up the glass. "Hit me again."

"I was only gone for twenty minutes. Do you mind if I ask...?"

"This would be number four, plus a few shots. Are you asking me if I'm hammered? Because my answer to that would be an unequivocal 'not yet.'"

"You know you can't crawl into a bottle of booze to solve your problems, though. Am I correct?"

"If I was trying to solve my problems, you might be. But you've missed the other option."

"Which is?"

"My problems aren't solvable. Too many years, too many faces. Too many lives lost or taken, my finger on the trigger too many times. There's a policeman back in DC who was just doing his job. He probably had a family, kids, friends..."

"It's not your—"

He didn't let her finish. "But I thought it wise to lure Gerry Dahlen into the E Street Tunnel, a crowded and enclosed space, to avoid a police chopper." He was shaking his head. "I'm such an asshole."

"Bob... years of drink, it causes depression..."

She was about to put a consoling hand on his shoulder, but he turned her way first, irritated. "Why?! Why do you continually insist on trying to help me, Nurse Dawn? What part of 'I can't be fixed' isn't getting through to you?"

The bartender came over with a fresh glass of draft. "Miss?" he asked.

Dawn blushed a little, she was sure. "Miss" made her feel young. "I'm okay, thank you."

He pointed to the sign behind the bar that read No Loitering, but looked sheepish about doing so. "Just so you understand, it's policy that customers need to make a purchase to stick around. If I make an exception" – he gestured over his shoulder – "one of these idiots will throw it in my face for months."

"I get it," she said. "I'll have a cup of... do you have tea?"

"Best green tea Lipton ever stuck in a bag."

"That'll do, sir, thank you."

He nodded and left to make her drink.

"Let me guess: you don't drink alcohol," Bob said.

"Oh... an occasional glass of wine with my friends. But mostly... no. When you work with people using it to ruin their livers, it becomes easier to avoid temptation. Or self-medication, in some folks' cases."

He took a swallow of beer, then wiped residue from his lip stubble with the back of his hand. "Is this the part where you tell me how many lives I've changed and all the people who count on me? The part where George Bailey discovers life is wonderful and not the egregious piece of shit that it actually is?"

She frowned and leaned a forearm on the counter, studying him. "Bob, have you ever spoken with any of the other clients at the clinic?"

"Clients? You mean bums, right? Your word, remember."

"Whatever. Answer the question."

"Not really. I've seen a few out on the street."

"Do you know what a nurse or secretary at that clinic makes for a living? I can guarantee you, it's not much."

"But they do it out of love?" Bob said, his expression bordering on contempt.

"No. No, they do it out of fear. They do it – I do it – because the West Loop is my community, the place I live, where my friends live, where a lot of good people live. And when one part of that community hurts, it affects everyone. And on some level, each one of us figures if we just let that go – if no one is the person who at least tries to do the right thing – everything eventually falls apart."

"I don't have a community," he said, "and I've never helped anyone."

"If you say it enough, I guess it must be true."

"It is. I'm a menace. I hurt people."

"Also true. You sure put a beating on those boys at that corner store..."

"There! You see? My point exactly. One of those kids almost lost his hand..."

"And the kid behind the counter almost lost his life. He would have, is my guess, if you hadn't saved him. Bob, when on earth are you going to stop being terrified of the man you were, and start recognizing the man you are?"

He pointed his half-empty draft glass at the television behind the bar. A news report was showing a mugshot of the dead officer. The volume was down or inaudible over the rest of the bar. Underneath the photo it read "Sgt. Edward Purcell, 48." "Tell that to his loved ones! Tell that to the people who'll never be able to talk to him again, never hug him again..."

"Did you shoot that man?"

"No... Dahlen shot him. But he was aiming at me..."

"And did you ask that man to take up a job in a dangerous occupation, where any shift on the street could prove fatal?"

"No, but—"

"But nothing! How many more lives would this Dahlen

character be responsible for ending if he isn't dealt with? How many more families like Marcus's would be torn apart by his greed and selfishness?"

"Are you arguing acceptable losses with me?" he asked. "You?"

"I'm telling you not to bear the consequences of other people's choices. Just because you could stop something bad from happening doesn't mean you always will."

"Dawn..."

"Just... listen, okay? Last winter, at the clinic, we had this guy come in regularly, Old Fergus. He wasn't really that old, but he looked ancient and decrepit after years on the street. I tried to get him to go to the shelter when the snow came, because he wasn't taking care of himself. And they held a spot for him for weeks. But eventually, they had to give it to someone else. And sure enough, a few weeks later, they found Fergus not far from your old flop on North Peoria, froze to death."

"That's... I mean, it's shitty, but I don't see..."

"Do you think I blame myself for his death, Bob? I don't doubt I could have done more. We all can, all the time. But sometimes life gets in the way. There were half a dozen like him that week and the week after. And all of them, other than Fergus, made it through a brutal winter because of the folks at the clinic guiding them towards the right decisions."

"And that's good."

"It is. But we can't save everyone. We do what we can, Bob, not what we'd like."

"So you just... what, keep trying, but never really fix anything?"

"Welcome to real life. I try to do the right thing all the time. At least that way when I fail, I can still look myself in the mirror instead of wallowing in self-pity and the narcissistic notion that only I can save the world... or worse, that no one deserves saving but myself."

"My teammates..."

"You tried to save them... and you failed. But you didn't make their decisions for them, and you didn't betray them. That was your old associate Mr. Dahlen. You know who you did save? Me, Bob. You saved my life. And Marcus's life. And then we drove for ten hours so that you could save Ginny Smalls, too."

She got up from the stool as the barkeep arrived with her tea. "Can I get that in a go cup?" she asked.

The bartender snorted derisively but turned around to fetch some Styrofoam.

"I'm going to go back and eat my now-cold burger," she said. "When you're all done drowning in your own self-importance, think about where I would be – where that boy would be – if you'd quit before you even started. Think about how many more people you get a chance to do right by... but only if you don't quit now."

She got up and headed for the door, leaving him to nurse the glass of draft. There wasn't much else to be said.

She crossed the quiet parking lot, hoping it had had some effect. If he didn't come around?

We'll cross that bridge when we come to it, she told herself.

When she got back to the room, Marcus had already finished his enormous burger and the fries and the apple pie. Dawn squinted at him as he bunched up the wrapper and tossed it, basketball style, into the trash. "Did you bother inhaling while you ate, or...?"

"I was STARVING," he insisted. "But I left yours, so there's that..." He nodded towards the door. "Is Bob..."

"We'll see," she said. "He's just thinking some things over, is all." She walked over to the bureau and picked up the brown paper bag.

Behind her, a key scratched the lock.

A moment later, Bob opened the door.

He looked sheepish, but gestured towards the bag. "Got any spare fries?"

Dawn smiled and nodded. She didn't mind sharing.

58

Bob woke early, sunbeams slipping through gaps in the curtains, tracing paths to the second double bed. It was seven o'clock, and the others were still sleeping.

He showered and shaved, the face in the mirror still carrying the weight of self-doubt.

But he knew what they had to do.

She was right, of course. He'd fallen into the trap of self-pity, of thinking he was doing the world a favor by running away from his past.

Away from Maggie.

But there were plenty of Ginny Smalls out there, plenty of kids like Marcus.

He'd seen the files before he left, or what Nicky Velasco could access, at least.

He'd learned of the damage the agency and Team Seven had wrought over two decades. It had been true then, and it was true now.

Running away wasn't helping to fix any of it.

He got dressed. By the time he left the bathroom, the others were awake, and Dawn had the television news on.

"You need to catch this," she said, motioning for him to come and watch. "I take it this is the individual in question?"

The photo was of Gerald Dahlen at a society function. Under it, the scrawling headline read "Report claims contractor sold secrets."

"Your newspaper friend went right to work," she said.

"I called him from the bar last night, before you decided to tag along," Bob said. "We had a nice chat."

"You missed some of the story while you were in the bathroom. They said he's expected to be charged with working as an unregistered foreign agent, espionage and possibly treason."

The anchor was wrapping up the short story. "Officials with the Justice Department intend to question Dahlen as soon as possible. Sources have told WJLA News that his whereabouts are presently unknown, but that Dahlen will likely not be allowed to leave the country pending charges."

"Dude is going to jail," Marcus said. "I guess this means we win."

Bob was less sure. "I'll believe it when he's behind bars – which, given the dirt he likely has on Team Seven and its overseers, isn't likely to happen."

"You think he'll cut some sort of deal?" Dawn asked.

"I think if it's clear he's going down, he'll meet a mysterious 'accident' en route. That or they let him skip, knowing he can't come home. But it doesn't matter. As long as he still hasn't been convicted of a crime or cut off financially, we have a target on our backs."

Marcus was puzzled. "But... why? They have evidence. They have the recording..."

"They have a recording given to them anonymously, with no sourcing, no chain of evidence, no warrant. At the very least, they'll need Ginny to testify to its authenticity. As long as she's alive, Dahlen won't quit trying to find her. Given my colleague Nick's resourcefulness, he probably won't be able to, not any time soon. But he knows we *did* find her, or we wouldn't have Smalls's evidence."

"He'll assume you could lead him to her," Dawn said.

"Once again, this is the part where I tell you both it'll be safer to be far away from me," Bob said. "Even if he's eventually behind bars, he has people on the outside. The charges and hearings could take months."

Dawn turned off the TV. "What are you suggesting, Bob?"

"I need to find him before he finds us. He'll be moving heaven and earth to pull it off."

"Bob..." Dawn sighed.

"I know, I know, 'Don't blaspheme.'"

"I was going to say, 'Maybe it's time to leave this to the authorities.'"

"I don't have to kill him," Bob said. "I can turn him in."

"But if they can't find him..."

"... then they're looking in the wrong place." Bob took out his phone. "When I questioned Eddie Stone, he mentioned they were watching Dahlen's properties. But he didn't mention the resort."

"Resort?" Marcus asked. "Like..."

"Back in the day, all of the senior officers at the SAC had getaway spots. Kennedy's was in Jackson Hole, Wyoming. Dahlen's was a resort his father owned, on the Finger Lakes in upstate New York, about thirty-five miles south of Ithaca."

Dawn looked doubtful. "That was a decade ago. Why would he hold onto it when he has so much money now?"

"Why get rid of it? He certainly didn't need the cash from a sale. When I was checking up on his company the other day, it mentioned a home in California, a private hangar.

Stone mentioned those as well, as locations they had under watch…"

"But not the resort," Marcus said.

"He needs a place to operate from unimpeded."

"So… we're going to upstate New York…"

"I'm going to upstate New York. You two are staying right here."

Dawn wagged a finger his way. "Oh no, uh-uh! We've been over this…"

"His cover as 'Brighteyes' is blown. He also knows what the leak was and who leaked it. You two will no longer be priorities. That means it's better to stay away."

The nurse sighed. "Man… you just do not get it, do you? We are in this together!"

"It's not safe. If I need help, I can ask Al."

Dawn's hand shot up to her mouth in shock. "Oh! Oh Lord! I forgot! Professor Temple was going to come and look for us in DC. He called while you were going after Dahlen."

She crossed her fingers behind her back as she said it. It was better if Bob didn't know she'd doubted him and had made the call.

Bob dialed Temple's phone frantically. If he'd walked in on Team Seven's operation at the warehouse, there was no telling the danger he was in.

Temple answered on one ring. "Where the HELL are you!? Are you aware that things are busting loose here?"

"Sorry, bud. We had some unwelcome arrivals in DC and had to get out of Dodge. I take it you got out of Congress Heights okay and saw the news?"

"I did, though the place was crawling with Metro police. Did you see the part where Gerry Dahlen disappeared overnight? Feds haven't found him yet."

"Cast your mind back," Bob suggested. "Back in the day,

his old man had a resort in Ithaca, not far from your little cabin. In the Seneca Falls area."

"He needs a base of operations, and he has no one to turn to," Temple conceded. "You might be right."

"We need to head up there."

"Or you could just turn him in, tell the feds where you think he's hiding."

Bob lowered his voice and strolled away from Dawn and Marcus, out of easy listening range. "You think that will settle anything? Even if he doesn't beat the charges, he has enormous resources."

"True."

"You know where this is headed," Bob said.

"I do. It sounds like you do, too. Just remember when it comes time to choose between him or you, that you make the right call. He who..."

"... hesitates is lost. Yeah. Never gets old, that one."

"You never really learned it. I'll meet you there," the professor suggested. "You can stay at my place."

"That's not necessary."

"But it is. We go back too far for me to turn my back on this now. And besides... you need me to let you in. Front door lock sticks like a bugger."

He'd have made any excuse to help, Bob figured. "You ever get tired of telling me what to do?"

"I do not," Temple said. "Besides, I may not be as young as I was, but I'll be more help than the two you have with you now."

"They're coming, too," Bob said. "I know, just... don't ask! She's like a pit bull in a nurse's smock sometimes. At worst, you can keep them occupied while I take care of business. We're driving, so we won't need it until tomorrow, assuming I'm not wrong and he doesn't get picked up somewhere in DC today."

"I needed a break from city life anyway," Temple said. "I'll fly up this morning."

"Semper fi, Sarge."

"Semper fi, Bobby."

He ended the call. "We're going to New York, I guess."

Dawn was nodding, hands on both hips. "Uh-huh. A 'pit bull in a nurse's smock'?!"

59

Andrew Kennedy swung his driver through the tiny white golf ball. He watched it soar off the ninth tee box, a slice causing it to curve away from the verdant green of the fairway.

It bounced once a foot before the rough, then settled in the first cut of longer grass.

It was just past ten in the morning, dew still settled on the emerald blanket that sprawled out ahead of him.

"Damn it. Must be sliding my hips left, opening up the club face," he muttered.

"Or maybe you're just never going to play on the PGA Tour," a familiar voice intoned.

He turned to hand his caddy his club. A few feet beyond them, Stone had seemingly appeared from nowhere, seated on the bench by the ball washer.

How does he do that? "It's not about the score, it's about getting better," he said indignantly. "And networking."

Stone rose to his feet and put his hands in his pockets. "It's a little chilly for golf, isn't it? And you're not networking, playing by your lonesome."

"It's also a good place to clear my head and see the big picture," Kennedy said. "Thank you, Tom. Go find my ball, and I'll meet you on the fairway in a minute or so."

The caddy complied, hefting Kennedy's bag as he strode down the fairway, the golf cart left behind for his employer.

"Now..." Kennedy said, fishing a pack of Camels from his pocket and lighting one. "What, pray tell, brings you out this morning?"

"Six hours, Andrew? On top of the four hours Singleton had me tied up? That's not a debrief, it's death by slow torture."

Kennedy held up both hands in mock surrender. "I'll make sure they take it easier on you the next time a washed-up spy gets the drop on you and ruins our operation. Okay?"

"Very funny. Did you catch the morning news or CNN, by any chance?"

"I did. It was a decent likeness of Singleton. They made him look like the actor from *Better Call Saul*..."

"Bob Odenkirk," Kennedy said. "I would've said more Bruce Campbell, the *Burn Notice* guy."

"Yeah! Interesting take."

"Not really," Kennedy said. "Eddie... you know I have all sorts of time for shooting the breeze with you, because we've been doing it for decades. But... like I said, I came out here to clear my mind. The morning news?"

"Hmm? Oh... yeah. What do you want me to do with it? I could call Metro Police and tip them Bob's identity."

Kennedy thought about it for a moment. "Too many potential complications. Bob's sitting on a wealth of information about the Strategic Activities Center, some of the things we've had to do, some of the people we've employed. And from what I hear, all they have is the description. Dahlen's driver isn't talking either, so... better to just find Singleton and kill him."

"That's proven difficult up until now."

Kennedy shrugged. "He was well trained. Score one for preparedness. It doesn't change the fact that he knows far too much to be running around free... or perhaps talking to the *Post*."

"True enough."

"He had no compunction, obviously, about leaking Dahlen's audio."

Stone looked skeptical. "Are you sure we need to handle this? We've got a lot of friends in local law enforcement. If they pick him up, we could always arrange an accident while he's inside. An Epstein, perhaps."

"Loose lips, Eddie, loose lips... Just play it straight for now. Track him down and take him out." Down the fairway, his caddy was standing patiently in the rough. Kennedy gave him a small wave to let him know he wasn't forgotten.

A twosome with a cart pulled up behind the tee box.

"I have to play on or let them play through," Kennedy said. "Anything else?"

"Dahlen. What about him?"

"He's in the wind, sure, but he's not going anywhere. Every port of entry has his details, and his private jet is grounded. We've managed to freeze most of his domestic accounts already..."

"Which means fuck all," Stone said. "I'm sure he's got money squirrelled away in every tax haven on the planet."

"True, but the mobility issue is important. We've tried all his properties?"

"We have. We know he left Leesburg field in his chopper yesterday, but no flight plan was filed. We have a hit from its radio beacon just outside Allentown, Pennsylvania, but nothing after that."

"What about his old man?"

Stone's brow furrowed. "He's been dead for nine years, Andrew."

"But he still has holdings, through the family foundation. As I recall, he had a resort in the Catskills, or something like that – one of those swanky lakeside joints the Jews from Brooklyn used to go ape for back in the day."

"It got past us." Stone sounded irritated with himself. He checked his watch quickly. "I have a conference call I need to take in a half hour. I can't miss it."

Kennedy nodded towards the fairway, then strolled over to the electric cart and settled into the driver's seat, his expanding waistline just fitting behind the wheel. "That's why we're a team, Eddie. Check the place out. Send someone from Buffalo or New York to see if it's viable. Get back to me when we have something."

He stepped on the accelerator, leaving Stone behind on the tee box.

60

They were just past Philadelphia, a few hours into the new day. Marcus had once again fallen asleep on the back seat.

Bob was driving, which he hadn't done much in ten years. It felt liberating, covering a long distance at speed, the low rumble of the road under them, the radio on gently. The streets of Chicago's West Loop had become a familiar home, but it had been a small piece of the world where little seemed to change.

The NPR show was playing Chicago blues, which suited Bob just fine. It had run through guitar-laden tracks by Luther Allison, Otis Rush; Andrew "Big" Brown had just finished an up-tempo shuffle.

Dawn looked up from the map she'd been studying. "Hmm," she said, eyeing the radio.

"What? You don't like blues?"

She sighed a little and shrugged. "Not so much. My father loved it. I mean, I get it... life's hard sometimes, and people like simple, catchy songs. I figure that playlist is a little... well..."

"What?"

"I mean... I thought you boys liked all that Stevie Ray Vaughan and Allman Brothers and such..."

"Many do. Most of them didn't grow up in Chicago," Bob reasoned. "I was sneaking into Buddy Guy's club when I was seventeen. A little Jimmy Johnson, some Jimmy Burns..."

She went back to studying the map. "Give me some Beyonce any time..." Her finger traced the map. "Bob... if I'm getting this right, Professor Temple's cabin is nearly an hour away from where Dahlen's resort is located."

"Yep."

"So... when you agreed to us helping... you were really planning to keep us at arm's length, far away from any problems."

The tone suggested she didn't approve.

"I'm not babying you, Nurse Dawn. But you've seen the kind of people we're facing. If you're with Al, I know someone has your back. When I'm working on Dahlen—"

"And by 'working,' you mean extracting a confession and leaving him for the authorities."

"Of course," he said, probably too quickly. "Anyway... getting close to him isn't going to be easy. One will have a much easier time than two or three. Even if you come along and wait somewhere, you're isolated and without protection. At least at Al's, you have someone looking out for you."

"Well, okay, I guess." But she didn't sound as if it was okay.

In the back seat, Marcus began to snore loudly.

"Oh Lord..." Dawn muttered. "A few hours of that will be fun."

"How angry is he at me?" Bob asked. "The fact that I didn't tell him about Richie and Janet..."

"He's hurt. We talked a little before you disappeared at the motel. It was sort of a sucker punch, Bob. He's always felt like an outsider in his own home, and then someone comes along and takes away the only two people who loved him... and then he begins to doubt whether even *that* was true."

"They loved him, Dawn, believe me. I remember when they took him in as an infant."

"Well, I know that, and you know that. But put yourself into that boy's shoes. His whole world has collapsed in a matter of four days."

Bob wasn't sure how to broach the idea that had been fomenting since DC. "When this is all done, he still has nine months left before he turns eighteen."

"Uh-huh."

"We'll need to find him somewhere to go."

"Yes."

"Or... if someone who cared about him was willing to take him in until then, at least, they could help him, offer him some guidance. You've heard him talk about cars and engines and stuff. A degree in mechanical engineering, if the financing could be arranged... that would see him into adulthood in pretty good stead."

"Yeah," she said, "but he has no family. Where are we going to find someone who..." She stopped talking. Bob had taken his eyes off the highway and was staring at her pointedly. "What? Oh... oh, no! I've been a mother once already. I did my time." She softened her tone slightly. "It didn't turn out so well."

"Really?" Bob said, turning his attention back to the road. "After everything you told me about not giving up and not taking the blame for the choices of others?"

"Oh, I know I'm not to blame for Maurice's death. But... I know you know what it's like to lose a loved one, because of your fiancée. Try to imagine what it's like to lose your own child. I've never felt so empty, Bob. Never. And that emptiness, that hole, it's still inside me. It's buried a little deeper, because if it was like the days after it happened, I wouldn't be able to function. But it's there, and every day it tries to drag me down again."

"Yeah..."

She glanced sideways. He had a sickly look, forlorn. He took one hand off the wheel to tug at the pale blue scrunchy around his wrist. "What? This is the second time I've talked about my boy that you've looked real... well, it's hard to pin down, Bob. I'd say hurt. You looked real hurt, both times."

"It was unfair, what happened to you..."

"Yeah... but I noticed both times, you pulled on that scrunchy you've got around your wrist, there. I've been a caregiver for some time, Bob. I know a coping mechanism when I see one, a habit. Why? What's that about? Why does Maurice's death set it off?"

He stared ahead bleakly, as if the road weren't there. "Yeah..." he said finally, sighing slightly. "Yeah. Well... Maggie gave me one of these, sort of like this one, same color... That was a week before she died. I had it... kept it all these years... until a few weeks ago, when the elastic must've given out. I was probably drunk at the time, and I lost it. And it was the last thing she gave me."

He was talking around the point, she knew. "But that's not the same one, so... I don't understand, Bob. What's so—?"

"She bought herself a pink one. She said she figured when she gave birth to our baby, whichever one of us had the right color got to pick the name."

Dawn's mouth hung open in shock. It had been right in front of her the whole time. He hadn't said it, but the pieces were there, the jagged memories, bitter remnants that had torn his soul from his body and left him adrift. "She was pregnant when she died."

He nodded, but didn't elaborate. Instead, he breathed in sharply through both nostrils, tilting his head back slightly, warding off any desire to cry. He held it in, burying it as best he could.

"Bob..."

"It's the past," he said. He looked down at the scrunchy. Then he took his hands off the wheel for a moment and removed it, tossing it into the door's map pocket, to his left. "Maybe it's better if I just let it go."

She put a hand on his. "Never let them go, Bob. Never. The pain? Sure. That's always there. But the memories of who she was, who you were together? That's everything that makes this life worth living. Don't ever let that go. I do not believe she would want that for you, Bob. I believe she loved you, and... I don't know; I don't know why she left you, any more than I know why Maurice disobeyed me and went out with his troublemaker friend again. But I do know that you cannot let pain define you. You are owed more than that in this life. We all are."

He nodded briefly, tersely. "I'll... yeah. I'll think on it, okay? But you have to think about Marcus."

"I have. And... Okay, I admit, I'm also having trouble letting go. And that's what it feels like."

"So... you don't object to looking out for him. You're afraid of losing Maurice each day that you see him... or the possibility of losing someone else you care about. About not being enough to keep him safe forever."

She bowed her head slightly, rubbing her hands together nervously. "Yeah. Yeah, I guess. And I have responsibilities, a job, assuming they take me back after this."

"You had those when your son was alive, too. I bet you managed just fine. I bet you manage at most things just fine."

He caught the hint of a smile.

"You know," she said, "if you were a few years younger and not a trained killer on the run from the government..."

Bob nodded a few times. “Are you flirting with me, Nurse Dawn?”

“Nope. You’re my patient, and that would be unprofessional. Plus… you’re kind of pasty and tall and not my type.”

“Gee. Thanks.”

She punched him gently on the upper arm. “You know what I mean, you big jerk. Still… I’m happy you stumbled into our clinic, Bob. All of this – everything that’s happened since Marcus showed up in Chicago – I wouldn’t wish it on anyone, including the three of us. But the fact that you’re helping, doing good, not just huddled in an alley somewhere, giving up? That makes me a little happy, yeah.”

Bob couldn’t help blushing a little. It had been a long time since anyone really cared that much, or that he felt deserving enough to accept it.

He still wasn’t sure about that part.

“Maybe we can talk about what to do with Marcus later, then.” He wanted to leave the door open for her. The boy needed someone like Dawn, with a good heart and the self-discipline to do the right thing.

“Maybe,” she said. “We’ll see when we get there.”

61

ITHACA, NEW YORK

The resort conference center had been mothballed for two years.

It was a sterile, drab, concrete building on the edge of the lakefront property, converted from a 1960s office and retail space. The nearest homes were two miles away, acres of trees its only neighbors.

When they'd arrived a day earlier, the chopper touching down on the center's landing pad by Cayuga Lake, Dahlen had made getting the building up and running his small support team's first priority.

It hadn't been used since being shuttered for rentals two years earlier, but the communications suite still contained enough recent technology to let him touch base with his worldwide operations.

By the evening, a larger support team had flown to Syracuse, then driven down to the resort nestled on the southern tip of the lake. He had twelve men, along with Gustav – although his shabby performance at the airport lent serious doubt to his value, his long military and agency record notwithstanding.

It would have to do, he thought as he stared out the sloped floor-to-ceiling windows of the second-floor lounge. It had the best views and the nicest environment, so he'd had the office desk from the first floor moved there, his computer set up so that he could look out onto the lake.

So much work. So much effort and time. So much money. All of it facing imminent destruction because of Bob Singleton.

And because of his own choices, Dahlen knew.

He removed the sling around his wounded arm. The bullet was gone; the damage stitched. The pain of moving it was a small price to pay to remind himself not to allow it to happen again.

He had no guilt over his actions because he knew they were justifiable. He knew the services Critical Safety provided, the trained personnel, were essential to national security and foreign military operations. Yes, he had grown fat off the spoils of war. But at the same time, his company had saved civilians, ended conflicts before many thousands more were injured, helped topple evil regimes.

Surely, all of that is more than enough payback for Tehran?

He turned pensively away from the window and looked back across the vast room. A life-sized oil-on-canvas portrait of his late father, ensconced in a library wingback chair, hung from the far wall.

Kenneth the Great. Even in the place he loved most, his expression was dour and cold. He wouldn't have thought twice about taking the Russian-American fixer's money to tip the Iranians. *Twenty million to prevent one scientist from moving to America. Who wouldn't have made that deal?*

The Iranians had betrayed him, of course. They'd promised they wouldn't burn Team Seven or take retribution after the mission's failure. But they'd arranged for him to pay off a second informer, Excelsior, for operational details nonetheless, details that Dahlen – barely involved with the agency by then – couldn't access on his own.

Now the men's fates were tied, he believed. If he was going to go down, Excelsior was potential leverage, or someone who could be blamed. Perhaps, more immediately, he was a tool that could be employed to finally deal with Singleton.

His personal secretary ascended the top step of the broad, carpeted staircase that curved down to the first floor. "Sir, the video conference call is ready for you."

"Thank you, Rene, I'll take it up here."

"Of course, sir."

He wandered over to the far wall forty feet away. The monitor was an older plasma model, but high-definition nonetheless, and nearly eighty inches wide. It flared to life just before he reached it. He glanced over his shoulder to the bar adjacent to the stairs, where Rene was operating a remote control, then returned his gaze to the screen.

An image sprang to life. It was a man, based on the shorter hair and frame. But his features were obscured in shadow, a dark room barely lit so that Dahlen could make out one edge of his head and torso.

"It's been a long time, Excelsior."

"Not long enough." The voice was disguised by a scrambler.

"Isn't this all a little cloak-and-dagger, given that I know who you are?"

"Perhaps. But if you're recording this to use against me in some manner, well… it's one less piece of evidence now."

"Hmmm… I suspect with modern technology, they could figure out a way to identify you, nonetheless. Still… I can't say I blame you."

"What do you want? I've done everything you've asked of

me so far. The deal was if I helped you with Singleton, my name would never cross your lips."

"And I intend to stick to that," Dahlen lied. "Still, I'd be more inclined to place faith in your efforts if you took care of him for me."

"Do your own dirty work."

"Did you see the news this morning?"

"I did. You're in a lot of trouble."

"Kennedy knows you're around. Even if my lawyers can extract me from all of this, they'll question me about you."

"I imagine they will. Will they go black on it, though? I can't see them waterboarding a guy facing federal prison time already. Bad for publicity. And if they don't go that far, you have no reason to break our deal. Unless you're naive enough to think they'd honor any agreement they cut over getting both of us."

"Don't worry about me," Dahlen insisted. "In case you haven't noticed, I'm the one of us who parlayed Tehran into greatness. I've built my company into a business leader that will soon top a billion dollars in valuation." He began to pace from side to side, holding in his irritation at having to deal with such a lesser pawn of a man.

"My private shareholders are some of the richest men in America. I hope to be at the helm long enough that my wealth eclipses that of my father. I'm not going to let a broken, blunt instrument with a Good Samaritan complex ruin it. If you're tipped to his presence, I want to know about it the second it enters your right ear and begins to ping around your undersized brain. I would hate to think you might let him get close to me, in the hopes he tackles his issues in the old-fashioned, judicious manner of his Team Seven days. Am I understood?"

"Crystal clear."

Dahlen flicked his hand towards Rene, and the secretary shut down the feed.

"That will be all for now, Rene." He waited until the secretary had left, then limped back to his desk. He'd ordered Gustav to put the word out that there was contract work available. Within a few days, he expected, a few dozen mercenaries and private contractors would be looking for Singleton. Then the matter of Excelsior's compliance could become moot very quickly.

62

The old twin-rut track ran through the pine trees west of Seneca Falls on a right-of-way. The car kicked up a steady train of dust.

Dawn had taken over driving a few hours earlier, and the cloud of debris was making the rearview mirror useless.

She glanced over at Bob. He had a strangely puzzled expression. "What's going on, Bob?"

"Hmm? Oh... yeah. Just... I'm amazed by how little it seems to have changed up here in fifteen years. Everywhere else is going insane, but it's still quiet here, still isolated and peaceful."

"That's because nothing happens in the middle of the woods," Dawn noted. "Unless you're a deer, in which case I imagine there would be a lot of running."

His puzzled expression returned. "What's got you so chipper this afternoon?"

"Well... I wouldn't say 'chipper,' because we continue to be in heaps of trouble. But I had a good chat with the Lord this morning about our predicament and decided I'm going to focus on the positives for as long as possible. Such as, all of us still being alive. And... I have to admit, it sure is pretty up here. I mean... if I'm going to be killed by a psychopathic former CIA agent-turned-millionaire, I'd rather it be in Chicago. But this'll do."

Marcus took off his earbuds. "There are a lot of trees."

"And no high-speed internet," Bob said. "I imagine you're going to be a joy to deal with."

"Man..." Marcus sighed.

Bob gestured ahead. "His access road is on the left about a hundred yards."

The side road led down a slight slope, which curved slowly to the left, back towards the lake. At the bottom of the trail, the trees were cleared around a two-story log cabin, with a wide chimney of concrete and stones running up one side. Bob could just about make it out through the trees, a few miles away.

A pile of logs was neatly stacked at the bottom of the chimney in a makeshift pyramid pattern. Just ahead of them, Temple was using a small hatchet to split logs, tossing each finished product onto the pile with expert precision.

He stopped when he heard the car's brake pads squeak slightly. He buried the hatchet in his makeshift cutting block. His long-sleeved undershirt was sweat-stained, and he pulled off a rough and well-used pair of leather work gloves.

Bob parked the car. Temple was smiling, small nods of approval at seeing his visitors.

"Well, aren't you all a sight for sore eyes!" he announced as they climbed out of the car. "I don't know if you tried getting me on my phone for the last few hours, as the reception here is so damn spotty, and... well... you know."

"We do," Bob said. They hugged briefly. "Good to see you, bud." He looked past his old friend to the house and woods. "Any issues?"

Temple shook his head. "Not a peep. Come on, let me help you with your..."

"Bag," said Marcus. "We have one bag. Don't worry, I've got it."

He walked past both men towards the side door.

"Charming young man, that one," Temple said.

"He really is usually more polite, Professor," Dawn said. "He's just had some bad news about your internet speed."

"Ah... gotcha. Have to go into town for anything important of that sort."

A gunshot rang out, clear but not close.

Bob turned towards the woods. "That sounded like a rifle. Thirty-thirty maybe."

"Hunters," Temple said. "Woods are full of 'em right now. They get warnings about straying too close to private property, but it still happens from time to time. Worse is when they use leg traps to try to catch deer and such. Totally illegal and dangerous; I almost stepped on one last week."

He led them into the cabin. It wasn't fancy: a flight of stairs ahead of the door leading to bedrooms upstairs, a long living room to the left, an entrance to the kitchen beyond it, a bathroom to the right.

"I'll just take your bag upstairs," Temple said. "You folks grab a bench in the living room, there, and when I get back, I'll put on some java."

He left them to settle in. Dawn took a seat on the wide sofa that faced the fireplace.

Bob wandered immediately to a row of pictures on the mantel.

"Is that... that's you, isn't it?" Marcus asked.

Bob lifted the framed photo. "Yeah. Yeah, that's Maggie and me, just after we met. I haven't seen this in... I don't know, a long time."

The woman was smiling, happy, her arms around him, her chin on his shoulder.

"You look so young," Marcus offered.

"That's usually not the first thing you want to mention when you pick up an adult's fifteen-year-old photograph, dear," Dawn mentioned gently.

"We were twenty-five, twenty-six. Something like that. We came up and spent the week with Al after his wife went into long-term care in the city. The specialist treating her was in New York."

"Difficult times," Temple said, from the doorway. "I haven't had many visitors over the years since, but we did buy a couple of cots for that purpose, so I've set them up in the spare room at the end of the upstairs hall."

But Bob was enraptured by the photo, barely paying attention. "Yeah... sure," he muttered. "Maggie..." He looked forlornly at his dead fiancée's image. "They say you're supposed to get over grief after two years, but..."

"In my experience, you never really do," Dawn said. "That's one thing we have together: we've all lost the most important people to us. But we've found each other. You make your own family, in my experience."

The professor leaned through the door. "I'll go get the coffee. Then I imagine Bob will want to do some planning, take a look at what I have in stock."

Dawn waited until Temple had left. "He wasn't talking about food, was he, Bob?"

"No. No, Dawn, he wasn't."

63

The man with the binoculars leaned against the boat rail to steady them as he studied the building on the lakeshore.

It was sunny but cool. He checked his watch every ten minutes and noted any movement, tapping details into a file on his phone.

His earpiece buzzed. "Epsilon here."

"What's his status?"

Stone had arrived just a few hours after the team the night prior. They'd been told Dahlen likely wasn't going anywhere, for a few days, anyway. They were surprised the big boss had decided to make an appearance so soon.

"I think he's on the second floor of the conference center, sir. He's obviously cocky about his safety, as he's right by an enormous window."

"Fits his MO," Stone said. "Points of egress?"

"Three major, one lesser. There are emergency exits on the north and south sides of the building, along with the main doors on the west side. North side seems most likely, as it's less than fifty feet from there to the chopper pad."

"We'll want to shut that side down, then. What's the lesser option?"

"There's a boat launch and dock attached to the east side. But there's nowhere to go on the lake, no major waterways easily connecting that he could use, not with any efficacy."

"We have points on the road in?"

"Completely covered, sir."

"Alpha, are you getting all of this?" Stone asked.

A third voice entered the conversation. "Yes, sir, we're ready to roll at a moment's notice."

"Good. Good work, gentlemen. We'll wait until after dark tonight and disable that chopper. Washington expects the warrant to be ready by this time tomorrow, at which time we pick him up. Remember: if there's any sign of a third party, particularly Bob Singleton, I need to know before the man is six feet from you. Am I clear?"

"Yes, sir," the spotter on the boat confirmed. "We'll keep our eyes peeled."

He barely knew Stone, but Epsilon felt a cold shudder down his spine when the man addressed him, like a pronouncement from death itself.

64

It took several minutes to find the right dirt roads needed to drive around the bulk of the resort's vast perimeter.

By the time he returned to his starting point, a few hundred yards from the entrance, Bob realized just how easy it would be for someone to slip away.

The main buildings were surrounded by a few hundred yards of clear-cut scrub. But beyond that lay acres of marshy forest land, the spindly white pine and poplars often bunched so closely and canopied that the sun disappeared, the light between them imperceptible.

It defined his task more thoroughly, however. His best chance would be to catch Dahlen somewhere near the clear-cut, to ambush him coming out of one of the buildings.

But that led to the question of which building. Even with Al's borrowed binoculars, he couldn't see them well enough to discern movement patterns.

Maybe, then, we go with whichever is closest to...

He swiveled his head slowly left, panning the binoculars until he found it.

Bingo. The helipad is closest to the conference center, so that's option number one.

He'd found an old PDF of the resort's layout before leaving. At least, then, he could avoid the main roads and likely guard locations when he entered the property – which was inevitable. He didn't want to go in blind, without reconnaissance of opposition numbers and their possible weaknesses. But the visibility problem demanded it.

He raised the glasses and scoped out the main building again, trying to anticipate points of ambush or surprise. The conference center was a lump of gray cement, a three-story rectangle of uninspiring concrete, small windows, form following function.

It was designed to make money, not memories, which probably explained why it had eventually failed as a business, he figured. No one came to the lake just to do business, something neither Dahlen nor his late father had realized. It had an ideal location; it had privacy; it had access to everything cottage life could offer. It just lacked any semblance of a heart.

He checked his payload in the kit bag on the passenger seat one more time. Retirement notwithstanding, Al had kept an unhealthy amount of weaponry on hand.

He'd opted for the folding rifle and scope, because despite what he'd told Nurse Dawn, he thought the chances of catching Dahlen and turning him over to anyone were remarkably slim. Then she'd spotted him loading it into the bag, and it had been relegated to its place in Al Temple's gun locker.

The Beretta pistol was low caliber but effective and well suppressed. The stun gun and steel-reinforced wrist ties would help keep guard casualties to a minimum, which she had demanded.

The SUV was parked in a small clearing of trees, across

the road from the resort and a few hundred meters from the exit. It gave him a clear view of anyone coming and going, but little of tactical value.

Across the road, a car pulled off to the verge and parked temporarily, the occupants not getting out, exhaust fumes from the tailpipe suggesting a running engine. Bob craned his neck as he tried to see the men in the front seat.

He finally got a look at the driver, but didn't recognize him.

He was chatting in animated fashion with the man in the passenger seat, but also obscuring Bob's view of him.

Damn it. It's probably a couple arguing about their vacation plans, Bobby. Chill out. This is a long-haul exercise, not something that'll be resolved in a few hours this afternoon.

He wished Al's cabin were closer. He didn't want to drag his old mentor into even more danger, but the numbers were likely to be heavily against him. *You need him to protect Dawn and Marcus. Focus on the positive: yes, Dahlen probably has a dozen gunmen ready to shoot you dead on sight... but the only guy you actually need to handle is him.*

He hadn't given up on his promise to Nurse Dawn; if there was any chance of getting Dahlen to give up Excelsior and confess, it might even be enough to get a reprieve on his own termination sanction from Andrew Kennedy.

The driver leaned forward slightly to adjust the car's front seat, and Bob spied his passenger clearly for the first time.

Speaking of possible traitors... Hello, Eddie. Long time no see.

65

Dawn finished going through the kitchen cupboards, opening and closing the last with a flourish. "My goodness… when you said you didn't have much in the house, you clearly meant 'mostly dishes and cutlery, but no food.'"

"Unless you count the carton of milk in the back of the fridge," Temple offered. "Fortunately, I kept the temperature real low, so it's a bit icy. Otherwise… it's eight-month-old cheese, at this point."

"I know, I smelled it as soon as I opened the door."

Temple glanced towards it. The fridge door was open. "Huh. Airing it out?"

"If I don't, everything we make will be tainted by that odor. Still… you need some baking soda to really eliminate the remainder."

"We have as little baking soda as everything else," he admitted. "But there's a general store three miles down the road."

"Any chance of Gerald Dahlen or his men stopping in there?"

He chuckled. "Unlikely. It's a little rough around the edges for a rich boy like Gerry. Besides, he's thirty-odd miles south of here. No reason to make it up this way."

"Then… I need to borrow your car," she said.

"Ah… no. Bob made it clear you two are supposed to remain under wraps."

"You just said yourself there's basically no chance of my being discovered. Right?"

"Well… sure, but…"

"But nothing! We don't know how long we're going to be here; we have zero decent supplies, and the boy in the next room eats like a locomotive furnace in need of coal."

"Then I should go…" Temple began to say.

"And leave Marcus with me to protect him? Professor, I've never fired a gun in my life and don't intend to start now."

Temple sighed a little, as if he'd been asked to turn off a favorite show. Then he rummaged in his pocket and handed her the keys to his Ford Bronco. "She's the older wide-body, and she guzzles gas. I've had to rebuild the engine six times, but she has power for towing and carrying, and she can overtake well. Just… be nice to her, okay? The clutch can be a little sticky."

Marcus entered the kitchen, coffee cup in hand, just as she accepted the keys. "Where are you going?"

"The store up the road. You need anything?"

He didn't appear much happier than he had been that morning when they arrived. "I'm fine." But he didn't look fine.

"Is he always—?"

"He was good until he lost his internet," Dawn explained. Then she frowned. "I wonder what Bob likes to eat. We've had nothing but fast food for days."

"In the old days, he was a meat-and-potatoes sort of guy," Temple said. "But he had a lot more muscle then. I don't imagine he's that picky, though, given where he's been eating for the last decade."

"I guess not. Still... it would be nice to make something that would cheer him up. He looked pretty down after he saw that picture."

Temple looked grim. "Maggie. I thought about putting it away before he got here; then I figured maybe he'd notice it by its absence. But... yeah. I guess he loved her as much as I loved Evie."

Dawn walked over to the kitchen counter and gathered up the small pile of reusable bags Temple had retrieved from storage. "Nothing wrong with that. Maybe I can scare up some pork chops, see if that puts a smile on his face."

Temple studied her as she walked to the kitchen door. "You're a good woman, Nurse Dawn," he said. "If he was going to stick his fool neck out saving someone, I'm glad it was you."

"Me too, Professor," she said before walking out and making her way to the front door. Perhaps a little guy time would be good for Marcus, she figured. On the few occasions that his deadbeat father had made an appearance, her son, Maurice, had always brightened up.

She frowned as she reached for the door handle, realizing how deeply she felt for the boy. It wasn't the same as being a mother to your own child, and maybe that was what his parents had reckoned with. But there was something there, nonetheless, something that made Bob's suggestion at least worth considering.

The boy deserved at least that much.

66

In a sense, Bob knew, he was lucky.

It wasn't the odds; his first tour through the woods adjacent to the resort had spotted at least six guards on patrol.

But Dahlen had clearly never prepared the property to be a place of last resort. The perimeter fence that cut through the surrounding trees was old-fashioned chain link, without alarms. It was also dilapidated in numerous locations, partially collapsed, never repaired. There was also no sign of CCTV cameras, although he expected that would change the closer that he got to the buildings.

He'd borrowed a brown mock turtleneck and a pair of slacks from Al for the recon. He'd considered waiting until nightfall, but they had no idea how long Dahlen would stay. Stone's team keeping tabs on the exits meant government pressure would come to bear sooner than later.

He'd covered a few acres by the time he got back to his starting point.

He checked his kit load, silently cursing himself for listening to Dawn and leaving the rifle behind. He held the bag open. The suppressed Beretta would be useful while limiting the attention it drew. An abundance of reinforced wrist restraints and thick black electrical tape would help keep guard injuries or fatalities minimal – assuming he could isolate the men he was facing.

The stun gun would lower the risk of strong opposition in each case. A set of powerfully jawed bolt cutters, a flashbang grenade, a pneumatic lock punch, some nylon rope and a mini crowbar rounded out the kit.

He'd left his shoes in the car, a mile away. The forest floor was dense with twigs, broken tree limbs and other noisy detritus, and trying to remain silent without reducing his movement speed drastically was impossible.

Instead, he'd opted for two pairs of thick nylon socks and soft-soled slippers, another suggestion from Al. The idea was to move swiftly and quietly, use the density of trees to reduce the number of opponents before Dahlen knew it had happened, and isolate him.

He pushed through the forest, remaining low, using the wider tree trunks as cover, checking visual cues from the first sortie and his compass to make sure he was in the right location. He leaned around the base of a green ash and waited.

Guard number one, ten o'clock.

The man was walking a short pattern, boots crushing leaves as he checked for movement to the west, towards the road, as well as east towards the buildings. He had an MP5 submachine gun slung around his neck, stock braced by his left arm.

After a few minutes of pacing, he stopped and tapped his earpiece.

"Collins, perimeter five checking in. Nah, quiet as a mouse, chief. Yeah. Two days of this? Are you kidding... no. No, fine." He paused and listened to the voice on the other end. "I have a sandwich with me. Yeah, yeah, okay." He tapped the earpiece and continued on his way.

Bob shadowed him, staying parallel but a few feet behind the man, edging nearer as the trees allowed. He waited until a particularly wide cedar offered maximum cover. As the guard stepped beyond it, he leaned in quickly and hit him with a jolt from the stun gun.

The man went down hard, collapsing in convulsions. Bob dropped to his knees and flipped the man over in one smooth motion, pulling a set of wrist ties taut. He reached around the man and slapped a strip of tape across his mouth, making sure to wrap it around the man's head once to be sure he couldn't easily work it off with facial movements and saliva.

The guard had recovered, and he began to struggle. Bob grabbed him by the back of his jacket collar and leaned back with all his weight, dragging the smaller man, in a sitting position, until his back was against a tree.

He passed the nylon rope through the loop created by the man's arms and secured him to the tree trunk, his captive trying to yell unsuccessfully through the tape.

For good measure, he secured the guard's ankles with another steel-reinforced tie.

"Shhh..." Bob suggested. He reached down and plucked the earpiece from the man's head and stuck it into his own ear.

He needed to move quickly. The guards were running a perimeter line of defense. They were far enough apart to cover the few acres necessary, but close enough that at points of their patrol they would be able to see the next man in the line, make visual confirmation the line was intact.

That would fall apart within minutes if "Perimeter Five's" absence was noted.

He picked up his bag and crouched low, scurrying through the woods in a wide curve until he was behind the second man. He followed the same procedure, waiting until he'd cleared a wide tree before reaching in with the stun gun.

The man's weapon wasn't around his neck. As he convulsed from the shock, his loose grip tightened. But instead of holding on firmly, it squeezed the weapon from his grasp.

It landed loudly on the forest floor, snapping twigs. Bob paused for a split second, anticipating the sound of men coming his way. But he knew he didn't have time to worry about it, and set about restraining the man.

A few moments later, he was following a line of trees to the third. He shadowed his target again. He was about to reach around the tree and shock him when his earpiece buzzed. "Anyone else hear that?"

The voice was in muted stereo, one version transmitted through the earpiece, the same sound coming a split second later from four feet away, where the young guard was trying to hail his associates.

"Collins, did you catch that?" the guard asked. "Collins?"

Bob suspected that if he answered, he was so close the man would hear him speaking, assuming he didn't immediately peg it as the wrong voice. His other choice was to catch the man while he was still focused on the call-out.

Bob darted around the tree and leaned in with the stun gun. The young man was more alert than anticipated, turning side-on to reduce his target profile, punching down and away, hammering at Bob's exposed wrist, the stun gun flying out of his hand.

The guard tried to swing his weapon towards him. Bob pushed the barrel up and away with his left hand, stepping and throwing a punch with his right that caught the guard on the side of the chin and dropped him to one knee.

He was down.

But he wasn't out.

The guard slapped at his earpiece. "Perimeter breach at three," he barked. Bob hit him again with a short right cross, this time connecting hard, the guard crumpling, unconscious.

He secured the man's wrists but got no further. He heard twigs cracking and leaves being crushed underfoot from somewhere to his right.

They were coming for him.

67

Inside the converted conference center, Dahlen's attention was glued to the giant screen on the wall.

CNN had picked up the *Post*'s story, but had done little other than supplement what was already known with talking-head opinion pieces.

He wanted to be confident that his lawyers and handlers in DC would get him information before it hit the news, but so much of what happened next would be up to the Justice Department.

They'd been alerted to the warrant application by a federal court source and had tried to challenge it, unsuccessfully. But the government had withdrawn it at the last moment to make additions and amendments. That was not, his lawyers insisted, a good thing.

He had two days, at most, before it would be necessary to flee the country.

The government's best efforts to prevent him crossing international borders would be easily overcome with money. But the forty-eight-hour window was also a final chance to track down Singleton and Ginny Smalls, eliminate any corroborating witnesses, and render the audio recording moot.

His secretary, Rene, scampered up the stairs. “Sir, we have a perimeter breach in the woods. At least two of the guards are down, possibly three.”

The woods?

The government would come down the main road, warrant in hand. Either would require a response, as he had no intention of being taken into custody. But taking out the perimeter guards was the kind of approach he’d expect from a solo operative or small team.

Singleton.

“He’s here,” he muttered.

“Sir?”

“Send everyone we have except six and ten. Have them on the entrance in case this is a distraction for something larger. Everyone is on a shoot-to-kill order at this point. Am I clear?”

“Yes, sir… but…”

Rene was always reluctant to speak his mind, Dahlen thought. “Out with it.”

“Perhaps it would be time to evacuate you to a new location.”

They’d booked a handful of rooms at a hotel in Buffalo, the backup plan calling for a night border crossing into Canada, followed by a private jet charter taking them from Montreal to Paris.

But once they’d committed to that route, he’d been warned, any chance of immediately clearing his name would be ruined.

“I’m fine,” he said simply. “Gustav has the lakeside door?”

“Yes, sir.”

“Keep an eye on the front entrance and keep me apprised,” Dahlen ordered. “If we need to leave quickly, we’ll take the chopper.”

Rene nodded, but appeared nervous. “Of course, sir.”

The secretary jogged back down the stairs.

Dahlen walked back to his desk and opened the top drawer. He took out the Glock and chambered a shell. He hadn’t fired a gun in years before the tunnel incident, but it had reminded him of the sense of power a sidearm provided. Perhaps Singleton would beat the odds and reach him; he doubted it. But if he did, Dahlen told himself, he would regret his impudence.

Sometimes, if you want something done right...

68

Stone kept an eye on the road exit. They hadn't seen any movement in two hours. There was still no word on the warrant, but he knew it would come that day. Washington knew how important the timing could be with a target as wealthy as Dahlen.

His headset crackled to life. "Epsilon checking in. I've got movement through the trees. Looks like the guards are riled up by something."

"What's your sense, Epsilon?" Stone asked.

"They're moving quickly. Whatever it is, it's not wildlife or a tourist. Weapons are readied, and the three guards in question have moved into a triangle to cover each other."

They were supposed to stay put and avoid procedural breaches by staying off the property. But Stone had been a spook for nearly a half century, and his hackles were raised.

Something serious was going on.

Zeta was sitting behind the steering wheel. "Might be a diversion, sir. He'll know by now that we're watching the road. If we venture into the woods..."

"Point taken." Stone nodded towards the entrance. "Take

us in, but do it slowly. If he's trying to flee, we might be able to block the road sufficiently and slow him down enough to stop this from turning into a chase."

Zeta nodded. He started the SUV's engine and trod lightly on the gas, pulling them directly ahead, out of the clearing and to the edge of the road. He checked for other traffic, then drove across the pristine asphalt to the resort entrance.

Stone took out his Smith and Wesson M&P 9 mm pistol and checked its load. "Keep it to a crawl," he advised. "He's not going to try to escape by boat, as the lake is cut off from proper egress. If he comes shooting around a corner, we need to block passage and get out of the vehicle as quickly as—"

He didn't get a chance to finish the sentence, a burst of machine-gun fire raking the cab, bullets smashing through the safety glass of the windshield, peppering Zeta's torso but missing Stone. He ducked low, trying to minimize his target profile.

Zeta slumped over the wheel, a bullet hole through his throat pumping out consistent spurts of blood. His dead weight slumped forward on the brake pedal, the car jolting to a halt.

Stone didn't stop to see if Zeta was alive. The chances were slim at best, and they were under attack. The bullets had sprayed the windshield from left to right, suggesting a firing position northwest of him.

Instead, he opened the passenger door and crept out, closed it while staying low, then circled around to the back of the truck, chambering a shell in the pistol.

A moment later, he heard footsteps on the gravel roadside. A man's voice called in the incident. "Perimeter six to base, we have visitors. Yeah... SUV. Looks like just a driver... I'm going to take up position here in case of a follow-up. Say again?"

Stone couldn't hear the other side of the conversation. "Sure, of course," the guard said.

He heard gravel crunching again, louder as the man approached the driver's side. The door opened. "Looks like mil-spec gear, sir. He has an earpiece, so someone's in contact, and they'll know something has gone wrong. Recommend Perimeter Ten joins me to defend the position. Uh-huh, that's a roger, base. I'll expect him shortly."

Stone ducked low to check the direction of the man's feet from under the car. He was turned due northeast, possibly to rifle through Zeta's jacket. Stone knew if he stepped out of cover, he risked being spotted by the man's partner on approach. But he wasn't going to get a better chance to get the drop on the guard.

He drew the sheath knife from his ankle scabbard. He raised himself to a low crouch and scurried quickly around the left rear corner of the SUV's bumper.

The guard heard him a few steps before he reached him and was turning as Stone swung his arm up, ramming the knife into the man's midsection and pulling up hard, using the blade's serrated edge to tear the man's innards out of place. The guard's eyes widened in an expression of puzzled distress. Stone pulled out the blade and quickly swiped it across the man's neck, severing the carotid artery.

The guard dropped to his knees, clutching his throat, gurgling as the air from blood-flooded lungs gurgled out of the slashing wound. Stone rescued the man's MP5 from around his neck just before he pitched over, face-first.

He'd wanted to keep it even more silent, take him from behind and scramble his basal ganglia, the nerves at the base of the brain and top of the spine. But improvisation was par for the course.

Perimeter Ten stepped out of the trees, his weapon still held low. He froze for a split second, shocked by the sight of his comrade bleeding out on the gravel. Stone raised the MP5 and sighted him center torso, squeezing the trigger once for a half second, then again, both bursts riddling the man with bullets, his torso jerking spastically as he collapsed.

Stone tapped his earpiece twice to open all channels. “Papa Bear says look alive, gentlemen, the target zone is hot, and Zeta is down. All units converge on the conference center. Epsilon, what’s the status on the bird?”

“She’s still sitting on the pad.”

“Keep an eye out for runners. He’ll try for the chopper first. Try to pin him down there until we can snag him.”

“Roger, Papa Bear, Epsilon out.”

Stone scampered over to the second guard and recovered his MP5. He checked his perimeter, but the vicinity was clear. He trotted over to the edge of the woods and partial cover, walking parallel to the road, towards the conference center.

His instructions from Kennedy had been clear, to wait for the warrant and let justice take its course. But Dahlen had killed one of his men and shot at him.

It wasn’t pure sentiment; Zeta knew the risks.

But it was definitely personal.

69

The three guards were in a triangle formation, separated by twenty-five yards or so, sweeping through the woods. If he opened fire on one, Bob knew, he would have no way of retraining on the others before they found cover or returned fire.

The MP5 was loud, and in the darkened woods, the muzzle flare would give away his location immediately.

Trying to take them bloodlessly was now a lost cause, he knew. Dawn wasn't going to like that.

Can't be helped.

The two front men in the inverted triangle were a complication, the distance between them tricky. He needed some room to work. Bob turned and stayed low, scurrying back as quickly as he could without alerting them to his location until he'd put thirty extra yards between them.

He took out the nylon rope and the flashbang, hoping that their slow sweep gave him enough time to set up.

He tied one end of the rope to a small tree, then skittered sideways, drawing it wide across their eventual path. Halfway along, he drew his knife and hacked two or three inches of moist dirt free from the ground. He planted the flashbang, then secured it by packing the rest of the mud around it. He could hear their boots again, crunching the undergrowth even as they tried to remain silent.

He twisted the pin on the flashbang and pulled it out, keeping the trigger depressed as he wrapped the nylon three times tautly around the grenade's top end, the trigger held down by the pressure. He kept it taut as he drew the line out ten more feet, securing the other end to another sapling ten feet away.

He heard a voice, someone whispering. They'd gone off radio, correctly assuming he'd be listening. They were close. He picked up his bag and hurried back another fifteen yards, taking a position behind a wide tree trunk.

It took the men another thirty seconds to reach the line slung less than six inches from the ground. A guard's foot caught it, but experience kicked in, and he yelled, "GRENADE!" even as he tried to dive from the blast radius, his associates reacting a split second later.

The flashbang blew, the effect dissipated outdoors. But that hadn't been its main purpose, which was to force the men to prone positions.

Bob wheeled around the tree, the MP5 sight raised to eye height. He shot the first man before he'd even tried to rise, the second as he rolled over to regain his feet.

The third, the point man who'd triggered the device, scrambled behind a nearby tree before Bob could sight him.

Instinct kicked in, his feet breaking into a run before his brain had even sent the message: *Go now; he'll be blind.*

As he reached the tree, an arm swung out wildly, a large blade held in a backhand fighting grip. Bob ducked away, the blade just missing his midsection as the crouched man fought to regain his vision. He kicked down hard, heel finding the man's forearm, the knife knocked free.

The guard rolled away and came up on his feet. His vision had to be obscured by tears, Bob knew, but not badly enough to miss the hulking shape ahead of him. The man went into a balanced martial arts stance and bounced forward into a front kick.

Bob raised the MP5 and shot him through the chest.

Assuming his initial count had been good, that was all six of the perimeter guards, he figured. He checked his compass and the sun's position. He was close, he knew, just a few hundred yards from the center.

There would be more men, but first he had a chance to make up some ground. Dahlen would be aware from the third guard's alert that something was wrong. With a little luck, his arrogance would keep him from immediately fleeing.

There was still time to finish it.

70

Rene sprinted up the stairs. "Sir, we've lost contact with the perimeter guards."

"How many?"

"All... all of them sir."

Dahlen rose from his desk. He picked up the headset and put it on. He tapped the earpiece. "Base to five, come in, five."

The line remained dead.

"Base to seven, come in, seven."

Still nothing. Six and ten had been separate from the rest, near the driveway, on the extreme north side of the property. "Base to six," he called out. "Come in, six; what's your status?"

Nothing.

He pulled off the headset. "How many men do we have left on the buildings?" He opened the drawer and took out two extra magazines for the pistol.

"Four, one on each corner, sir, along with Gustav and myself."

"We're heading for the chopper," he said. "You have the lead, Rene, and Gustav has my six."

Rene radioed the other man to meet them at the front

doors. "Sir... perhaps I should stay here to slow down anyone who—"

"Shut up," Dahlen ordered. "It's a fifty-yard dash to the pad, Rene, and I pay you handsomely to rein in your cowardice. Now let's go!"

They bolted for the stairs and jogged down them. At the front entrance, Rene removed a submachine gun from a rack and slung it over his neck. Outside the doors, Gustav arrived. He held them open as the two men joined him outside. "How quickly can you get her up and us out of here, Gustav?" he demanded.

"With normal checks, ten minutes. Without them? Cold? Two, but—"

"But nothing. I suspect we don't have ten minutes. Gentlemen, your job for the next five minutes is to keep me alive. You will both be handsomely rewarded if you do your job. We stay low, and you keep your eyes east. Nothing's coming from the lake that we need to worry about. Got it?"

Both men nodded.

"All right, gentlemen. It's time for us to make ourselves scarce. Lead on, Rene."

They began their run to freedom. They'd be safe again in a few hours, Dahlen told himself. But if he had to run, he would lose his company, his reputation. Most of his fortune, however, would be intact.

Revenge could still be best served cold.

71

Stone neared the clearing at the edge of the road in, where the forest gave way to the parking area by the main buildings.

He tried to get a glimpse of the conference center entrance, where Epsilon had seen the majority of bodies enter a day earlier, but it was cut off slightly by the adjacent building.

Before he could change position, Epsilon called in, voice terse. "We've got runners, three making a dash..."

"Take one and three," Stone ordered. Dahlen was a tactician and would protect his point and flank, at the least.

He saw them a split second later, a tall, thin man with a gun slung over his back. He'd run two more steps, perhaps halfway from the building to the chopper pad, when Epsilon's .50-caliber sniper bullet sheared the top of his skull off like a sharp knife cutting a melon.

Dahlen appeared right behind him, a pronounced limp slowing him. He staggered to a halt at the sight of his associate going down.

Another man was just behind him, running in a sideways

gait, trying to keep an eye on their six, but almost bumping into his boss as a result. The second man caught Epsilon's second bullet square, the massive power of the sniper rifle blowing him backwards off his feet, the figure dead before he hit the ground.

Dahlen froze for just a few moments between the two corpses, unsure of the direction to take, doubtless terrified. Instead of turning around, he knelt quickly beside the second man's corpse and began fumbling for something.

Keys, Stone thought. *He's searching the man for the copter's ignition key.*

Stone did a wide visual sweep of the parking area to the far tree line. A guard was making his way towards Dahlen, but was fifty yards behind him, at least, in front of the main office building. Stone raised his gun and let out three short bursts, the second taking the guard down.

The man began to struggle to his feet. A gunshot reported from the tree line near him, and the man pitched face-first to the ground, dead.

Another guard appeared a few feet beyond him, rounding the building's corner, then screeching to a halt at the sight of his dead friend. Stone was about to sight him and fire, but someone beat him to it.

He tapped his earpiece. Dahlen was up again and running unevenly, his limp slowing him, towards the chopper. "Status report."

"Alpha here, sir. We're in the woods. The perimeter guards are all dead or restrained."

"Head for the parking lot. By my count, we've still got four bogies in the vicinity. Leave Dahlen to me. Wait a second... how far off are you?"

"About three hundred meters by my estimate, sir."

Then who shot the other...?

Singleton.

He looked the other way. Dahlen had reached the chopper and was climbing in. "Roger, Alpha, proceed as directed, with caution. Flush out and remove any more obstacles. Out."

He left the tree line and ran towards the helicopter. In any moment, they'd have company. He wanted to end it without witnesses.

Stone was twenty yards away before he could see through the chopper's sun-dappled Perspex bubble. The cabin was empty. That meant...

Dahlen popped out of cover from the other side of the chopper and fired three shots from the pistol. The first missed, but the second struck him in the thigh, and Stone felt his leg give way, his body pitching forward as the third bullet struck him in the shoulder, spinning his torso slightly as he went down, the MP5 flying from his grip.

Shit... always hurts like hell.

He tried to right himself, but Dahlen was already a few feet away, the pistol raised. "Bad move, Edward," the businessman chided. "Just because I prefer not to doesn't mean I've forgotten how to shoot."

"Just do it," Stone grunted through gritted teeth. "We've all heard too much from you already."

"Goodbye, Edward," Dahlen said, his finger tightening on the trigger. "I doubt greatly you will be missed or remembered."

72

Bob emptied the magazine, and the fourth man guarding the main building went down. Unlike his friends, he'd tried to make a dash for the parking lot and a vehicle. He hadn't been any more successful.

He tossed the MP5 aside and drew the pistol from the speed holster at his waistband, chambering a round.

He sprinted past the main administration building. Sixty yards away, he saw someone running towards the chopper, unable to make out who from behind.

Dahlen popped out from behind the chopper and opened fire, his pursuer going down hard. There were two other men lying ten feet away.

Someone had launched an assault. Chances seemed good that it was Team Seven, given Stone's presence. Bob ducked behind a nearby sedan. He moved to the car's back corner and checked to see if Dahlen had spotted him.

The businessman was standing over a prone man who'd risen to his elbows. It looked like...

Stone.

The easiest route was to just let Dahlen kill him. *Eddie's as much a murderer as he is. He's as bad a seed as they come.* He just had to let it happen...

You promised me, Bob.

Dawn's voice barged into his thought process once more.

Well... shit. He raised the Glock and squeezed the trigger with steady, even pressure, letting the explosive gunshot surprise him.

The slug caught Dahlen in the shoulder, staggering him into a trip. The pistol flew from his grip as he slammed, back first, to the concrete surface of the helipad.

Bob sprinted his way. Both men were trying to rise. Stone seemed unable, as if he'd caught a slug in the lower torso or leg, and something wasn't working as it should.

Dahlen was showing surprising resilience. He dragged himself to his knees and rose, unsteadily, his head turning frantically as he looked for the pistol.

He spotted it and staggered that way. He'd just about reached it when Bob raised the pistol again. He'd never been a great shot on the move; nobody was, really. He compensated by aiming center mass at the man fifteen yards away, emptying the remainder of the seven-shot magazine.

Bullets struck Dahlen in the torso and legs, and he collapsed to the ground.

Bob pulled a fresh magazine from his pocket and reloaded. He ran past the prone Stone, who had managed to turn himself onto his stomach and was crawling towards a pistol a few feet away. Bob stopped for a moment and kicked it aside. He walked the last few feet to Dahlen calmly.

The man hadn't given up. Bleeding from multiple wounds, he was nevertheless reaching back, behind him, his hand scrambling to find the pistol he'd dropped.

Bob put a foot down on the free arm and pinned it. "You're done."

Dahlen stopped struggling. He was panting for air, his

eyes dancing from pain and blood loss, dizziness setting in. "You... you fucking shot me... again... Can't end like this..."

"You made your choices, Gerry. It ends now, or you'll be back, causing more havoc."

"I told you... I have money..." Dahlen said. "I have so much money. It's... it's yours. All of it. My accounts... gold... stocks and bonds..."

"I don't want your money," Bob said. He looked around quickly, scanning the tree line. Stone's team wouldn't be far behind. "I want the name of Excelsior, your treacherous partner."

Dahlen coughed, and a trickle of blood spattered the corner of his lips. He pushed himself to a seated position. "After all these years. So irrelevant," he said.

"Not to me. Not to the men who died because of your betrayal. They deserved better."

"Excelsior was—"

The gunshots were deafening, from right behind them. Stone had propped himself up and emptied a magazine into Dahlen's prone figure.

Dahlen fell back, unmoving.

The elderly agent was panting, exhausted and bleeding. "You don't get... to kill the bad guy," Stone gasped. "You don't get shit."

Bob felt his anger swell, the cold and calculated indifference of being operational giving way. He raised his pistol to Stone's head. "You son of a bitch, he was going to..."

"He fucking shot me!" Stone spat, rising to his feet, leaning his weight on his good leg. "And our old business is our old business. You're not agency anymore, Singleton. I'd..." He staggered sideways but held his balance. "I'd fucking shoot you myself, but I owe you for saving me."

"That and your gun is empty."

Stone was wobbling. He looked down at the pistol, the

slide completely withdrawn, the chamber empty. He tossed it aside and slumped to his backside. “Go,” he said. “There’s a Jeep with a body in it on the main road in. Put it into ‘park’ before you remove the body, he’s holding down the brake, and the engine is running.”

“I don’t understand...” Bob said. “What’s the angle, Eddie?”

“You get one favor for saving me, and this is it. I look the other way until Friday. Then you’re back to number one on my hit list. You feel me?”

Bob took a split second to decide. Killing Stone wouldn’t fix anything; it wouldn’t prevent Kennedy or Team Seven from wanting his head.

Besides... he’s old and arrogant. When we meet again, I like my chances.

He took off running towards the north road.

73

Marcus was bored beyond belief. The lack of Wi-Fi meant that using his phone and its tiny data allowance for videos was out of the question.

Temple's TV was limited to an antenna, which picked up one non-digital-only channel, in fuzzy fashion, from Syracuse.

Temple had offered board games, but that seemed like the most mind-numbing thing he'd ever heard of. Instead, he'd decided to browse the bookcases in the living room for something to read.

"See anything that appeals?" Temple asked from his perch in the wingback chair by the fireplace. He had an open paperback on his lap and a cup of tea on the side table.

Marcus shrugged. "I don't really know. I don't read much. If you want, I can rebuild your Bronco's block again..."

"That's okay. I think it'll hang together for a while." Temple looked slightly amused by the kid's distraction. "If you'd like, I can fish out some of my comic books from when I was a kid..."

Marcus frowned at the word "kid" and felt a pang of irritation. In truth, it seemed like a great idea. But he didn't want the man thinking of him as someone young and stupid.

"No, that's fine. I'm sure there's something here I'd like... something with some action in it, maybe?"

Temple chuckled. "You and Bob, both looking for a constant distraction."

Marcus smiled at the man's soft reminiscence. "He really is important to you, isn't he?"

Temple furrowed his brow and considered it seriously. "He's the closest Evie and I ever had to a kid. He lost his parents at fifteen, joined the Marines at eighteen. After that, I was the adult in his life. So... almost real family, I guess."

"We make our own family; at least, that's what Dawn says. Right?"

Temple's serious expression hadn't changed. Perhaps he was a little embarrassed by personal stuff, Marcus thought. "Sure, kid," the professor said. "Something like that."

Marcus had spotted the cartoon artwork, black line drawings on white cardstock, framed and behind glass, when they'd first arrived.

But he hadn't really bothered studying them until he was close up.

They covered a six-by-three-foot section of the living room wall. Some were obviously professional, superheroes from Marvel and DC comics, originals signed by the artists, some characters he didn't recognize. A few others were as good, or almost as good, and signed simply "Temple."

"The spoils of my misspent youth."

He turned. Temple was behind him, holding a pair of cups of coffee.

"You're allowed this stuff, right?"

"Coffee? I mean... yeah, sure." He accepted a mug.

Temple shrugged. "In my day, kids weren't allowed coffee.

Or sugar. Or... come to think of it, we had pretty much no rights whatsoever."

"That sounds... awful."

"Yep. Well... I can't complain. My uncle was a good man. Too good."

"Too good? You said something about him in Chicago..."

"You pay attention! It's a fine trait, kid, makes you seem polite by default. You can use that. Yeah... My uncle Walt was the neighborhood piggy bank, I guess you could say. Every lowlife knew he was a soft touch, every schemer."

"Weird. I'm sorry, I mean... that sounds difficult."

"Long time ago, kid, long time ago. He always figured he'd turn things around, that all his generosity would come back to him someday, lift us all to a better lifestyle or something. But that's not how life works. Not typically."

"Is that why you joined the Marines? To toughen up?"

Temple sipped his coffee. "Hmmm. Yeah, I guess. Something like that."

"And Bob?"

The professor gave a curt shake of his head. "No, that was... that was somewhere between necessity and social programming."

That lost the young man. "I'm sorry... I don't..."

"He had nowhere else to go; poor school grades not from lack of intelligence but from constant distraction. These days, maybe, they'd say he was a little ADHD, some hyperactivity, hyperfocus on his interests. But more than that, Bob's father instilled a sense of nobility in the kid before up and dying on him. Bob's conscience is large and rampant."

"It bothers you that he worries about others so much?"

"That he beats himself up for every mistake he ever made? Yeah. It's not just sentimental, Marcus. It... makes him vulnerable. That's what opening yourself up to the problems of others can do. I wish I'd taught him better."

His resigned sadness was uncomfortable. Marcus turned back to the art. "Did... you really draw these? They're amazing."

"Yeah... I had them in my study in Chicago for years. But Evie really enjoyed them, so after she passed, I moved them here. Helps keep her around a little."

One picture was nearly two feet across, Temple having completed a group image of a half-dozen superheroes at the same time. "They had the Avengers when you were young? That must have been..."

"I get it; I'm practically a zombie," Temple said dryly. "Sure they did. I drew that in, let's see... I'd say '73, give or take. I'd have been ten or eleven. Submitted it, too."

"You sent your stuff to Marvel?"

"Yep. They didn't buy any of it, but I got some encouraging letters from the editor-in-chief."

"Stan Lee?"

"You know about Stan the Man?" Temple sounded surprised.

"Knew. He died. But he made appearances in the movies first..."

Temple frowned. "I haven't watched them. That's a shame. Still, he must've been older than heck. I haven't really followed any of that stuff since... geez, before the Marines, I guess."

Marcus followed the line of pictures to the end. The last was a framed photo of Stan Lee himself. "Wow. He looks so young there. I mean, sort of... younger, anyway." His eyes traced the photo to the bottom, where the comic legend had left an inscription. "To Allan, Keep working on your art and you'll make it, True Believer!" it said in black marker. "Sincerely, Stan Lee."

He'd signed off with a single word.

"Excelsior!"

Marcus couldn't help but take a short, sharp breath.

It couldn't be a coincidence, he knew.

His hands began to tremble, his stomach instantly flipping end over end from butterflies.

He backed away a step. He needed to get out of there immediately, get away until he could tell Bob.

"You okay, kid?" Temple asked.

Marcus glanced at him. Temple was studying him. He flashed a quick, weak smile. "I think the first cup of coffee isn't sitting too well."

His hand was shaking, and he slopped some coffee onto the floor. "Shit."

Temple waved him away absentmindedly. "I'll get it. Maybe you should take a rest, kid. Put your feet up for a few minutes." He nodded towards the sofa.

Marcus didn't know what to say. He wanted to flee, but his legs felt weak. He took a few steps and sat down on its edge. "Yeah... Yeah, I guess."

"I'll just get a cloth..." Temple said. He left the room through the kitchen exit.

Marcus waited until he was through the door and willed his legs to work. He ran for the front entrance, then realized he had no way to get out of there. Bob had one car, Dawn the other.

He needed to buy time. "Professor, I'm just going to get some air," he called out.

"Fine," Temple yelled back.

Marcus opened the front door and staggered out. He looked both ways, hoping an idea would spring to mind. But he felt numbed by panic. He stumbled down the steps and walked around to the side of the house, past the woodpile.

Run into the woods. Anything. Just go. He needed to stall for time and figure out how best to handle the discovery. He needed Bob and Dawn.

The click from behind him had become familiar in the days prior, the sound of a gun being cocked.

"I'm going to need you to turn around slowly, kid," Temple demanded. His voice was calm and even.

Marcus did as commanded. Temple was holding the gun casually, but was too close to miss.

"Stupid mistake on my part, leaving that photo up," he said. "Ego that he wrote back, even all these decades later. I'm guessing from the way you reacted that Bob told you about Tehran, and you just did a little mental math."

"You're Excelsior," Marcus said. "You're the one who betrayed them."

Temple looked matter-of-fact about it. "I'm sorry it has to come to this, kid..."

Marcus felt like crying, like dropping to the ground and curling up in a ball. But he forced it down. He needed to keep calm, like Richie had... like his father had taught him.

"You don't need to kill me, Mr. Temple. I don't know anything, really. I won't say anything."

Temple was shaking his head gently. "Believe me, kid, if we had another route out of this, I'd take it. I'm not a bad guy, Marcus. Bob could tell you that. But sometimes in this life, we have to look out for number one."

"So... you're just going to shoot me? I'm a kid."

"You're a witness. In the end, we all have to choose, Marcus. We either do for others, or we do for ourselves."

Marcus's pulse was racing, his heart beating a mile a minute, the stillness around them and the slightest of breezes only accentuating his sense of vulnerability. He needed to keep the man talking, figure out something. There had to be a way out.

"I thought you were supposed to have some sort of warrior code. Bob is always talking about doing things for the right reasons..."

"He does that, yeah," Temple said. "I can't let you go, kid. If I do, I'm done, and you know it. You'll tell Bob, and he'll either try to kill me, or he'll turn me over to Eddie Stone, and then I might as well already be dead. I'm not going out like that, kid. I'm sorry..."

He raised the pistol.

The crack of a hunter's rifle caught them both by surprise, coming from close by in the woods. Temple's head swiveled that way reflexively. Marcus jumped sideways, praying. His body was stopped short by the log pile, his hand finding the handle of the hatchet. He yanked on it and threw it in one motion, remembering in that split second a similar failed effort back home.

Temple turned in time to see it flying towards his head. He bobbed his head sideways, and the hatchet flew by him harmlessly.

Temple stepped forward and hit Marcus with a backhand, the weight of the gun smashing into the side of his head, driving him to his knees.

"Goddamn hunters," he muttered. "Thanks for that, kid... Ah! Uh-uh, stay on your knees! I guess I should be happy you tried that. It'll make me feel a little better about this."

He lowered the tip of the barrel so that it was aimed directly at the top of Marcus's head. "Goodbye, Marcus. I'd tell you it's been fun, but I'd be lying, so—"

The log seemed to come from nowhere, smashing into the professor's head, knocking him face-first to the ground. Dawn was panting from excitement, holding the makeshift weapon by one end in her right hand.

"Are you okay?" she said. She rounded the prone figure and helped Marcus to his feet. "We need to get his—"

Temple rose to all fours, shaking his head to clear out the cobwebs. He hadn't let go of the gun.

Dawn reacted instinctively. "RUN!" she screamed.

They bolted past him, towards the Bronco.

A shot rang out, the wing mirror on the passenger side blown clean off. They ducked down into cover, behind the car.

They could hear him, not far away, as he walked over. "You can't stay in cover, and you don't have a gun. If you try to get into the car, I'll gun you both down before you get the chance."

Dawn whispered urgently, "We have no time, and we need to distract him." She took off her shoes. "I'm going to throw my shoe that way..." She gestured. "It'll only give us a second as he gauges what it is. But the second it leaves my hand, you head for the woods, got me? Try to zigzag a little, make yourself hard to hit."

He nodded frantically.

Dawn tossed the shoe, and they ran. Whether the move worked or not, Marcus couldn't be sure. But the first shot rang out a split second later.

"GO!" Dawn bellowed. They reached the nearby tree line and kept going, Marcus pushing branches aside for them as they ventured into the darkness of the forest.

74

Bob got back to the cabin after twenty minutes on the road. He'd expected flashing sirens in the car's rearview mirror, a rapid reversal of Stone's decision.

But it had been a quiet drive, a strange, sudden come-down from the scene in the woods.

His hands were trembling again slightly, and he pushed the demand for a drink out of his mind.

He wasn't sure how to explain it to Dawn except to tell her the truth: that while he hadn't killed Dahlen, he'd been about to, and had had to kill other men. She wasn't going to like it, but at least they were free. At least they were safe.

He steered the car down the dirt road to Al's. She seemed to like his mentor, so perhaps Al could help convince her what he did had been necessary. Al had always been a pragmatist at heart.

The Bronco was parked a few feet from where it had been, he noticed. *Probably went to get supplies... which means actual food for supper.*

He stopped the car and put it into park. He took off his seatbelt and climbed out, pushing the door closed.

The clunk of the door slamming shut accentuated how eerily quiet it was. He wondered how they'd managed to keep the kid busy. He walked toward the house.

Halfway there, he stopped.

A single woman's black, flat-heeled, toeless shoe sat in the middle of the parking area.

He glanced over at the house.

The door was ajar.

He looked back at the Bronco and noticed the other shoe next to the driver's-side door. A few feet past it, the wing mirror lay in the dirt.

Something was wrong.

Bob drew the pistol from his waist and cocked it.

He ran to the front door and pushed it open, stepping to the hinge side, instinct preparing him for the possibility of an ambush. Bob peeked around the doorjamb. The place was silent.

"Anyone here?"

There was no answer. He stepped in cautiously, treading softly on the wood floorboards, aware any sound could give him away. He followed the hall and checked the door to the living room.

Empty.

The kitchen and bedrooms followed, with the same result.

They would have left a note. They would have given me a sign. Something is seriously wrong.

He left via the back door and walked around the house. The hatchet that had been buried in the woodpile was lying fifteen or twenty feet from it. A single log sat a few feet closer.

A struggle, perhaps?

His phone began to buzz. He retrieved it from his jacket pocket. A text message popped up on the screen. It was from Marcus's number.

In woods near lake. Prof is excelsior. Help.

Bob's head reeled, and he felt dizzy. He stared at the screen, dumbstruck.

It couldn't be.

The kid had it wrong somehow.

It had to be a misunderstanding of some sort, an argument that got out of hand.

He texted back, awkwardly:

where are you?

Don't know.

Bob tapped with his index finger, trying to go slowly enough to avoid mistakes.

Find landmark. Hide there. Heading for lake.

He had to make sure the kid and Dawn were safe, first and foremost. Then they'd clear it up. They'd clear up whatever was frightening the kid.

He pocketed the phone and ran west, into the woods.

75

Dawn and Marcus sprinted through the trees, leg muscles straining against the changing grade, the ground softening slightly as it sloped down towards the banks of Cayuga Lake.

Somewhere behind them, a man's voice was barely audible over the wind and rustling branches. "There's nowhere out here to hide, no cover. Let's talk about it, okay?"

Dawn stopped running and looked around frantically. "He's... He's not wrong, though," she said, getting her wind. "It's just trees. Eventually he's going to see us."

"Bob said to find a landmark so he can find us," Marcus said. "We need something big, something..."

He turned in a semicircle, looking around as he talked. Dawn's eyes widened. "Look out!" she yelped. She shoved him sideways and pointed to the forest floor.

The steel trap was a circular band of rusted iron, the top edge lined with serrated teeth. "Holy shit..." Marcus muttered. "What the fuck is that?"

Dawn gave him a harsh stare. "Really? Now you start swearing and blaspheming when we most need help?"

He looked flustered as he gestured at the device. "That thing could've taken my foot off."

"It's a trapper's snare, like the professor mentioned," she said. "I saw a thing on them on PBS. It wouldn't take your foot off, but it might've broken your ankle."

"Great. Now we have to worry about where we step."

The voice behind them boomed slightly louder, "I'm going to find you soon enough. Let's just speed this up and talk this out, guys, okay?"

"We need to move," Dawn advised.

They scurried down the slope, stopping short when they reached a high muddy bank. The lake lay just beyond. Dawn's eyes searched the water frantically for someone in a boat, a day tripper, anyone.

It was deserted, just wind-assisted whitecaps rippling the surface.

She scoured the shoreline. Perhaps a half mile away, an old wooden building sat next to a small dock. "There. There might be something we can use as a weapon, or a place to hide, I guess."

They followed the shoreline, reaching the building a few minutes later. It was the size of a barn, its lake side open to the water, wide-open doors giving way to boat ramps.

They ran inside. The interior was dimly lit by the sun through the smudged front windows. Two stacks of wooden rowing boats filled one side of the room, while on the other side, a twenty-foot Shetlander sailboat took up half the bay.

It was overturned so that the hull could be worked on, propped up slightly above the ground on cinderblocks. Beyond it, a flight of steps led to a second-floor balcony overlooking the first level.

"Look for a weapon, anything we can use," she suggested.

They scoured the room, lifting objects off the hanging wall hooks: a net, sets of oars, life jackets.

Marcus held up an anchor on a chain. "Looks pretty deadly to me."

Dawn glared at him. "You can barely pick it up. What are you going to do with it, bargain our way out by parking his yacht?"

"Good point." He set it down and stared hopefully at the balcony.

"No, we're not going to try dropping it on his head," she said. "Be serious, child, Good Lord..." She picked up a putty knife that had been left by the upturned boat. "It's something, anyway. I can't believe I gave that man our gun."

A cracking sound broke off their search, wood snapping somewhere nearby outside. "He's coming around the front," Dawn said. "Back door! Now!"

They ran to the door facing the woods. It had been blocked off with a wooden bar and was locked.

"Shit!" Dawn muttered. "Excuse me."

They heard the rustling of leaves being crushed, footfalls near the ramps. "Quickly!" she commanded. "Under the boat!"

There was barely room to scurry under the wooden Shetlander and take cover. Dawn ducked low enough to watch the entrance, a pair of legs rounding the corner moments later.

"You in here, folks?" Temple asked from twenty feet away. "There's nowhere else out here to hide, so I figure you just might be. I know this boathouse well, used to store a canoe here. They lock the front door to discourage trespassers, but it's the only thing out here, the only place to go..."

His pace appeared cautious as he walked in. "Now, I'm betting you don't have any sort of gun or knife on you, or Dawn would've used it back at the house..."

Marcus kept his tone to a whisper. "I'm going to run for it, try to get him to follow me. Draw him away. Then you run the other way once we're clear."

"NO!" Dawn hissed. "We wait for Bob."

Marcus took out his phone and texted Bob frantically. "Boathouse, by the..."

Then he lost his grip, the phone tumbling from his hand and clattering off the cement.

The feet stopped moving. A second later, Temple was jogging toward the back corner of the room.

"No other choice," Marcus said.

"No! Wait..." Dawn managed. But he had already rolled out from under the far side, coming to his feet quickly, sprinting for the front exit.

Temple spun in place, and a shot rang out as Marcus whipped by him, flying out the door and tearing towards the woods in his bare feet.

A moment later, Temple gave chase.

76

Temple followed Marcus, the older man breaking into a trot as he cleared the building.

Dawn waited a few seconds before rolling out from under the boat.

Her eyes searched the room desperately for something they might have missed. She needed a weapon, something she could use to save Marcus, something more dangerous than a putty knife.

Her gaze fell on the upper balcony. They hadn't had time to look there.

She ran up the stairs.

The space was nearly empty. The shelves were bare except for a giant canvas tarpaulin stretched out over a pile of unused lumber.

She pulled it back and picked up a two-by-four board, hefting its weight. It could do some damage, she supposed, but it wasn't much.

On the wall next to the shelves was a small glass-and-metal cabinet. She ran over to it and pulled it open. The fire extinguisher was half-sized but had some weight to it despite being small enough to swing like a hammer. Dawn pulled it out of its clip and headed back towards the stairs.

She ran down them and around the upturned wooden boat, to the wide boat launch door.

She was about to round the corner when Temple stepped out in front of her.

Dawn reacted first, swinging the fire hydrant with all her strength.

Temple turned in mid-swing, letting the extinguisher hit him in the flesh of the shoulder. He swung a hard backhand with his pistol, catching Dawn flush and sending her sprawling.

Temple walked in calmly after her. "It was a brave idea, but as soon as we were outside, I could see he was alone," he said. "He has nowhere to go, no resources. It won't take me long to find him once I've dealt with you."

Dawn tried to scurry backwards along the floor, to round the corner of the row of boats and find cover. But Temple took two quick steps, reaching down and grabbing her jacket collar, his strength belying his wiry build as he hauled the woman to her feet.

"Time to end this," he said. He raised the pistol.

They both heard the sound of rustling footsteps. Temple spun on his heel and pulled the nurse in front of him as a shield as Singleton rounded the corner, pistol raised.

"You treacherous bastard!" Bob muttered. He circled around Temple, moving inside the room. His former mentor turned in unison, keeping Dawn ahead of him.

"Now... you know me well enough to know I don't want to shoot this nice lady, Bobby," Temple warned.

"I know you? I FUCKING KNOW YOU?! Tell me what I know, Al. Tell me!" Bob was shaking his head in a mixture of disbelief and disgust. "How could you? I'm your oldest friend. You brought me up; you brought me into the agency..."

"I didn't want it to go down like this," Temple said. "You know what you mean to me. You were like the son that Evie and I never had..."

"SON OF A BITCH!" Bob snarled, his anger growing. "You betrayed the Team! You let Tyler and Jon die. You let me think it was my fault. For what?! FOR MONEY!?"

Temple's exasperation grew. "FOR MY WIFE! FOR EVIE! She was dying, Bob, and nothing was working! And we were drained, done! The money was all gone, everything I'd worked nearly twenty years to build. But there were still things we could try, experimental drugs..."

"So you sacrificed two good men... and Richie... and Janet. And Smalls. And... and me." Bob felt the energy drain from his body. It couldn't be true, but it was.

And it couldn't stand. He raised his gun hand.

The older man stepped further behind the nurse and returned aim. "Don't do it, Bob. Don't even think it. I have you dead to rights, but you might hit the woman."

"And that would be fine with you, wouldn't it? We were nothing to you..."

"SHE WAS EVERYTHING!" Temple bellowed. Then he softened at her memory. "She was everything. So yeah... I took the money. There wasn't supposed to be any ambush. They were just going to hand over a decoy, arrest a couple of team members, maybe exchange them later. But they switched plans on me. And you know what? If I thought it would've saved Evie, I'd have pulled the trigger on Gaines myself. We were all expendable, all ready to give our lives for something bigger. But there was nothing more important than her."

"And when we got back, you were the one who 'warned' us, told us Kennedy planned to clean house."

"He did! He gave the contract to Dahlen, who gave it to

me. He already had me in his pocket, but I didn't want any of you to die..."

"Instead, you told him you'd finished us off."

"I gave you a chance. I pointed them to four John Does at the Chicago morgue. If they'd pushed it, you'd have been dogmeat, maybe me, too. But they didn't."

"And we went to ground thinking we were safe. Everyone except Smalls, who refused to hide. Back in Chicago... I figured they'd traced the kid's car somehow, but he was parked blocks from the clinic. You led Dahlen's team to us..."

Temple raised his chin haughtily. "That's the job, Bob. That's what it is, kill or be killed. You think I want this? No. I tried like hell to avoid this; if that hadn't been the case, I'd have taken you all out myself back in Chicago. But it is what it is." He swung the barrel back to Dawn's temple. "Now, we're getting out of here. You even think about..."

"You take another step," Bob said, "and I will kill you where you stand."

Temple began to slowly back away, towards the ramps, dragging her with him. "No. No, you won't."

Bob looked past him, hoping upon hope for a last-second save, a hunter passing or someone on the lake spotting the standoff. "Don't you goddamned move..." he warned.

"Or... you could do the big thing: your life for hers," Temple said. "You drop your piece, and I'll let her walk."

"Don't do it..." Dawn warned. "He won't let me go."

"I know," Bob said, his weapon level and steady.

"Please..." Dawn pleaded. "Don't hurt me, Professor."

"You're not going to shoot me, Bob," Temple said. "You want to, but you can't risk hitting the woman. You were never that selfish. He who hesitates is lost, remember?"

"She'd be ashamed of you," Bob muttered. "Evie would be ashamed of you for all of this."

Temple ignored the dig. "We're going now. If I hear you

behind me, I'll shoot Dawn in the femoral artery, let her bleed out slow. You feel me? I still get the hostage, but her odds of surviving decrease drastically."

He dragged Dawn backwards, the nurse making it difficult. He smacked her on the side of the head with the gun. "Go dead weight on me again and maybe I'll just shoot you here and take my chances."

"Do as he says, Dawn," Singleton cautioned. "I'll figure out a way out of this."

"Not this time," Temple said as they reached the exit. "I knew eventually I'd have to teach you the lesson you never seemed to get, Bob. That you always have to look out for number one."

"You dirty son of a bitch."

"Last offer: put the gun down and take the inevitable. You aren't going to make it a week with Team Seven looking for you anyway. Let her have a chance. I'll let her run, give her a five-minute head start. It's a chance, at least."

Bob began to reach down to place the gun on the floor. "I'm putting it down slowly..."

"DON'T DO IT!" Dawn screamed. "You know he's lying. You know you can't trust him."

"I have to give you a shot at making it out of this," Bob said. "What happens to me... it's not important right now. Just do as he says..."

Temple pulled the pistol away from Dawn's head and aimed it at Bob. "Sorry it had to be like this, Bobby. I'd say 'semper fi' for old times' sake... but I lost the faith a long time ago."

Bob squinted, anticipating the sting of the bullet, knowing he'd probably hear nothing, that Temple was too good a shot at ten feet to miss a bullet through the brain, that it would strike him so fast the sound wouldn't register.

Marcus stepped around the corner, his hands raised,

swinging a heavy object with all his might. The rusty old leg trap sprang closed as he buried its teeth into the side of Temple's head, the device flying from his hand, snapping tight on the professor's skull.

Temple screamed with pain and staggered backwards, dropping his pistol reflexively, both hands coming up to his head to try to pry the mighty trap loose.

Bob grabbed the pistol off the floor and aimed center mass, emptying the magazine, Temple's torso riddled by bullets, spasmodic as he staggered backwards from the impacts.

He fell to his knees, blood pouring from his facial wounds, an incredulous look on his face.

Then he pitched over sideways and lay still.

77

They went back to Chicago that evening, Dawn and Bob sharing the driving for the ten and a half hours, a straight shot from Ithaca along Interstates 90 and 86.

They didn't talk much.

Marcus kept quiet in the back seat, sensing that maybe Dawn was giving Bob space. He hadn't said more than a handful of words since the boathouse.

At the cabin, he'd used an old number to contact Edward Stone through the agency, leaving him an anonymous message with Excelsior's real identity and where they'd find his body.

When they'd left, Dawn had asked what they were going to do next. He'd answered simply, "I'm going to take you two home."

Marcus wasn't really sure what that meant anymore.

He knew they'd be looking for him, police probably fearful one of his parents had killed him in their "murder suicide." He'd have to explain that somehow.

Dawn's idea seemed best, that his father had dropped him

off with her, an old family friend, a week earlier. That he was oblivious to what had happened.

Then she'd said she could see about helping him sell their house, using the money to go to college in a year.

"You're going to be just fine," she'd told him during a pit stop for dinner at a burger joint, using a paper napkin she'd moistened to wipe barbecue sauce off his face. "You're almost a grown man."

But he didn't feel it. He felt like everyone was about to drift away. He should've felt free, unburdened by being chased by lunatics with guns. Instead, he just felt empty.

They got back to Dawn's apartment just before six in the morning. Bob parked the car at the curb. "Well... here we are," he said.

"I guess so," said Dawn, the tension of imminent separation setting in. "It's a good thing we left before the weekend. I'm still going to have to call Dr. Girard, hope he doesn't fire me for missing two days' work."

He nodded towards the building. "I'll carry the bag up for you."

Normally, Marcus figured, she'd have protested and done it herself. Instead, she smiled wistfully and said, "I guess."

They followed her up the stairs to the third floor. Dawn opened the door, then stood in the doorway for a few moments, drinking in the familiarity. "It feels like forever. Like a different place in the world."

She led them in. The apartment opened directly into a small, tidy living room. "Let's at least have a coffee before you decide to disappear on me. Good?"

Bob nodded. He looked awkwardly nervous as he settled on the sofa, Marcus thought, like he knew it shouldn't just end there. He perched himself on the edge of the armchair. There was nothing keeping them together anymore, nothing but bad memories and a mutual appreciation for surviving.

Bob watched Dawn walk through the connecting door to the kitchen. Then he glanced back at Marcus. “I’m just going to have a word with her, okay? Hang tight.”

He got up and left the room.

Left out of the conversation again, Marcus thought. That’s what adults did. If they thought he was ready to be out on his own, they had a strange way of showing it sometimes.

He didn’t share their confidence, anyway. He wanted time to roll backwards, to reset the clocks to a week earlier, when his life was boring but normal. When he still had a family, a daily walk to school, idiot friends.

Dawn appeared from the kitchen, bearing a mug of coffee in each hand. She walked over and handed him one. Bob followed, carrying his own.

They both sat down. “Marcus...” she said, sounding unsure of herself, “how would you feel about coming here to stay with me? I mean... I know I’m not the most fun in the world, and it’s not the same as—”

“Yes,” he said, nodding frantically. “I mean... yeah. I think I’d like that.”

Bob smiled. “You can’t save them all,” he said. “But sometimes...”

Dawn gave him the evil eye, but it was half-hearted. “Boy’s going to be eighteen in nine months...”

“But he’ll need all the help you can give him. It’s not an easy world,” Bob said.

She glanced away for a moment, and Marcus followed her eyes to the sofa table, under the gilt mirror on the far wall. A picture of a smiling boy in his Sunday best sat there, alone.

Then she lowered her gaze to the floor. “I think that would be just fine,” Dawn said. “Just fine.”

Bob drained half the coffee in one swallow.

"What about you?" Dawn asked. "You'd better not tell me you're going back to that alley off North Peoria."

He smiled gently at that. "No. No, I think I'm done with giving up. But" – he rose to his feet – "I do have to get moving. Things to take care of."

They nodded, but Marcus felt a slight emptiness again at the notion. Bob walked over to the door.

They followed, Dawn holding it open for him. "You'd better stay in touch, though," she said.

"As I can," he said. "There are still a lot of people out there who want my head, my former employer chief among them. You might still get a visit from them, as they'll be looking for me. You're prepared for that?"

"As well as we can be," Dawn said.

"So... you're just going to run?" Marcus interjected. "That doesn't sound like much of a life, Mr. Singleton."

"One, call me Bob, for crying out loud. I think we're at least that close, and I keep asking, and two... I'll have to do just that. For a while, anyway."

"Where will you go?" Dawn asked. "Never mind. Let me guess: knowing that could put us in danger."

"Yep. Stone and Kennedy have no reason to come after the two of you. They know I won't have given you anything that could hurt them, because of the potential fallout. But you can be sure they'll keep an eye on you, hoping you'll lead back to me somehow."

"You deserve better than just avoiding men who want to kill you," she said. "Everyone needs a purpose, Bob."

"I've been thinking about that, too," he said. "I did a lot of damage when I was with Team Seven. I contributed to them hurting a lot of people. There are a lot of Ginny Smalls out there... people left without family because of no fault of their own."

"People like me," Marcus said.

"Yeah, kid. People like you." He turned towards the corridor. "But I'll make sure I stay in touch. Okay?"

Marcus nodded.

"You call me when you're feeling low, Bob," Dawn demanded. "You hear me?"

"I will."

"You know where you're headed first?"

"It's probably better if you don't know the details," he said. "But I figured I'd start by finding Jon Rice's parents and brother, tell them what really happened to him. It's not much, but they deserve that, at least. The same is true of Ellery Azadi."

"You're a good man, Bob Singleton," she said.

Bob turned on his heel and made his way down the corridor. "Not yet. But I'm working on it," he said before disappearing around the corner to the stairwell and the street beyond.

78

It had been difficult, saying goodbye.

Al Temple's betrayal had made it that much harder than it needed to be, a second round of loss after one of the worst moments of his life.

He tried to see his mentor's decision for what it had originally been: an act of desperation to save someone he loved. That, Bob could understand.

Everything that came after was harder to ignore.

At the townhouse he'd sublet to Temple, he parked the car at the curb.

He got out and checked the street both ways, looking for any signs of team surveillance, the street empty save for other parked cars, the wind gently billowing roadside tree branches. It had begun to drizzle cold rain.

He didn't have long to get moving, he was sure. Stone's seventy-two-hour window still had about two days' grace in it, assuming the man stuck to his promise.

Staying at the townhouse was out of the question. It wouldn't take Stone long to figure out who actually owned it. At some point, he knew, he'd have to arrange to sell it.

Renting it out wouldn't work; eventually, any income would lead back to him.

He mounted the steps and inserted the key.

But the door was already unlocked.

His right hand dropped instinctively to his waistband to ensure the pistol was still there.

Bob pushed the door slowly open, unable to avoid a slight squeak from the hinges. He closed it silently behind him and took a few steps into the hall, then peeked into the living room.

"Took you long enough to get here."

Eddie Stone was sitting in the armchair by the fake fireplace. He had a paper cup of coffee in one hand, a pistol in the other.

"I thought I had seventy-two hours," Bob said.

"You do. This is just a courtesy call to tell you I got your message about the professor... and to let you know how quickly and easily we can find you."

"Ever the showman, Eddie."

"I take it you're not here to stay."

"Am I still on the clock?"

"You are."

"Andrew Kennedy signed off on this?"

"I don't tell him everything. I'm sure he doesn't tell me everything."

"Okay." Bob nodded to the other rooms. "I'm just here to pick up a suitcase from the hall closet. Some things I need before I head out."

"Any plans?"

Bob smiled. "Now... I know you like to be a man of your word, Eddie, but that doesn't mean I trust you that much."

Stone smiled. "Smart. After Friday, we'll be coming for you."

Bob smiled back, but didn't answer. He walked back to the

hallway and opened the closet, taking out the Samsonite hard-shell case that had sat there for years, waiting for the moment he had to flee.

"Thank you for Temple," Stone said as Bob rolled the case out into the hall. "That must have been difficult."

"In the moment? In the moment, it was just business. And if you do manage to track me down... you'd better come with more than you showed at the cemetery. Or send someone younger," Bob said. "Otherwise, the next time I won't be so accommodating."

"Message received and confirmed," Stone said. "I'd wish you good luck, but it's against my principles."

Bob picked up the case and walked to the front door. He opened it and looked out to the street, yellowed leaves blowing across the asphalt, gusting into the air, sticking on the chain-link fence that surrounded the soccer pitch on the other side of the road.

He was going to miss Chicago.

"Dawn and the boy..."

Stone shrugged. "Not our concern. I assume you weren't dumb enough..."

"Not a word."

"Smart. Keep it that way and avoid us for long enough, maybe the right people will figure you're not such a problem. Maybe they'll even decide we should stop looking."

"Take care of yourself, Eddie. I'll see you around."

"Not if I see you first, Bobby. Not if I see you—"

Bob stepped outside, not hearing the end of it, pulling the door closed behind him. The air was cool, light rain coming down, drops cascading gently from the townhouse's gutters, running down the wrought-iron front rail.

He walked down the steps and opened the car's back door, tossing the suitcase onto the seat. He looked back at the red-brick townhouse once before slamming the door. He rounded the car and climbed in behind the wheel.

The engine fired up immediately, the heater coming on.

It would take a while to get over Temple. He needed to get moving. He put the sedan into drive.

The sedan pulled out onto West Drummond Place.

He would head south, away from the city, away from surveillance cameras and urban decay. He had debts to pay, worthy people who needed someone's helping hand. It wasn't going to be easy. It was a dangerous world, with old enemies aplenty.

But he owed himself the chance to make amends, at least. Dawn had convinced him of that.

He'd given up once, but that wouldn't happen again.

He'd become an old hand at avoiding trouble.

Now, it was time to go looking for it.

ABOUT THE AUTHOR

Did you enjoy *Code Red*? Please consider leaving a review on Amazon to help other readers discover the book.

Ian Loome writes thrillers and mysteries. His books have been downloaded more than a half-million times on Amazon.com and have regularly featured on the Kindle best-seller lists for more than a decade. For 24 years, Ian was a multi-award-winning newspaper reporter, editor and columnist in Canada. When he's not figuring out innovative ways to snuff his characters, he plays blues guitar and occasionally fronts bands. He lives in Sherwood Park, Alberta, with his partner Lori, a pugnacious bulldog named Ferdinand, a confused mostly Great Dane puppy named Ollie, and some cats for good measure.

Printed in Great Britain
by Amazon